Praise for the works of ...

Don't Let Go

Georgie and Tyler are wonderful characters and the way their relationship changes from purely professional to a romance is lovely, with good pacing. This is a clever book on many levels, and it really kept me on my toes, intellectually speaking. It was both challenging and heartwarming in equal measures, and I absolutely loved it.

-Rainbow Book Reviews

Nothing is quite so refreshing as something completely different to the norm. *Don't Let Go* is a traditional romance, set in the corporate world and with a twist of a corporate intrigue to add to the action. What makes it unusual is that the main character in both the romance and the corporation is a veteran who has suffered a traumatic brain injury and is suffering from a range of seemingly catastrophic aftereffects.

-Lesbian Reading Room

Queen of Hearts

...is a sweet romance about finding love when you don't expect it and recognizing that everyone deserves a happily ever after. I was impressed with how Wright was able to give such a large cast of characters their own distinctive personalities and prevent so many female characters from blending together. This is a robust cast of side characters who bring humor and drama to the story. *Queen of Hearts* is an entertaining romance. It was such a quick read for me because the scenario is so appealing. A reality TV show full of interesting and beautiful lesbians looking to find true love is something that I would clear my schedule for. This book is a lovely break from the daily grind and if you're looking for something light and fun, check it out.

-Lesbian Review

Cause and Affection

I have come to expect intelligent, flawless writing from this author, and this latest book does not disappoint. As with her other books, this one is well-populated, but everyone has a role to play. No extraneous characters.

This is so well-written and compelling that I wanted to both find out what would happen next and didn't want it to end!

-Gayle T., *NetGalley*

The author has given us not only well-drawn characters but two very determined main characters. One is a little surer of what she wants than the other, but their dynamic is so real, that their determination carries the plot through the slower parts. It's not all roses and unicorns though. There is pettiness, jealousy, courage, understanding, ambition and greed here. There is an undercurrent of society-induced hesitation about a business leader being a lesbian, but trust me, it works out better than you expect in the end.

-Carolyn C., *NetGalley*

Illusion Lake

Other Bella Books by Sheryl Wright

Cause and Affection
Don't Let Go
Queen of Hearts
Stay With Me

Illusion Lake

Sheryl Wright

BELLA
BOOKS
2021

Printed in the United States of America on acid-free paper.

First Bella Books Edition 2021

Editor: Katherine V. Forrest

ISBN: 978-1-64247-118-2

Acknowledgments

Writing, much like flying can be a solitary endeavor. That is, right up to the moment you land, then a whole host of folks jump into the fray, some unseen and many often unknown, all dedicated to making sure the aircraft is in tip-top shape and ready to go again. This book has seen much the same treatment, being handled by several unseen editors and production staff intent on making sure the story is perfect before it reaches your hands. For all those unseen helpers I thank you so much.

To Jessica Hill and all the gang at Bella Books, thank you so much for your support. Knowing you will consider my proposals makes the act of writing a book so much less daunting. Pairing me with an editor of Katherine's station and experience has made the entire process both painless and ever encouraging. Again, thank you doesn't really cover it but it's all I've got, at least until the world rights itself and we can all meet again.

For Katherine V. Forrest, amazing author and editor extraordinaire, *Nia;we*. Your insights and extraordinary skill and patience have taken my story and made it incredibly better. For those who know me, just think about how often you need to put me back on track every time I start pulling at threads or allow details to send me down the rabbit hole. Skillfully, Katherine has saved this book and me from doing just that. My OCD may make me susceptible to savoring the details but once again, Katherine has dug me out. A sincere thank-you, even in Mohawk, does not come close to what I owe you. Please know I'm learning so much from you and treasure every letter and every editorial note. Oh, and as requested, I pried out the Caps Lock key from my keyboard ☺

A Special Note on Timing

I wrote this book back when we were planning to meet in New Mexico for the annual Golden Crown Literary Society convention. Then COVID-19 happened and the world changed overnight. I won't speculate on how things will change but they will. No matter what befalls each of us during this time of change, I can only hope for love for each and every woman out there. While my partner has worked hard to keep me and my compromised immune system safe, I wish everyone the same: Safety, security, and love. After all, when it really comes down to it, what else is there that truly matters?

Stay Safe and Stay Sane.

Sheryl

https://sherylwright.com

For Elmo,
who taught me to use a level, swing a hammer,
and operate the lawn tractor. No boys needed.
And for Nanny,
who never gave up on me.

PROLOGUE

Mile after mile, for the last hundred miles, dried out and frozen cattle pastures and the interstate were her only companions as she drove southwest into New Mexico. With no schedule to follow, she had pushed hard, not to get here, as much as her need just to be going somewhere, doing something, anything. It had taken thirty-two hours of hard winter driving, broken only by a restless night stay at a cheap hotel, to get here from Toronto.

Here.

It wasn't much to look at.

When Elliott Snowmaker pulled herself from her beat up Jeep and took stock of what was left of a once bustling airport operation, her heart hurt almost as much as her back. The only runway that looked usable was littered with small stones and junk that probably fell off cars racing here illegally. The only buildings left standing were a boarded-up wood shack, a dilapidated brick building with peeling gray paint identifying it as the airfield's fire station, and an enormous rusting Quonset hut, probably a relic of World War II, was the only hangar left standing.

The painted lettering on the Quonset hut doors, like the rest of the place, had been left to fade and peel, but it was still legible: *Elliott's*

Aircraft Restoration. We Specialize in Warbirds, Antiques, and Vintage Airplanes. All Makes and Models Welcome.

There was no denying this was the place. As soon as she did the paperwork it would be all hers. Question was…what the hell was she going to do with it?

CHAPTER ONE

Kiva Park set her cell phone to speaker, placing it on the desk next to a framed photo of her dad grinning and hugging his two daughters. It had been taken only last year, and she marveled to think how important it was to have the latest snapshot of them so close by. Absently, she listened to her sister on the phone while sorting case files. Swinging slightly side to side in the deep leather of her father's office chair she could admit she was enjoying this break from her normal, far more intense routine.

Her father's office was decorated much like her own back in Toronto, meticulously kept with custom mahogany furniture and two walls of dark wood shelves stacked with legal volumes. It certainly was a contrast to the storefront it occupied in the center of town. She was listening and absently agreeing with her sister Shay as she rambled on and on, shucking off her heels, examining her bare toes, considering whether it was time for a pedicure,when suddenly the volume of the call hiked.

She blushed, stammering her denial, "I…Yes, I was listening! Please don't get upset. I heard everything you said. I just, I just don't know what to tell you, sis." Nothing was worse for her insecure and newly single big sister than thinking she couldn't be bothered listening to her problems. Kiva's problem wasn't an unwillingness to listen, but frustration at hearing the same complaints over and over.

"Shay, I know you're having a dry spell, but at least you're not sitting here in nowheresville with no place to go, and no one to do."

There was a huff from the phone, followed by a gentle laugh. "Ah, I can see it now, the fastest lesbian in the West dying of frustration as she wilts in that dust bowl we escaped from. You must be fading there."

Now it was Kiva's turn to huff, but she had to agree. "Tell me about it. I've been here so long, I'm actually starting to entertain thoughts of monogamy and even, wait for it…settling down." In actuality, she'd only arrived a few weeks ago but compared to her very active social life back in Toronto, Illusion Lake, New Mexico was as mind-numbing as it could get.

"O—M—G! I knew spending the winter handling Dad's practice would have this effect. What are you hoping for?"

"Are you kidding? I'm hoping to get out of here unscathed and return home a normal red-blooded and single lesbian. You know what they say about our mother, 'Kerry Ann O'Donnell was destined for bigger things,' and that goes for her daughters too. Even if I wanted to stay, Illusion Lake can't handle three lawyers and I can't see Dad retiring anytime soon."

It was easy to hear her sister's lighthearted laugh. A great improvement over whatever she was bitching about a moment ago. Kiva leaned over her chair to put her heels back on but straightened up at the sight of dried grime covering the heels and toes. Groaning, she knew her careful egress through the muddy unpaved parking out back was not as successful she'd hoped. Maybe she should park out front from now on, main street parking tickets be damned. Grabbing a tissue, she dabbed at her expensive Italian slingbacks, brushing away much of the claylike buildup. "Of course I get all sorts of ideas around the perfect woman scenario, but it's silly."

"Amuse me, why don't you," her sister suggested. "Come on. Why don't you ever just say out loud what you're looking for? I mean, you know what Mom says. 'You have to see it before you can have it.'"

"That's the thing. I don't want to see what I can't have. Besides, it's more about the type of woman. I'm restless all the time. It's not fair to settle down with anyone when I just can't keep still."

"You can't keep still because you haven't found the right woman or as Mom would say, *the one*."

"Oh God, you do sound like her," Kiva warned her sister.

"Yeah, but maybe she's right this time. I mean, did you ever give it a try? I'm talking about going old school and really letting yourself see things the way she taught us when we were kids."

Now it was her turn to huff. "How do you think I got through law school and managed to pass the bar in two states and one province?"

"Yah, that was cool…" Her sister seemed to sense she'd gotten off track. "No, wait. Don't change the subject. Let's do it now. Close your eyes and describe the perfect woman, the one who could settle your restlessness."

Kiva felt a rush of heat at the thought. They were close, but no way was she close enough to talk about sex with her straight sister.

"Whoa, whoa, whoa there, knucklehead. I'm not talking about sex, and don't deny that's where your head went."

"Did not!" Kiva laughed at herself. She sounded like a teenager. "You're killing me here, you know that?"

"Stop making excuses, for God's sake, and stop thinking about sex for five minutes."

Lowering her head, she smiled. Her big sis always got her, even when she didn't understand herself. The truth was, much as she liked to play the field and pretend she wasn't into long-term relationships, things had gotten stale. It seemed like the more women she met, the more they were the same, cast from one of three molds: the Fixer Uppers, the Rescues, and the Payment Plans.

The Fixer Uppers were the women who were making a good living and settled in their careers but usually at a cost. They needed attention in some area, like the Victorian houses in her neighborhood at home always needing fixing—trim painted, windows replaced, something. She had long given up on the idea that any of those women wanted the updating, or anything changed about themselves. If they had, they would have gone out and done it themselves.

Of course, they were much easier to deal with than the Rescues. Rescues could go on forever about their childhood wounds or how their last lover destroyed their confidence and trust and how the right woman could save them. She had long since decided these were not really women in pain but nutbars whose needs were thinly disguised demands. They wanted everything without any responsibility or work on their part. After all, they would say, "You have to understand, I'm a victim," or some such crap. They clung to their victimhood like a badge of honor.

At least the Payment Plans admitted up front they expected her to foot the bill, tend to their every whim. It would be one thing to be in a relationship and share the burdens of life, but a whole other thing to take on someone else's financial responsibilities simply because somewhere along the line they had decided that doing or contributing less made them somehow worth more. She never got it. Maybe it was how they were raised. As much as she and Shay joked that their mother was on the crazy side, she'd always insisted they understood they were responsible for themselves.

"Okay." Kiva gave in with just the right hint of dismissal. There was no need to let Shay know she'd been putting off this very exercise, scared about where her deep, dark internal thoughts might take her. Their mom was a spiritual woman and a lifelong student of what she referred to as the universal mysteries. Yes, she was a New Ager through and through, introducing her girls to meditation as toddlers and hypnosis as soon as they were old enough to sit still to use their imagination as directed. They were so practiced each could move themselves into and out of the suggestive state without effort. She set her now pristine heels on the floor. "Give me a sec," she said as she got comfortable in her dad's office chair, closing her eyes and letting her head roll back in complete relaxation.

Shay asked the standard opening question. "Where are you?"

"In my perfect place."

"Great. Are you safe and alone?"

"Yes."

"Good. Now I want you to see yourself celebrating your fiftieth wedding anniversary. Can you see the cake, the friends and family gathered around?"

"Yes."

"I want you to feel how happy you are and how much you've achieved. Listen to the people gathered with you as they tell you how impressed they are. Allow yourself to feel the achievement they see. You have enjoyed a stellar career. You have personal fulfillment. And you have enjoyed the most spectacular relationship. Can you feel everyone's praise and know it's true?"

"Yes."

"Good, that's good. Now I want you to look around. Can you see your colleagues and how happy they are for you?"

"Yes."

"Nice work. Now look around your home. Can you see that it's everything you ever wanted?"

"Yes."

"Perfect. Now, look around again. Do you see children or grandchildren?'

"Yes...holy shit! I have grandkids!"

"Easy now, let yourself relax again and smile at your grandchildren. Now take a look at the woman beside you. What do you see?"

"Nothing."

"She's holding your hand and smiling at you. What do you see?"

"Noth..."

"Relax and feel yourself there. Is her hand warm or cool in yours?"

"Warm."

"Good. Is her skin soft or rough?"

"Soft, rough, both I guess."

"Perfect. Now turn to her and tell me what you see. Is she as tall as you? Taller? Shorter?"

"Taller, but just a few inches."

"That's perfect. Let yourself see her gray hair but remember back to when you first met. What color was her hair then?"

"Blond, dark blond."

"That's good. Now tell me how she keeps it, short, long..."

"Short and straight but not too short. Her bangs are in her eyes, and I want to lean over and brush them away for her..."

The old-fashioned buzzer on her desk rang, and she reluctantly opened her eyes. "Sorry, Shay. Duty calls. We'll have to leave make-believe for another day. Will you call me on the weekend and tell me all about Dad's blind date?"

"You got it, kiddo. Just promise me you won't dismiss any propositions from slightly taller blond women who need their bangs cut."

Kiva laughed her off the phone. "Gotta go," she said. She picked up the probate file and the note from Ian Guerrero, her father's legal partner, and walked to the door. She read the client name again, to be sure she looked professional even if this was a simple discharge. "Elliott Snowmaker. I'm Kee..."

The woman walking across the small waiting room was good looking in a handsome sort of way, the same height as Kiva, thanks to Kiva's three-inch heels. Her straight hair was dark blond with light yellow highlights just brushing her ears and falling in her eyes. As the woman's head tilted just slightly, Kiva shook herself from the idea her sister had just planted and cleared her thoughts, adding with more authority and some discomfort, "I'm Ms. Park. I'll be representing the firm today in the matter of your uncle's estate."

"Great-uncle," the woman corrected, offering her hand.

Kiva tried not to scowl at her forgetfulness. It wasn't the woman's fault she and her sister had been playing silly games on the phone thirty seconds ago. She accepted the outstretched hand, then almost dropped it when it felt as real as the experience she had just described. No way could she tell Shay about this! She would say this was destiny or some such bull.

She waved at the seat across from her desk and sat down, feeling entirely off her game. The best way to handle this, she decided, was to get through the inheritance information, hand everything over, and be done with her. She spotted the Post-It note stuck to the file and remembered Ian wanted to talk to the woman too. Something about making an offer so she could get out of town and back to wherever she was from sooner than later. That certainly worked for her.

"As I said in my letter, I'm here to discharge your uncle's estate and—"

"Great-uncle," the woman corrected again.

She sucked in a breath to keep her cool. The woman hadn't done anything wrong in correcting her. "Sorry. Yes, you said that. Great-uncle. Now before we start, I'll need to check your ID and verify you are who you say you are. Nothing personal."

The woman obediently dug into a leather portfolio and handed over a Canadian passport and an FAA pilot's ID book.

Excusing herself and taking the documents from the office to copy them, Kiva headed to the break room. She would typically hand stuff like this off to Sofia, her father's receptionist/assistant, but needed a few minutes to compose herself. Heading to the back room that also served as a kitchenette, she copied the various IDs for the legal record, then looked longingly at the fresh coffee. No, she'd ask her client if she wanted one before she poured herself another.

Maybe she'd call Shay later and give her hell about this situation. It was probably just her subconscious playing games. Maybe she'd caught a glimpse of the new woman in town, and her mind suggested her features to fill the conjuring her sister had orchestrated. Or…last night she had dinner at the rib place out on the highway across from the only hotel in the area, and she probably spotted her there. Yes, she was sure of it now. That must be how her imagination had come up with such a perfect match. Amazing how much the mind took in.

Slipping back into the office she resumed her seat, saying in passing, "Welcome to Illusion Lake, New Mexico. When did you get in?"

"Actually, I just arrived."

That didn't make sense. Kiva must have seen her before. "Are you staying at the Big Pine Inn?"

"I just checked in." She gave Kiva a sheepish look, then explained. "I left Toronto late and pretty much drove right through. I wanted a shower and to change before we met. Once I have the keys, I'll move into my great-uncle's apartment."

Hmm. That didn't make sense. Maybe she had seen a picture of the woman. Perhaps there was one in the file. She flipped it open.

"I can certainly give you the keys today, but you may want to stay at the Big Pine anyway. You do know there is no house included in your inheritance?"

She nodded.

"Do you know what you've inherited from your uncle?"

"Great-uncle."

"Yes, sorry. It's what I meant. And I'm sorry for your loss." She scolded herself for being a little late with that sentiment. She was completely off-kilter and needed to focus. "Let me get you a coffee. What's your preference?"

"I'm kinda coffee'd out. Any chance I could get something cold? Water, pop?"

Smiling, she nodded, making her way from the office without another word.

Why is this so hard? Just grab her a Coke, get a coffee, relax. The sooner she's out of your hair the sooner this ridiculous thing comes to an end. Why on earth did I let Shay talk me into that mumbo-jumbo of Mom's?

When she sat back down across from the woman, she was back to her old self. "Ms. Snowmaker, I just want to say again how sorry I am for your loss." Her practice at home was focused on juvenile criminal law, but here, with her dad and Ian the only lawyers in town, they did a little of everything and wills and estates took a big chunk. When she agreed to take over his practice so he could take a long overdue break, she had been looking forward to this part of the work. Dealing with young offenders was starting to weigh on her, and this had sounded like a good gig.

"No need. We weren't close. Not with us each living at opposite ends of the continent. I had no idea he would leave me anything. Frankly, it's all been a bit overwhelming."

That information didn't exactly mesh with her understanding. Flipping to the man's last will and testament and the photocopies of the ID she had taken, she carefully compared the two. "You are Elliott Annabelle Snowmaker, great-niece to Elliott Moreno?"

"Yes." She grinned somewhat irreverently. "But please don't share that 'Annabelle' thing with anyone."

She nodded but wouldn't ask. She could sympathize. Her mother had saddled her with Kiva, the name of a traditional Dené healing lodge she had visited while pregnant with her. "Can you explain your familial tie?"

She nodded, seemingly unfazed by the questions. "Elliott is my maternal grandmother's little brother."

Not a lot to go on. She had to accept the explanation, as the relationship was detailed right there in the opening of his bequest. "It would seem your great-uncle Elliott…"

"Elmo," she corrected. "I only know him as Elmo."

"All right, Ms. Snowmaker—"

"Elliott."

"Yes." This was getting tedious. "I'm happy to refer to him as—"

"No. Sorry. I mean, call *me* Elliott, *please*. That's what everyone calls me."

That information stalled her thoughts. Elliott was a cute name, and it sort of suited her. Knowing it was her turn to reciprocate, she stalled then skipped over it, unwilling to trade on common names. Something about being casual with Elliott scared the hell out of her.

"Are you named for him?"

"I guess. I never asked. I mean I know him best from all my Nanny's stories, but we only met on special occasions."

"I take it you're the only grandchild?"

"Sorry, no. First of nine and before you ask, I have no idea why Elmo left everything to me."

She sighed, trying to put all the information in order. "I have to ask, should we be expecting any challenges from your siblings, cousins, aunts, uncles, or other family members?"

Elliott looked to be giving the question serious thought, finally shaking her head. "I can't see it, but you never know. Frankly, I'm not sure my cousins even know Elmo is dead much less that he had anything of any value. Most of my aunts are gone and like my father, none of their husbands ever stuck around. I don't know what happened to Elmo's wife, but my grandmother was sure their divorce was finalized more than thirty years ago.

Kiva hated to push when it came to the tumultuous topic of family, but she needed to be prepared. "And your mother and surviving aunts?"

Seeming to get where she was going with her line of questioning, Elliott sat straighter, explaining, "My grandmother is Elmo's only surviving sibling. Anything I gain, she knows I'll share with her. As for my mom and Aunt Vicky, well...they haven't had anything to do with me since I came out and I have every confidence my grandmother will return the favor when it comes to sharing this situation with them. Besides, I've already stopped at the airport, and I can't see a lot of value to fight over."

Kiva nodded. "Elmo's estate has some valuable aspects but more so on paper. We'll go over that, and I'm glad to hear you have some idea of what you're facing."

It took another hour to pore over the estate papers and go through the details required by the courts, state inheritance laws, and federal tax requirements. Initially, she hadn't expected to spend as much time on this business, but Elliott Snowmaker was a bright woman and asked detailed and essential questions.

"Now all we need to do is get everything signed, then I'll take you next door to see Ian Guerrero. He can explain the penalties for breaking the airport lease and go over the offer the county is considering and—"

"Wait. What's the rush?"

Caught off guard, Kiva almost stumbled before explaining, "I was told you were in a hurry to get things settled and head back up north."

"By whom?"

"Uh, I'm sensing a problem?"

"There may or may not be one. First, though, I need to know who it is you're representing."

She was stunned by the question. In the twelve years she had been practicing law, no one had ever asked her that. She'd had a few criminal cases where the client accused her of not getting them the best deal, but she'd never had anyone ask whose side she was on. "I'm representing your great-uncle's estate."

"And if I wanted you to represent me, would there be a conflict?"

"I..." She paused, actually thinking it through. "Not that I know of. Why do you ask?"

"No." Elliott Snowmaker held up her hand like a cop calling a traffic stop. "Business first, Ms. Park. I'm asking if you will represent me in all matters related to the holdings I have inherited and do so unequivocally and with all prejudice."

"I don't... You do know an action taken *with* prejudice is *final*? Is that what you want?"

"Yes. Now answer my question. Please."

Damn, she was a forthright woman! Stalling for all the world to see, Kiva finally said, "Normally I would require a retainer."

Before she could say more, Elliott counted out crisp one hundred dollar bills, ten of them. "Will that suffice for now, Ms. Park?"

Reaching for the cash she suspected had just been issued by an ATM, she counted it out loud, then said quietly. "I have no idea what you're up to, but it's clear this is a pay-to-play game. Just so we're clear, I'm officially representing you, and yes Ms. Elliott Snowmaker, I'm all in."

CHAPTER TWO

Elliott sat quietly, letting the lawyer open a new file and prepare a receipt. It hadn't escaped her that Miss Stuffy Dress hadn't bothered to reciprocate on the first name thing. It fit in perfectly with everything else she was learning about this place. The whole town seemed aloof and suspicious. She'd checked into the Big Pine Motor Inn only to receive the third degree from someone she assumed was the owner, who questioned her as if she was checking in for a quickie or to host a motel party. She was way too tired and alone for the first and certainly too old for the second. Now the lawyer was giving her the business, and that was after that damn real estate agent had shown up at her door, pounding away until she answered, hair wet from the shower and eyes still blurry from the drive. Did she want to discuss what was going on? *No, not yet.* Even dead tired, she knew when she was being bushwhacked.

"First thing. Can you sit in with me and the other lawyer? Sorry. I'm tired and can't remember his name."

"Ian. Ian Guerrero. He's a partner with the firm."

"And does the Park part of Deegan, Guerrero, and Park mean you are too?"

Looking surprised, the stuffed shirtdress of a lawyer shook her head. "Actually, that's my father. I'm just filling in here while he takes his winter break. When he is here, it's just him and Ian. Sally Deegan retired a few years ago but she still comes in for the odd special client."

That gave Elliott some relief. *So, she may not be part of the regular pack of suspiciousness.* "Ms. Park, do you know what this Ian wants from me?"

The lawyer tilted her head. "Why do you keep calling me that?"

Elliott took in the woman behind the desk. She liked her face. High cheekbones and rich auburn hair that trailed to just past her shoulders gave her a look that matched her profession. Her face was freckled from the sun, and her eyes hinted at Asian ancestry. Maybe her surname was from a Korean forebearer. She was wearing a shirt-dress, although Elliott often thought they should be called coat-dresses because they looked more like tailored jackets cut extra long and shaped just right. Her shoulders were square, escaping the kind of stoop associated with deskbound workers. Maybe in her legal practice, away from this place, she spent more time in court. Somehow, she could see it.

"That's how you introduced yourself. I haven't been invited to address you as anything but Ms. Park."

Blushing, Kiva rushed out her hand again, explaining, "Kiva. Kiva Park and I'm so sorry. I guess I imagined I would be handing you your file and the keys and that would be it."

Elliott nodded, a smile easing her strain. "Kiva, nice. Should we go and hear what Ian has to share? I'm not trying to rush things, but I'm cranky, hungry, and tired and not in that order."

"Oh, of course. You mentioned the drive. Yes, yes, let's check in with Ian. We can put off walking the property and going over the holdings in the hangar till you've had some rest."

She nodded, following Kiva, the not-so-stuffed dress-shirt after all. Elliott may have been exhausted, but she had to admit the view was more than worth the walk. Forcing her exhausted brain to work and her overwrought libido to take a break, she accepted Ian Guerrero's hand before plunking herself in a chair, glad to see Kiva sit down right beside her. Whatever was going on, which was probably only happening in her brain, she didn't want there to be a question as to whose side Kiva Park was on.

Ian waved at the woman beside her. "It's okay, Kiva. You don't need to stay for this."

"Actually, I do, Ian. Please, you said you wanted to make things simple for Elliott?"

Watching as he considered the situation, Elliott sat quietly trying to size up the man and decide what her new lawyer thought about her father's legal partner. He backed into his chair then pulled it forward but not right to his desk, maintaining a distance. She was having a hard time deciding on his age when it hit her that he was wearing a toupee. *Why do guys do that?* She guessed it was better than a comb over, but the jet-black wig just looked wrong against his scraggly gray sideburns. "Yes, well, Ellie—"

"Elliott," she corrected.

He staggered but recovered quickly. "Yes, of course. Okay, let me see." He sorted through several folders on his desk. She wasn't sure if he was having a hard time finding what he was looking for or stalling for time. Finally, he opened the top desk drawer and pulled out the only papers there.

"Yes, here it is. When I heard about your uncle's untimely death, I took it upon myself to look into the airport lease and see if there was any wiggle room. I'm sure Kiva's mentioned old Elliott signed a lengthy lease with some serious penalties. I know there isn't a whole lot in the way of value in the estate and, well, I didn't want to see Kevin's girl here," he said, nodding towards Kiva, "facing a mess like this. And I think I may have worked out something with the county. Now, it's not a done deal, but I explained you weren't interested in taking over Elliott's failing business or his debts. And they're open to a small settlement. Actually…" He tried but failed to pull off the gosh-darn-good-guy look, explaining, "There's a chance we may be able to get those old boys to waive the cancellation penalties altogether."

Elliott pushed her chair back, needing to distance herself from Ian Guerrero. Knowing there was no way she was agreeing to anything this snake was peddling, she forced herself to not walk out. Instead, she allowed a sense of amusement to creep in and sat silently waiting to see how her new lawyer would handle him.

"I'm sorry, Ian. Did you say you opened negotiations with the county on behalf of my client?"

His face paled, then he growled. "Remember your place, Kiva. You're just filling in for Kevin. Old Elliott was his client."

"I may just be filling in, but Elliott Moreno or, more accurately, his estate, is my father's client. I think that gives you some latitude in this situation, but this Elliott, Elliott Snowmaker, is my client. Before you resume any negotiations, I need to be brought up to speed and then my client and I can decide if the firm can or should retain any involvement."

He started sweating, but charged back in. "I'm just looking out for you both. The last thing you want is for little Elliott here to be on the hook for forty years of penalties!"

Standing, Elliott turned her back on Ian Guerrero. Nothing pissed her off more than being referred to as "little Elliott," especially by some dipshit dirt water lawyer. "This discussion has to wait until I've had eight hours sleep. I'm so exhausted, I'm not sure I can find my way to my car, much less the motel."

Kiva nodded and stood. "Let me walk you out and point you in the right direction. We can listen to Ian when you've had some rest."

She followed Kiva through the small reception area and out to the sidewalk. Elliott was prepared for the woman to stop there, but Kiva was smart, spotting her dusty, dirty Jeep parked just two spots down and headed right for it. She stepped down from the sidewalk on the far side of the vehicle then wheeled around at the driver's door.

"You knew something was going on and you didn't warn me?"

Elliott pinched the bridge of her nose. An oncoming headache was the least of her problems. "Ms. Park…"

"Kiva!"

Elliott smiled at the fiery retort. "Like I said, I just got here."

"But you knew enough that something was up and that you should hire me, trust me, and that I wasn't part of whatever may be going on?"

Sighing, she nodded. "Quick explanation?"

At Kiva's crossed arms and toe-tapping, she decided the basics would suffice, at least for now. "I knew your dad was Elmo's lawyer. Great-uncle Elmo used to send my grandmother copies of all his important papers. You know, for someone to keep them safe. So, when I got the letter from you, I looked you up. Then I got here and checked into the Big Pine Motor Inn like you suggested. I wasn't in my room twenty minutes before some real estate agent was banging down my door."

"Who?"

Pulling from the back pocket of her jeans a business card the crass agent had shoved in her face, she handed it over. The lawyer looked at it carefully, lines creasing her brow.

"I know Erica. She usually deals in housing. A hangar isn't exactly in her repertoire. Please tell me you didn't sign anything."

"Are you kidding? The woman couldn't even explain what she was interested in. She tried to tell me she was just there to welcome me to town and deliver her condolences for my great-uncle, who she referred to as 'Good Old Elliott.'"

"Good Old Elliott? More like Good Riddance Elliott." She crossed her arms, taking a careful look around before explaining, "I hate to be the one to tell you, but your uncle wasn't exactly well liked by everyone. I mean they respected him but to these people he was always an outsider. You know, 'that weird guy who lives at the airport,' sort of thing. Why Erica pounced on you, I don't know."

Elliott wasn't surprised to learn Elmo was still an outsider here. Her grandmother was a private person too. Their shared and painful upbringing taught them to keep their distance. Now that looked to be for a good reason. "So, are you the least bit interested in figuring this out? I mean, if it cuts too close to home, say so now, and I'll bring in an outsider."

For her part, Kiva looked to be considering her options carefully. Finally, she sighed. "I'm pretty much as outside as you're going to find around here. And I'm curious to know what this is all about."

"What about your practice and Ian Guerrero?"

"Like I said, it's my dad's partnership, not mine, but I'll have to do some due diligence around overlap to be sure you're covered. Do you want me to come out tomorrow and take you for a tour of the property?"

"As a matter of fact, I do. If for no other reason than to have a witness as to what we find." She watched Kiva nod. She looked so serious, it made Elliott feel sorry for her. "I take it you've been out there already?"

"Actually no. The initial survey and inventory was already completed when I arrived. Now I'm sorry I didn't pay more attention."

Clicking the unlock button on her key fob, Elliott wasn't sure what else she could do now. As much as she was enjoying standing in the winter sun chatting with the enigmatic Kiva Park, she was beyond exhausted. *In another world, I would ask her to dinner. Right now, I'm so tired I can barely stand on my feet.*

Elliott asked, "Would you like to join me for breakfast or meet me at the airport?"

"Do you even know where to get breakfast around here?"

"Not a clue, but anything has to be better than a PowerBar and iced tea. Which is pretty much all I have in the car."

Kiva cracked a slight grin. "Meet me at the Crow Diner at eight," she said, pointing across the street and diagonally from where they were standing.

Elliott climbed in the Jeep. Lowering the window, she offered a handshake. "You're on, counselor. See you in the morning."

* * *

Kiva watched as Elliott backed out and pulled away in her overloaded Jeep. It was time to have a frank discussion with her father. Checking her watch, she knew she couldn't get away with leaving this early, and there was no way she was going to call him from here. Marching back in, she decided to play at whatever game Ian was involved in. Then she spotted him in her office at her desk going through files. "Can I help you?"

He stopped his rifling. "Just checking to be sure everything was signed and properly closed off."

"Actually, I have an appointment with Elliott tomorrow. She wants me to go through the contents of the hangar with her. She's a little overwhelmed and not sure what to do with everything." That seemed to be the right answer, judging by his wolfish grin.

"Yes, that's perfect. You go help her figure out how to get rid of all that old junk. I'm sure she'll be happy for the help. Anything to get her out of here and back to her real life."

Kiva picked up the files associated with Elliott Moreno's estate, stuffing them one by one into her briefcase. "I don't know if I'll need these tomorrow, but as Dad would say, 'better to be prepared.'"

Ian backed out of the office, empty-handed. Then stopped.

"Yes, of course. Wait! Is that why she gave you the retainer? To cover the extra hours needed to sort out old Elliott's junk?" Kiva glanced at her desk, already knowing the cash was gone. She watched his eyes as he grinned, explaining, "Don't you worry, little girl." His yellow teeth were giving her the creeps. He patted his shirt pocket. "I'll just run this over to the bank before it closes."

After another two hours of making endless changes to several wills and estate plans, she gathered up the documents she had managed to snag relating to the airport and adjoining properties and let herself out the back door. It was midwinter and even though she now called Canada home, she was still caught by the day's bitter cold. Here in the north of New Mexico snow this late in March was gone but the ground was still frozen and the sun often warmed the surface enough to muddy up the back alley where they parked their cars. Sitting in hers, she waited for the heater to ramp up and thought about Ian's behavior.

Her parents had befriended him when they settled in this backwater, and she had known him since birth. Of course, it was a different place back then. The airport was part of an active military base, and the town flourished with soldiers spending their money on everything from movies and dinner to housing and rentals. When the base closed, the town began drying up.

There had been a big push a little over a decade ago to revitalize the community, but the recession and the real estate market crash had brought it to a painful halt while taking the savings of most of the townsfolks involved or invested in the idea. She didn't doubt it was time for a fresh look at reviving the local economy, but whatever Ian was involved in, he was playing his cards close to the vest. Too close. And if Erica Dunbar, the local real estate agent, was stalking Elliott Snowmaker, she knew it had to be significant. That woman had been the queen of the low-ratio mortgage and had cost more folks their homes than Kiva could imagine. Whatever they were up to, alone or together, she had a feeling the quiet and forthright Elliott was standing in their way.

Elliott.

Kiva couldn't for the life of her say what she was expecting, but the unassuming woman who had walked into her office wasn't it. Long used to considering her time in Illusion Lake, Mirabal County, as a dry patch, she had to rein in her interest. She had read the notes her father left on all his outstanding cases and clients. She knew Elliott was a pilot for some charter airline up north. Of course, everyone in town knew that. Old Elliott was always bragging about his niece. Or grand-niece, as Elliott herself would have corrected. She hadn't really known the elderly Elliott well enough to say more than hi and ask how he was on the few occasions they bumped into one another.

She'd always liked old Elliott. He was kind and gentle but not too attentive or creepy like other old men she had met as a kid. And he remembered things. He kept a Christmas card list and never failed to send her a card every year. It always featured some old plane on the front and a personalized message inside. He always wished her well in school and offered his congratulations on her achievements. When it came to the Park girls, her dad bragged to anyone who would listen but old Elliott was the only person in town who ever remembered, much less bothered to say as much. When she graduated from law school, she was surprised and delighted to receive a desk clock as a gift from him. It featured a bear cub and propeller, a Piper-branded gift he said was to remind her how time flies. *Yes, Elliott. It sure does.*

It never took long to drive home from her dad's office, but by local standards it was downright long-distance. Getting to the state road took no more than a few minutes and once there it was all of six or seven minutes more to the family home on the far side of the lake, a legacy of her maternal grandmother. Her Gran had bought the old farmhouse in complete disrepair and had spent several years renovating it all by herself. To say the O'Donnell women were tough was an understatement. The large two-story house, with its clean wood siding, handmade shutters, communal attic, mature garden beds and wraparound porch always felt like home to her. She loved the place and had fantastic childhood memories. It was one of the few properties in the county that had retained any value.

And her dad had been smart, buying out the property next door a decade ago. That house wasn't much more than a cottage, but it sat on five acres. These days he was renting it out to a down-on-his-luck veteran in exchange for maintaining both properties. Now the family home, neglected after her mother's move to California, was awash in winter flowerbeds and tended lawns in a region mostly parched dry or brushed in snow. It was a pleasure to return to, and a big change over her small condo in Toronto.

Parking her car alongside the house, she walked around the back, waving at her neighbors before climbing up the stairs to the big wraparound deck and heading inside. It was tempting to just grab a beer and stretch out on the couch, but she wanted to get out of her work clothes.

Upstairs, she headed for the guest bedroom. There were four bedrooms to choose from since she had the place to herself for the entire winter, but somehow this room, even with its mauve paint and the hand-painted flowers her grandmother had added, felt extra welcoming. In jeans and a T-shirt, ready to tackle her work, she trotted downstairs, heading to the open kitchen and grabbing the cold one she'd promised herself. Plunking herself down on the couch, pulling out the files she had taken from the office, she looked for something she had spotted the day she arrived but hadn't thought much about at the time.

The proposed airport redevelopment plan had seemed like a long shot when she noticed it. There were always plans to redevelop the airport, ever since the Air Force had handed the property over to the county almost thirty years ago. While a few of the houses in the one-time private married quarters had been sold off, the military had bulldozed most of the other buildings. Those that hadn't been removed had been pulled down by the county when they couldn't rent them out. One of the few successes had been old Elliott's business. He was the first to sign on and the only one to last all these years. And he had worked at it, running everything from a flying school and charter service to finally focusing on his vintage aircraft restorations.

Reading through the preamble of the redevelopment plan, she knew she'd missed something significant. Money. That had been the common denominator in every previous proposal. Now it looked like the county had an investor on the hook, and her father's law partner was facilitating the deal. No wonder Ian was so hot to get "little Elliott" to agree to renege on her great-uncle's lease.

Taking a second to enjoy her beer, she watched out the big rear windows as Mark and Andi, her dad's tenants and probably the best thing to happen to him in years, played with their kids at the edge of the frosty lake. Some old teacher of hers had explained that Illusion Lake was once a wide river that had become landlocked. The only reason the five-mile-long skinny lake hadn't completely dried out like most of the region was a deep aquifer that fed it all year long. Still, even with the constant replenishment, she could see a marked change from the shoreline she had known as a kid. It wasn't that noticeable, maybe a few dozen feet, but even without a background in science she could appreciate just how much more water would be needed to bring the lake back to its original dimension.

Opening old Elliott's file and skipping past several letters, pages, and documents, she found what she most wanted to see, the county lease for airport access. Elliott was in a unique situation. At some point over the last thirty years, the county had sold more than half of the vacant land on the east side of the old base. Old Elliott was smart, buying both the hangar and the land it was on along with more than one hundred acres which started right at the edge of runway fifteen. It took time to read through it and absorb the gist of the contractual obligations. When she was done, she knew two things. Her father was still a consummate professional, always putting his clients first, and the county was screwed if they thought they could renege now.

Flipping back to the summary document her father had written, she noted Elliott Moreno had first leased airport access in the eighties, during the early days of downsizing, a precursor to the base closing. He had signed back-to-back ten-year leases until 2009. That was when the blowback from the housing crisis really hit the economy worldwide. When the other airport leases had failed to renew, the county must have panicked; they offered old Elliott a fifty-year contract and they attached enough penalties and riders to make one's head spin. Still, she recognized her father's hand in the provisions. Someone was apparently stuck on the fifty-year timeline, but the penalties were reciprocal. That meant the hefty fees they could leverage against old Elliott if he reneged could also be held against the county if they tried to squirm out early too. No wonder Ian was trying to pull a fast one on little Elliott. *I must stop calling her that.*

She began calculating the penalties on the long yellow pad she had removed from her case when she remembered a schedule included in the attachments. It only took seconds to find it, then skip to the current year. The penalties worked like a mortgage schedule. The longer the lease was honored, the lower the penalty for breaking it. With close to forty years left on the lease and no death provision, either party was on the hook for eighty percent of lease payments due, less the cost of living increases worked into the leasing rate.

Finding the correct line in the penalty schedule, she read across the page and almost gasped at the number: $444,800! That was the penalty the county could charge Elliott if she wanted to break the lease. It was also how much they would owe her if they wanted her gone.

"Holy shit!"

CHAPTER THREE

Elliott wasn't bothered by the stares as she made her way to an empty booth in the busy diner. She nodded and offered her greetings, taking no offense at the reluctant responses. After all, no one had a clue who she was. The waitress was quick to reach her table, hoping no doubt to learn why she was here so she could share it with everyone else.

"What can I get you, hon?" she asked, sliding a plastic-covered menu onto the table.

"Someone's joining me, but I could use a coffee while I wait."

"Sure thing."

Slipping around the counter and grabbing the coffeepot and a mini stainless-steel pot of fresh cream, she was back in a flash. She flipped the already set cup over on its matching saucer and filled it to the brim before heading down the line of almost full booths to top up coffee for all the regulars.

Expecting the third degree, she smiled, realizing that the waitress, like the folks she was now quietly exchanging words with, were all waiting to see who would join her. She was still grinning when Kiva Park walked through the door. Today she was wearing a power suit in dark colors. The contrast with her soft curves and lithe frame added a feminine air to her strictly business look, while stirring something in Elliott. She stood to welcome her breakfast companion, saying loudly enough for the diner patrons, "Ms. Park, thank you for joining me."

Kiva's eyes widened slightly, then she offered a grin to match her own. The woman was indeed bright.

"Thank you for inviting me, Ms. Snowmaker. Shall we get to business or have breakfast first?" This she said in an equally professional tone and again loudly enough for the folks present to get an earful. Sliding into the booth across from Elliott, she opened her briefcase but waited until the waitress had delivered her menu and filled her coffee cup before she asked in a more conspiring tone, "So how was your night?"

"I slept pretty well, considering the place is like party central. I guess that's what happens on Friday nights when kids have no place to go."

"Oh no! I'm so sorry."

Elliott waved her off. "We were all teens once. I guess it's the one standard whether you grew up in a city or a small town."

"I take it you were a city kid?"

It was easy to think this was a different woman today, playful and talkative. "Oh yeah." Elliott smiled, then hid behind her coffee cup before admitting, "As wild as they come. Drove my mom crazy. How 'bout you?"

"I wasn't exactly the wild one. That was my sister, but I must admit I did tag along with her to a few parties out at the Big Pine before we moved up north. I had no idea things hadn't changed on that front."

The waitress was back and asking Kiva how she was settling back in. Elliott was reminded that the woman sitting with her didn't live or practice here fulltime. She had been assured of that yesterday, but somehow getting confirmation mattered to her. Circumstances were confusing enough without having to decide who she could trust. She didn't exactly have a great track record at picking the trustworthy. Her last breakup had been a hard lesson, teaching her that the friends she believed in and supported weren't as dependable as she imagined and the promises made between two people supposedly in love meant nothing when one of them was unfaithful and had been from the start.

Looking at Kiva sitting across from her shuffling some papers, she could only hope she wasn't wrong about this one. Last night, taking advantage of the free Wi-Fi, she had researched her new attorney. This wasn't Kiva's first visit home, but it was her first time taking over her father's practice. She was licensed to practice law in this state and several others, but up till now her part-time forays had been to assist her father in cases requiring a litigator. It seemed her dad, Kevin Park, preferred the office over the courtroom and had taken advantage of his daughter's skills especially in ugly cases involving children. She had been so good, with an unbroken winning streak, that her father, and by extension his partner, was often able to settle even the most contentious matters out of court on the strength of threatening to bring in Kiva. Elliott blurted, "I'm not a good judge of character."

Stilling the papers she was sorting, Kiva was smiling. "Then it's a good thing you hired me." She added, "I know you're suspicious and you're right to be. I've done some digging, and we should talk about it, but," she lowered her voice and, leaning in, said, "not here. Once we get to the hangar, I'll go over everything I've found, and you can explain what all these things are." She pushed the inventory list over to Elliott and pointed to the highlighted items.

Though she wanted to concentrate on the list, Elliott found it hard to look past Kiva's hands, her thin long fingers, her skin so healthy and soft. Her nails were manicured but what caught her eye was not the nail polish so much as how short the nails were. She said without thinking, "It must be hard to be here all winter without your partner, I mean…"

Looking taken back, Kiva didn't comment. Instead, she brushed the papers aside as the waitress set down their breakfast orders.

"That was fast. Thanks," Elliott said to the waitress as she checked their coffee levels and set down a bowl of salsa, then grabbed a bottle of ketchup from an empty table.

"It doesn't take long to scramble eggs," Kiva remarked, unceremoniously pushing the ketchup bottle away. "Would you prefer salsa for your eggs? Gale makes it fresh everyday."

"I'm a plain-Jane kind of girl. Just a little salt is as adventurous as I get."

Kiva smiled at her. Elliott wasn't sure why, but she took it as a good thing as Kiva smothered her eggs in salsa before digging in. Kiva said, "I got used to this kind of thing growing up here. It's a pain at home, trying to find the things I like."

Elliott nodded. She knew the woman was right, but times had changed a lot. "It's easier to find a good falafel than tapas. That's for sure."

That comment seemed to draw interest from Kiva. "You live in Vancouver, right?"

"No, the company I fly for, did fly for, is headquartered in Vancouver. I live in Toronto too." She watched Kiva's eyebrows rise. It was easy to guess she hadn't spent much time researching her new client. Elliott didn't know if she should be pleased the woman was focused on her great-uncle's estate and whatever was going on regarding the strange behavior of Ian Guerrero, or disappointed she hadn't been considering her in more detail. "I did say I researched you. I hope you don't think that's, I don't know, stalkerish?"

A smile lit Kiva's face. She ate more of her eggs before finally commenting, "No. I'm glad you did, and as far as a partner, that's ancient history. You must have hit on the Osgood Hall Gala write-ups. That was almost four years ago, and yes, times change. What about you?" she asked conversationally while indelicately chowing down on her salsa and eggs and moaning with pleasure at each bite.

Elliott pushed past her enjoyment of listening to the sounds of Kiva Park devouring her breakfast and concentrated on the question. "Ah, partner, yes. I mean no. Like I said, I'm not a good judge of character, so relationships have always been a big disaster for me. I mean, it's not like I haven't tried but, well, women don't seem to go for me and the few that do…let's just say, most see a meal ticket or something like that, and it just makes me resentful when I figure it out."

"Which I assume is always too late?"

She nodded, remembering that Kiva hadn't hiccuped at the mention yesterday at her coming out to her family. *Note to self: Never play poker with this woman.* "So yes, no partner. Frankly, I'm not sure I can afford another mistake on that scale. You saw that heap I'm driving so I don't have to tell you about the rest, do I?"

Kiva's eyes narrowed. "You need a better lawyer. There is no way I would have let some money-grubbing little bitch take you for all you're worth much less tarnish your reputation."

Maybe she *had* done her due diligence. "You know?"

Kiva nodded. "I did my research too. And unlike you, I am an amazing judge of character. I can tell you right now, I know you wouldn't hurt a fly and you absolutely didn't deserve what she put you through. As a matter of fact, I was going to ask, since I'm representing you, would you be okay with me taking some action on that point? I can't get the case reopened, but I can get the unfounded allegations axed and keep her from spreading her lies and continually harassing you."

Elliott set her fork down, swallowing the emotions that threatened. "You believe me?"

Kiva nodded.

"I… no one, not even my so-called friends, believed me."

"That's the thing with abusers and psychopathic behavior. They use bits and pieces of the truth to pad their lies. It delivers a realism lesser minds can gravitate to or fall for. I bet there were times when even you had to shake your head, thinking it sounded true."

Unwilling to trust her voice, Elliott just nodded. It had been such a nightmare. One she was willing to do anything to stop. She had fallen for a gregarious bartender, a woman so outgoing and friendly that she readily filled the voids in Elliott's solitary life. The cost, though, was quickly apparent. When it got to be too much, both financially and emotionally, her partner instantaneously became the victim and played it for all the world to see. Elliott thought she could bow out quietly, taking on the extravagant debts her partner had rung up in her name, but the woman was not so easily dismissed. Suddenly all the people she believed were friends were questioning her behavior, accusing her of everything from abandonment to domestic abuse, and spreading it far and wide.

Living on her cousin's couch to wait out the storm, Elliott had been keeping a low profile. Then one morning in flight ops, she was getting her weather briefing and passenger loads for her scheduled flight to Mexico City when two cops marched in and put her in cuffs, making sure everyone in the place heard them read the charges of assault, theft, and arson. Once in the police station and confronted with evidence of her ex's car being torched and the woman being slapped around in the alley behind her bar, she had shown the cops her flight schedule, explaining that her crew overnighted in Mexico City, and that's where she was when the alleged attack had taken place. They kept her in an interview room for hours while they confirmed with the airline and then with the hotel in Mexico City that she had indeed checked in and checked out the next morning for the return flight. They even went so far as to interview her captain for confirmation she was on the plane and the crew to confirm she was at the hotel.

Weeks later, video footage from the convenience store across the street from the bar surfaced showing her ex leaving the alley and climbing into a cab around the time the fire had been called in by neighbors. The footage clearly showed the night deposit bag pinned under the woman's arm and smoke coming from down the alley. Her ex had claimed Elliott had battered her, taken the night deposit to fuel her drug problem, then set fire to her car.

Once the police received the bloodwork for Elliott, they knew she wasn't a drug user. Then with the video from the convenience store, they searched the apartment now shared by her ex and her new girlfriend. It had turned up considerable incriminating evidence, including the empty night deposit sack.

Even after her ex was arrested she never gave up the lie, claiming Elliott must have planted it all. While the police were no longer fooled, their friends still were. It hurt like hell and the damage was done, especially at work. They had furloughed her without pay while they investigated her ability to maintain her flight schedule and ordered her to receive counseling to ensure she was safe to fly, citing depression as a factor in keeping her grounded. She wasn't depressed, but she was embarrassed. Her only crime at work was a failure to maintain a schedule, her arrest causing her flight to be delayed while they found another pilot to take her place. The ultimate sin in her line of work, her reputation was solidly and wholly ruined. Even if they finally recalled her, she wasn't sure she had the chutzpah to stroll back in the door.

"I'm so sorry all that happened to you," Kiva said emphatically. "It never should have, none of it. I think it's time you take on the airline too. Your furlough was unfounded and undeserved. In my opinion, they targeted you because you're a lesbian. If they suspended every straight male pilot suspected of abusing a domestic partner, they'd lose a quarter or more of their workforce. And I promise when we're done here, if you let me, I'll dig into the entire case and fix as much as I can."

Still not trusting her voice, Elliott just nodded. It was an interesting sensation to trust this woman. After everything that had happened, she wasn't sure trust would ever figure back into her repertoire of feelings, but here she was and if nothing else, she knew she could trust Kiva Park.

* * *

Kiva drove to the airport, her new client following in her own car. They had gone through the highlighted items on the inventory list, but even with explanations from Elliott she wasn't sure what half the items were. It didn't really matter, nor would it matter to the probate, as the will stipulated clearly that everything be handed over to young Elliott. Still, she wanted to be thorough and to be sure, after everything that had happened to Elliott, that she was protected. Last night she had spent time on the phone with a friend in the Metropolitan Toronto police force getting the skinny on Elliott's situation. She had already accessed and read the court files. The little bitch who had framed her managed to get off just because the bar owner was a friend and wouldn't press charges. They had let the arson charges go too, with insufficient evidence to prove that she had set the fire herself before climbing into a cab. The allegations of abuse were also suspect, but cops were always antsy around domestic violence, so the accusations had managed to outlive indications to the contrary.

On the phone with a detective sergeant she often worked with, she listened to their discoveries about Elliott's duplicitous ex-partner with disgust, knowing there was little law enforcement could do to protect a person's reputation.

"I'm sorry, Kiva. I wish the law worked differently. I think your client's a good person, but she got involved with a bad crowd and she's paid a big price. I said as much to her."

"You spoke with her?"

"I did most of the interviews. I think she's a gentle soul who believes in the good in others. I told her so when I drove her home the last time they brought her in. I'm embarrassed to admit constables from fifty-one division took a new complaint from the ex without checking the open investigation notes. The poor woman had taken some work at the Island Airport at night, doing maintenance and stuff. Constables cuffed her coming off the first morning ferry, on her way home from work. Those dumbasses didn't even think about how she would have gotten out to the burbs to carry out an alleged attack when you can't get off the island once the night ferry docks."

"You drove her home?" That was something a rookie cop might do, but not a senior detective.

"No, to her car parked at the ferry dock. I felt like a real shit. I mean, here she was, still in coveralls and covered in grease. It took all of ten minutes for a PC to check her alibi. They have frigging cameras everywhere over there. They had footage of her working on private aircraft all night."

"Oh, that's so horrible. I didn't know she took a non-flying job after the airline suspension."

"Not like she had a choice. They suspended her flight medical on suspicion of depression. I did a little digging, and even with the counseling ordered, there's still a two-year cooling-off period required before they'll let her back in the air. I have to say she took losing that crappy, do-anything-to-pay-the-bills job at the Island Airport better than I would have."

"She lost that job too?"

She heard a confirming groan from the crisp digital connection. "They freaked when the constables showed up to check her alibi. They sent her a text letting her go. She got it while she was in my unit and I was driving her back to her car."

Kiva had thanked her friend for the information and ended the call, more determined than ever to correct the injustice heaped on the head of the quiet and reticent woman she was starting to get to know. *Why didn't you fight harder?*

But then, fighting was the original accusation. As Kiva drove through the gates of the airport, gates that should have been closed and locked and never were, she took stock of the whole situation. She needed to be sure of Elliott before she went to bat on all the outrageous accusations inflicted on her. But her first priority was old Elliott's estate. She needed to concentrate on that today, that and deciding what was better, getting her out of here or taking on the plans Ian Guerrero and his cronies had for Elliott's new holdings.

CHAPTER FOUR

It took a minute for Elliott's eyes to adjust to the dim light of the hangar. She pushed its big rolling door open wider and from the threshold took in what she had not expected. The list of items on the inventory had been vague at best, but nothing could have prepared her for what she saw. Laid out in assembly-line precision were three primarily wood fuselages and a fourth more modern looking warbird, all in various stages of restoration. Across from them were the wing assemblies. She couldn't make out any powerplants, but welding curtains and tool chests divided several sections where the light from the open door didn't entirely penetrate. The hangar was big, a lot bigger than she expected. She could imagine parking three or four small business jets in here. And the place featured galleries running down each side. One looked like it housed a skinny row of offices while the other side could be parts lockers, enclosed in chain link fencing. It was easy to imagine that not much had changed from the days when the place belonged to the military, except for the wooden airframes. She was sure even they predated the giant Quonset hangar.

"I know it's a lot."

Elliott turned to see Kiva standing beside her. She had forgotten she was there. "Do you know where the power is? I'd like to turn on some lights and look around if that's okay."

Kiva smiled to help her relax. "Of course. This is all yours now. You can do as you like." She held up a mini Maglite, clicking it on and leading the way. "I found a layout drawing in the files, so we have a hint."

Elliott followed her up the gallery stairs on the office side and to the end of the long gangway. A large and modern electrical panel was mounted against what must be the rear of the hangar, facing the airside of the airport. Kiva held the flashlight, letting her do the honors. Section by section, fluorescent lights lit up all through the long narrow line of offices, and she could hear the mercury vapor lights warming as they hummed to life above the open hangar. She was giddy to see everything on the floor but reined in her enthusiasm, wanting to follow whatever plan Kiva had in mind.

"Want to look around up here?" When Elliott nodded, Kiva started back along the gangway between the offices and the diagonal hangar wall. "I don't know what we should expect, but I understand your uncle was living up here."

The first door she opened was to a sitting room. It was easy to imagine this once being an office. The next was the same size and converted to a bedroom furnished in what looked like surplus military furniture including a precision-made single bed. "Is this his..." Elliott was taken aback by the bedroom, unable to see her great-uncle living in such an impersonal space.

She felt a hand touch her arm, calming her. "I don't think so. According to the layout plan, this was intended as a guest room. Come on. Let's keep looking." She led them past the men's room that had been converted into a spotless bathroom with a shower, sink and toilet, even if the door sign had never been changed. Next was a double-sized office.

Opening that door, Kiva signaled for Elliott to enter first. Unprepared and already a little emotional, she stepped into a much longer room that had been converted into a library. Maybe it had started as a file room or reference material gallery, but either way the result was outstanding. Almost shaking with excitement, Elliott moved to the first set of steel shelves that lined every wall and randomly pulled down a book. She took in the cover then replaced it and pulled down another. Moving along the wall, she repeated the process, soaking everything in before finally exclaiming, "This must be one of the most complete aviation libraries around. I mean, he's got everything you can think of from Curtiss on up."

Kiva smiled, pointing. "You missed the Zane Grey collection on the bottom shelf."

Overwhelmed, she took in the windows overlooking the hangar floor, the opposite twenty foot wall lined with books and the military-grade couch, recognizable by its wooden arms and blue leatherlike coverings, pushed under the open windows. "Do I have you or your firm to thank or was Uncle Elmo really this fastidious?"

"Surprisingly enough, your great-uncle kept the place this way. From what my father told me, old Elliott spent his last few months in a care facility up in Amarillo, but we had someone do a little dusting after inventorying the place. That's all it needed. I'm told he kept this place spotless and organized right from the start."

It was a lot to take in. "I could spend a month just in this room. What else is up here?"

"Just his bedroom. Are you ready for that?"

Elliott nodded. She had to see everything and have a chance to sit down and talk about whatever was behind Ian Guerrero's hurried offer to buy her out. "Lead on."

Elmo's bedroom was surprisingly removed from the military holdover in the rest of the place. It was a little crowded, with a matching set of antique pieces. Elliott ran her hand over the footboard of the burled-maple sleigh bed, with its vintage four-point blanket in the distinctive blue, yellow, red, and green stripes of the Hudson's Bay Company, still looking fresh against the natural white virgin wool, perhaps a tribute to his ancestry. Taking in the matching maple table and bureau dresser, she noted that the only thing missing was a dressing table. She remembered her grandmother telling her Elmo had once been married. "I don't know exactly when his wife left," Elliott said more to herself than Kiva. "I just know they didn't have kids. Nanny said he missed that, missed having kids of his own."

Kiva opened the wardrobe at the end of the room. "I'm not sure what you want to do with his clothes, but if you need a hand, just let me know."

"I need a hand with everything, but you must get that a lot with clients."

"I do, but most of mine are young offenders and sometimes their families. Estates are not my forte but…I've taken an interest in this case. Besides your uncle—sorry, great-uncle's—unique holdings, there's more going on here than what either of us expected. My notes say there's a kitchen downstairs. Why don't we have a look at that? Maybe we can find the coffee, and I can show you some of the paperwork."

Elliott nodded, waving a hand for Kiva to lead the way while she took one last look around Elmo's most private place, his bedroom, wondering if he had been lonely all these years. She felt the crunch of her own singleness. Was it easier for men? It hadn't been easy for her grandmother, but she had sworn off men long ago, and it looked like her little brother had done the same when it came to women. After all she had been through, swearing off women and relationships only made sense, yet the hole it left felt insurmountable.

Reaching the bottom stairs, she could see two of the airframes Elmo had been working on. Work…undoubtedly a better cure for her melancholy. Maybe what he had built here was worth considering, exploring, even continuing. It was certainly a better option than going home.

* * *

Kiva poured two mugs of coffee, apologizing to Elliott for the lack of cream. "There's some powdered creamer here. Maybe it was just easier to keep. My father says he usually ate dinner at the Crow Diner, so maybe he didn't bother with much else."

Opening the fridge to discover only a case of Molson Ex, Elliott asked, "Was this cleaned out too?"

"Not that I know of." The implication hung between them. "I think he knew he wouldn't be coming home from the care facility." Setting her cup on the scratched and worn Formica surface of the table, she traced a finger along the old chrome edging tape encompassing the table trim before pulling out a chair, a match to the one Kiva had taken. The chairs' legs were a copy of the table, with chrome hoops for each leg. Even the chairs' backrests were finished in some sort of plastic cloth with a similar pattern to the Formica top. She smiled to think this was probably a very fancy kitchenette fifty years ago.

Elliott seemed reticent, even removed, from the situation. Maybe this was all too much. It was hard to gauge how people would react to a loss. Still, by Elliott's own admission she hardly knew the man. "You seem upset, too upset for someone who never really knew your great-uncle."

"I'm…I guess I'm…I don't know what I'm feeling, but you're right, it's only partly about losing Elmo. I guess I'm struck by how solitary his life is, was. I think he may have been like my grandmother. The thing about her is her unwavering belief that she can never trust anyone. Well, that and her assertions that she would never place herself again in a position where she has to kowtow to some man. I think Elmo was in the same place when it came to trust and his heart. Nanny once said she didn't think he would ever get over Aunt Alice leaving him. Now I'm sitting here in this place, and this whole thing he's got going is so amazing and perfect, and part of me just wants to jump in and take over where he left off, and the other part is scared shitless. I keep thinking I'll end up just like them, alone and compensating by devoting my life to my work."

Elliott cradled her coffee mug and tinkered with the spoon, eyes on her actions. "I'm not saying that's a bad thing. I'm just saying...I don't know what I'm saying."

Kiva listened, reading the emotions and intention of her words clearly. "Maybe you're not ready to give up on love."

Turning the saddest of blue eyes on her, Elliott seemed to agree. "Am I that easy to read?"

"Don't ever apologize for being human. I'm sorry to hear your Nanny and old Elliott gave up on relationships. I for one don't want to give up on the idea of that one special person." What she didn't say and would never admit was that the picture of that perfect someone her sister had drawn out of her, and the sullen woman sitting across from her, were a perfect match.

Oblivious, Elliott continued, "I don't believe in love at first sight. I guess that's cynical, but attraction can be deceiving. I'm not saying chemistry doesn't play a part, but there has to be more, at least for the long run. That soulmate business—is there such a thing? I mean, do we really have one perfect partner out there waiting to be found or is it just something the greeting card companies made up?"

Kiva grinned at the image. "Yes, it's all a made-up fantasy we've been sold but what a beautiful fantasy. Don't you think?"

Looking very much like she was starting to relax, Elliott offered a lopsided grin. "I believe you may be the smartest person I've ever met."

"Good, because we may need all my smarts and everything you have to figure this out. The first thing you need to know is you now own the hangar, its contents and close to one hundred acres of land this side of the runway. Just ten years ago your great-uncle signed a fifty-year lease. It's like nothing I've seen and very unexpected considering his age." She pushed the papers over, folding them to the requirements list first. "These are the joint responsibilities. Old Elliott was responsible for maintaining a fixed base operation, which is stipulated as a maintenance facility without fuel. Do you know what that means?"

She nodded. "He's just promising to service aircraft that land here, offering repairs and such without running a fueling truck. Translated, it means any plane landing here won't be able to buy gas, but they can get an oil change."

"Okay, I get that. Next, it says he has to host a radio room."

"No problem there. A radio room is basically someone to talk to since there is no tower. It's not a requirement to have a radio operator or even listen in since this airport simply requires pilots to announce their intentions on a set radio frequency. I'm guessing we'll find a radio setup somewhere and 'hosting' simply means he's supposed to allow airport staff access when needed. Are there any airport staff? I mean, the runways are dangerous in their current condition."

"What do you mean?" Kiva asked.

"I took a quick look around yesterday. Zero-nine and maybe Two-one look close to being out of action, gravel and bits of rubber have been tracked all over. I suspect kids have been out here racing at night. Still, the FOD risks are extremely high."

"FOD?"

"Sorry, foreign object damage. Stuff that can be sucked into intakes and rip engines apart or chip propellers beyond repair. It's not such a significant risk with small piston aircraft, you know, little bug bashers, but it can still do some expensive damage. Do you remember the Air France crash that permanently grounded all Concords?" Elliott asked, continuing without waiting for an answer. "That was caused by a small piece of trim which had fallen off the previous departing aircraft. It was about the size and shape of a school ruler."

"You're kidding right?" At Elliott's firm shake of her head she shivered involuntarily. If a little piece of metal could take out the fastest civilian airliner, just how safe was it to fly? Forcing herself to focus on the job at hand, she did pat herself on the back for starting to understand all this air stuff. She took the pages back from Elliott, flipping to another section. "These are the responsibilities of the county. I didn't understand it when I read it, but it makes more sense now… Let me see, yes here it is. Section three, the county will maintain and keep a minimum of one runway, it says nine slash twenty-seven…"

"Zero-nine, Two-seven. Those are the magnetic headings for each direction of the runway. Ever notice the numbers at the start of the runway?" When Kiva nodded, she explained, "They are the first two numbers in the magnetic heading, so zero-nine stands for ninety degrees or east. I would have preferred they keep One-five up as well. It's the one just outside the hangar door, but it will work as a taxiway too."

"Got it. Okay. So according to this, the county needs to take care of at least one runway and you're saying that's not happening?"

"Not from what I've seen. We'll need to take a walk and have a closer look, but I wouldn't want to take a chance on landing here. Not till someone's had a sweeper clean the place up and the potholes filled."

This was so interesting. Looking over the rest of the requirements, she already knew without having Elliott explain that the county was failing on several points. "Do you think old Elliott could have serviced aircraft? I mean if someone was brave or stupid enough to risk landing here?"

Nodding again, she confirmed, "With just a cursory look so far, I don't see a reason why he couldn't. Whether he wanted to is another story. He looks to have had his hands full with the projects on the floor. Still, if someone landed and was AOG, there's no reason he, or me, couldn't get them back in the air."

Smiling, Kiva reached over, putting a hand on her arm. "Okay, I'm going to get you to stop with the pilot talk for a bit, at least until I'm clued in, but to make it simple, I'm just going to assume that means you could fix a plane if it were needed. So, tell me, in your opinion was old Elliott in violation of the lease agreement?"

Giving the question careful consideration, Elliott read the list over, finally shaking her head. "No. Other than dropping dead before the lease was out. And like I said, we haven't found the radio room yet, but he was just supposed to host it, not operate it so a handheld two-way would have counted, and I'm sure we'll find one here somewhere. If not, I've got one in my flight bag."

Hmm. It was a lot to consider. "Okay, let's go have a look at the rest of the place and find that radio room thing they're talking about. Then we need to talk about what you want to do. I have a feeling everyone has plans for this place, but they don't mean a thing until I know what you want."

They spent some time venturing through the opposite loft, eventually finding the radio room along with the parts stores, a room dedicated to large drawing files including an old-time microfiche reader and a large-scale printer. Like the rest of the place, everything was organized and fastidiously kept. The rooms below the loft weren't as clean, but when Elliott explained the nature of the lubricant sump and other aspects, she understood it would be impossible to make these places look any more decent.

The most interesting event was their tour of the main hangar floor. What had been defined as "aircraft salvage" turned out to be several vintage aircraft in various stages of restoration. She watched Elliott's eyes light up at discovering the identity of each model, especially when she realized the engines for each one—she kept calling them powerplants—were whole and completely rebuilt. It looked like old Elliott enjoyed working on engines most as he had taken on that aspect of each restoration first.

Before returning to work, Kiva made a note of each airplane make and model to get an idea of what exactly Elliott was sitting on and how difficult it would be to unload them if that was her intent. When she reached the office, she was glad to see Ian was out and took the time to do some swift research. The smallest of the planes, when finished, could garner over a hundred thousand dollars, while the largest, the de Havilland Mosquito, would potentially be worth millions. It turned out there were only two of them on the planet that were flying. If Elliott could get it rebuilt and back in the air, she could expect offers of over ten million.

By late afternoon Kiva was buried in work on a divorce agreement when Ian chugged back in. He wanted to see Elliott and preferably today.

"Not going to happen," she said without so much as taking her eyes off her computer screen.

"Goddammit, Kiva! There is no time for your bullshit. I need to get this done, and you shouldn't be keeping that girl on a string. Close this up and cut her loose."

Standing, she squared off against a man she once thought of as an uncle. "I don't know what your problem is, but that woman and her inheritance are none of your business. She hasn't decided what she wants to do with everything out there or if she even wants to sell, so back off and give her some space."

He looked like he was close to an aneurysm but seemed to understand he couldn't make progress fighting with her.

"I'm just watching out for her," he blustered. "The last thing either of us would want is for her to get stuck holding the bag on that broken down hole in the ground. I just want to help. I talked to the county, and they're willing to make a deal and let her off the hook with the penalties. I'm sure she's having a hard time, losing her uncle and all, but she's better off letting me get rid of all that junk for her. I bet I could even find someone to make a good offer for the hangar too. She could probably walk away from this thing unscathed and with a good hundred grand in her pocket."

While the airport or more correctly the access roads and the runways were county property, most of the land the old base covered had long been sold off part and parcel, including the last standing hangar. "A hundred thousand dollars for the contents of the hangar, the building itself and connected land?"

He seemed to choke. "There's nothing there worth any real value. The best I could do is get the hangar sold and maybe a few bucks from the scrapper for all those old engines."

He looked sincere until she met his eyes. There was no way she would let Elliott fall for this crap, no matter what was behind it. And as far as there being nothing of real value, she had spent an hour on the phone with curators of the Smithsonian Air and Space and Canada's National Fight Museum. The guy from the Smithsonian had estimated the value of a complete DeHavilland Mosquito could easily hit ten million, while the guy from Ottawa offered her a million Canadian dollars for the incomplete project, as is, sight unseen. "I'll talk to her, but she needs a few days to process."

He backed away, his smile viperish, leaving her feeling a chill. "Do that, then let's bring her in here and get everything closed and done. As a matter of fact, I'm sure she's in a hurry to get home so I can have the firm buy out the hangar and hold it until the realtor can get it sold."

"Why would you do that?"

"It's the least we can do for old Elliott. He was a good man," he said as he left the office.

She listened as he checked in with Sofia, their joint admin/receptionist, before returning to his office. Slouching back in her chair, she tried to relax. It was hard to wrap her mind around what was going on. Yes, there was a redevelopment plan on the county books for the airport, but there always was. Yes, the economy had recovered so that could be a factor in someone wanting to do something with the property, but there had to be more. What galled her most was Ian's belief he could fool the younger Elliott into thinking her great-uncle's estate was worth a measly hundred grand. Maybe her father had been duped into thinking the contents of the hangar were worthless, but she knew better now, and Elliott certainly did. No wonder Ian wanted to make her an offer sight unseen. Why he was still sticking to it now that Elliott had toured the hangar she couldn't understand, and offering for the firm to buy her out was not only unprecedented, it was unethical.

She needed to talk to her father about this, but she couldn't contact him now, not with Ian in hearing range. Instead, she sent a text to her sister. She'd get her to feel him out. More than that, she wanted to know why he'd dumped her in this mess without so much as a warning.

Please, Dad, please tell me you didn't know, and you're not part of this.

CHAPTER FIVE

Elliott walked into the motel room and flopped down on the bed. She hadn't made it to the Crow before closing time and had settled for grabbing some chips and pop from the gas station on her way back from the airport. After spending the morning with Kiva going over the inventory and the lease details, she had stayed at the hangar while Kiva returned to her father's office to take on Ian Guerrero. That was a relief. Much as she would have liked to see that, she was too emotionally invested in what Elmo had built. He had created so much more than the original estate papers had said.

Item listings like "Various aircraft dismantled/wreckage" turned out to be the restored fuselages and unmarried wings of four different aircraft. Even in their disassembled state, they were each worth a small fortune. She'd stood next to the fuselage of the smallest of the four, running her hand along the brand new varnished struts. Elmo had been meticulous in his work and his bookkeeping. Inspection stands near each aircraft contained drawings and loaded binders and logbooks detailing every aspect of the restorations.

The smallest airframe belonged to a pre-war de Havilland Gipsy Moth. The next, also pre-war, was a Boeing Stearman with logbooks from the US Navy. Beside it was the only warbird not built with a wood frame, a Supermarine Spitfire, another valuable find. Not as valuable as the Mosquito but still worth more than any scrapper would understand. The most priceless and significant of the lot was the almost completed fuselage and separated wing assembly of a Mosquito. *Salvage my ass!* Even unfinished, she knew of a half dozen aviation museums who would give their first-born for a chance to own it.

It didn't take long to search the rest of the hangar and find all the pieces of each aircraft including the powerplants mounted on engine stands. She was starting to understand old Elmo's methodology. Unhurried to meet demands, he worked at one type of job at a time, and woodworking looked to be the most recent concern. It wasn't her specialty, but after taking a careful look at each aircraft and the work yet needed, she was sure the fuselages were ready for stuffing and then fabric. The maintenance logs all showed inspections on the airframes, which were good to go for the next stage of assembly. After taking a careful look around the loft, she knew he was missing a few parts needed to complete the assembly of each aircraft. Most of the instruments were there, and the electrical harnesses were laid out on big sheets of plywood in the stuffing room, but little things here and there were still missing. She had to wonder if it had been money or time holding him back.

Finding parts for these old warbirds could be a challenge; they usually called for a small fortune. Besides the hangar and his personal possessions, Kiva hadn't mentioned any bank accounts, and she could only presume cash had been the deciding factor. Still, there was enough of everything in the stockroom to finish the Gipsy Moth. That was something she knew she could do and it would fetch a good eighty, possibly ninety grand when finished. Maybe she could get that one done. It would give her a little cash and some room to decide what to do next.

The airport lease was paid up for the year, so that wasn't an issue and between her unemployment insurance and her credit cards, she figured she could cover the electric bill for the hangar, at least for a while. It was strange that old Elmo had managed to buy the hangar and a good chunk of land around it. Counties usually hung onto a windfall like a military base. From what Kiva had read to her, Elmo had leased the hangar up until 2009, when the last agreement was drawn up. Mirabal County officers had signed the lease only after Elmo bought the land the hangar sat on with the old Quonset-style building included. He'd also purchased several adjacent lots. She couldn't blame him. They had gone for a song. It looked like the county had divided up the entire base into housing lots. Aside from Elmo, only a few others had been purchased at the time. She could only imagine that few people around here could afford to buy much less build after the housing crunch hit. Kiva had explained in detail how the current airport lease wasn't for the building but for runway access and its continued use. It wasn't how most counties or municipalities handled the acquisition of military establishments, unless they were cash strapped. It was impossible to know the exact circumstances. It certainly lent to the mystery Kiva had glossed over.

Kiva. She was something else too. Smart, kind, and yet so distant. It was if she was watching from afar, listening, learning but not judging. That was new. How long had it been since someone new didn't immediately judge her? It was all she'd been asking for lately, and it felt strange to meet someone who was so willing to listen.

Was she holding back on making a judgment or merely holding her judgment back? She would have to ask if she wanted to know. But asking was opening a can of worms. She was working so hard to let that whole episode with her ex go, to keep it from rotting her soul.

Perhaps being here was the best thing for her. She could work on the Gipsy Moth. Raise a little cash. Find a home for the other projects, then head out in the spring to start fresh. Kiva had said she would take on her case at home. She couldn't fix what was done, but if she could help repair her reputation or get her flight medical clearance back, that would help. With it, she might be able to return to the airline. Without it, she would need to rely on US medical clearance to get a job, and that would mean staying in the States or more likely, going overseas.

Everyone was short of pilots. Her inbox was flooded every month with offers for jobs in distant places like Bangladesh, Indonesia, and others so desperate they were accepting first officers with as little as five hundred hours. One recruiter had told her that with her flying hours, she could put her in the captain's seat on a 757 today if she were willing to sign a two-year contract. A winter here in Illusion Lake, then two years in Bangladesh might be a small investment in getting her life back. It would be lonely, but she had been lonely before. She could do lonely again.

Looking around the motel room, she suddenly felt claustrophobic. After the long drive and her restless night, the last thing she wanted was to sit in this room staring at the tube. Grabbing the duffle she hadn't bothered to unpack, she checked out and headed to the Jeep.

There was a perfectly usable if impersonal guest room in the hangar and more than enough distraction to keep her busy for the evening and all night if need be. She could unpack all the junk she had been carrying around for the last few months, get comfortable, and spend more time nosing around. It was her place now so why not. It sure beat listening to the local teens partying all night.

* * *

Setting her beer down, Kiva stretched out on the couch, staring out the window at the lake. According to her dad, the world had recently discovered Illusion Lake, and suddenly the offers for large development plots were pouring in. He had received several offers for her mother's family home, the place she was currently enjoying, and even more for the little cottage next door with its extra acreage. Her dad had no intention of kicking Mark and Andi out of their small home when they were just getting on their feet, but he was thinking of severing the lot and contracting Mark to build a new home. It would be on the opposite side of the cottage and if Mark and Andi wanted to rent or rent to own, he would let them then demolish the one they lived in now, increasing the land around their existing family home.

As for the airport and old Elliott's estate, when she spoke with her dad earlier in the evening, he admitted he hadn't been out to the hangar. Ian had done the initial survey, and he had trusted his findings. She didn't break his bubble on his partner's behavior, but did ask how life was treating Ian. Her father noted his recent divorce and speculated that he might be a bit overextended with his two youngest boys in college, but he wasn't worried about Ian.

When she mentioned Ian's offer for the firm to buy the hangar, he assured her Ian probably had a buyer in mind, as it was not ethical for the partnership to make such an offer. He suggested she drop in to see Gent Koehler. Besides being the mayor of Illusion Lake, he owned the only bank in town and would have a better idea if someone had their eye on the old hangar or the airport redevelopment plan. She didn't mention that she thought old gentleman rancher Gent Koehler was the creepiest guy in town. She wouldn't put her money in his bank and she certainly wouldn't subject herself to a face-to-face meeting. Just knowing he and Ian were thick as thieves was all she needed to know. Influence and power be damned, she wasn't talking to Gent. Her father had sounded so confident on the phone, but she herself wasn't so sure.

There was another way. She called the person she had been avoiding since she arrived. Erica Dunbar was a gossip and a flirt of the first order, but she was the go-to source for everything real estate in the county. And Erica had already hit Elliott up, offering her card within an hour of her arrival. Kiva wasn't ready to tip her hand, not yet, but she did need information. Maybe playing the helpful attorney to Elliott was her next move. She reminded herself to be cautious. Whatever she said to Erica, the whole town would know within the hour. Discretion just wasn't something the woman understood.

"KIVA!"

Here we go. "Erica. How are you?"

"Oh, good God, girl, I've been missing you! I can't believe you've been home what, two weeks already, and you haven't called. And what's this I hear? You're already chasing the new gal in town? Oh gosh, I think she's so hot, you know, in a brooding soft butch sort of way. What's she like? I mean, I already introduced myself, but she was a little cranky. Which, I admit, is to be expected, but still, you know what I'm getting at, right?"

"Erica. Take a breath, will you?"

"Oh gosh, sure thing. I'm just so excited to hear from you."

"Me too, buddy, and no worries. I meant to stop by as soon as I settled in."

"I hear you arrived just in time to handle old Elliott's estate, not to mention the Murdock divorce. I can't believe those two didn't make it, but you know how fiery Maria is. I just knew she would be way too much for Bryan. Tell me, in all confidence, is it getting ugly?"

Kiva smiled to know her old friend hadn't changed. "You know better than to ask. Client-attorney privilege."

"Oh shucks, of course. Oh, and you just missed the whole thing with Sandy and Max Guerrero. Evidently, she tried to toss him out, but Ian pulled some legal beagle thing and tried to force her to leave the kids with good old Max. You should have seen it! No way was our good Sheriff David Dias going to let that fly and have his daughter and grandkids in harm's way. He showed up at their house with every deputy in tow, and removed Sandy and the kids at gunpoint. Well, I don't know if anyone actually pulled out their guns, but it still sounds like it could have happened.

"What else, what else... Oh, did you hear about the fight that bastard Gent and I had? Of course you did. You were always the smartest of us all. I wish you'd got here a month ago. Can you believe him, and Ian too, pullin' this whole exclusive stunt? I'm so boiled over.

I actually tried to hit old Elliott's niece up for the option before that bastard could get his offer in. But really, I took one look at that poor girl and couldn't do it. I guess I'm just too soft. Besides, she's so cute. Please tell me you haven't bagged her already."

"Erica! She's my client, not a conquest. Besides, I've got some good news for you. She hasn't signed with Ian." She didn't bother mentioning why or that she had no idea what Ian and Gent were doing.

"REALLY?"

Kiva pulled the phone away, rubbing her ear. "Don't get your hopes up just yet. She wanted time to think, but she's not a fan of the deal either."

"Well, duh! Who would be? The only ones set to profit are Gent, Ian, and that developer from over Dallas way. I don't even think it'll bring any jobs in, at least none local. Honestly, I can't see how the county's even considering it. I mean, we need an airport for future economics and all, don't we? And making everything private and all gated for some uber rich folks just doesn't do much for the town. I mean, I might make out okay with listings in the future, but that's a long ways down the road. Ian says I'm crying over spilt milk, but I just don't see where it's fair to us folks who've been living here during the hard stretches. No offense."

"None taken. I know I've been lucky to have my practice up north but being back has me rethinking it."

"Oh, Kiva girl, tell me you're home for good. Goodness knows we could use you. Not that your dad ain't a good man, but his heart ain't in it anymore. Well, not since the heart attack. We were all so happy to hear you were coming home to take over and I'll admit I've been hoping you'd open up this whole business so as we can all get a fair crack at it. It just galls me that Ian and Gent think they got a right to take the whole pie."

Storing away the comment about her father having a heart attack, she told Erica, "I'm not sure if I'm back for good. Dad just wanted the winter to get his health back, but we'll have to see how he does. And I think you're right about this whole business with Ian and Gent. They certainly are behaving like it's a done deal."

"See! I knew you'd have something to say. Now when can we get together? I'm living out at the old Ramos place, and you've got to see what I've done with it. I know! Why don't you bring young Elliott for dinner Tuesday night and we can all put our heads together and figure a ways to make this deal work for the whole town and not just those two sons-a-bitches? Whatcha' say? Come by around five, five-thirty or so?"

"You're on. We'll see you then." She ended the call, tapping in a short text for her sister.

"Just spoke to Erica…You are so dead!"

She pulled out the last version of the airport development plan. This one showed a housing development and small industrial allotment on the land Elliott now owned. If she heard Erica correctly, Gent and Ian had some deal that needed the entire airport property with no room for any runways. And it sounded like it was a done deal with only Elliott's holdings and the airport use agreement standing in the way. First thing Monday she could visit the county planning office, but that would alert anyone involved that she was interested in the plan or suspicious of it. There had to be another way to get the information she needed without Ian or Gent getting wind of it. She needed time to formulate a strategy.

Staring at the lake, hoping for inspiration, it finally hit her: any large-scale redevelopment would need to file an environmental plan. While the EPA had been gutted in recent years, the filing was still required even if it was just a formality. And those plans were public documents. Heading to the kitchen, she took a seat at the island counter and booted up her laptop.

She loaded the coffeemaker with fresh ground decaf, retrieved her phone and tabbed to her contact details, remembering that Erica had invited her and Elliott to dinner on Tuesday. All the conflicts she had experienced with Elliott during their first meeting sprang to mind. The woman was frustratingly reserved, yet there was a certain vulnerability…

Elliott answered the call with a briskness that bordered on rude, then her voice seemed to soften. "Ms. Park. Sorry. Kiva. I was trying to answer with my elbow. You're on speaker. I hope that's okay."

"Uh, can I ask where you are?"

"In the hangar. I'm trying to get an even coat of urethane on the wing spars of the Gipsy Moth. I have to say, I haven't the skill with a brush Elmo had."

"That's probably just practice." She could almost imagine Elliott nodding.

"I just had the nicest conversation with my grandmother. Turns out she used to sew all the envelopes for Elmo's refurbs. She spent an hour talking me through all the finer points of sewing canvas."

It was easy to appreciate her enthusiasm. "I'm not sure what an envelope is, but I'm guessing it has something to do with the aircraft fabric?"

"You're right on point, counselor. Good for you."

Listening to the competing sounds of the coffeemaker hissing in her kitchen and Elliott clinking what she guessed was a brush in a glass jar, she asked, "Is she going to sew the…envelope for that little plane?"

"I wish. She says her place is too small for that kind of work, but I think it's really about her arthritis. She's sending me some samples, her old machine, and a huge pair of pinking shears. That's pretty much the only stuff I haven't found around here."

"With all that material you found? I'm surprised."

"All I can figure is he has someone doing the sewing locally." Elliott switched off from speaker. "So, to what do I owe the pleasure?"

What a contrast from the annoying woman who had walked into her office Friday morning. "I promised I'd get to the bottom of things, which I'm still doing. Do you remember that real estate agent you met when you arrived?"

"Met? *Hmm*, more like accosted by, but yes."

"I know her. We were childhood friends. She may have the inside scoop, but it comes with a price."

"Oh," she groaned, "I'm not going to like this, am I?"

"It's just a dinner invitation. You do eat?"

"How good of you to notice, and yes, if chatty Cathy is a friend of yours, I can sit through dinner and a personal interrogation."

Snickering despite herself, Kiva could admit, "Erica is a handful, but she means well. So, she's invited us for dinner Tuesday night."

"How about I buy you breakfast Monday morning and you prep me for her cross-examination?"

It was hard not to smile at her description of a social engagement with Erica Dunbar. "Deal. Should I pick you up or meet you at the Crow?"

"I'll meet you there. That way you can point me in the direction of a grocery store. I think I'm pretty much at my limit with gas station burritos."

The image of Elliott roughing it out at the hangar did worry her. "At least you have beer in the fridge." It was nice to hear her chuckle of agreement. "Okay, I'll see you Monday morning, then set you on the path for groceries and anything else you might need."

"Anything?" Elliott asked, her tone mischievous.

Grinning, she ignored the question. "Breakfast."

"See you then."

And she was gone. Kiva poured her coffee, considering the lighthearted exchange. Why was it always the ones who wouldn't stick around who piqued her interest? Or was it Erica's interest that had aroused hers? Pushing the questions aside, she sat in front of her computer searching the EPA records for proposals and applications. If they were going to sit down with Erica, she wasn't about to let her know they didn't have a clue what was going on. She needed some facts to work with and fast.

CHAPTER SIX

Waking before her alarm, Elliott stretched in the old military-issue twin bed. It reminded her of her own service and the difference in housing for folks serving in the ranks and their officers. This was definitely an officer-grade bed, although probably the type used in training barracks. She allowed a moment of nostalgia until she remembered the service was still testosterone-fueled, even in the enlightened Canadian Forces where being out had been protected by civil and military law since 1986.

When she first viewed this spare room, she remembered her quarters in Edmonton; this room wasn't much different. Being posted to the west was not her first choice, but that was where she was needed, and that was where she had gone. Though she'd been the squadron punching bag, she might have stayed beyond her first five-year commitment but even in a liberated military, service was still a sausage fest. At least she'd had the chance to serve in Afghanistan. Airlift wasn't exactly high risk, but it was what she could do, and she was proud she'd had a chance to serve.

Climbing from the bed, she automatically went to work making it, including the prescribed hospital corners. It was habit, and she had a feeling that had been the same force driving Elmo too. Last night she had closed the single pane windows that lined the wall facing the hangar floor, worried that the fumes from the polyurethane might bother her. Now she opened them wide and was pleased to note the smell had dissipated. The stuff Elmo used was all top of the line.

Yesterday, when she decided to start where he'd left off, she found the paint and sealants room on the other side of the hangar just as organized as the rest of the place and stocked with polymer adhesives and a variety of weatherproof polyurethanes. One wall of the prep room was lined with mixing charts, the application for each carefully added in Elmo's exacting print. Procedures were always changing even in the restoration business, and it looked like he understood that too, with newer charts pinned over outdated product directions. It would be her job to keep at that now; she'd start with research for low volatile organic compound sealants for future restorations. Most volatile organic compounds were much more harmful than most people understood, delivering carcinogenic compounds to all those close enough to smell the product, and some smells were unavoidable. Odor from the finish would dissipate soon enough, but she'd have to smell this stuff on a regular basis so better to be safe and find the best products to eliminate or at least reduce the harmful VOC issues for restoration work.

Restoration was such a funny word. The way she felt this morning, rested, rejuvenated, made her think it might apply to more than the warbirds down on the floor.

She rushed to dress then headed straight for the wings of the Gipsy Moth. Elmo's workbook called for three coats of varnish on the spars. She was sure he'd already applied two, so she just needed to finish this last coat. Most people would want to err on the side of caution and complete all three themselves, but every coat, regardless of how thin, added to aircraft weight and in a tiny bird like this, weight was everything. After a careful eyeball inspection, she only found one small drip mark, something she could easily sand out.

Elliott was so excited with her achievement she wanted to call Kiva and tell her all about it. Stopping in her tracks, she reminded herself of two facts. Kiva was only here for the winter, and Elliott hadn't decided if she herself was going to stay much longer than it took to get the Gipsy Moth out the door. If she went back to flying, even if Kiva could sort out her medical, she was most probably headed to Bangladesh or some such place for a minimum of two years. Two years was a long time, even for her.

Pushing those thoughts aside, she made a plan for the day. She would finish the varnish of the wing spars and, if there was time after that, she would inventory the non-powerplant-related mechanicals like the landing gear and the flight control cables.

First thing tomorrow, she would meet Kiva. She wasn't sure what spurred her to ask her to breakfast. It wasn't like she needed an update. Whatever forces were at play were out of her hands and being handled by the lawyer, but that didn't stop Elliott from wanting to spend time with her. Last night on the phone she'd felt like her old self, maybe more like a teenager full of life and mischief. It had been a long time since she'd seen that part of herself. A grin etched across her face. There was no denying, even for her, that something had changed, something big. *Welcome back, Elliott.*

* * *

Spotting Elliott's Jeep among half a dozen pickups lining the main street, Kiva smiled at the thought of the woman warming a booth for them. Yesterday's research marathon hadn't garnered any facts but did provoke even more speculation. She reined herself in as she parked her car. "This is not a date," she growled. Still, she couldn't hold back the smile when she walked into the diner to find Elliott sitting at the same booth, head down and deeply engrossed in a book. That just seemed so much like Elliott. Slipping into the bench across from her, she enjoyed the warmth her arrival produced.

Without preamble, Elliott turned the book for Kiva to see. "Isn't this cool? It's a complete diary of a Jenny restoration. You know, the Army Air Corps flew them during the first war. Did you know the original variants didn't even have seatbelts? And most of the time these guys flew without parachutes. Can you believe that?"

Kiva grinned at her enthusiasm. "What am I looking at here?"

"Oh, that's the joinery for the engine mounts. It's so hard to believe they were building lightweight wood structures that could withstand the vibration from those old piston engines. Although I have a feeling the Curtiss engines were better than the rest. Did you know Curtiss got his start with the AEA, Alexander Graham Bell's aviation think tank, funded by good old Ma Bell herself?"

Kiva waited while the diner owner poured her coffee. "The usual for me, Gale. Have you ordered?" she asked Elliott.

"Uh, no. Um, scrambled, bacon, rye. Thanks."

Shaking her head at how Elliott's attention was completely on the book, she offered a wink. "Thanks Gale," and turned back to the woman across from her. Even with the book oriented toward Kiva, Elliott was tracing the outline of a diagram with her index finger as if she were memorizing every inch.

"Ma Bell, who—was she his wife, mother?"

"Mabel Bell was a scientist in her own right. She was also hearing-impaired. Alexander started out studying hearing impairment, ended up with his own school in Boston. She began as his student, became his wife. When he wanted to conduct scientific research, she talked her dad into backing him. He was brilliant but disorganized and she transcribed all his research and filed every one of his patent applications. Without Mabel, he probably wouldn't be remembered today."

It was hard not to enjoy every moment of Elliott's enthusiasm. "I've heard the old quips about Ma Bell. As if Bell Telephone was run by some crotchety old woman. I had no idea there was a Mabel involved. She founded a study of aviation science? When was this?"

"Around nineteen hundred was when Alexander took an interest in flight. Everyone agreed flight was impossible and would destroy his name in the scientific community. But she couldn't dissuade him, so she brought in a team with experience in combustible engines and that sort of thing. Glen Curtiss was one of those men as was a lieutenant named Selfridge from the US Army's aerial test division who has the distinction of being the first passenger to die in a crash of a Wright Flyer flown by Orville Wright."

She listened intently, letting the story and Elliott's enthusiasm enthrall her completely. Minutes later, Kiva sat back as Gale slid their plates in front of them. She thanked the waitress then said with gentle recognition, "You're liking this, all this history and learning new things about these old airplanes?"

Elliott nodded, easily conceding the point. "I have to admit I thought I'd just drive down here, sign some papers, clear out Uncle Elmo's personal stuff, send the rest to auction or the scrapper but, well, I'm feeling so...I don't know how to describe it..."

"Optimistic?"

"I love flying, but there isn't a lot of room in a scheduled flight to really enjoy yourself." Grinning irreverently, she revealed, "For some reason, the passengers don't appreciate that sort of thing. They don't pay good money for you to do loops around clouds or delay them with an aerial tour. After a while, it kind of takes the fun out of it. I mean, I'm still proud to tell people I'm an airline pilot, but the job's not much different than piloting a ship, except more complicated and with a lot more federal oversight."

Kiva agreed. "I can see where that would take all the fun out of it. What about that little plane you're rebuilding—sorry, restoring? Could you fly that when it's finished?"

"I could, and I plan to."

"What about your flight medical? Sorry, that's none of my business."

Elliott smiled at her. "Yes it is, and I think you should know I'm okay with anything you might want to ask. Here's the thing. I have two pilot's licenses and two medicals. One in Canada, which is the one suspended." She added with a mischievous smile, "Don't worry, counselor, it's perfectly legal. Working for an airline operating in Canada, that's the one I use for work. But my American license and medical is an optional thing I went and got on my own, and it isn't affected by what happened up there. And yes, before you ask, I reported everything that happened to the FAA. They saw no correlation so I can fly here legally, and I intend to do just that. I have the ratings and experience to act as my own test pilot. So, once the Gipsy Moth is ready, I'll take her up and put her through her paces."

Kiva plastered a smile on her face, but something inside felt like it was burrowing a hole in her gut. The thought of Elliott taking out one of those wrecks, even fixed up, was more than frightening. She pushed her half-finished breakfast away, making room to pull some papers from her briefcase. "I printed this out last night, but I'm not a map person. Can you help me decipher it?"

Pushing her empty plate aside too, Elliott began lining up the printed-out segments, creating a larger map. "This is a street map with a development plan overlaid."

"That's what I thought, but I'm not sure what most of the markings mean. I've highlighted a few things I did recognize, like the hangar and runways."

"What are these squares over here?" Elliott asked, pointing to the northeast side off the lake.

"Oh, that's my mother's house where I'm staying right now, and that smaller square is the cottage next door. My dad bought it years ago. It's a perfect location, on the other side of the lake."

"Not anymore."

"I'm sorry. What do you mean?"

"This plan overlay depicts a change in the elevation of the lake. Is the lake very shallow by your house?"

"Yes, it's amazing. It's soft sand all the way across, and I don't think it gets deeper than ten feet at the halfway mark. As kids, Shay and I would drag the swim platform my dad built as far out as we liked and still be able to touch bottom when we wanted."

"It sounds like fun," Elliott said, but her face didn't match the words.

"What are you not telling me?"

"I'm not sure, and I need a topographical chart and more room. Can we go to your office?"

She shook her head. "That wouldn't work, and I don't know where to get the map you want."

"I can download it from the USGS website and Elmo has a large-scale printer. Can you come to the hangar?"

Checking her phone for the time, Kiva knew she had a full schedule. Feeling an uncharacteristic displeasure at letting her down, she explained, "Sorry Elliott but not today. I have two appointments and a motion to file. How about I pop by tomorrow, say mid-afternoon? Would that work? I mean, we could go over your findings and then head out to Erica's together."

Elliott agreed, her smile returning. "Can I keep this plan view? I may need to draw it into the topo chart to make sense of the whole thing."

"Of course," she said, grabbing the check Gale had slipped under her coffee cup. She paid for their breakfasts and walked her out of the diner. "So, I'll see you tomorrow."

In addition to filing the motion she mentioned to Elliott, she would meet her divorce client today and face off with the husband and his lawyer. She would also sit with an elderly couple who were exploring options to sever their farm into several plots to divide among their kids.

She also needed to have a talk with her father. When he asked her to take over so he could have a break, he'd mentioned he was under the weather and that rest was a strong suggestion from his doctor. Never once had he uttered the words *heart attack*.

She had to wonder how much Shay was holding back. After all, it was her sister who put the bug in her ear to take the winter off from the heartache of working with kids whose greatest crimes were being born the children of incompetent and sometimes abusive parents. She always found it disturbing that any two straight assholes had the right to procreate without even the simplest test or requirement to prove themselves competent. Yet two gay men in a loving relationship would need to stand on their heads and spit nickels for the chance to adopt an unwanted child.

Before she could decide what needed to be done first, Ian marched into her office. His face was as haggard and hostile as it had been on Friday. "When are you bringing her in to sign over the hangar property? Dammit, Kiva! It's already Monday, and I want those papers filed today."

"Then I think you have a problem because she isn't interested in signing over anything. At least not yet. Besides, I can't for the life of me understand why you're in such a hurry. What exactly have you got up your sleeve?"

"She has a life to get back to, and as far as I'm concerned, it's your job to help her get there. Just how long are you going to string this along?"

"As long as she needs."

He seemed to growl, like he was ready to bite, then said, "Don't turn this into some sort of conquest, Kiva. If you intend to bed the woman just do it and leave the rest of us God-fearing folks out of the mix." He spun from her office and disappeared.

She got up and shut her door. She had known Ian all her life and never once had he made a comment about her sexual orientation and certainly not about who she did or didn't sleep with. That could only mean one thing. This was personal for Ian, and the stakes were high.

She opened the private Gmail account on her phone and sent a note to the investigator she used with her practice in Toronto. If she was going to dig into Ian and his cronies, she couldn't risk using anyone from around here. She gave him Ian's details, name, address, and asked for a full background check, her primary interest his business and holdings. Now, she had just enough time for a quick chat with her sister. There would be no hypnosis session today.

As soon as she answered, Kiva launched in without preamble. "Shay? Why am I the last to hear Dad had a heart attack?"

She listened to her sister's soft chuckle. "I told him you'd figure it out. What can I say? He still thinks he can protect his baby girl."

"'Nuff with the baby girl crap! You tell our father I intend to kill him the next time I see him."

"Yeah, he loves and worries about you too. You know, you've made him so proud by coming down and filling in for him. I can't tell you how much he hates you being back in T.O. Well, when Trump was in office he did say he thought it was safer having you up there, but still, especially since Mom's moved to California, he's having a harder time with the distance."

"Oh, for God's sake, Florida's less than four hours flying time from Toronto and I can go direct. You can even get a direct flight from there to here but to get from New Mexico to Florida you can waste an entire day making connection after connection. Travel wise, I'm closer to him living in Toronto than you are in Fort Lauderdale."

Shay still sounded amused. "*Touché ma sœur*, but reality and the old man are never on speaking terms when it comes to his kids."

Kiva groaned, mostly for effect, but her shoulders relaxed. "How is he?"

"Good, really good. As a matter of fact, he's out playing golf with Jasper Tong."

"What?"

"Relax. The cardiologist said it was fine if they just play nine holes and I concur. Tomorrow they have a boat rented and they're going up the Intercoastal to do some catch and release."

"Sounds more like catch and release beers?" Listening to her sister laugh, she let loose the last of the tension she'd been holding. "Okay, I get the message. I'll stand down for now but no more keeping secrets from me. You may be the oldest and a big fancy doctor but I'm not a baby anymore, Shay. Can you two try and remember that?"

"You got it, sis. You want me to tell him the jig's up, or you wanna pop his bubble yourself?"

"You go ahead. You can play the heavy with Dad better than me."

"So how's it going? Are you still taking flak from Ian?"

Deciding how much she wanted to share, she finally asked, "Does Dad have any idea what he's up to? I mean, if he has some insight, now would be the time."

"I did mention it after your call the other night, and we had a long talk. He admitted Ian's not been himself for some time, but assumed it was the divorce. Now he thinks he may have missed something important."

"*Hmm*. Listen, sis, I'm going to make a suggestion here. One I need you to gently, very gently, plant. I think he should consider dissolving his law practice, at least the partnership with Ian, sooner rather than later."

"Holy fuck!"

"I said gently. You do understand the concept of discretion?"

"Well, yeah but…never mind. Do you really think it's that bad?"

"Honestly, I haven't got concrete evidence yet, but my gut is telling me Dad should run, not walk, as fast as he can."

"Ouch." She could hear her sister exhale loudly. She always did when she was thinking but couldn't find an easy answer. "Okay, here's what I'll do. I'm going to let him know you're really liking being at home. So much so, you might consider sharing a practice with him. Just not one that includes Ian Guerrero."

"I don't know, Shay. It doesn't feel right to get his hopes up."

"Oh, I know, but I also know you've had enough of teeny-weeny criminals, not to mention the snow."

"You do recall that it snows here too?"

"Not like it does up there. Besides, a few years doing general law would be good for you. Don't answer yet. Just think about it, and I'll get him to do the same."

She gave in. Her first appointment was due any minute. It was time to get her head back in the game and console a woman about the breakup of her marriage and prepare her for what would come next.

CHAPTER SEVEN

Tuesday, the twenty-eighth, Elliott printed carefully, making notes in the work journal Elmo kept. She had finished the final coat on the spars, installed the steel wing wire mounts and pulled the electrical harness through to add wingtip lights and a strobe to bring the old bird up to FAA code for navigation. Next, she'd test fit the wings and install the instruments and panels. That was all she could do until an FAA inspector signed off on the next stage of inspection. Once that happened, she could think about adding fabric.

Looking over the work yet to be finished, she knew she still had a number of steps to complete. The rudder wires had been pulled through and tie-wrapped to the places where they would connect to the still-to-be-attached rudder. Same for the elevator controls. The mounting plate for the stick was sitting on the work desk and the major items remaining were the instrument panels, seats, and, of course, the engine. Even though it was signed off on and hanging from a hoist and ready to mount, she wanted to run the engine before she dropped it in. She'd read through the inspection requirements several times but couldn't decide if the engine was supposed to be installed before or after the airframe inspection. Better to check first. Even though she was a licensed airframe and electrical mechanic, she had never worked a rebuild, much less a restoration. She wanted to get this one right from the start. Instruments next, she decided.

Two hours later she was sitting in the kitchen, the original panel drawing spread out across the old chrome table. She was drinking her coffee when her phone rang. She smiled to see the number and tapped it to answer, "Elliott's Aviation Restorations. Time makes them old, I make them fly."

"Well, that's some greeting." Kiva's voice rang clear, a smile easily suggested. "I take it you're enjoying the challenge?"

"Challenge is the right word. I'm trying to decide if going old school is a disservice to the pilot who buys the Gipsy Moth or if I should give them all the best modern tools for safe navigation."

"I'm not sure what that means, but I have a feeling you'll figure it out. Is that what you're working on, some navigation things?"

"Yeah, I thought I'd assemble the instrument panels today, but I'm not sure if Elmo's design is the best choice, even if it is historically accurate. I mean it will look good, but as far as flying, I'm not doing anyone a favor."

"I can't even begin to offer any advice, at least not without you explaining much more."

"Oh boy, I don't want to bore you to death."

"It sounds like an interesting debate, but I think you would have to show more than tell. The reason I called... I wanted to invite you out on the weekend for dinner. Dad's big old barbeque is sitting here unused, and I hate to fire it up just for me."

"Well...since you put it that way. I would hate to think of you burning all that fuel just for one lonely steak."

"Ouch. Sorry. Didn't mean it that way."

"I'm kidding. Besides, it will be good to show you what I put together. I've printed out the topographical charts and added in the details from the development plan. I haven't figured it out yet, but... I'm thinking, if we put our heads together, we'll have a better chance of getting to the truth."

"Sounds perfect. Listen, are you still good for tonight at Erica's? I mean, she can be a lot to take all at once."

Delighted by the concern, she was glad Kiva couldn't see her wide grin. "Thanks for the warning, counselor. How about we work out some secret hand signals, you know, in case my head is about to blow and I need you to get me out fast?"

"Now that sounds smart. Oops, my next appointment is here. Am I still picking you up?"

"That's the plan. Just come in and find me. It'll give me a chance to show off my very fine brushwork."

"You've got it, Ace. See you soon."

Elliott looked at her phone, reading the Call Ended message. How was it a simple phone call could make her feel so...

Steady there, old girl. She may be kind and easy to look at, but she's just being friendly... I think.

* * *

Elliott's head was starting to buzz. She wasn't sure if it was the third glass of wine or the shrill of Erica's incessant, often suggestive patter. God, the woman could talk and talk. She wasn't unkind, but apparently she didn't get as much attention as she craved. She just knew it wouldn't be coming from her, no matter how many times the woman overstepped her boundaries.

Having learned long ago that she was the only one responsible for saving herself from these situations, Elliott wasted no time removing Erica's hand from wherever it landed or adding more room between them whenever she got too close, which was more often than anyone had ever tried with her. When Erica's hand landed in her lap for the umpteenth time, she stood, looking to Kiva. "I'm sorry to cut the evening short, but I have a lot of work planned for tomorrow. If you're still willing to drive me back, I would like to go. Now."

Looking confused by the sudden announcement, Kiva then caught on. "Yes, of course. I forgot you mentioned your schedule."

"*Oooh!*" Erica wailed. "Why don't you stay? I can drive you back to your hotel in the morning. Besides the last thing you want to do is try to sleep at the Big Pine. That place has been party central since we were kids."

It was a relief to hear Erica still thought she was living out of the local motel. At least she wouldn't have to worry about having her show up at the hangar, at least not yet.

"Sorry, but I'm very OCD about my surroundings. I need things a certain way, or I can't sleep."

Offering her most alluring smile, Erica moved in for the kill. "Who said anything about sleeping?"

Thank God for Kiva weaving her way between them, halting Erica's advance. "Thanks for dinner, Erica. It was great to catch up, we'll have to do it again sometime." Reaching back and hooking Elliott's arm, Kiva pulled her towards the door.

Before they were safely out, Erica yanked Kiva back. Unfazed, she tossed Elliott her car keys. "I'll be right there."

Heading down the stairs as fast as she could go without running, Elliott tried to pretend she couldn't hear Erica's outburst.

"Why are you being such a bitch? Just because you saw her first doesn't mean she's all yours!"

"Oh, for fuck sakes, Erica. You're drunk and in case you didn't notice, Elliott isn't a prize you can claim or put dibs on. She's a person and one who very politely tried all night to let you know she wasn't interested. Frankly, I don't know what's wrong with you. I'm going to assume you've had too much to drink and leave it there. Good night."

Watching Kiva march down the porch stairs, Elliott wanted to thank her for coming to her defense, but Erica was Kiva's friend, and she probably hadn't expected things to go the way they had. She waited until Kiva pulled the car out onto the county road, before offering, "I take it your friend has changed."

She could feel the tension radiate from Kiva. "Erica was always a handful but…"

"I bet she's always been a handful. No worries. We all have one friend like her."

"I doubt that, but thanks all the same."

"Actually, while we were sitting there I remembered a bartender I used to know, back when I was flying for Bearskin Airlines."

"Bearskin?" Kiva laughed and chanced a quick look. "You just made that up."

"Nope. It's a commuter airline operating north of Lake Superior. You know which lake that is, right?"

"You think I don't know my Great Lakes?"

"You'd be surprised how many people get them mixed up. It's the largest of the five, the one on the top left that kind of looks like a moose antler."

Kiva grinned at the image. "You really flew up there? What was it like?"

"Lonely. Rugged. Beautiful. Oh, did I mention lonely?"

Kiva drove, quieted by the thought. "I was twelve when we moved to Toronto from here. It was complete culture shock, but at least I had grade eight to make friends. It was so much harder for my sister. She'd just turned fifteen and started grade ten without a friend in the world. This is a tiny town, and we knew everyone here."

"I'm so sorry. Did your parents break up or was it a job thing?"

"Both. My dad was heartbroken, so he dragged us home to live with his parents. They have a big house in Koreatown, and he took a job with Legal Aid at Old City Hall. We got to know the core pretty well."

"I grew up near Koreatown," Elliott quietly offered.

"Really? Riverdale or Cabbagetown?" she asked, assuming it was one or the other.

Choking slightly, Elliott admitted, "Regent Park."

Kiva glanced at her thoughtfully, before turning her eyes back to the road.

"Surprised?" Elliott asked.

"Um, yes. Sorry! It's just that you don't meet many articulate, successful graduates of the projects, especially Regent Park. No offense."

"None taken. I know I'm an anomaly and I don't often admit to being a Regent. Besides, most people think only people of color live in housing projects. They have no idea how different it is in a place like Toronto."

"Actually, I never thought about it, but you're right. My father used to call it the United Nations of poverty. Sorry."

"Hey, don't worry. At least you get it, and it sounds like your dad does too. Can I ask, what brought him back here?"

"My mom. In a nutshell, she's a restless spirit. They love one another, but she can't keep still, and he can't keep up. He came back when I was in law school to try and reconcile with her and set up a practice. It's one of the reasons I took the bar here and in Ontario. You know, just in case."

"Well, that worked out okay. And I'm sorry it didn't work for your parents. Would you ever think about staying? I mean as far as small towns go, this isn't a bad place. You might not see the kind of cases you get at home, though."

"As for cases at home, I could do with a few less. My last client was an eight-year-old boy who found a gun and shot his baby brother."

Kiva sounded so defeated that Elliott had to ask, "Why on earth would the cops press charges? Please tell me this wasn't a race thing."

Sighing, she shook her head. "The boy was white—well, mostly— but his older brothers were all in a gang. And the gun was traced to a gang-related homicide. They suspected the eldest brother and thought holding my client would push him to take responsibility, but he just sat in the courtroom, day after day, never saying a word. I tried everything

I could think of to get my client to open up, but he clung to his loyalty like it was all there was in the world, no matter how scared he was."

They drove in silence until Kiva turned onto Airport Road, making their way to the hangar. Elliott was feeling the buzz of three glasses of wine and took a long moment to question what she was seeing, what looked like the corona of an early morning sunrise.

Beside her, Kiva noted the sight too. "What is that?"

Like a bell going off in her head, she knew. "FIRE!"

Kiva hit the accelerator. Seconds passed in slow motion as they skidded around the parking lot entrance across from Elliott's hangar. Flames from some heaping pile were licking the street-side doors. "Call 9-1-1," Elliott ordered, jumping from the car and heading right for the fire.

She couldn't get close, the heat pushing her back. Wood shipping pallets and other garbage had been stacked against the tall wooden doors that covered this end of the Quonset hut. She hadn't left anything near the huge panel door and especially not this one. The airside door was of the same construction but skinned in aluminum for protection in case of aircraft fires. This side had probably never been done because no one could see a need. This was intentional.

Running around the hangar, Elliott struggled to unlock the pass-through pedestrian door and raced to the room where all the safety gear was stored. She grabbed the two largest fire extinguishers and a knockdown device, the chemicals inside designed to be released from within the fire, robbing it of oxygen from the inside out. With it pinned under her arm, she struggled with the two extinguishers, moving as fast as she could to the front.

Kiva ran to her, grabbing one of the extinguishers. "I called them," was all she said.

That didn't bode well. Who knew how long it would take for a volunteer fire department to respond? The flames had climbed high enough to blacken the single pane windows across the very top of the panel doors. Once those windows blew, the fire could work its way into the hangar, threatening everything of value.

Moving in as far as the heat would allow and pulling the pin of the knockdown device, she pushed herself another ten feet forward. Missing would mean the difference between saving the hangar and losing everything. Pushing in just a little more, she lobbed it in underhand, seeing it disappear into the top of the pile of flames. Frozen in place and praying for the thing to work, she felt something tugging at her and realized Kiva was pulling her back and away from the fire.

A popping sound was barely audible, but a spray of what looked like white powder went everywhere. She held her breath, letting Kiva hold her back, both watching as the flames died down and the inferno became a smoldering mess. She squeezed Kiva's hand and pulled a pin from her extinguisher, moving in and working to douse the fire still burning at the base of the pile.

Kiva, who was doing the same thing with the second extinguisher, warned, "We're not getting to the stuff in the back."

She wished for the umpteenth time she hadn't consumed so much wine. She emptied her extinguisher then gave her keys to Kiva. "Bring the Jeep over here. Right here. Face-in," she ordered.

Taking Kiva's extinguisher, she emptied it out too, then made the run back around the hangar, grabbing the last full-sized unit, along with a grappling hook.

Back street-side, she noted some of the kids who raced on the runways had gathered to watch. She waved them in and ordered them to follow Kiva to gather every remaining fire extinguisher, no matter how small. As they started to jog after Kiva, she grabbed one of the younger ones and pointed to the Jeep. "Get in and do exactly what I say." He looked scared to death but followed her orders.

From the back of the Jeep she grabbed the winch kit, attached the controller and the grappling iron to the steel cable, and ran to the fire. The knockdown device had smothered much of the outside fuel along the edges of the pallets and the other garbage piled against the big door. Pushing herself to get as close as she could, she heaved the long iron hook high, then retreated and, using the wired controller, pulled the slack out of the line and began slowly winching the pile from the door. She knew she wouldn't be lucky enough for it to stay together, but several pallets pulled away, and she let the winch drag them clear. She ordered the teen behind the wheel to reverse and pull their catch away. By then the gang was back. Kiva, realizing what she was doing, set them to work getting enough of that separate fire out so Elliott could retrieve the grappling iron. She dropped it when she felt her hand burning and Kiva stopped her before she could try again.

Rummaging in the hatch of the Jeep, Kiva located a pair of heavy leather work gloves and handed them over, demanding, "Put these on." Then she ordered the kids to hold on and stay back until they broke the fire down more.

Elliott handed Kiva the winch control. "This button is to give me slack. This one to pull." She ran back toward the doors, lobbing the hook once again, then stepping back and giving Kiva the signal. Again, only a few pallets came loose but it was working, and the kids were getting the drill, taking turns putting out fire in the separated piles of wood and junk.

It took five more tries until the pile of debris was pulled away from the hangar doors. Still, fire licked at the old wood. Looking around at Kiva and the kids, she knew they didn't have much left to work with. She remembered the old aircraft extinguisher. It was nothing more than a fifty-gallon cylinder on what looked like wagon wheels, but it would work. Signaling to the kid still behind the wheel, she ordered, "Drive around to the other side." She followed, running as fast as her tired legs would go. Grabbing the keys from the kid, Elliott unlocked the large airside panel door. The old red rig stood nearby. Together they pulled it out and Elliott clipped the bar loop to her hitch, explaining, "Drive carefully back around. There's no pin, so I have to stand on it to keep it on the hitch." He looked scared, so she reassured him as he headed to the driver's door. "You can do this."

He drove cautiously to the front of the hangar, and she would have bet he didn't as much as take a breath the whole time. The other kids helped her push the rig into place, and she let fly, working the base of the flames up. It took the entire tank to knock it down, but when they were done, they stood in awe of their accomplishment. Some of the piles they had pulled away still burned but without threat to their surroundings.

While she gathered and checked the mostly spent fire extinguishers, Kiva went into lawyer mode, gathering the kids, getting their names and assuring them they had done a hell of a job. "You're heroes and damn fine young men and women in my book. I intend to put your names forward to the county for commendations." She made sure they each had her card and they began to slip away as sirens were finally heard approaching.

Elliott stepped up beside her, checking her watch. "Twenty-two minutes. Is that normal?"

She shook her head, "None of this is normal. Before they get here, I have to ask, and I know they will, did you leave that mess, the garbage and pallets, like that?"

"No, of course not."

"Where were they?"

"I have no idea. I don't know when or where to put the garbage out, and I only have a few used rags and empty urethane cans that need to be disposed of. And those should still be in a fireproof bin in the paint prep room."

"What about the shipping skids? Where were they?"

"I didn't have any, inside or out, other than the two with parts sitting on them in the engine bay. I did notice some over by the Fire Hall this morning when I went for my run. None of the airport volunteer firefighters have responded, is that the county fire department?" she asked, turning to the fire engine making its way around the parking area to pull up next to where they were standing.

Grabbing her arm before she could approach the truck, Kiva warned her, "Elliott, I have a bad feeling about this. Please say as little as possible."

She nodded as the first firefighter reached her. "Move that Jeep out of the way and get back. We'll handle this."

Elliott jumped in her Jeep and moved it back into the parking lot. She grabbed the bag that held the winch kit, ready to gather it all up and store it away when a thought hit her. She looked around quickly, then reached up and pulled the SIM card from the dash cam. The device had enough onboard memory to allow the fire department or the sheriffs to download a record of everything that happened. First, she'd see if anyone was interested in the truth before she would offer proof of reality. She left the bag and controller for the winch on the hood and trotted over to join Kiva, who was now going head-to-head with a white-helmeted firefighter and someone in the green and tan uniform of the sheriff's department.

Elliott accepted the outstretched hand of the fire chief. He seemed sincere as he explained there would be a lot of questions when it came to determining the cause of the fire.

Kiva then introduced the local sheriff. Elliott recognized the look in his eye and knew trouble was brewing. Surreptitiously slipping her left hand into Kiva's, she felt her freeze then comprehend the gesture. She was passing her dash cam SIM card to Kiva. As she did, she offered her right hand to the sheriff. Instead of shaking her outstretched hand, he snapped a handcuff on her wrist, then swung her around, snapping the other wrist behind her back.

Kiva, now in possession of the SIM card, protested. "Sheriff, really? This is uncalled for."

"Not from where I'm standin'. This sure looks like arson to me, and until the chief here says different, I'm taking missy here into custody."

"Elliott had nothing to do with this, she was with me this evening. As a matter of fact, if it wasn't for her valiant efforts things might have been much worse."

"Think what you like, Kiva. You always was a bad judge of character. My bet here is your new lez-be-friend's been a little disappointed with old Elliott's big heap of junk and thought she could ring in some insurance money to make up for her comin' all this way!"

Kiva looked like she would protest more but Elliott gave her a subtle shake of the head. "I would be grateful if you would lock up here when the fire department is done. My car keys are on the hood."

She took in Kiva's incredulous look, then watched her march to the car and grab the keys. The sheriff led Elliott to his car, then tossed her in the back like any criminal or drunk and closed the door, walking away to rejoin one of his deputies who was already taking pictures of the scene.

Kiva casually shoved the SIM card into her pocket. She wanted nothing more than to jump into her car, race home, and look at what it contained. Gathering the loose items that were part of the winch, she noted the tiny flashing light coming from the housing around the rearview mirror. Anyone would assume it was part of the alarm system. Now she knew it was a dash cam and hoped upon hope that Elliott had it set to record all movement and not just when the engine was running.

Normally, she would have handed it over to the police as evidence, but she suspected whatever was going on was tied to the offer Ian had been pushing. At dinner with Erica, the realtor repeatedly complained of the unfairness of Ian and Gent Koehler, the local banker, keeping her out of the big housing deal. How they expected to sell out some gated community with no jobs in the area made no sense to her.

Standing here looking at how fast they had arrested Elliott, and with not so much as a pretense of an investigation, told her this was much, much more than a housing deal. Right now she needed to find a judge and convince him or her to hear a motion for bail for Elliott. Storming to her car, she checked the time on her phone. Already after midnight. She didn't want to leave, didn't want to see Elliott cuffed and sitting in the sheriff's unit, but she couldn't help her from here.

Grabbing a Sharpie from the console of her Mustang, she marched to the police 4x4 and not waiting for the sheriff, who she knew would interfere, threw open the rear door and leaned in. "We're going to figure this out, but first I have to get you bail. I'm going to file for bond, and…" She checked over her shoulder, confirming her suspicion that the sheriff was heading her way, "I'm going to check certain things out and see if I can have this whole thing tossed."

She leaned in and pushed Elliott forward, then scribbled something on the arm cuffed behind her. "That's my cell. Call me as soon as they give you a chance and make sure they do."

"That's enough, Kiva!" The sheriff pulled her away. "You wanna talk to your little friend, you're gonna wait for visiting hours like every other piece of trash around here."

"For your information, I am talking to my client." She didn't elaborate, especially when it looked like that information surprised him. *Good.* First, she would drive to the sheriff's office for a copy of the charges he intended to file. Then she'd need to find a judge who would take her call at this time of night, decide who she could trust. She slipped her hand into her pocket to be sure the SIM card was still there. All she could hope was the quality and angle allowed her to see who was or wasn't directly involved.

Instead of heading for her office, Kiva drove to the house. It was farther than the office but safer, and she had brought her laptop home. Besides, she was starting to worry about her privacy, or more accurately, her client's. She had no idea who set up or supported the network at work and if her emails or files were protected or could be spied on. This whole thing stank of desperation. For the life of her, she couldn't figure out how grabbing the hangar and the extra hundred unused acres included in Elliott's holdings and eliminating the runways entirely was so crucial to their plan.

Pulling into the driveway, she noticed lights on next door. Mark was sitting on his deck and bundled in a parka, having drinks with a few friends.

He waved to her. "You remember my brother Jake, and those two goofs are Jesus and Mac. We served together in Afghanistan and Iraq."

She waved back, telling them, "Hi, guys, welcome to the lake, and thank you for your service."

Mark got up from his porch and came over to her. "Listen, some guy came by earlier. He was kind of poking around, and I know it's none of my business, but I kinda promised your dad I'd keep an eye out and everything and, well…"

"No worries. I appreciate everything you and Andi do around here. I couldn't handle the place without your help. So what did this guy want?"

"He claimed to be your boyfriend. I strongly suggested he come back when you were home."

"My boyfriend? Mark, you know better than that. Did he give you a name or card or anything?"

"Nope. Just jumped back in his truck and hightailed it out of here." Taking in Kiva's face, he said, "I take it there's some sort of trouble going on?"

Making a judgment call, she nodded. "Between you and me, someone's targeting my new client. They just tried to burn down the hangar at the airport."

"Young Elliott's place?"

"You've met her?" she asked, incredulous.

"Andi did yesterday. She was in the Cash and Carry buying supplies when Andi was working. Andi thought she was really nice. She also thought she was batting for the other team?" he asked, offering a look of brotherly hope.

Ignoring his matchmaking, she said, "Yes, young Elliott is very nice and in trouble. Whoever's targeting her has already convinced the sheriff she's involved in the fire even though I told him she'd been with me all evening."

"How bad is the hangar?"

"Looks like the old wood doors took most of the damage. We managed to get it under control before the fire department finally showed."

"Listen, about this guy. He really put me off. He was driving a shiny new Escalade, but his clothes looked like thrift store stuff and something else. They smelled."

"Of maybe…accelerant? Gas?"

"Something like it. I'm sorry I didn't get a name, but he got all edgy after I didn't buy the boyfriend thing."

"No, you did great. Thanks."

"Kiva, I wanted to ask you something, but now's not the time. I'll…"

"Is it about your two friends?"

He looked embarrassed. "It's just, they're having a hard time and I was wondering if, well…"

"Yes."

Looking confused, he started to ask, "Wait…what?"

"Yes, I know how we can put them to work. Right now, in fact."

"Now? What…" He looked back toward the deck and his friends. He smiled back at her. "Sure. What are they gonna be doing?"

"Just tell them it's right up their alley, and it comes with housing so get them to grab their gear and meet me at my car in twenty minutes. And Mark, thanks so much. You've saved me once again."

He drew himself up, looking very much like the soldier he once was. She watched him trot back over to the guys, ordering as he went, "Duty calls. Drop your beers and grab your gear! Kiva's got a job for you and housing too. You lucky bastards!"

Letting herself in the door, she went straight to the security monitor, rewinding the recording to an Escalade pulling up the driveway. She watched as a young man she didn't recognize got out. He tried the front door, then walked around the far side and looked to be trying to force the back door when she saw Mark move into camera range. There was no audio on the security cameras her father had installed a few years back.

She sucked in a breath when the stranger shoved Mark aside but his two friends moved and the unknown male retreated to his truck and backed out quickly. She used the on-screen editing controls to mark the start and end of the sequence, selecting the time stamp to be displayed, and sent a copy to her Gmail account.

He had shown up at almost the same time they had arrived at the hangar. Thank goodness for Elliott's constant time watching— a habit, she explained, from always having to record takeoffs, landings, and navigation waypoints to the exact minute.

Kiva started the coffeemaker and grabbed the old picnic basket from under the island and pulled out the large thermos. The guys would need coffee, and she didn't know what Elliott had stocked in her canteen-turned-kitchen. While the coffee brewed, she sat down at the computer.

Relieved to see the video player open automatically when she inserted the SIM card reader, she noted it began to stream from the start of the recording. She checked the time stamp; it contained twenty-four hours of footage. She used the loading time to pack the picnic basket, the makings for sandwiches, then filled the thermos.

Back at the computer, she advanced the footage to the time closer to when she picked up Elliott. She could clearly see her Mustang out front and Elliott locking the walkthrough door to the hangar and jumping in. The footage was high quality and Elliott's Jeep was parked far enough away to make out most of the hangar. Far enough that she could see for herself that Elliott was right. There wasn't as much as a garbage bag out front and certainly no shipping pallets or skids. She stopped the playback and noted the time stamp, then set the video to fast forward.

While it played, she opened another window on the screen and copied the entire recording and saved it to her Google Cloud account. She continued watching intently until she marked the start of the next arrival, then pressed play. She almost choked when she recognized Jake's truck pull up out front. Holding her breath, she prayed that Mark was not involved. Watching Mark's brother get out of the cab, again she sucked in air, relieved to see he was alone. The back of his pickup was loaded high with skids and other garbage. He undid several straps, then backed up by the doors, and climbing up, started kicking and tossing everything in a pile. When he was finished, he got back in his truck like it was nothing and drove away. She marked the time again and started to fast-forward. She didn't have to wait long until the Escalade pulled up. Again she noted the time, slowing the footage to grab a headshot of the driver. He wasn't alone. She grabbed a frame and sent it to the printer and copied it to her Gmail. Hitting play, she almost threw up when she recognized his passenger.

Jose, Gent Koehler's son, climbed from the other side of the Escalade. He joined the driver at the back hatch, then both men carried cans to the pile of debris. She grabbed another screen pic and sent it to the printer and copied it to the cloud. She also noted they each wore gloves. After they poured the contents of the cans on the pile, they wrapped each can tightly in pieces of an old wool blanket. It was easy to recognize—the Hudson's Bay blanket that covered old Elliott's bed. They snugged the cans down under the back of the pile, and she could only assume it was to preserve them as evidence. She had a sick feeling she knew where those cans came from too.

Someone other than Elliott must have keys to the hangar. Between the distinct four-points blanket she knew no one else around here would have, and the cans which she was sure had Elliott's prints on them, not to mention the fact the wool was an excellent barrier against fire, there was enough evidence to support the sheriff's charges of arson.

Without the dash cam footage, she wouldn't have a hope of defending her. Even with it, she would have to be smart. Thinking about her options, she apologized aloud, "I'm so sorry, Elliott, but I think the best way to play this is let you spend the night in lockup." She needed time to be sure of who all the players were. Forcing their hand now would only make things more desperate for Ian, Gent, and whoever else was behind this.

She copied the last clip and sent it off, then shut down the laptop and stuffed her notes and the printouts in her attaché case. She raced upstairs and loaded an overnight bag with clothes and her toiletries. Back in the kitchen, she made sure the surveillance system was still recording, then grabbed her purse, attaché case, and the picnic basket and headed out.

The guys spotted her and ran to grab her bags and help her load her car. They wanted to follow in their pickup, but even with just three beers, they couldn't risk the sheriff pulling them over and, she told them, they were probably being watched. That straightened them up, and they climbed in the Mustang, sobering as they did so.

On the short drive back to the airport, she explained who Elliott was, how she had just inherited the hangar and business, and that someone was framing her for arson and maybe even insurance fraud, which carried a minimum five-year sentence in their state. She didn't explain how she knew other forces were at play, just that Elliott had been with her all evening, so she was witness to her innocence. They didn't seem to need reassurance. They just wanted to get to work and debated back and forth about how they would secure the area and break up their duty shift. She had been right about this being right up their alley.

Nearing the hangar, they could see the fire truck was gone, but the fire marshal's car was parked where it had been and the fire marshal herself was carefully sifting through the debris. Several work lights on stands illuminated the area, and a portable generator hummed as she worked, carefully photographing her findings.

Much as Kiva wanted to stop and talk, she had a bad feeling the hangar would not be empty. Sure enough, the sheriff's car was there and the walkthrough door wide open. "Okay, guys. This could get ugly. Stick with me. We need to kick this bastard out before he starts planting evidence."

"You think he's involved? The *sheriff*?" Jesus asked. He was in the back seat and last to climb out of the car.

"I'd bet my life on it."

"Ouch!" he said.

Seconding the thought, Mac reassured her, "We've got your back."

It didn't take long to find him. He was in the guest room, and Kiva could see it was the one Elliott was sleeping in. He was tearing apart her books and had already gone through her personal papers and what looked like several journals. Unabashedly, he looked at her and grinned. "Looks like your lez-be-friend's got a history of crazy. Bet you didn't know she lost her job up north for bein' sick in the head?"

"Put that stuff down and get out!"

"Get off yer high horse, kid. I got cause, and you know it."

"Actually, Dias, you don't, and unless you have a warrant to search the premises, I suggest you put everything down and leave now."

He grinned suggestively until he noticed the muscle backing her up. Mac stepped into the room and stood tall. "Have you got that warrant, Sheriff?"

"You're way outta line, boy. But I see old missy here has you on a short chain, so tell you what. I'll just take these here papers and be on my way." He moved to leave with Elliott's journal and her pilot's logbooks, but Mac stepped in his path.

"Like Ms. Park said, if you don't have a warrant, you don't get to take anything. Your badge doesn't give you the right to break the law."

Sheriff Dias looked like he would argue until Jesus stepped into the small room. Dias spat tobacco juice on the polished floor, shoving the papers in Kiva's hands. "You just made a big mistake, Kiva, one even your slanty-eyed daddy can't fix." He pushed past them and strode out.

"Bastard." Kiva handed the keys for the double-barreled locks to Jesus and nodded for him to follow the sheriff.

Standing by her, Mac noted, "Some days I miss the Army. It may not be perfect, but at least they do a better job of weeding out little racist turds like him. You okay?" She nodded, starting to pick up the mess in the room when he stopped her. "Maybe we should photograph everything first?"

Exhaling, she took a minute to get her emotions under control. "You're right. Thanks." Sighing, she muttered, "I've been living in Toronto for so long now, I almost forgot what it could be like here."

He nodded, and she observed his own faraway look. Pulling out his cell phone, he offered, "Why don't you let me document everything here. I know you want to talk to the fire marshal. I'll make sure Jesus has your back."

She nodded thanks and headed back down the stairs. Remembering the portion of the dash-cam video showing the arsonists using a cut-up Hudson's Bay blanket to protect the planted evidence, she backtracked to Old Elliott's bedroom. Sure enough, the blanket that had graced his bed for decades was now missing. She grabbed a few shots with her phone, trying to think of who else could have copies of the keys. Then she remembered her father saying Ian had completed the inventory of the hangar contents. Ian! He had access. He had time. And he could have easily had copies cut, several in fact. Which begged the question, why not start the fire inside?

At the bottom of the stairs she looked out at the contents Ian had described as salvage. Remembering Elliott's enthusiasm and her appraisal, she knew the four aircraft, even in the mid-restoration stage, were worth a small fortune.

That could only mean Ian was working his plan from two ends. He wanted the hangar for his land deal, and the contents for their value. She'd bet his land development partners didn't know he was playing them on the hangar contents. Still, that wasn't her concern right now. Getting her Elliott out of this mess was. *Her Elliott?* Ensuring Elliott's safety, not to mention her own, was going to be a much more significant challenge.

First thing tomorrow she would find out just who was involved in the land deal. She had already discovered that a shell corporation had purchased much of the vacant land in the area and held options on almost every other property around the south half of the lake. Strangely, they had no interest in the northern half where her family home was located. And they wanted the airport, all of it, though she couldn't figure out why. Having an airport was the primary draw to the area for any of the few companies who were considering development, but lack of skilled labor and the distance to a major center had all been the factors that had kept other companies and developers away. One thing she did know now: not only were Gent and Ian involved, but she'd bet Sheriff Dias was too.

Letting herself out the airside door, she walked around the hangar, heading for the area the fire marshal was working. "Hey, Mary," she called from the taped off perimeter.

Mary Rinaldo's face lit up to see her old grade school friend. She walked to Kiva, a smile on her face and camera strung around her neck. "If it isn't the long-lost Parkette. How are you, buddy? I didn't believe it when Erica said you were back in town but here you are, and I hear you're defending a crazy ass arsonist? What's with that?"

"Nice to see you too, and before you jump to conclusions, I have evidence for you and I'm counting on you to add it to the public record."

Mary nodded back toward the charred pieces of wool blanket and the cans of urethane. "I hate to break your bubble, but I got lots of evidence too."

Kiva handed her the SIM card, then pulled from her back pocket one of the screen-captures she had printed out.

Mary unfolded the paper, moving closer to one of the light stands to look over the picture. "Kiva, this doesn't prove anything."

"That's just one frame from the entire evening captured on video. When you play the footage on that SIM card, you'll see I picked my client up at five. Two hours later, Jake Coe pulls up and dumps all that crap against the door. Then he leaves."

"Mark's sleazy brother?"

"That's the one. I have coverage of my home security system showing him pulling into Mark's an hour later."

"Please tell me he's not involved. I always thought Mark was a good guy."

"Not from what I could tell."

She sighed. "Who's this other guy? Maybe your client's boyfriend or something?"

Kiva grinned at that idea. "Not a chance. She's definitely playing for our team. I don't know who he is, but if I'm not mistaken, the other guy is Jose Koehler, Gent's youngest son."

"Yah, I heard he flunked out of college and was walking around like he's hot shit, telling everyone he's got some big ass job lined up. What's the video show?"

"They pull up, pour accelerant all over, then wrap the cans nice and tight and snug them down low. I can only assume it was to protect the evidence. Did you dust for fingerprints?"

"Didn't have to. Whoever handled that stuff had finish all over their hands. There's perfect ridge detail everywhere. I was wondering how anyone would be so stupid, not to mention wrapping the cans in wool. There was no way enough air could have got to them even with the heat. Dias was telling me your client has something wrong with her head, so I put it down to plain old stupid. Sorry."

"No worries. I know what he's selling."

Mary walked to her car, grabbed an envelope, and marking up the evidence info, time, date, where she obtained it and from whom, sealing the card inside. "So, I'm thinking you want me to go burst Dias's little bubble, tonight or what?"

"Actually, I was hoping you would take your time. How long does it normally take you to process a scene and hand over evidence?"

"Something like this, two maybe three days. Why?"

Kiva leaned against the fire department vehicle, trying to decide just how much she was willing to share. "Something's going on, something bigger than a fight for the hangar. Have you noticed anything suspicious happening lately?"

"More suspicious than this?" She leaned on the door, thinking things through. "Actually, now that you mention it, there's been a rash of fires. Mostly uninhabited houses, a few summer places that are empty this time of year. I mentioned it to my chief, but he brushed it off to kids with nothing better to do."

"They wouldn't happen to be centered around the south half of the lake?"

Mary's eyebrows raised. "How? Never mind. I don't want your speculations to interfere with my investigation. Here's what I'll do.

I'll hold off filing this until Friday, Monday if you can't get in front of a judge till then. I'm assuming you'll want your client present, so let's aim for Monday. I'll need that long to pull out the other reports of suspicious fires and arson centered around the lake and meet you in the Fifth District Court."

"What makes you think I can't get Elliott out till Monday?"

Still looking surprised, Mary said simply, "Dias shipped her down to the Lea County Correctional Facility. I thought he would have told you that."

"Why the fuck?"

"I know! I thought it was an asshole move too, but he went on and on about her having a record as a violent offender and needing to send her to a Level Three facility. There's only two of them in New Mexico. It's the closest. When he explained she was all fucked up in the head, well, it almost made sense."

"Oh, geez, Mary. You could have led with that!"

"Hey, I just investigate suspicious fires. I'm not all-knowing, you know?"

Kiva looked around in near panic, trying to decide what to do next. She turned for the hangar door, then turned back, pulling her card from her back pocket. She nabbed the pen Mary had used to complete the evidence envelope and scribbled her cell phone number on the back. "Only call me on that. Don't call the office whatever you do, and Mary, thanks for sitting on this till Monday. I'll see you in court."

* * *

Elliott was carsick from being bounced around in the back seat of two different police cars. It was easy to guess they weren't taking her to a holding cell in the county sheriff's office. By the time the deputy opened her door and pulled her out, her head was pounding and she was working everything she had not to puke. Half walking, half being dragged into the detention center, she made it to the intake desk to be screamed at to stand on a pair of painted outlines of feet. With the taste of bile burning in the back of her throat, she tried to politely say, "I'm sorry but…"

"Speak when you're spoken to!" the male deputy spat at her.

"I'm going to be sick."

"I told you to shut the fuck—"

She leaned over, vomiting on the floor in front of her. A rough hand grabbed her by the neck, dragging her towards a holding room while she gagged from the vomit still in her throat. She landed on the floor of a cinderblock room. There were other prisoners here, including men. There was no toilet, no garbage can, or anywhere else for her to dispose of the vomit she couldn't hold back. Crawling to a corner she was determined to keep her upchuck away from the others. It wasn't until her stomach as empty that she noticed most of the occupants were in worse shape than her. *So, this is the drunk tank?*

A filthy skeletal-looking woman was jonesing in the far corner. Closest to her was a guy she bet was homeless and happy to be here. He gave her a weirdly polite smile. Beside him was a heavyweight suit who looked like he'd had ten or twenty too many. She choked, having a hard time clearing her nose and throat, finally surrendering to the fact that she had no choice but to blow her nose into her shirt and wipe her mouth.

So she rolled down the sleeve of her once crisply pressed white shirt and wiped her face before clearing the vomit from her nasal cavities. Only then did she notice how dirty her shirt was, blackened with soot from fighting the fire. She shook off her revulsion at herself and folded the sleeve to cover some of the disgusting mess.

She wasn't sure how long she had been sitting, eyes closed, head back against the block wall when she heard the electronic lock on the door click open. Hopeful for a reprieve from the stench of the small room, she watched as a bulky corrections officer, hauling an even larger man in a fireman's carry, came into the room and dumped him on the concrete floor.

Because she was beyond tired, it took Elliott a millisecond to comprehend the unconscious man's head was about to be acquainted with the floor with concussive force. She wasn't fast enough or big enough to prevent his shoulder from hitting the floor with breaking force but managed to grab his head. Pain registered on his face and his eyes opened in shock. In that split second, she saw something more, something that forced her to replay every first aid course both the military and the airline had mandated that she attend.

Quickly checking his pulse, she noted his eyes were open but didn't follow her movement. She sniffed at his breath. This guy wasn't drunk.

"Call 9-1-1!" she ordered before the CO pushed the door closed.

He looked back at her, shouting, "The guy's just drunk!"

"He's not drunk, asshole! He's having a grand mal seizure." At the CO's indifference, his antipathy, she added, "You don't want this on your record and I *will* report it. Call 9-1-1! NOW!"

He looked to be frozen. Maybe he was too low in the pecking order to make life and death decisions. He finally conceded, "I'll get someone to take a look at him."

"I'm a medic! This guy is going to be brain dead by the time your boss gets his ass in gear!"

That stopped him. He pulled the door open, asking, "You're military?"

"Yes. Look, I've seen this before. We haven't got much time!"

He took a deep breath then smacked something outside the room. Red lights lit up the intake area and a corrections officer with sergeant stripes rushed to his side. "We got an army medic, says this guy's having some sort of seizure and could die."

The sergeant instantly picked up a phone, demanded a rig be rolled immediately. "Soldier!" he demanded. "What do you need?"

"Someone needs to check his effects for medication or a medic alert card."

While he shouted orders, she followed her own advice, pulling up his sleeves looking for a bracelet. Then unfastening a few more buttons on his shirt, noting that the skin around his face and neck had a blue tinge she hadn't noticed before. It was hard to pick up with Black victims but easy when compared to the color of his chest. Pulling up a thin silver chain around his neck, she found a MedicAlert pendant. Several allergies were listed on top of severe epilepsy. Seeing the blue condition worsening, she laid her ear against his chest, then swore. When the sergeant returned, she was struggling to give him mouth to mouth. "I can't keep his airway open. I need someone to position his head."

The sergeant got down on his knees, pulling his head expertly into position while calling for the other CO to bring the portable O2 and the defibrillator. "We've lost his pulse," he informed her professionally.

"Dammit!" was all Elliott had time to say, moving to his chest, ripping the starched shirt open, beginning compressions. She was counting aloud when she spotted something out of the corner of her eye. "Behind you!" she automatically warned. The sergeant turned just in time to block an attack from the skeletal crack addict. He had her down and cuffed in seconds, turning his attention back to Elliott and the patient as the other CO rushed in with the ordered equipment. Now the sergeant set up the oxygen, snapping a mask on the man while ordering his attacker be placed in some restraining device they rolled to the door.

Between the events of the evening, fighting the fire with less than optimal equipment, her carsickness, vomiting, and being stuck in this putrid room, she knew she couldn't keep the compressions up much longer. Luckily the medics barged in and took control. When she sat back, her arms were so fatigued they felt like Jello, and her hands were shaking from the adrenaline. It took a few minutes to get the man stable, and two paramedics, the sergeant, two COs and her to get him on the stretcher. Then they were gone, and the automatic door closed in her face.

She sat down on the cold bench. With the crack addict gone, it was just her, the filthy homeless man, and the drunk guy in the expensive suit. The suit had snored through the whole thing, and she imagined some high-priced lawyer would soon bail him out. The old homeless man patted her gently on the shoulder. "You did good, kid," he said before moving to the empty bench at the end of the cell and stretching out to sleep.

Closing her eyes, she let her head rest against the wall. Justice, she knew, was a waiting game. Kiva had everything needed to prove her innocence. Still, judging by how quickly she was arrested and the fact they had taken her out of the county as soon as they could, she suspected her lawyer and friend was facing an uphill battle. All she could hope for was quick processing and she had a feeling no one in the Mirabal County Sheriff's Department was in a hurry to inform Kiva of her whereabouts. That meant she needed to be in the system to be found, and until they processed her in, she didn't exist.

Please Lord, if I was going to wallow in obscurity, why couldn't it have been in a clean shirt?

Because it was night, Elliott wasn't moved to the women's pod after processing but to holding, a prison-type dorm with several cells and two stainless steel octagonal tables in the common area. She was given a vinyl-covered mattress and personal hygiene supplies including a roll of toilet paper and told to find a bed. There was no corrections officer present and the only panic alarm was on the wall near the exit. She wouldn't have minded the time with nothing to do, but she wasn't alone. The crack addict from the drunk tank was there, along with another woman who she could see was also displaying similar signs of withdrawal.

After spending a long night trying to stay out of their way, the next morning Elliott was moved to the women's pod along with the exhausted drug addicts. The pod was quiet, with only a few posturing inmates claiming one was the pod boss. Elliott nodded her respect, promising she had no beef and would defer to them. The other women asked her questions, and she answered and tried to fit in. They wanted to know what she was in for, and she was truthful, admitting she'd been charged with arson. They shared their charges too, including their excuses or why they didn't think their arrests were fair. Most were guilty of what Elliott would call poverty crimes. Things like stealing clothes for job interviews or some shit their kids just had to have.

By the time dinner was served, the drug addicts who had crashed all day came alive, and the balance of power shifted. Night was hell with noise levels rising and zero chance for sleep. On top of that, the skeletal crack addict with whom she'd been in the drunk tank kept telling everyone Elliott was a cop, because she had warned the sergeant of her attempted attack. While the petty criminals kept their distance, the drug users shifted into high gear, determined to prove their suspicions. Finally, Thursday morning, she was taken in orange scrubs to attend her bail hearing. Standing in shackles, she didn't exactly cut an image of the young honest professional.

Kiva only had a minute with her before the hearing and asked her to choose. "I can push to give evidence now and maybe get you bail or hold back our cards until Monday's hearing when I can have the fire marshal ask for the charges to be dropped."

"Do we have to put all our cards on the table to get me out now?"

"Yes."

"I'll wait."

The court clerk stood. "All rise for Fifth District Court Judge, the Honorable Katherine Forrest."

Elliott wasn't surprised when the judge set bail higher than either she or Kiva could raise. At least she had set the hearing date for Monday as they had hoped. Being led away from Kiva felt like leaving a part of herself behind. Turning from the back door to the courtroom, she was relieved to see Kiva watching her. She looked both determined and reassuring. Elliott returned the look. It was easy to believe in Kiva even if the situation felt out of control. All that could be done now was to be inconspicuous and wait things out. She wasn't sure what Kiva could achieve in four days, but if it brought them closer, that worked for her too.

Locked up and alone, she spent her time considering all the work to be done in the hangar and trying not to think about the enigmatic and enticing Kiva Park. But Kiva was her lawyer. Even if there weren't rules against anything between them, Kiva would be heading back to

Toronto in the spring, and no matter what she decided to do, Elliott knew she could not go back there, at least not for a few years. That offer to fly 757s in Bangladesh was looking better and better.

For the rest of Thursday, Elliott managed to stay under the radar of the troublemakers. Some of them had shared the same transport for their own court appearance, which had led a few to give up the idea that she was an informer or, worse, a cop. Then Friday afternoon, a new inmate was processed in. She walked in like she owned the place. She showed signs of a tough life lived and hard drug use. And she wasn't in withdrawal. Either this new inmate had been clean long enough to recover, or she was still high.

Not liking either option, Elliott knew she had to keep the peace. This wasn't like Vegas where what happens there stays there. If she got in a fight here, there was every chance she would be charged and this already hellish experience would get worse.

In the cell farthest from the crack queens, as she now thought of them, she moved her mattress from the bottom bunk to the top. It smelled like piss, but it would give her some advantage if attacked in the night, and the pod was a busy place all night. The crackheads had received e-cigarettes with their commissary allowance and judging by the smell wafting from the shower cubicle of an upper cell she had a feeling they were smoking the filters as they giggled and carried on. She couldn't tell if the new woman was partaking or just standing guard, but she kept taunting Elliott.

She called herself the pod boss and kept marching into Elliott's cell with her drug addict followers in tow, rummaging through her stuff and demanding she hand over her measly issued items. Sitting cross-legged on the top bunk, Elliott refused to engage and certainly wouldn't make the mistake of surrendering anything to her. It wasn't that they needed anything. It was a power game, and she wasn't going to play.

Besides, the CO who processed her in had already shortchanged her. Elliott had been issued a plastic cup, the toilet paper, and a toothbrush but no toothpaste, soap, shampoo, or even a towel. Wearing the issued underwear and scrubs, she had prison Crocs for her feet and nothing more. Every time she got down from her bunk to have a pee, the new pod boss would walk in and watch, making comments and calling for her bitches to join in the fun.

Elliott had managed to stay clear of them Friday, Saturday, and most of Sunday, but that night, after the dinner trays arrived, the atmosphere got tense. The trays were heavy plastic, probably blow-formed like plastic gas cans, but filled with poly insulation as a method to keep the food warm. Not only was the design a complete failure as a warming device, the inmates had learned how to pry the tops and bottoms apart. By late evening, Elliott knew they had received some contraband. They were high and fearless, and she was the only thing they would focus on. The night of hell was about to begin.

CHAPTER EIGHT

Monday morning, while breakfast was delivered, a corrections officer ordered Elliott to grab her gear. Hoping this meant she was to be released, she moved with speed but soon learned she was being taken with several others for a court appearance. She shuffled into a waiting minivan as ordered and sat silently for the ride. At the courthouse, the van drove inside a loading door and Elliott, along with the others, was moved to a holding cell. One by one, the others were taken up for their appearance. When they returned, each prisoner was placed in one of two other cells. Elliott, the last to be led up, stumbled into the bright and airy courtroom. Her entry door didn't open directly into the courtroom but into an enclosed box with another bench.

She stood tall, unwilling to sit or put a foot wrong. From inside the plexiglass-enclosed box, it was hard to hear what was being said. Watching as the prosecutor supplied file after file to the clerk stirred a feeling of panic that she forced herself to control. No one looked at her, and no one asked her anything. Thank goodness Kiva was there and looked to be countering whatever materials the prosecution kept producing.

Sheriff Dias was sitting behind the prosecutor and looked to be getting upset, insisting on objection after objection. She watched as

Kiva provided her files and reports. Hopefully the dash cam in her Jeep had captured the actual culprits responsible for the fire. Judging by Dias's constant outbursts, he was not pleased with how the hearing was going.

Finally, a woman in a fire department uniform was sworn in. She presented page after page of photographs as she explained the details to the court. Not knowing what they depicted, Elliott could only hope the woman was presenting a case for her and not against. Still, judging by Kiva's warning look, it wasn't going well. The fire department woman moved a TV monitor mounted on a rolling stand to where the judge could view it. It was easier for Elliott to see than hear what was going on through the plexiglass wall. She watched as the footage from her dash cam was played. The uniformed woman, who Elliott had finally heard identified as the fire marshal, played a clip of her exiting the hangar, locking up and getting in Kiva's car. She then played another clip in which a young man pulled up in a pickup truck loaded with old skids, scrap wood, and other garbage and piled it all against the hangar door. Finally, she watched with the court as another vehicle pulled up, two men added several items she couldn't identify from where she was standing then set the fire.

For the first time since Elliott was taken into custody, she could breathe. She felt lightheaded with relief. It wasn't entirely over. There was more to and fro, and Kiva made several more motions, but finally the judge dropped her gavel and ordered the case dismissed. For the first time since she was marched into the enclosed appearance box, the judge turned to her, apologizing for the county and the state, and ordering her immediate release.

But "immediate" was a legal term, not a practical one. A court officer opened the door leading to the holding cells and led her back downstairs. He placed her in the second cell where she waited with the other detainees who were to be set free. Finally, two court officers and a corrections officer led her and the other two back through the corridor to where the corrections van was waiting. They boarded silently for the drive back. Once they pulled out of the building, the CO explained they were returning to the corrections center to collect their personal belongings, change into their own clothes, and be processed out. Elliott finally allowed herself a moment of calm. Kiva had done it. Now it was time to figure out what was really going on.

* * *

Kiva stood leaning against her Mustang parked at the curb of the Lea County High Security Corrections Center. She knew this was where Elliott would exit and wanted to be the first person she saw. The early morning hearing had been pushed back supposedly to accommodate Sheriff Dias, who had evidence to support additional charges. When they finally stood before the judge, she was shocked to see Elliott's condition. Her hair was flat and dirty, her forehead still streaked with the remnants of soot, and she looked like a ghost. She could only guess that she hadn't slept. Still, it was the gash across her forehead that frightened her the most. What the hell had she been through? Watching her exit from the detention center, she could see some life return to her face, but she couldn't help but crinkle her nose as she got close. "Oh my God, the smell..."

"Trust me, I feel even worse. Um," she looked down at the dirty, stinking shirt, asking, "You wouldn't happen to have a clean T-shirt? Actually, a dirty one would be better than this."

"I...how about the T-shirt I slept in last night? Is that too gross?" Kiva's worry disappeared the moment she saw Elliott's irresistible grin.

"That actually sounds like heaven."

Kiva grabbed the offered T from her overnight bag, handing it to the woman standing at the curb in nothing but her sports bra. There was no missing the fresh bruises and scratches over her chest and back. "What the hell happened in there?"

Elliott was smiling. "It doesn't matter now. I'm out, and if I heard right, you got the charges dropped?"

"Yes."

"All of them?"

She sucked in another breath. "I don't know what Dias has up his sleeve, but we need a plan, and we need to figure out what they're up to and fast. Come on. Get in the car," she ordered, heading for the driver's side.

Elliott held up the dirty shirt. "Can I toss this, or do you need it?"

About to ask her to put it in a nearby trash can, she realized she could use it for added proof Elliott hadn't handled the accelerant that night. She backtracked to the trunk, emptying a plastic bag to stuff the shirt in, hoping the plastic would trap the smell. Now, taking a long careful look at Elliott, she asked again, "Are you sure you're okay?"

"I'm tired, bruised, filthy dirty, and hungry as a bear, but I'm out, and that's all that matters."

Smiling, Kiva slipped the car into drive. "A lot happened over the weekend. Do you want to eat, shower, or talk first?"

Looking down at the wrinkly T-shirt, Elliott grinned, asking, "Roswell Seventy—*aliens*? Please tell me it won't take us seventy years to solve this mystery?"

Kiva grinned as she wheeled the car onto the main drag. "Since there are no aliens involved, I think we may be okay."

"If it won't embarrass you too much, do you think we could find someplace to eat? Someplace you never have to go to again. You can tell me what's happened and then I have to see what's left of my hangar."

Pointing to the IHOP sign just up ahead, Kiva smiled. "If it works for you, it works for me."

A few minutes later, Elliott stood in the ladies' restroom, taking a careful look at herself. She had managed to scrub off the rest of the soot, not to mention the dried blood from her face, the soap leaving a terrible sting across her wound. Amazing what you could do with some soap, water, and a mirror. She scrubbed her teeth with her finger and was relieved the five days without toothpaste hadn't left them looking too bad. Not much more she could do on that account, but she did rinse her hair in the sink using the harsh soap. She finger-brushed her hair back and walked out with her head held high. The collar of her T-shirt was soaked, and the wet hair was dripping on her shoulders, but Elliott didn't care. Seeing Kiva's kind and sympathetic smile was all she needed. "Do I look better or worse?"

"Better. I know you're probably jonesing for a shower, but I'm glad you want to talk first."

Elliott waited while the waitress delivered coffee and took their order. "Never in my life would I have imagined it could be that bad. Fuck, hell week in basic training was a cakewalk in comparison."

Kiva held up her phone. "I've been making a few discreet inquiries and I have news for you. I think you were targeted. I think Dias arranged to have an inmate transferred there with the sole intent of getting you into a fight and stacking charges against you. Elliott, I don't know what you went through or how you kept your head, but instead of walking out with extra charges, you took a beating. You also received a commendation."

"I did?"

"You saved a man's life, and not any man. He's the Congressional Representative for the state of New Mexico." She held up a hand. "I want the whole story, but first I want to put your mind at ease about the hangar. I've hired security. Not your average police cast-off types but two veterans. They served with my neighbor Mark. I trust him, and I trust them. They've done some basic repairs on the big door, they changed all the locks. I'm sorry to tell you, someone else had keys to the hangar after you took possession and they removed several items and placed some in or near the fire as evidence against you."

Wrapping her hands around the porcelain mug, letting the heat of her coffee act as proof she was alive and free, Elliott asked quietly, "Do you know who's involved yet?"

"I have my suspicions, but we'll get to that. While I was waiting for your release, I got a call from your grandmother. She was worried sick. She was also a fount of information. You were smart to give her my number."

Elliott held up her arm, showing off the still readable Sharpie-written numerals. "You were smart to give it to me. And for the first time in my life I'm thankful I'm not the first grandchild to call her from jail. She's okay, right?"

Smiling, she nodded, "She's a trooper. She was worried you'd get in 'deep doo doo,' as she called it. She told me you were always getting in scraps as a kid, always the defender of other kids who couldn't stand up for themselves. She's very proud of you."

"Well, I'm just glad she can't see me looking like this. When I was little she was always the first to throw me in the tub after each of those 'doo doo' incidents. Evidently, getting in fights is okay as long as you scrub yourself clean afterward."

Kiva sat back as the waitress served lunch. "Eat," she ordered with affection and watched as Elliott began devouring a high stack of blueberry pancakes. She sipped her coffee, realizing just how easy it was to be with this woman. She was kind and strong and somehow unpretentious. More than that, there was a spirit about her, an indomitable force that gave her courage. "I'm proud too," she added quietly.

Elliott swallowed a big mound of pancake. Offering her trademark grin, she teased the compliment away. "*Aaah*. Now, you're going to make me cry."

Kiva took her hand. "Don't worry. It'll be our secret."

For a moment Elliott looked vulnerable. Then, just as quickly, the weakness was gone, replaced with something else, something more hopeful. She squeezed Kiva's hand. "Okay, I'm ready. What did Nanny have to say?"

It took another thirty minutes and a gallon of coffee before she shared everything she had learned. Some of what she'd heard led her to locate Old Elliott's bank account. She didn't have a figure, but the bank had suggested it was a respectable amount. He also had a safety deposit box which had not been detailed in the will. Her grandmother suspected old Elliott had some insight into what was going on regarding the redevelopment plan and had stored that information safely away from Ian Guerrero. Just months before his death, he had moved his money out of the local bank to a chain bank up in Amarillo. It took Kiva only one call to verify the story.

"Will we have time to drive up there after I've had a shower and changed?" Elliott asked.

"I don't think we can make it today. The drive back here took close to two hours. Add another two to get to Amarillo…I think we should head back to town; you can get some rest and I'll go back to the office and clear my week. And I'll see if we can make an appointment with the bank for tomorrow." Realizing she was still holding Elliott's hand, she gave it a squeeze before letting go. "Ellie," she said before realizing she was using the pet name Elliott's grandmother used. "I promise you. We're going to get to the bottom of this and soon."

She watched Elliott blow out a long breath. "I know thank you doesn't really cut it but, thanks all the same. I don't know what I would have done if you weren't here."

CHAPTER NINE

Elliott bounded down the hangar stairs to the canteen. She'd showered, slept, showered, eaten, then slept again. Now it was bright and early Tuesday morning, and she was fresh from yet another shower and ready to get back to work or at least get to work on figuring out what the hell was going on. She halted when she spotted the two men making breakfast. "Gentlemen."

They both jumped, turning to face her and coming to attention, offering a joint "Ma'am!"

"Whoa there, fellas. I appreciate the show of respect, but I'd prefer you just call me Elliott." They shared a look but didn't respond. "Okay, why don't we start with your names again. Sorry, I wasn't quite myself yesterday."

The closest of the two offered his hand. "I'm Michel MacMillan. I go by Mac and this is Jesus Ortega, ma'am." Mac pronounced his given name in the French fashion, hinting at a Cajun ancestry, before offering his companion's name in authentic Spanish intonation.

Shaking his hand, and offering a friendly welcome, she said. "It's nice to meet again, Mac, and you," she shook the taller man's hand, "I'll confess right now, I'm completely and terribly Canadian. I can pick up any French name, but for me, Spanish is right up there with

Klingon. So, help me out here; Hay-Zeus or Aye-Zeus?" she tried to pronounce it as Mac had.

Jesus grinned, enjoying her discomfort. "You know," Mac offered, "that would work. Why don't you call him Zeus?"

She smiled, "Whadda'ya say? Will Zeus work for you or will you make me resort to using Sarge?"

"Either is great, ma'am."

"Oh no," she said, shaking her head. "I'm sure everyone in town has the sheriff's word that I'm some jailbird nutcase. With a rep like that, no way are you sticking me with that ma'am nonsense."

He gave her hand a good shake, and with a grin, asserted that he liked Zeus just fine. "You up for a big breakfast, Cap?"

Deciding that Cap was a better moniker than ma'am, Elliott smiled, enjoying the prospect of having these guys around. "Well, I thought you'd never ask." She poured herself a coffee and tried to help without getting in the way, listening as they went through the chores they had done since arriving.

"Changing all the locks was a good start. I wish I'd thought of it earlier. After breakfast I need to drive up to Amarillo. I was thinking of buying one of those video surveillance systems while I'm there. I was just going to go on to eBay after I check my email, but I think we should put it in ASAP."

Both men agreed it was a necessary addition. As they ate breakfast, they discussed the number of cameras, where they could be installed and whether she should invest in a wireless system or run cables. "I'll grab everything while I'm in town. I think we can run it all off my laptop. It's an older model, and I just use it for email. Think I'll need a backup hard drive?"

Jesus nodded. "I'd suggest a terabyte backup, and we may need a signal booster for the Wi-Fi. Show us where you want to set everything up, then I'll have a better idea of what we need. I should take a look at the router too."

"My laptop's in the blueprint room, you know, the room with the large-scale printer and the microfiche? I figured we could keep it there unless you want to set up a dedicated..." Taking in their shared look, she asked pointedly, "What's wrong?"

Mac began, "Kiva wanted to see the maps you'd done for her with the development plans. She was sure that's where you'd have left them, but there's nothing there. No plans, no local maps, not even the stuff she printed out for you."

"And no laptop," Jesus added. "Sorry, Cap. If they have that stuff, they have a good idea what you've figured out."

She wanted to swear or throw something. Getting mad wouldn't help. "I take it you haven't seen my phone either?"

They shared a look again, "We assumed you had it on you."

She huffed in frustration, then shook her head. "I think we better take a good look and see what else is missing."

They both sat in silence.

"What now?" she asked. "Look, if you men are going to work with me, you better get used to just spitting out stuff like this. I don't need things softened or mansplained!"

Mac nodded. "Kiva told you about the blanket. The fancy one they took, right?" At her blank stare, he elaborated, "They took an expensive wool blanket, one with different colored stripes on it and wrapped the accelerant tins in it to keep your fingerprints from burning off the cans of varnish they hid as evidence. Sorry."

"The Four-Points trade blanket?" At their joint nods, she swore, then said, "My great-uncle received that blanket as a wedding gift." Elliott sighed. "I have a feeling we have a lot more to worry about than an old Hudson's Bay blanket." She took an object out of her wallet that looked like a thick business card except it was square, not rectangular.

Picking it up, Zeus asked, "Is this what I think it is?"

"When you travel as much as I do and you're as forgetful as I sometimes am, it's best to be able to track things. If one of you will download the app, we may be able to locate my laptop and my phone. Who knows? We may hit pay dirt."

Jesus had his phone out and downloaded the GPS tag-tracking app in seconds. Elliott accepted his phone and signed in before selecting the correct tags to track. "It's limited to crowdsourcing, but it's better than the proprietary apps that require the devices to be turned on to track."

It only took a minute, but she had a location. "And the hits just keep on coming," she announced rhetorically, before saying, "I think we better call Kiva."

* * *

Just getting in her car as her phone rang, Kiva noted the caller ID and was immediately worried, "Jesus. Is everything okay?"

"Hi, Kiva, it's Elliott. Have you got a minute?"

"Yes, of course. How are you feeling?" Before she would let Elliott answer, she rushed ahead, "I'm sorry I didn't come out last night, but I thought you could use the rest. I hope you didn't think I was avoiding you?" *Why am I rambling?*

"What? Oh, no. Thanks. I was exhausted. I gobbled down the supper the boys made and went right back to bed."

"Oh. Good. I mean I'm glad. Ah, what can I do? I mean, you called?"

Elliott's voice was full of mischief and charm. "You're teasing me. That's okay. Yes, I ate, showered near a half-dozen times, and slept. So, thanks for that. Listen, you're not at the office, are you?"

"No. Just on my way. Do you need something? Is everything okay?"

"Could you pop 'round here first? I mean if you have time in your schedule?"

"Actually, my week is open now, so sure. Anything you want to share, or should I just hurry over?"

"Why don't we wait till you get here?"

"On my way."

Pulling into the parking lot on the street side of the hangar, Kiva was pleased to see scaffolding erected in front of the charred door sections. Some segments had already been scraped and primed, others looked like they were ready for removal and replacement. It was a relief to know the guys were working while Elliott was gone. She could only guess that whatever she had to share was not going to bring her joy. She had already set aside most of the week to get to the bottom of whatever was going on. Preparation for any case was key, but it was the action of the courtroom, the actual battle of intellects and wills that thrilled her.

Not to say she wasn't enjoying running her father's practice. Just last week she sat with her divorce client at her side, face-to-face with her abusive husband and his smarmy lawyer. Carving the two into shards of the crap they were had been an enormous pleasure and such a relief for the woman she was protecting. It was hard to get battered women through these confrontations, but they had prevailed, and her client was immensely relieved. That was a big win in her books. Now it was time for a win in this business too.

Walking carefully through the hangar's step-through door, she stopped to watch Elliott and the guys. They were working together to maneuver the delicate-looking top wing to fit onto the frame of the smallest of the aircraft, the Gipsy something. *I've got to make a point of remembering these things.*

That thought made her feel an unexpected warmth. *Careful Kiva. This one is catch and release only.* It was too easy to take in her muscle tone, the look of her shoulders, arms, the curve of her waist as she moved the skeleton of the top wing, using some sort of hook and chain hoist suspended from the ceiling. She pulled at the chains and led the thing into place while the guys each guided a wing tip. As Elliott called out directions, she noted her precision and command. She never scolded or berated them when they got it wrong or asked questions as they moved. It was clear she was in command and these soldiers Kiva had hired responded naturally, as if they had worked or trained together for years.

"That's it. Hold!" Elliott ordered. "I'll slack it up, then we can have a better look at the fit. Call out if the pressure increases or falls off. Remember, you're just directing it in place, not holding it up. Ready?"

"Ready left!" Jesus answered.

"Ready right!" Mac called out.

"Here goes." Elliott began slowly hauling on just one chain.

"Weights off, on the right," Mac called out.

"Zeus?"

"It's a little heavier. Can you come down a bit more, Cap?"

Kiva watched as Jesus waved and jumped like a kid, announcing the wing seated. Wanting a closer look at their progress, Kiva strolled over to join in the fun. "You guys are making real progress. This thing is starting to look like a real airplane." Watching Elliott's short blond hair bob in her eyes like some sixties' surfer filled her with affection.

"It's just a dry fit but look! It's perfect."

Kiva couldn't hold back the smile or her delight in their achievement, Elliott's achievement. What was it with this woman? "I hate to break up the fun," she announced tentatively.

"Not at all. Why don't you join us in the canteen? I know it's the kitchen now, but I can't get used to calling it that. Yeah, the guys were having a laugh too." She waved for them to follow. "Let's give our report to the JAG." Both men grinned at her use of common military terminology, the military designation for lawyers as members of the Judge Advocate General's command.

In the kitchen, they all poured coffees and doctored them up. "Sorry to drag you over here, Kiva. I hope I'm not screwing up your schedule." Elliott pronounced it in the Canadian fashion—_shed-u-le_, without the hard C sound—and that had both guys teasing her. "Yeah, yeah, laugh now. Just you wait. One day you might need someone to help you pronounce something in Inuit."

"Whatever is going on," Kiva told them, "we have the week to get to the bottom of it. Maybe not figure it all out in that time, but if we take any longer the situation may escalate and not in our favor."

"I know what you mean," Mac said. "I talked with Mark last night. Jake showed up at his place around dinnertime. He was wasted and cut Mark a new one. Said the sheriff wanted to know why he was out here at the hangar and accused Mark of spying on him and us of trying to make his life, well… You get where I'm going."

"I do, and now I'm worried for Mark, Andi, and the kids."

With real concern, Elliott asked, "You don't think he'd do anything to hurt them?"

"I never would have, but I'm not sure how deeply involved he is. I'm hoping he's just a pawn. Did he say what the sheriff said?"

"Mark said he was too wasted to make much sense. He had the impression Dias was trying to hang the whole thing on Jake. We got the feeling he knew what was going to happen but didn't think it meant anything or that it was part of something bigger."

Nodding, she agreed it seemed logical. Elliott added, "Kiva, a few more things are missing than just empty cans of varnish from the trash and Elmo's wedding blanket…"

"It was his wedding blanket?" Concern was written all over her face. "Oh, Elliott, I'm so sorry."

"It's okay. Nanny was just as surprised to learn he had kept it all these years. Anyway, they took my phone, my laptop, all the papers I printed out and worked up, with the overlays of the redevelopment plan you gave me and the plan itself."

"What else?"

"I'm not sure yet. It'll take me a few days to make a full inventory. Luckily Elmo kept great records. I would have already started but…I just wanted to get something accomplished first. And there is something else."

Jesus opened the GPS tracking app and handed his phone to her. "Elliott has trackers on all her important gear."

Accepting the phone, she looked closely. "And it just gets better and better," she said, swearing under her breath. Picking up her own phone she tabbed to her contacts and pressed connect.

"Hi, Ian, it's Kiva. No, I'm just running errands. Listen, I've cleared my slate for a few days. I'm thinking I'll take a break, maybe hang out at the house, you know, get some reading done… Yes, we finalized the divorce… I thought I'd run into Tucumcari today and get that filed… Actually, I need to do some shopping. Can I get anything for you?… Sure, I'll pick up the stationery order. Anything else?… No, Ian! I will not push her. You'll just have to wait. I'll see you later this week."

Ending the call, she turned to them. "We have a choice to make. We know Ian Guerrero is involved and now we know for sure Gent Koehler is too. The question is whether we can trust Sheriff David Dias, or do we have to take things up a level and get the state authorities involved?"

CHAPTER TEN

It took over two hours to properly search the hangar and check for other missing items. Luckily old Elmo had kept immaculate records of all his work and everything he stocked. While Kiva and Zeus walked the upper corridors, Mac and Elliott covered the items which required aviation knowledge. They searched the floor and found the airframes untouched and the same with the engines in the area curtained off by welding screens.

The propeller stores turned out to be a problem. All the fixed pitch props, the type that could be mounted on walls and fetched a reasonable price at auction, were gone. As certified new propellers ready for use, they would cost a whole lot more to replace. The only other items missing were personal, Elliott's electronics for a start. In her room, pages had been ripped from her journals. She hated how deeply she had divulged her most private thoughts in those pages, including her attraction to Kiva. *More fuel for the fire.*

After they amalgamated their short lists, it was decided that Kiva would take Elliott into Amarillo. Kiva had a hunch she wanted to follow up. She was not a member of the Texas Bar Association and hadn't been able to search corporate registries in the detail she could within the New Mexico state system. She was confident she could bluff her way through the red tape if she were there in person, as she wanted to research newly formed companies and find banking information. Like the adage "Follow the Money" she was doing just that. She also wanted to search the Texas DMV records for the tag associated with the Escalade and the unknown driver captured in the dash cam footage of the hangar fire.

Elliott had other things to do, but Kiva had insisted they take one car. She wanted to be there for her when she opened the safe deposit box, and in case there was anything else she could help with. Elliott hadn't argued. The thought of taking a two-hour drive alone with Kiva was both exhilarating and nerve-wracking. Behind the controls of any aircraft and in all weather conditions she could conquer the air with confidence, and if anything, she lived for those flights where the weather was challenging or conditions required her to really think. Yet a few hours alone with this astounding woman had her on the edge of hyperventilating.

In the car she tried to stay relaxed as Kiva chatted about the case, the items they found missing from the hangar, and whether old Elmo was simply meticulous by training or suffered from OCD.

"I can be like that. OCD, I mean," Elliott admitted. "When you travel for a living, it's easy to misplace things along the way. You have to create a system or habit of where you place your stuff in each hotel, even when you eat and work out, or it just doesn't happen."

"Is that why you put the GPS trackers on all your gear?"

"It's easy to lose your wallet when you're tired and have to pull out ID or credit cards all the time. After the first time it happened, I memorized all my accounts and ID numbers. In a way that wasn't such a good idea."

"Out of sight, out of mind?"

She nodded, offering a grin. "After I lost my ID a second time, I ordered the trackers. They offered a deal if you bought a dozen and I love a deal."

"You didn't really memorize all your ID numbers, did you?" Kiva asked teasingly.

"Both my FAA and my TC Airline Transport Pilot's license numbers, my driver's license number, my employee number, my pilots' union number, my social security number, my Ontario Health Card number, and my Social Insurance number. I can also recite the VIN on my Jeep and the serial number of my hunting rifle, my bank accounts, and my credit card."

"Okay, I want to ask about the rifle, but first let's go back to the Social Security card. I'm assuming you mean an American SSN. How did you get that?"

"My mother is American. Sorry, I should have mentioned that before."

"American? But I thought you said she lives in Peterborough?" Kiva asked in apparent confusion.

"Oh sorry. Peterborough, New Hampshire, not the one in Ontario. She's originally from Buffalo. My grandad, and I guess great-uncle Elmo too, worked for North American Aviation until they closed their doors in the seventies and Buffalo lost all the aircraft factories. Grandad moved up to Toronto to take a job with de Havilland. I don't think it was a big thing back then for Americans to move north. Actually, he had a joke about it. He liked to say, all he had to do to immigrate to Canada was prove he could handle a canoe."

"My great-grandfather immigrated to Canada after the war. The Korean War," Kiva said. "He has a similar joke, that the test was proving you could make love in a canoe. We kids loved that story, but when he told it, he'd get a slap to the back of his head from my great-grandmother."

"I bet," Elliott said, smiling at the thought. "It's funny how so many people from so many places can come to one country and share the same cultural experiences. I wish more Americans could grasp the idea." She asked, "So I guess your mom is the Yank in your family tree too?"

"You bet. Irish American right out of Boston, but she had the wanderlust. She met Dad at a baseball game in Toronto or more precisely at a bar while the game was playing. She'd driven up with a bunch of girlfriends but couldn't get tickets. So they ended up at a bar."

"Let's see…Wild American girls looking for fun and to follow the game, *hmmm*… My guess is either Wayne Gretzky's or the Loose Moose."

"Oh my God! You hit it on the head. The Loose Moose," she confirmed with astonishment. "She says it was love at first sight."

"Nice," was all Elliott was prepared to say. She knew Kiva's parents were divorced and so it might be a sore point. You never knew with people. Some adjusted and adapted while others carried the failure of a parental relationship like it had something to do with them or worse, as if their feelings hadn't been taken into the mix.

Seeming to comprehend, Kiva placed her hand on her thigh, giving it a squeeze. "Hey. No worries. They parted ways with very little grief and a very long time ago. They originally settled down here to be with Mom's mother. Mom was studying Shamanism, and eventually it took her to California. I think she wanted us to stay, always making sure Dad understood the house was his too. Without her though, he was heartbroken and he wanted more support for us. So we packed up and moved to Toronto to be with his family. Talk about total shock."

"Torontonians, Canadians, or his family?" Elliott asked gently.

Kiva hummed at the remembrance. "The family part we were ready for. Dad was always close to them and they by extension to us. And I think we were better prepared for how different Canadians can be, but the vitality of Toronto, after this sleepy town…Wow! Now that was different. It was harder on Shay. She was starting grade ten as a complete outsider. For me, it was easier. I got to start high school with a bunch of other kids from all over the city who were just as new to the core as we were."

Elliott asked, "You said your mom is in California. What's she doing out there?"

"She's a professor of Integral Studies. And don't ask me to explain. Whenever I talk to Mom, she's always so excited about some tiny bit of ancient knowledge some elder has imparted." She talked about her mother's blossoming spiritual beliefs and why they were important enough for her to pack her bags and leave and why neither she nor her dad held a grudge.

It was fascinating and completely out of her wheelhouse. Elliott had never really talked about her own spiritual beliefs. It wasn't something that came up between pilots, even at thirty thousand feet with the world just blotches of lights and dark, and a field of stars stretched out before them. Pilots simply and silently took in the universe and enjoyed the view.

She was enjoying the view here too. Of the woman behind the wheel. Kiva was like a vision from a favorite Federico Fellini movie. She could see the scene in her head, Kiva standing on the edge of a precipice, a silk scarf holding her auburn hair back from the tireless wind, her open Fiat Spider idling close by, and her contemplating the death of her peasant lover and wanting to follow her over the cliff.

"Elliott?"

Caught out, she fumbled, "Ah, sorry. What were you asking?"

"Do you want me to come in with you?"

They were stopped, and she realized they had reached the bank where Elmo had moved his accounts to and secured a deposit box.

"Would you? I mean, I think it...I might need you to look through the safe deposit box. If there's anything there or if they challenge my access."

Kiva marched into the bank with Elliott on her heels. Bypassing the tellers, she headed for the management area, presenting her card and asking to speak with the account manager. As soon as he heard Elliott's late uncle's name he disappeared in a flash, returning with the branch manager.

A middle-aged woman introduced herself and invited them to her office. After verifying Elliott's ID, she opened a folder on her desk, at the same time offering to Elliott, "I'm sorry for your loss. Mr. Moreno only moved his accounts here last year, but he certainly was a pleasure to meet and speak with on his visits to the branch. There isn't a single teller who doesn't have a story and kind words to share."

Awkwardly, Elliott thanked her. "I owe him so much. I had no idea he would leave me anything."

The branch manager looked surprised. "Considering the size of the bestowment, I'm shocked. I hate to ask, but I will need a copy of the Deposed Will before releasing any information or funds and of course, a portion must be set aside for the IRS."

"Of course," Kiva said, reassuring the woman and supplying the necessary documents while reminding her they had already been filed with the court and other authorities as required. After they discussed other legal matters, the woman finally opened the file and presented several forms for Elliott to sign and Kiva to witness. Once that was done she passed over several final papers.

"These are all the statements for your uncle's accounts. You will see there were several attempts to access his checking account following his passing, along with charges to his credit card. We have reversed them all and notified his credit card company to stop automatic charges. As for his accounts, we still have these unauthorized attempts."

Kiva looked over the statement Elliott held out to her. "Why isn't the bank investigating this? They're not for insignificant amounts." One she was looking at was for close to ten thousand dollars.

The woman smiled with grace. "We've found that family members sometimes try to access accounts prematurely or use the deceased person's credit cards to cover funeral expenses. For that reason, we usually wait to be sure the attempted withdrawals weren't made by someone with legitimate needs. I know it's not quite letter-of-the-law, but we deal with mostly families in this branch. The death of a loved one is hard enough without losing access to the breadwinner's accounts. In this case," she added, "when we didn't immediately hear from the beneficiary, we reversed the withdrawals and froze the accounts. Would you like us to begin an investigation?"

"Judging by the amounts involved, yes. Frankly, I can't believe you waited this long."

Looking unfazed by the criticism, the manager agreed, setting her copies of the highlighted statements aside. "And just to be clear, you are sure you, Ms. Snowmaker, or any of Mr. Moreno's other family members, have not tried to access these accounts?"

Elliott shook her head, still staring at the statement. "My grandmother and I are all he had left. I have cousins but they never took an interest in Elmo and vice versa."

Kiva said, "Ms. Snowmaker was not aware Elliott Moreno had any accounts here until two days ago. So no worries where that's concerned."

"That's good then. Now we will need to discuss where and how to best transfer the accounts. We sure would like to see you continue banking with us. Of course, if you're planning on heading home anytime soon, we can suggest a bank up in Canada. We do have some contacts there. Just let me know your plans, and I can look into it for you. Now, would you like to open Mr. Moreno's safe deposit box, or do you have questions about these accounts?"

Kiva turned to Elliott, about to suggest they check the box before they made any decisions. Judging by her pale complexion, she was already overwhelmed. "Might I have a moment with my client, alone?"

"Of course. You take your time now. How 'bout I fetch you all some coffee?"

"That sounds perfect. Thank you," Kiva said, watching the bank manager leave and waiting until the office door was closed. "Ellie? Are you...*oh shit!* Please don't barf. Just breathe, sweetie. Just breathe." She coached Elliott through a deep breathing exercise and wiped away an errant tear. "You're okay. Just keep breathing."

Elliott nodded. Unable to speak or at least not willing to break from the breathing pattern, she waved the statement. There was real fear in her eyes and apparently a lot of confusion.

Calmly Kiva read through the entire statement. She had only taken notice of the highlighted unauthorized transactions, missing the totals all together. "Holy fuck!"

Elliott nodded, leaning forward to put her head between her knees. Finally, she spoke up. "How?"

Trying to calm herself as well, Kiva rubbed soothing circles on Elliott's back. How in the world had Elliott's great-uncle accumulated so much wealth? Twenty-eight million was a hell of a lot of money for an old guy who restored airplanes for a living.

She read through the account statements and the investment summary. It could be that old Elliott was simply a smart investor. If he'd stayed out of the housing market and avoided the investments that had gutted the rest of the nation's assets and mutual funds, not to mention most of the world, he could have done very nicely for himself. "Maybe he was one of those few smart investors who saw the housing crunch coming and knew enough to short the market?"

Coming up for air, Elliott nodded. "Nanny said something about him always going against the trend in his investments. I don't remember any stocks or bonds, unless they're in the safety deposit box. Maybe if we go through all his papers, we can figure it out?"

"There's nothing in the estate papers regarding an investment account. You think that will make you feel better?" she asked. She still had her arm around her and moved to gently massage her neck.

Nodding, Elliott sucked in a deep breath. "I don't know what to do with all this. I don't want to make a mistake. I also want to see what's in the box."

"First, though, keep breathing and don't worry. I'll help you with all of this. I promise. Okay?" She watched Elliott nod, then signaled for the bank manager. She carried in coffee for them all and chatted with Kiva as Elliott got her bearings and tried to relax and come to terms with her sudden wealth. They decided to keep everything set in place in this same bank but transferred into Elliott's name. The manager was delighted and relieved when Kiva informed her that Elliott was indeed a US citizen and didn't require a battery of foreign account releases and federal forms completed on top of the regular red tape. While they tackled the tax forms, she let Elliott sit quietly and read through the legalities of the transfer. Finally, the last task was signing for the transfer of the safe deposit box.

Once they had the key, Kiva reached for Elliott's hand. "Let's go have a look. I promise you're ready for whatever else Elmo has put away."

In the vault, the manager, after she and Elliott used their keys, took out the box and set it on a nearby table and left them to open it alone.

Inside was a large envelope, and a set of car keys. Real old-fashioned ignition keys on a Chevy keychain with an attached paper tag. On it was an address, written in what Kiva now recognized as Elmo's frail hand. Kiva took out the envelope, laying the contents on the table.

She enumerated, "Ownership and insurance for a…nineteen-fifty-three Chevrolet. A storage lease, entry passcode, and a lock combination for a rental locker paid until the end of this year, and…a letter addressed to Constance Green. Your grandmother?" Elliott nodded. "And one addressed to you. Would you like to open it?"

"No," she said decisively.

"Okay…I know. We should get some lunch and let you acclimatize to everything. Maybe call your Nanny and have a chat?"

"You don't mind?"

"Not at all. I need to stop by the courthouse this afternoon, but that can wait." She placed the contents of the box in her bag, and called to the waiting clerk to lock the box.

When they climbed into the car in the cool northwest Texas winter sun, Kiva pressed the button to lower the Mustang's convertible top and pulled out onto the main drag. She'd find someplace with comfort food on the menu and draft on tap. A good burger and a beer were always excellent when she was stressed out, and she had a feeling they would work for Elliott too.

CHAPTER ELEVEN

By the time Elliott was composed enough to talk, she had made a good dent in her burger and finished her beer. "You know this American beer tastes like water."

Kiva gave her a one-sided grin. "Don't let them hear that. Folks around these parts take great pride in their beer. Almost as much as their beef."

"Oh, I'll give you that. The beef is absolutely the best. The only time I've had beef this good is when I was stationed in Alberta, but this beer…" she rolled the last few dregs in the tall glass, "not so much."

"I know. It's the opposite of home. I bet it's why old Elliott got your grandmother to ship him down a case of Export every month." She watched as Elliott signaled the waitress and ordered a coffee. Then she asked gently, "Are you ready to read your letter?"

Elliott nodded "It's just…I had no idea. If Nanny knew, she never said. And…it really changes a lot for me."

"How so?"

Struggling to contain her emotions again, Elliott finally met her eyes. "When I walked into the hangar, it was like…like someone had handed me the keys to the kingdom. After my life had completely fallen apart, I suddenly had everything—anything I could dream of.

Holy smokes, that Mosquito alone was like, wow!" She let out a small, telling breath. "Except the treasury was empty. I had every imaginable passion at my fingertips, well, vocational passion," she added with a grin, "but I was scratching my head trying to figure out how I could afford it."

"What was your plan?" Kiva asked. "I mean, I'm getting to know you, and I have a feeling you always like to have a plan."

"Yeah. It's a pilot thing. 'Make a plan. Make it work.' I figured I had enough money between my employment insurance and my credit cards to get me through a few months. If I could get the Gipsy Moth finished and sold, I could stay and afford to finish the Boeing Stearman next."

"Employment insurance would have cut you off as soon as they figured out you were out of the province."

Elliott nodded. "That's why I figured I only had a month or two at best."

Kiva raised her coffee mug in salute. "Good plan." She looked around to be sure they had some semblance of privacy. "You ready?"

Elliott tore the top edge of the envelope, then stalled. "Please don't think me a wimp," she said, pushing it across the table. "Would you?"

Kiva removed the folded pages, knocking loose a couple of photographs.

Elliott scooped them up, examining them closely, handing them over one by one. "That's Elmo and me."

Looking over the first photo, Kiva was consumed with a sort of pride and pleasure. "When was this taken? I mean you couldn't be more than four or five years old here?"

Nodding, Elliott pointed to the back where someone had carefully handwritten the date, including Elliott's age in brackets. "I think that was taken at the Heritage Warplane Museum. Whenever Elmo was up visiting, he and Nanny used to take me places like that."

"You look to be in your element."

Elliott finally started to smile. "That's the Tutor Jet, you know, the one the Snowbirds fly. I remember how proud he was that I already knew which hand belonged on the stick. My grandmother said he lifted me into the cockpit and I grabbed the stick, put my left hand on the throttle control and started making jet sounds. I guess, there was hope for me right from the start."

Kiva picked up the second photo. "And this one. Oh, my goodness. You look so young."

Elliott took a good look. "I forgot he came up for that. That was my graduation from Glider Pilot School at CFB Trenton. I'd just turned sixteen."

"I had no idea air cadets actually got to learn to fly. Your grandmother and Elmo look so proud."

"This one," Elliott said, holding up the last photo, "was taken soon after I qualified on the 737. I think I'd just finished my first scheduled flight. I walked out of flight ops, and they were standing there waiting to take me to supper. My captain snapped that. He was a cool guy. A big Norwegian. His name was Roald, and he just gushed on about me greasing my first landing with passengers on board."

"I bet old Elliott was proud as a peacock while you wanted a place to bury your head."

As if she'd been caught red-handed, Elliott colored. "Guilty as charged. Still, it was great to see Elmo and Nanny so proud. It was worth the razzing."

Kiva unfolded the letter. By the time she finished reading aloud to the end of the second page, she was fighting to hold back her own tears. Old Elliott had done more than just acknowledge his love and pride in his great-niece. He wanted her to know he had always known of the inequity in the way she had been treated compared to her siblings and cousins. He thought it was wrong, but his hands were tied. His only recourse was to support her vocation and believe in her.

"You never mention your family. Is it bad?"

Looking very much like she was trying to decide what to say, Elliott finally smiled. "I have two younger siblings. I think I mentioned my mother having nothing to do with me since I came out. My sister too. Actually, my sister tried. She wanted me to be her maid of honor at her wedding right up till my mom and aunts got a hold of that little tidbit. They all threatened her with not attending and that was it."

Kiva looked very much like she wanted to ask or argue or anything to change what had happened.

"No worries, counselor. My absentee father finally showed his face and talked Vicky into at least inviting me. I remember feeling like a complete outsider. I had my grandmother and great granny backing me up, and one aunt, but that was it. I still don't know why I didn't leave the minute we sat down for dinner. I found myself in the overflow room with the second and third cousins my mother considered equally untrustworthy for a good impression with her new in-laws."

"Overflow room?" Kiva asked. "Just how big was this wedding?"

"Three hundred and forty guests, eight bridesmaids, half a dozen flower girls. My mother was desperate to make a statement about her success which was all bull. And before you ask how they could afford such an extravagance, my asshole father set the whole thing up under one of his companies, paid a small deposit and not another cent, bankrupting the company responsible for the bill."

"Oh my God! That must have mortified you."

She let out a small bitter chuckle. "I remember walking through this crowd of strangers I once considered family and deciding it was time to leave. I went looking for Vicky to say goodbye and just as I found her, the photographer backs into the head table, knocking the ice sculpture over into the cake, breaking the blown glass bride and groom sculpture... I see your face. Yes, everything was over the top. Anyway, my sister freaks and who ends up being the one to talk bridezilla down from the ledge? Yup. All me. And just so you know, Vic's new hubby and family were appalled by my 'gayness' too. So, after I talk Vicky down, her new hubby suggests it's time I leave before I ruin the evening for everyone. I know! I have never wanted to punch anyone as much, but I agreed to leave. I was almost out the door when Vicky's perfect new hubby's brother and wife propositioned me."

"Are you kidding me? After everything, someone thinks you're threesome material."

"You got it. I ended up sneaking out the back only to run into my baby brother in the alley behind the Royal York, smoking an eight ball. I had no idea what to do so I called my dad. You know what, that bastard told me to mind my own fucking business."

Kiva sat back. "I have to ask, what happened with Mikey?"

"I pulled him into a cab and took him to rehab. I knew he wasn't ready, but I wanted him to know it was there and all he needed to do was walk in and ask for help."

"Did he?"

"Eventually," Elliott said. "More than once, but as he says, it's a work in progress."

So much to consider and Elliott had already suffered so much. Kiva picked up the papers, resuming her reading aloud. Old Elliott was an insightful man. He even mentioned the harsh reality of Elliott's soured relationship with her girlfriend, comparing it to his own failed marriage. He begged *my Elliott* to not give up, neither on flying nor on love. He was leaving everything to her because, in his mind, she was the only one who could understand the value of the gift whether she chose to continue his work or liquidate his holdings and return to the flight line. In the end, he said, only her happiness mattered.

Folding the letter away and carefully placing it and the pictures back in the envelope, she watched as Elliott finished her coffee, giving her time to digest everything she had heard. There was a kind of grace about her, something that belied the strong shoulders, muscled arms, and the floppy bangs she absently brushed from her eyes. She seemed stronger than any woman she'd met, yet vulnerable. Somehow complete in her strength and honesty. Yes. There was an honesty about Elliott, something beyond trustworthiness. Maybe it was authenticity or was it just plain goodness. *How unique.*

Accepting the envelope and adding it to the other items from the safe deposit box, Elliott asked her, "Can you look up where this storage place is? I want to head next door and buy a cell phone before I check it out."

Kiva was not at all surprised to find from her phone that it was only a few blocks away. "I can drop you off if you like." That smile was back on Elliott's face, the one that told her she was appreciated.

"I've got this. I'll get a phone and then walk over and have a look at what he thought was so important he couldn't store it in the hangar. I'll call when I'm done."

Kiva took Elliott's hand and gave it a warm squeeze. "I'm going to do some sleuthing of my own. Then I'll come get you and we can head home."

They walked out together, and she watched as Elliott headed across the parking lot to the cell phone store, tall and proud, like a soldier fearlessly facing the unknown. Kiva chided herself, realizing how emotionally attached she was getting. Her inner voice had warned her to keep her distance. Elliott had plans that wouldn't include her. Now she was seriously contemplating whether she had been wrong on that score. The woman was not like anyone she had ever known and that alone scared the daylights out of her. She grinned as she climbed back into the Mustang. She was scared, but nonetheless it was a good scare.

* * *

The walk in the midday sun was warming even with the cool temperature. Strange to think she was so far south, yet the weather was comparable to home. Maybe there wasn't much in the way of snow, most of which had already melted, but winter was winter, even here.

At the storage facility, she entered the code to pass through the gated entry. Locating the locker, she opened and removed the combination lock and raised the roll-up door. She suspected Uncle

Elmo had stashed his car here before checking into the care facility, but she had not expected this. Beside a car carefully covered with a canvas tarp, a shelving unit was stacked with AC Delco vintage Chevrolet parts, an old steel desk, and a wall-sized cork board. On the board were maps and layouts of Mirabal County, the airport, and Illusion Lake. One of the maps was a hydrographic survey, another a hand-drawn overlay of a development plan similar to the one she had made and which had gone missing. On the desk, centered on the blotter, was a handwritten note from Uncle Elmo addressed to her. She pulled out a battered wood school-style desk chair and sat weighing the letter in her hands, wondering what more Elmo could reveal. She carefully tore the envelope flap away, pulling out the folded pages.

Dear Ellie,

If you're here, it means I didn't recover from my cold. I had a feeling it might be more than I had in me, and I wanted you to be prepared. If you've read my Will and my letter to you, you know I want you to make your own choices and choose your own path.

If you choose to keep the hangar and the restoration business, be prepared. There are certain individuals out there who will do anything to pressure you to sell. Lots of folks around town think I'm a stubborn old man, but what I'm really doing is trying to protect them from being exploited. People get emotional and pretty stupid when it comes to money. And they'll put their trust in those cronies in charge before listening to a foolish old man like me. Being from up north, you know the value of water better than most ever will around here. So, take a good look through all the evidence I've got. Then decide what, if anything, you want to do.

Love,

Uncle Elmo

P.S. Since your Nanny gave up the sewing business, I've been getting a group of ladies from out on the Rez to sew my envelopes. I've switched from Duck Canvas to Ceconite. There's a manual in the top drawer along with a phone number and enough cash to pay for all the three cloth aircraft. Be gentle when you call. Those old gals were sweet on me, and it may be a shock for them to learn that I'm gone.

P.P.S. In case you didn't know, I couldn't be prouder of you than if you were my own. And the car engine could use a top overhaul. She's a blue flame inline six, so it'll be easy enough for you, except I could never find a new camshaft. And I just never had the time to order custom. There's a case of lead additive in the trunk. Make sure you use one for each fillup or she's gonna knock like hell. Have fun with her.

Love and respect,
Uncle Elmo, XXOO

Elliott's hands were shaking when she set the letter down. Not ready to take on the mystery on display across the wall, she turned to the car and pulled off the tarp.

"Holy shit!"

Before her sat a pristine white early model Corvette. Back in the restaurant, when Kiva was itemizing things from the safe deposit box, she'd read the ownership only identifying the car as a Chevrolet. Elliott expected, assumed she'd find a Biscayne or maybe a Bel Air convertible but a Corvette, not so much. Carefully climbing behind the wheel, she had to admire the rich red leather interior and its contrast to the white paint. It wouldn't have been her first choice, but she could hardly complain. Pulling out her new phone, she researched the model and was shocked to learn it was the first year of production and handmade. The paint color was Polo White, the only one offered in 1953.

Going over to sit at the desk to recover from her shock, she focused on reviewing the information Uncle Elmo had collected on the land development deal Ian Guerrero and the local banker, plus some unknown heavyweights, were eager to force her to accept.

Reading through file after file took almost two hours. It was a lot to digest. Sitting back, she sighed. *What have you got me into?* Tapping her fingers on the old desk, Elliott knew not all the answers were here but Elmo had amassed a lot of information. Much more time and help were needed for understanding the big picture. She stuffed the files in her messenger bag, adding to the bank records and the letters from the safety deposit box. Elmo had suggested several of the key players. Still, it would be Kiva who would better understand the implications both to her and the town. Opening the top drawer, she found the information where he'd said she would, the phone number and money to pay the sewing circle. She would call tomorrow and ask to visit to give them the bad news.

She stuffed the ten thousand dollars into the envelope she'd carried from the bank and tidied up, snapping a few pictures of the maps and drawings on the wall. She didn't know if anyone knew about the locker, but so far she was sure they were concentrating their efforts on the hangar. She now had a good idea that her property was somehow the key they needed. It was time to head back. She was about to call Kiva for a ride, then turned back to the Corvette, unable to resist.

Elliott popped the hood, then, searching the parts shelf, found everything needed to reinstall the pristine looking battery. With the positive terminal attached and tight, she snugged down the negative battery terminal, easily cranking it to a good ten foot-pounds of torque needed for a solid connection. She inserted the key in the ignition, pumped the gas twice to get the triple carbs to half choke, then turned the key. The engine chuffed and spit a little before finally turning over and rumbling to life. *Yes!*

After backing the 'Vette out of the storage locker, she pulled down the door and locked up.

She set the Super Glide transmission in gear and headed for the exit, enjoying the purr of the carbureted engine as she drove to the electronics store she had found on Google, while reminding herself she needed to call Kiva.

After buying what she needed, she sat in the car, thinking. *Kiva. How is it I'm so far from home and knee deep in whatever I'm in, and I meet you? How is it I could find everything I've been looking for, and you're here just filling in? What will I do when you leave?* Gunning the Corvette, she flew from the lot. In that moment, the solution felt both simple and altogether impossible.

Maybe I need to give you a reason to stay.

CHAPTER TWELVE

When Elliott pulled up to the hangar, the guys were on the top of the scaffolding, fitting the last replacement panel in place. She honked and waited, grinning. As they scrambled down, hooting and hollering over the car, she climbed out and opened the trunk to remove box after box of HD cameras. Other surveillance gear was jammed into the passenger seat. She'd bought out the store's most expensive system and all their extra cameras and accessories.

Jesus was the first to reach the car. "Holy hell, Cap!"

Stepping up close and taking a good look, Mac announced, "It's a Series One. I'm sure of it but which year?" Circling the car, he noted, "Single taillights, elongated mesh headlight covers, Corvette trim on the door but no side vent, *hmm*... don't tell me it's a fifty-four?"

"Oh, so close," she teased. "Fifty-three."

Both men groaned with pleasure, while Jesus asked, like a true gentleman, "May I?" He was standing by the driver's door.

"Have at it," she said, then asked, "Mac, will you help me get this gear inside?"

He opened the passenger door and dragged out the box belted in there and another stuffed below it in the footwell. Once they had everything inside, they unbolted the big hangar door and carefully pushed it along the steel track, opening it just two panel lengths.

"Nice work on the door," she commented. "All it needs now is a coat of paint and it'll look better than new."

"Listen," Mac said, "we were talking, and we thought it was time to paint the whole thing, the big logo, and the whole door. A real facelift. We know you're a little low on funds right now but since you're giving us a place to live and everything, we were thinking…"

"Hold on that for a sec," she ordered. "Just between us three, I've come into a little money. So if you want the job, you guys can stay on, you know, for a real salary and everything. It would mean doing a whole mix of jobs, including security."

"You mean like maintenance and maybe even helping with some of your work like we did with marrying the wings on the Gipsy Moth?" Mac asked.

"I know it's not your thing, but you might find some of it's not a chore and—"

"Are you kidding. Cap? We both think this is a hell of a setup. We're on board to help you keep it safe and do the work, whatever you need. Hell, we were gonna offer to do it for chow and clean sheets. Gettin' paid's a bonus." He stuck out his hand for her to shake. "Wait'll I tell Jesus!"

In the kitchen, she started to put the kettle on, then decided on a pop instead. She sat and thought about Kiva. By Kiva's own account she was only filling in for her father. Did that mean she would head home in a few months? *Of course it did.* Other than this threat to the hangar, Elliott could only presume there wasn't a whole lot of work for a lawyer in this one-horse town. Certainly not enough for three. And if Ian Guerrero was involved in whatever was going on, she was sure Kiva would not want to remain associated with him. Could Illusion Lake support two law offices? Would the town see Kiva as their salvation or just an upstart desperate to rob Ian of his clientele?

It would all depend. If Ian and the town's heavyweight banker Gent could spin this development as a win for the town, Kiva and, by association her father, would be the bad guys. Would things be different if she and Kiva could prove the plan would screw the town? Maybe. Still, it was hard to convince people of things that hadn't yet happened. Regret was shared in private while hope was in the public domain.

On her phone she pulled up the photos she'd taken in the storage unit. Looking over Elmo's findings, she had to decide who to trust. Elmo had believed the sheriff was clean but, much like the rest of the town, would go with the best story. Dias would want his old cronies to be right and her, the outsider, to be the problem.

She downloaded the GPS tracking app and checked the serial numbers for her stolen items. Much as she wanted to pick up a new laptop when she was in Amarillo, she had stopped herself. Hers was sitting just two miles away. It still hadn't been moved. Gent Koehler must be a complete idiot to think it was safe to keep it at the bank. He owned the local bank, held almost every mortgage in the county, and on top of that, the bastard was also mayor. No wonder folks around here completely trusted the prick. She considered herself lucky to never have met this stalwart of the community

Still not sure of her priorities, she grabbed the keys to her Jeep and headed out the door. Did she want to pursue Kiva Park even if she would disappear in a few months? *Holy hell, yes!* There was no question on that point. The real issue was, should she? *Like I'll ever know that answer.*

The other problem was deciding if she could trust Sheriff Dias. She stopped and sent a text to Kiva. *Unless you think it's a mistake, I'm going to Dias. I'm going to show him my GPS tracker and see how he reacts. Want to join me?*

The response was immediate. *I do. Can U wait?*

* * *

After looking at the tracker app and refreshing it umpteen times, Sheriff David Dias looked like he was ready to charge across the street to the bank and turn the place and Gent Koehler upside down. Kiva, sitting opposite him, suggested gently, "David, I can imagine you're disappointed, but I suggest you get a warrant. We need to do this right. If Elliott's correct and I think she is, there is much more going on."

He looked steamed. "You mean if I screw this up, you won't be able to use it as evidence later?"

"You have to accept that Elliott had nothing to do with the hangar fire. You have the evidence. Why haven't you picked up Jose Guerrero?"

He didn't answer, and she chanced a look at Elliott. When she offered a subtle nod, she shared what she suspected was the problem. "Let me guess. You took the video to Judge McCallum, and he gave you some song and dance about it not being proof or suggested that Jose was somehow being coerced?"

His silence gave him away.

"I'm sorry to tell you, but I have reason to believe McCallum is involved."

Swearing under his breath, Dias finally met Elliott's eyes. "I was given a whole heap of crap on you. It's not like you didn't look guilty. Still, that trip down to the Lea County Corrections, that was all on McCallum. He insisted. Said you were too dangerous for county lockup, what with your head bein'… well, you know what I was sold. Anyway, he wanted you in a Level Five facility. New Mexico ain't got such a thing for women. Lea County's a Three, and I sent you there. That's on me. With all the evidence I got, I was acting to protect my people. Still," he admitted, his shame clear, "my gut was screamin' that something was outta whack, but I trusted that man, trusted all of them, McCallum, Koehler, even Ian. For years."

"Who will you go to now?"

"When McCallum's gone fishing, I usually go down to the Fifth District Court. Unlike here, they got more than just the one Division, but I got my usual."

"Judge Tomlinson?" Kiva asked.

"Ah, shoot. Don't tell me…"

"Sorry," Kiva said, and elaborated. "I suspect others are involved, but I'm not ready to name them until I've done more research."

"Still…I think it's time you two bring me in on what you know. It ain't right that I'm the law and I ain't got a clue to what's goin' on here in my own town."

Kiva looked to Elliott. "You ready for that?"

She nodded. It was time to voice her concern and share everything Elmo had already found. "Look, Sheriff. The first thing you need to know is half that stuff they gave you on me is true, just out of context. You of all people must understand that no one's perfect and that things are rarely what they seem."

"Ain't that the truth," he said, looking resigned to having to trust the crazy in the head newcomer over his oldest friends.

Elliott couldn't help but feel bad for the man. "I want you to know I have no hard feelings. My great-uncle trusted you. I believe in Uncle Elmo. I want to continue his work and honor his legacy. Whether I can or can't may come down to you."

He nodded. "I got no problem with that."

Kiva took up where Elliott left off. "We haven't got the whole picture yet, but it looks like a consortium has been formed and they have a plan."

"I know all about the redevelopment plan. I can't see where some swanky gated community could be such a big deal."

"No," Kiva said, "it has to be more than that, otherwise why all this cloak and dagger? I need you to accept that Elliott has uncovered more information we're not sharing, at least for now, and I'll remind you that everything you do know is part of the public record and can be subpoenaed by prosecutors."

"I don't like gettin' half the picture." Shaking his head, he pounded his desk. "Damn it all to hell," he snarled, finally conceding, "just give me the CliffsNotes version then."

"Before we answer that," Kiva asked, "do you know anyone over in the land registry office? You know, someone you trust completely?"

"You know my kid works there. Why?"

"Isn't she married to Ian's son, Maxwell?"

"Was. They've been broken up for better part of a year now. I was hopin' they could work it out, but… Well, that boy needs to grow up a whole lot. I just don't see it happening anytime soon."

Kiva explained with gentleness, "David, sometimes the economics of a region can play into the behavior of breadwinners. Especially someone like Max, oldest son of a prominent lawyer. But sometimes a man is just a bastard. If Max has been abusive, you need to understand that behavior will not change, no matter what he promises you or your daughter."

He didn't comment, and she knew he wouldn't. A man like him would take his daughter having an abusive husband as his own fault. "Please let her know if she needs to talk, I'm always here for her."

"Right up until you run back up north. No way will she sit down with your daddy, and Ian Guerrero's her father-in-law."

Kiva reassured him, "Let her know all the same. And David, between you and me, I'm considering staying on."

That got his attention and Elliott's too. She wanted to ask questions but sat silently.

The sheriff said, "I just don't get what these boys are trying to do."

Kiva passed Elliott's phone to him. "That's a picture Elliott took of a new town development plan. It's conjecture, but it explains much more as to why they would want the entire airport and some of what they've planned with the land purchases they've already made."

He squinted at the large chart on the small screen. Standing and stepping around his desk, Kiva helped him zoom in on critical areas.

"I don't understand," he said, looking even more depressed.

"Neither do we." Returning to her seat, she offered, "That's why we need someone to quietly pull the land records and county overview from the registry office. And David," Kiva warned, "if she does this for us, no one can know, not even her boss over there."

He pushed his Stetson back, wiping his brow. "Okay, I'll ask her after dinner tonight. I'd ask you two over, but people would talk and we can't have them thinkin' I'm soft on this one," he said, tipping his head to Elliott. "At least not yet. Make sense?"

"Yes, it does," Kiva agreed.

They made plans to meet again. Next time he would come out to the hangar under the guise of questioning Elliott again, and Kiva would arrange to be there too. Now all they could do was leave the sleuthing to David's daughter and hope the records she uncovered would somehow bring this whole picture into perspective.

* * *

Elliott sat in her Jeep, still stuck on the idea that Kiva might be thinking of staying. It meant a chance that anything between them might be more than just temporary; something she had feared would hurt like hell when it ended. Kiva was just too, too marvelous for a casual fling. Falling in love with her and losing her would be shattering.

She saw the way Kiva looked at her, admired her physical strength and listened to her stories. Maybe Kiva thought she was some kind of superwoman when it came to aviation. Maybe she was. Still, when it came to love, Kiva would be her Kryptonite. The only way to survive one Kiva Park was to limit the exposure or take her to her inner Kryptonian world, where the exposure would be equal, and the risks would be to both their hearts.

Sitting in her Jeep, she tried to shake the fantasy away. Kiva was an alluring woman. Slender and shaped just right for Elliott's fantasies. Her Irish ancestry was present in the rich auburn of her hair and her love for life. The Korean was easy to see in her joy and sheer determination. Elliott smiled at her notion that Kiva embraced the heart of a poet and the intellect of a leader. As the guys would say, she was the full package.

Starting the Jeep, she shook her head at her ridiculous fantasy of a blissful relationship with such a smart, accomplished, and sexy as all get out woman. It was a fantasy, and silly. Hadn't she learned her lesson yet? *Nope. Not even close.*

Instead of heading for the airport, she turned the Jeep in the opposite direction. She'd buy flowers. Yes, flowers were a precursor of sorts. A silent announcement of the intention to court a woman. She groaned at her own internal language. *I'm a fool and I'm about to make a bigger fool of myself by chasing a woman I know is too good for me.* Still, she didn't turn around, the pilot in her automatically reciting, "Make a plan. Make it work."

When Elliott left the florist/garden center, she was excited about the delivery she had scheduled for the next day. So excited she almost went back inside to demand the flowers be ready now, so she could take them with her to dinner. While she was still in the store, Kiva had sent a text inviting her to supper at her place. That felt like a big step and something more.

Was Kiva telling her she was interested too or was this just business or a "hang with a friend" kind of thing? It wasn't like they had officially dated. They'd spent an excruciating evening with her old chum Erica. And they had enjoyed several breakfasts and coffee get-togethers. *Were those dates?*

Elliott groaned and started the car, leaving the flower delivery set for tomorrow, and fixed on grabbing a bottle of wine for tonight. In the ABC store, she took her time exploring the entire wine selection and finally settled on a highly rated California zinfandel.

When the door opened to Kiva's house, Kiva, dressed casually in skinny jeans and a tight V-neck sweater, looked so inviting, so gorgeous, it was hard to move, hard to breathe.

Kiva grabbed her arm and hauled her inside. "It's freezing out there. Get in before all the heat is gone." She reached for the wine still in the liquor store paper bag. "Zinfandel? A bold choice. And a perfect one for the ribeyes I picked up." Kiva casually pecked her on the cheek. "Come on in. I'm just putting the salad together. You can open this to breathe while I finish up."

Elliott followed her into the kitchen, rubbing the place on her cheek Kiva had kissed. *She kissed me. That means something, right?* Almost paralyzed with confusion, she forced a smile, deciding to enjoy the moment and worry later about what it meant.

Dinner service was set at the breakfast bar, and two amazing looking steaks sat on the counter ready for the grill. Elliott couldn't help but moan. "Wow. I have to tell you, I haven't had a decent steak in…well, I don't actually know how long. This last year hasn't exactly lent itself to steaks on the barbeque."

Smiling, Kiva handed over the corkscrew before returning to her task of ripping up romaine lettuce for the Caesar salad. "I hope you don't mind, I skipped the potatoes. I'm not a fan of all those carbs."

"Not at all," Elliott answered as she extracted the cork from the wine. "Although," she said with a smile, "I remember a ten-mile hike at OCS when we really needed carbs…"

Kiva grinned at the idea before donning her coat, ready to take the steaks out on to the deck to grill.

"Let me grab my jacket," Elliott offered, intending to brave the evening's severe drop in temperature with her.

"Actually, would you mind starting a fire? I'm sure that's something a big smart pilot can do. Everything's by the fireplace. I'll be right back."

Elliott nodded, liking the "big smart pilot" thing. Kiva had set everything on the brick hearth. Paper, kindling, starter logs, even long matches. She was lost in thought watching the flames lick up the starter logs when Kiva breezed back in. "That was fast."

"It never takes long. Come pour the wine, and I'll tell you all about my day. How does that sound?"

Elliott smiled at the domesticity that promised. "Absolutely amazing."

* * *

They spent an hour savoring their dinner and conversation before finally relocating to the couch across from the fire. They took their time with the bottle of wine, had moved onto coffee and were sitting close together and chatting like they had known each other for years.

Kiva, watching Elliott, listening to her, knew she wanted more. "You know, you can't drive back out to the hangar after finishing half a bottle of wine."

"Really?" Elliott was beaming at her. "What do you suggest?"

She smiled, a grin so mischievous and sweet before leaning closer to deliver her pronouncement with a tender kiss.

"*Hmm*. I think I understand," Elliott finally answered, before deepening the kiss.

Elliott's lips were soft, softer than she expected and the woman herself gentle and unassuming. Also cautious. Standing, she offered her hand, leading Elliott silently up the stairs. At the top, she pointed in one direction. "If it's too soon... I mean, if you're not ready, that's the master suite." She pointed in the opposite direction. "That's the guest suite, where I'm sleeping. I want you to join me, I mean, if..."

Elliott smothered her question with a searing kiss.

In the bedroom, Elliott's hands, already roaming the bare skin around her waist, tugged her sweater over her head. Tossing it to the floor, swooping in for another hot kiss. Her mouth was addictive, soft and full, fuller than she had appreciated. She kissed, then bit gently, before venturing deeper.

Kiva had been working her way through the buttons of Elliott's shirt when Elliott pulled it away herself, leaving Kiva in surprise at the black lacy bra. "This," she forced out between kisses while running her slender hands from Elliott's shoulders to her full breasts, "I did not expect."

"Will you be upset if I admit I wore it for you?"

"Hardly," she all but growled as Elliott dragged her silk camisole over her head. She waited for the moment that inevitably disappointed women when they realized how flat-chested she was.

Instead, Elliott's hands, palms open, slid up to cover each breast, moaning breathlessly, whispering in her ear, "God, you're perfect. Absolutely perfect."

When Kiva didn't respond, Elliott cupped her chin, tipped her head up. Foreheads touching, she begged, "Please don't be one of those women who thinks size matters. All that matters to me is the way you feel, and you feel magnificent and beautiful and absolutely perfect."

Then Elliott's lips were on her as she pushed her back onto the bed. She followed, inch by inch, hovering over her until her head felt the pillows and Elliott was on top of her. "Trying to top me, Ms. Snowmaker?"

Elliott laughed but didn't relinquish her position.

Kiva slid her hands around her back, unclipping the bra expertly. The smile she felt against her face emboldened her.

Elliott moved slowly, swooping in to savor one more kiss before tugging off her jeans, then lacy boy shorts. She stood, gentle and unassuming, waiting for Kiva.

More than aroused, she was caught staring, caught watching, salivating over Elliott's athletic form and froze to see Elliott watching her.

Elliott circled the bed, offering her arms and pulling her into a protective embrace. "It's okay to change your mind," she whispered in her ear.

Offering up the most convincing kiss she could muster, Kiva held on to her. When they finally came up for air, panting, she sucked in oxygen, needing to explain. "No…I mean…I haven't…I want this, want you. It's just been so long since…"

Elliott shook her head. "I'm such a blockhead. I've never asked you about any of your relationships. I should have asked, should have listened."

Still in Elliott's arms and feeling more than protected, it was easy to confess, "It's not really that. I haven't got the kind of negative history with women you've had to endure, it's just… It's just that some have complained…you know, about…"

"You don't have to do anything you're not ready for, and…" She placed a single finger on Kiva's lips, to stop her protest. "It's their loss. I look at you, all of you, and see the most beautiful, confident, and accomplished woman I've ever met. I'm sure a lot of women were in a hurry to get you in bed, but, Kiva, if they were somehow disappointed afterward it was their failure to see the real woman. I won't let that ever happen with us. No matter what does, or…" she grinned, "does not happen. You're the first woman who's ever really seen me, taken the time to really look inside, and I'm not going to fail to do the same for you."

Kiva pulled Elliott on top of her, aroused and feeling silly at the same time. "Don't tell me you have a thing for flat-chested Asian chicks?"

Grinning up a storm, Elliott answered, "Just the ones who save my butt, befriend me when no one else will, and make me crazy with desire."

Kiva struggled to get her jeans off, tossing them onto the floor. "In that case, I'm going to make you work to get my panties off."

Seeming delighted with the dare, Elliott pulled her back into her arms, promising, "Let's make it challenging. How about with my teeth?"

The moan that escaped would have embarrassed Kiva with any other woman, but somehow with Elliott everything was right.

Kiva listened as Elliott groaned softly in her half-awake, half-asleep reverie. Her hand traced down her back, the pads of her fingers as soft as feathers.

Elliott opened her eyes, and she immediately fell into a pool of blue, deep and alluring, somewhere between the sea and sky. A place the gods might dwell. She sucked in a breath and traced a finger along Elliott's kiss-bruised mouth. In those eyes she could see the change. Another wall had disappeared—maybe two or three—and in the depth of those eyes, she realized how little Elliott would ask of her, how little she would assume, and how much she would dare to hope.

Hope. Elliott was a creature of hope and dreams and stardust and kisses. Before she could think of what to say, Elliott found her lips. So this is what the arms of a lover who respected her, desired her, and saw her for who she was could feel like. She wrapped her arms around Elliott's neck. "I can't think of a better way to wake up."

"Better than coffee?"

"Better than coffee on Mars."

"*Oooh*. Now that's something. That really is."

CHAPTER THIRTEEN

Kiva sat in old Elliott's, now her Elliott's, reference library, the one converted from the double-sized office on the gallery of the hangar. Both entry doors, plus the windows facing the hangar floor, were closed to ward off the cold air. A small modern space heater, a contrast to the room's dated furnishings, buzzed quietly near the desk. She told Ian she would be working from home all week, and while she did have work to do that didn't involve Elliott, she was hard-pressed to spend time at home doing it. Sitting here now, she felt better just working quietly, knowing Elliott was nearby and safe.

Her phone chimed, its ringtone for her sister. She picked it up and asked with pleasure, "Is that my big sister, calling to check on me?"

"Is that my baby sister, pretending she has nothing to share with me?"

She groaned, "Oh, Shay, I do miss you...*sometimes.*"

"Yeah, yeah. I hear you're working from home?"

"Let me guess," Kiva said, putting her pen down and pushing back from the desk to stand. She could rest on the edge of the desk, be comfortable for her call, and keep an eye out the window, watching Elliott working diligently below. "Ian called Dad and complained?"

"Oh, you should have heard it! I thought Dad's head would blow. I had to take the phone away from him and remind Ian that Dad was recovering from a heart attack and that you were an adult and the person he should be discussing his displeasure with."

"Oh boy. How did Ian take that?"

"I have no idea. Dad grabbed the phone back, bawling me out for stepping in."

"Let me guess, 'You may be grown-up and a doctor, but I can still put you over my knee'?"

"Something like that. I wasn't worried so much as pissed off. I have every right to be. Ever since he got off the call, Dad's been stomping around, trying to decide if he should head home."

Looking out onto the hangar floor, Kiva had to decide what that would mean. "I definitely don't need the help on the work side. A few wills and one pending divorce case does not make for a busy schedule."

"What about the sale of the hangar? What's the hold up there?"

"Really, Shay? Not you too?"

There was nothing but silence from the crisp connection. Finally, sounding troubled, her sister asked, "Kiva, please tell me you're not involved with her?"

"I'm not involved with her," she lied, before admitting, "She sent me flowers today. And she's invited me to work from the hangar."

"Please tell me you're not falling for that, are you?" Shay pushed on without giving Kiva time to answer. "I mean, I think there are some things you need to know. Things about her…"

"Not you too?"

"Kee, please!" Shay begged. "I know she's probably the only lesbian for a hundred miles, but that's no reason to get involved with *someone*…well, someone with her issues."

"Her issues?" she repeated, mistrusting her sister's knowledge of Elliott's background. "I see Ian has been keeping you and Dad informed with his version of events."

"Oh, I imagine Elliott has an altogether reasonable version she's shared. Reading through the material Ian sent has given me a clear picture of this woman, and I have to warn you, kiddo, it's not good."

Kiva watched out the window as Mac and Elliott worked together doing who knew what to one of the wings of the old biplane. She didn't want to hear what her sister had to say. Didn't want to hear anything against Elliott, but logic and her need to be responsible outweighed any new loyalty. Convincing herself that she needed to be in possession of all the facts to best represent her client, she asked Shay to explain.

"Ian was worried about you. Putting Dad's argument with him aside, he seems to agree that this may be too much. Ian sent Dad some documents, and he passed one on to me to analyze. I know you're going to say I'm not a psychiatrist. You're right but I was worried about you, so I read her journal…"

"You what?"

"Look, I knew it would make you uncomfortable, but better me than a court-appointed shrink."

"What the fuck are you talking about?"

"Whoa there! I'm not the enemy. Ian FedEx'd a package to Dad. He wanted to keep him updated on the competency case against Elliott, and he asked that I have a read—"

"What fucking competency case are you talking about?"

There was silence again. Finally, Shay explained, "Look, Kiva, I imagine this is hard, but you know what I'm talking about: old Elliott's competency clause in his will. And I think it was smart. I've been reading this woman's journal, and I'm worried about you. She's clearly interested in you, and I don't think—"

"Shay, stop! First off, Ian is up to his eyeballs in whatever it is that's going on around here. Second, there was no competency clause in old Elliott's will. I should know, as I'm the one who discharged the estate and Dad should too. He wrote the damn thing!"

"You must be wrong. How did Ian get her personal records if he wasn't entitled to examine—"

"They were stolen the night someone set fire to the hangar. Several things were taken. I'm surprised they snagged her journal. I caught Sheriff Dias trying to walk out with all her personal papers including several journals. Of course, that was before Elliott provided him with proof of her innocence and Ian and Gent's involvement."

"You must be wrong. Ian would never…"

"Really, Shay? You're going to take his word over the truth?"

Her sister didn't answer. Kiva knew she wouldn't. If there was one thing Shay hated, it was being proven wrong. "I need you to pack everything up, no, I want you to photograph everything and make a catalog first. Have Dad witness it, then send it to me here at the hangar. Don't send anything to the office. And I think I have to risk upsetting Dad and have a long talk. Is he around?"

Her sister didn't sound happy when she revealed, "He's out by the pool with the kids."

"Go spell him while we have a talk."

"He's not going to be happy," Shay warned.

"I know, but better he knows the truth than be party to fraud and God knows whatever else is going on here."

While her sister went in search of their father, she looked out again over the hangar floor. Elliott was half stretched across the wing with Mac at the other end. They looked to be pulling or smoothing the loose fabric. The effort accentuated Elliott's shoulder muscles and her taut arms. She seemed so focused on her work, she was oblivious to the cold temperature in the hangar, wearing only a long sleeve T-shirt, the arms pushed up to her elbows.

This morning, just minutes before she left the house, a huge box of purple roses had been delivered. *So many roses.* Kiva was overwhelmed. She didn't know what purple meant—if it meant anything where roses were concerned—but the note said everything that mattered.

Something different for someone completely different.
Elliott.

Now her sister was privy to Elliott's innermost thoughts. While she longed to hear what she had learned, doing so would be a complete betrayal. How could Shay, or her father for that matter, fall for Ian's machinations? She understood where her father was concerned. He and Ian had been law partners for almost a decade. But Shay? It felt like a personal betrayal.

It also left her aching to know what Shay was so concerned about. There were always two sides to a story. Was her Elliott less than innocent in the drama of her last relationship? The detective sergeant she'd worked with in Toronto didn't think so, and she'd trusted the woman with much more delicate issues. Still, Shay was worried. What the hell had Elliott written in her journal that would make her sister question her honesty or her sanity?

She spent another hour on the phone, this time with her dad. That had been a revelation and at the same time innocently sweet. Imagine, him being worried for her virtue at this age? The real eye-opener was when she had to break his heart and tell him Ian Guerrero was a son of a bitch who was playing him and Elliott, and old Elliott had known a lot more about what was going on than any of them had uncovered so far.

She explained that the journal had been obtained illegally and that the last will and testament plus the other documents he was sent were forgeries, including stipulations not found in the authentic will. Her dad admitted he didn't remember all the terms of old Elliott's estate, never imagining his law partner would try to pull something over on him. To say he was floored was an understatement.

He'd conceded that he never really trusted Ian, but as a lawyer and as far as their practice went, he had always assumed the man would follow the letter of the law. It was one thing to posture for a client or err on their side, but he was rigorous in his application of the law and assumed Ian was too. This situation stunk, and he confessed he was torn between returning to face off with his law partner or letting Kiva rip him a new one.

That was new. Not his faith in her abilities, but his desire to knock Ian down more than a peg or two. He wanted to bring the Bar Association into the fray, even the courts. By misrepresenting their client, Ian had more than broken laws, he'd failed in his oath to the court and the state. Then, when he'd sent his fake legal documents to Kiva's dad to read, sending them by courier across state lines, he'd added federal charges to the mix. They were now talking felonies, and her dad wasn't sure how much longer he could keep quiet.

The first thing he had promised was to follow her lead. Sitting on evidence in a federal crime was not something he was comfortable with, and no, he wasn't prepared to send Elliott's journal back to her. It was evidence in a felony case now, and he wanted her to accept that and accept she had to inform Elliott of the situation including the fact that he had custody of her most personal document and that Shay, as directed by Ian, had read it and made clinical notes.

Off the phone, Kiva sat in thought, letting the noises of the hangar slowly drift back in. Down on the floor, the guys were helping Elliott with some new piece of equipment, one of the wiring layout boards it appeared, from what Ellie called the stuffing room, a place in the opposite loft housing a variety of large spools of electrical wire and connectors of all kinds. The board was on workhorses and they seemed to be adding new wires to some sort of test monitor on an adjacent cart. It was an intricate assembly requiring piece after piece from the large spool of thin wire as they called out numbers and lengths, then cutting each piece and laying it on the board.

Elliott looked to be crimping something on the ends. *Crimping!* She smiled.

Look at me. A week ago, I couldn't have named the most basic component of an aircraft. Now I'm noting things like transponders and navigation lights! Oh, Elliott, you do have an influence on me. Now I've got to interrupt your day and betray your tenuous trust.

* * *

It took Elliott another ten minutes to teach Mac how to measure, strip, and crimp the pins for the sensor harness connection to the new navigation display. The all-in-one virtual instrument panel would be mounted in the rear cockpit and just below the antique instruments. It would provide the pilot with modern navigation, including a virtual map display and communications capabilities. All in all, their little Gipsy Moth was shaping up to be a real winner.

Once she was sure the guys were ready to continue unsupervised, she convinced herself it was time to head up to join Kiva in the library. She was torn between wanting to see her and afraid she might be set to give her "the talk," letting her know she needed some distance, or suggesting they keep things professional at least for now. In her heart, she hoped they were headed in a more positive direction, but she had been wrong before. Besides the fact that they had both come here believing their time was temporary, now the underlying case with the county and the secret consortium added layer upon layer of complication.

Was Kiva one of those practical souls who put work first? Elliott certainly was or had been. When that changed she wasn't sure. Maybe Kiva was the catalyst. It certainly felt normal to have her working here. Better than that, it made her feel connected and not alone. The guys were living and working with her in the hangar, but it just warmed her to have Kiva nearby.

Tapping on the door to the library, she asked, "Are you ready for me?"

Kiva smiled from behind the old desk which was pushed sideways against the windows of the long narrow room. "You needn't be so polite. This is your house, but," she acknowledged with charm, "that's just who you are. *So*...so why don't we sit at the coffee table? I brought us up fresh coffees. Hope that's okay?"

"Okay? You don't have to twist my arm, and thanks. You're always so thoughtful." *So, we're being polite and thoughtful. Interesting.*

Besides the desk and all the bookshelves, there was an old Air Force issue couch, oval coffee table, and two chairs. Elliott sat down on the couch, expecting Kiva to join her there. When she chose a chair, she hid her disappointment. Picking up her coffee and carefully testing its temperature, she watched as Kiva got herself organized. This morning she had left Kiva's place feeling the afterglow and with a heady hope for a future together. But now...

Had Kiva taken the roses the wrong way? Whatever, she was sorry to see Kiva so uncomfortable. "Listen, I want to...look if I made you feel..."

"Ian sent your journal to my father. My sister was asked to evaluate it from a clinical standpoint. I'm sorry, Elliott. It was a breach of trust, but now that it's out there we need to act."

"*What?*"

"Also, it looks like Ian has forged an alternative copy of your great-uncle's last will and testament. To it he's added a competency clause."

"But wait...*what?* Are you talking competence, like I'm too crazy to competently manage Elmo's estate? That's ridiculous! You can have it squashed or whatever. Can't you?"

"Yes, in time, but these things sometimes take on a life of their own. The court likes to err on the side of justice, and if there is even a remote chance your uncle was concerned for your...*competency*, even just a witness, someone like Gent Koehler could speak to old Elliott's desire and will look good to the court. It could put you back in hot water. Don't worry, I plan to get out in front of this now, but I need to be prepared."

"You mean, you need to know what's in my journal?" she asked, now understanding the distance Kiva had invoked. Last night Kiva had stated that nothing would have happened between them if she was still acting as her lawyer but believed, as Elliott did, that they were working together to get to the bottom of what was going on. Now, she was the professional again and keeping her personal distance was a necessity.

Not at all happy that anyone had a copy of her innermost thoughts, Elliott kicked herself again for keeping a journal in the first place. Her ex's lawyer had tried to use her diary against her in the past. It had backfired, confirming her innocence and lack of knowledge in all the woman's outrageous acts and accusations. She had told herself she shouldn't risk it anymore. Yet she needed an outlet for her innermost thoughts. She'd always needed someone to talk to, some way to sort things out and without a confidant she had long learned that pen and paper were her best friend.

She got up and left the room without comment. There was no point in fighting the inevitable. Even if Kiva's sister were the consummate professional, it would be impossible to keep from letting little things slip. She had no idea when or how they had copied her journal, maybe between when she was arrested, and when Kiva placed the guys on duty. They could have taken it then and returned it before anyone was the wiser. At least Kiva's sister wouldn't know about the recent most passages of praise for Kiva or the longing she had recorded, detailing her attraction.

Coming back into the room, she placed her most recent journal in Kiva's hand and returned to her seat on the couch without saying a word.

"I don't understand."

"If they have my journal, it's a copy. I assume you need to see the original to know what I wrote?" There was no pleasure in her voice, and instead of explaining more or trying to understand Kiva's confused look, she picked up her coffee, gulping at the too hot liquid without tasting it.

Kiva looked over the cover, noting the opening date on the composition notebook. "How many journals do you have?"

Taking a frustrated breath, Elliott walked out again. She gathered all her journals from the bottom drawer of the dresser in the guest room. She'd been carrying them in her car for the last year until she arrived here. And now could finally imagine she had a home. She set them on the coffee table in front of Kiva and returned to her seat. She watched as Kiva picked them up one by one and then set them each aside. She went back to the desk, retrieving a pad of legal paper, returning to record each one, using the opening and closing dates on the front.

"Do you always use composition notebooks for your journals?"

"Yes."

"And always this brand?"

"As long as I can get it, yes," Elliott answered.

"And how many copies do you make?"

"Copies?" Elliott asked, clearly confused. "Why the hell would I make copies? They aren't exactly intended for public consumption." She was getting mad and, judging by Kiva's startled look, not doing a good job of keeping her emotions in check.

"Elliott, I'm sorry, it's just...I was led to believe Shay had your journal. *The* journal, not a copy. If there is a chance you have more than one, other than these concurrent volumes, I need to know."

"What you have in your hand is everything I have. I kept ones earlier, but they were stored in my mother's basement and she tossed everything when she moved back to the States."

Kiva tapped her pen on the yellow notepad. Then she placed a call. When the call answered she said simply, "Shay, grab that journal, will you... Yes... Now tell me what it looks like, yes, brand, everything...I see. Can you take a picture of the last four pages and send it to me? Yes...Send me that too...No, I'll explain later...Yes. Okay...Bye."

Grabbing the top book off the pile, she flipped it over. Below the ISBN barcode was the retailer information block: *Shoppers Drug Mart, Toronto. Made in Mexico.* She checked the others, one by one, and found them all the same. "Did you buy these all at once?"

"No," Elliott said, "they always have them in stock, so I just grab one when I need it. What's the problem?"

Kiva's phone pinged. She opened the email and looked through the pictures, finally handing her phone to Elliott. "Do you recognize that notebook?"

Elliott read the distributor details, "*Walgreens, Deerfield, Illinois. Made in Vietnam.* It looks exactly the same until you read that small detail."

"Is there any way you picked one up in Walgreens, say when you were on a scheduled flight, on a stopover at a US destination?"

"I could have, but I didn't. I always had my journal with me. It's a habit to carry it in my flight bag, especially after everything that happened with my ex. So, I wouldn't have needed to buy one at Walgreens. Besides, I started on the YYZ-MEX sched over a year ago. And before that, I was only flying domestic routes. Even if I'd done a transborder flight, I never would've had the time or a car. Stopovers are never longer than an hour, maybe an hour and a half. On layovers I take the crew transport with everyone else to whichever hotel we're in, and if I need anything I just grab it in the hotel store. I know it's crazy to spend seven dollars for a tube of toothpaste, but that's better than taking a cab to who knows where when I can be in my room getting some sleep."

"Take a look at the inside page pictures. Is that your writing?"

Elliott swiped the photo to the next one, then the next, then zoomed in to read a few lines. "It looks like it, but it isn't."

"Why do you say that?"

"Read it, Kiva. Even you lived in Toronto long enough to know that Canadians use 'about' where Americans don't." When it looked like she wasn't following, she read the line that had caught her attention. "'I'm intrigued with her name. When I asked, she put me off. I don't know what that means, but I'm interested in knowing more.' I would have said, 'I don't know what that's about, but I'd like to learn more.' Besides which, I do know what your name means, and we discussed its meaning and how your mother came to name you after the Anasazi healing lodge the second time we met."

Kiva was silent. Elliott had never done well with the silent treatment. She would prefer to argue it out than face a woman's stony reserve. Intent on letting Kiva make her own judgments, she endured the silence, watching her opening her latest journal, flipping through page after page. It looked like she was searching for something specific.

Kiva read quietly, finally closing it without comment. She looked upset and the last thing Elliott wanted to do was upset her more.

When Kiva finally met her eyes, Elliott offered kindly, "This must be hard. Here I am, spending the night, sharing my desire for you, sending flowers and telling you I'd like…I'd like to get to know you more, and you're stuck reading my journals and a fake version and trying to decide which one is real. Which of my most private inside thoughts are true and which is the bullshit version?"

"We can't."

She didn't argue. The last thing she could tolerate would be Kiva having to spell it out. She said, "I won't lie and say I understand. I feel bad you're stuck having to read what I've written. In the future, I'll keep my thoughts in my head and not on paper. No more journals and no more…"

Kiva met her eyes. There was no need for her to explain. There would be no romance. There would be no chance of something more. While the pain tore through her, she knew she wasn't ready to lose her completely, asking quietly, "You're still taking my case? I mean, if you want, I can find another lawyer. If that would be better for you?"

Looking sad, Kiva finally said, "No. There's no need. I took this case, and I want to see it through. Whatever is going on here affects more than you, and I owe it to the people of Illusion Lake. This may not be my home anymore, but it was home for long enough. I feel I owe these people."

And there it was. Kiva was staying on. Not for her, not for any hope for them, but for the folks who lived here. At least she said it, as clear as day. There would be no mistaking her professionalism for continued interest and there would be no more sending roses, or kisses good night, or making love.

Yes. That part ripped at her. They hadn't just fucked. They'd made love, and Elliott knew she needed to grieve for a relationship that would never happen. Space and time would help, but she'd had a taste of life on Mars and agonized deeply. Would she ever feel anything as intensely?

Deciding to box those thoughts away, she gathered the empty cups and trundled down to the canteen. She'd brew up a fresh pot for herself and the guys. She'd get Mac to take a cup up to Kiva, but that was all she would do. She wouldn't risk having her think she was… what was she doing? *Nothing. There is nothing I can do. My feelings have no place here, and she's made that clear.*

Her shoulders slumped while she waited for the coffee to brew. *It's for the best. She's too good. I knew that, and it's time I start accepting I'm just not partner material. Maybe it's karma. Probably what I get for all my years judging most women not good enough and only taking what I wanted. It serves me right that the tables have turned, and the woman I want is too good for me and in a place to judge me in return.*

CHAPTER FOURTEEN

After a day working at the hangar, Kiva returned home, but she still had work to do. Thinking about opening a beer, she changed her mind. This was work, not a casual read. She grabbed bottled water from the fridge and filled a glass with ice, taking both to the dining room table and settling in. Grabbing a fresh yellow pad of paper and her favorite pen, she was ready to begin a long night of reviewing documents.

Who am I kidding? She was about to read Elliott's journals, the recordings of her innermost thoughts. She'd had more than one case where journals and diaries were entered into evidence and as painful or humiliating for the child or mostly young teens, they spoke better to demonstrate a pattern of abuse than a young witness could verbalize.

This was different though. Elliott trusted her, and she couldn't help but think something was building between them. Indeed, their night together had been more than casual. What was it about Elliott? She had helped her past her deepest worries with an unsuspected tenderness. Their dinner conversation last night had been fun and light. It was impressive the way the woman could leave all her baggage and personal issues outside, never once letting the past interfere.

Not like her. She'd been on top of the world until things became intimate, then she'd panicked, worried about things other women had said or done to make her feel less than perfect. As she stood by the edge of her bed half-naked, her old fears began to close in, and Elliott at once recognized it. Walking around the bed naked as a jaybird, unafraid, she had taken her in her arms and offered to stop. *Who does that?* Worse was acknowledging this had happened before. One woman had dressed and stormed out, calling insults as she left. Another had tried to just ignore her discomfort, ordering her out of her clothes and forcing an overeager tongue down her throat, then trying to push two fingers inside her even though she wasn't in the least bit wet.

Elliott had recognized her hesitation, and somehow understood it. She had placed all the power in Kiva's hands and made sure she knew she could choose without fear. Elliott respected her. Other women did, at work, in court, but sexually? Not in years. And she had been playful and tender. Asking permission at every step, sharing her thoughts, and asking for hers. That was different. No one had ever talked to her during, through sex. She had felt more than listened to, Elliott made her feel worshiped. Choosing to use the case to put space between them—Elliott had understood that too and without question. Respecting her needs, her space. Merely promising to be there when she was ready. Yes, she was ready now *but…*

Kiva stared out the dining room windows at forty or fifty feet of illumination from the deck lights. Snow was coming down quietly. She had been so wrapped up in thought she had missed the change in the weather, missed everything happening around her. She had wanted Elliott to come home with her again, wanted so much more. And Elliott, it seemed, wanted her too. When Kiva cited the case as a reason to keep their distance, Elliott hadn't fought her. She'd just accepted it. Maybe it was what she wanted. Maybe she'd been disappointed after all. Maybe. Maybe all she ever wanted was a fling.

When Kiva revealed to Sheriff Dias that she might stay in Illusion Lake after her dad returned, Elliott had been even more attentive. Last night she said it was something she was waiting to hear. Like she didn't want what they'd begun to end. Kiva had been sure of it this morning. In any other situation, she would have been overjoyed. She recognized her deep feelings for her were different, deeper, more solemn than she'd experienced in the past. Maybe that was the real reason she had pushed back now. And she was both dreading and longing to learn if Elliott's journals would answer her hopes or her fears.

The first and oldest of the journals started just after her last relationship, during the time the ex had caused so much trouble. There was an aloof, impersonal air about the way she phrased things, and Kiva was more than halfway through when she guessed the journal had been the idea of Elliott's lawyer and it read like an itinerary of her daily activities, flight schedules, even what, when, or if she ate. She was covering the bases, going as far as to take receipts from the airport newsstands she stopped at for bottled water or the hotel gift shop where she grabbed overpriced necessities like toothpaste and tampons.

This wasn't a journal, it was a cover-your-ass book, and it made sense. It was also heartbreaking. What was it like to have to be so diligent in your actions, knowing your life was under such scrutiny and all from a woman who once claimed to love you? *Ain't love grand.* Setting it aside she made a few notes, pleased to know there was nothing there. In a way, she hoped the others would be the same. It would certainly make this process feel less invasive.

Book Two had started like the first, quickly becoming more personal as she detailed her humiliation at being arrested at work and in front of her colleagues. She had worked hard to earn their respect, respect that evaporated in a second at the sight of her being led out of flight operations in handcuffs. She continued to record her daily movements and kept adding the receipts for everything from breakfast at Chez Cora to stops at Shoppers and Canadian Tire. Every time she found a receipt from Shoppers Drug Mart, Kira checked it for the purchase of new notebooks to use as a journal. She wanted to prove Elliott's story that she only purchased the blank composition notebooks from them and only when she was ready for a new one. Sure enough, she found three separate receipts that proved she did purchase them there. It wouldn't prove that she was using only that brand, but it backed up her story. She also made a habit of recording what she was doing when she was online. That was interesting.

Googled: TC
Inspection Standards for fixed pitch propellers
Overhaul time for propeller mounting bolts, rings, and shims
Check Gmail
Googled: Black Book Values
My Land Rover
2004 Wrangler
2003 Cherokee

There were several numbers scribbled beside Elliott's neat printing of her search lists. No doubt she could perform the same searches and come up with similar numbers. She could also do a comparison on her computer using her Internet history. Even if the online history had been deleted, she knew a few tricks taught to her by some of her more astute young clients that would unlock a bevy of information. Elliott, she was sure, knew them too.

She slowed as she read through the retelling of the second arrest at the Island Airport. Elliott described herself as walking in a coma. She knew she hadn't done anything wrong and that the cops would figure that out too…eventually. She also knew her new employer, a hyper image-aware maintenance outfit catering to the city's elite with their private aircraft, would fire her ass for just embarrassing them. She described being numb and no longer caring. She'd lost her home to placate the woman, then her savings in defense fees. She'd sold her new Land Rover to eliminate her monthly payments. Without a reliable job, she'd picked up a winter beater with the cash she had left. Now she was sleeping on her cousin's couch and about to lose a crap job too. Her writing was self-accusatory, berating herself for being so stupid.

It was at this point where Elliott began to really open up, writing page after page detailing her upbringing. Her mother always blaming her for her loss of freedom, getting pregnant by accident. Elliott made a few jokes about that constant complaint.

How does one get pregnant by accident? I mean either you're having sex, or you're not. It's not as if birth control is brain surgery. And smacking me around from the time I could walk to make up for her mistakes—who does that?

Evidently her mom had a habit of having one man or another fall into her lady parts, accidentally making a baby. She laughed to read her use the phrase "lady parts." Only Elliott would write something like that.

Then there were the segments on her grandmother. These were sweet, the devotion evident. The two liked to talk, but her grandmother, Elliott mourned, never told her much.

Sometimes I wish Nanny would just spell things out for me and sometimes I'm so glad she hasn't. She's always let me figure things out in my own way. I can't think of anyone else who just believes in me. Maybe Aunt Linda? Certainly, Uncle Elmo.

In the first pages of the fourth and last journal, she announced learning of her great-uncle's death. Her first worry had been for her Nanny, his big sister.

This must be so hard on her. Elmo was her last living sib. Now it's just her, the last standing out of ten children.

It was interesting to read Elliott's memory of staying with the old girl as she worked through her grief, taking her out every day, touring her around all her old haunts from Regent Park to Saint James and every place in between. One night she took her upstairs at the Winchester House to the restored ballroom for an evening of swing. Elliott made sure to inform everyone who met them that her grandmother had danced in the club during the war to stars like Duke Ellington and Glenn Miller and listened to favorites like Alberta Hunter.

I want her to feel the joy of her youth again but more than that, I want her to know it mattered, her life matters, Elmo's life mattered. Maybe things didn't work out as expected but she made a difference in my life and I suspect for Uncle Elmo too.

Thanks to Elliott, Nanny was a celebrity that night.

It was after that, after that joint celebration of her grandmother's and great-uncle's youth, that they were ready to hear what the lawyers had to say. It was a little hard to read Elliott's harsh thoughts of those who shared her profession, but she understood. The woman had lost everything at the hands of the legal system, one in which she had been forced to prove her innocence. It was wrong and oh so backward, but it was a reality.

Kiva had long switched to pop for the caffeine to keep her focused and found herself with an empty glass when she reached Elliott's arrival in Illusion Lake. Getting up to grab a refill, she noticed the sun was rising. The reflection off the water sparked with magic, making the name, Illusion Lake, a perfect fit.

Forgetting the soda pop, she started the coffeemaker. *Might as well. I've got enough caffeine in my system to rocket to the moon. Time to add jet fuel to the mix.* That reminded her of Elliott's use of Mars as a destination of extreme happiness. "Let me take you to Mars," she had said. "Just you and me," she added. "Alone. Free of all life on earth that weighs on us; weightless. I want all of you, just the way you are, just us, thirty-four million miles from everything."

Who even talks like that? Yet it had worked, sloughing away all her fears, regrets and experiences to just let herself be. Be with Elliott. Involuntarily, her fingers had migrated to her lips. As she waited for the coffee to brew, her slender fingers began softly tapping. The effort at once evoking the pleasure from Elliott just by kissing her.

God, I miss her, want her. Why did this have to happen now, here, like this?

She braced for what Elliott would share about her and her dealings with her father's firm and their first outings together, maybe even their first night. *Or was it our only night? Am I ready to know?*

* * *

Elliott stirred from a sensuous dream of awakening in her bed with Kiva wrapped in her arms, their legs interwoven, her hair tickling her nose. She had been stroking the length of Kiva's back, her skin soft and warm. She had been on fire, all her skin, hot and wet and oh so wanting. In the dream they had made love for most of the night, their passion burning ever brighter. She had worried aloud that Kiva would tire of her, but she had laughed an amazing laugh, making sure Elliott understood she never would tire of her touch, of her need. Finally spent, they had fallen asleep together, intertwined and in love.

Fully awake and sitting on the edge of the single bed, Elliott tried to shake off the images. They were not together. They were not sleeping together. They couldn't make love again and they probably never would. Ian Guerrero and his machinations had seen to that. She knew people could get desperate when it came to money and deadly when it came to huge fortunes, but she never could have imagined someone fabricating legal, court-witnessed documents, much less having a journal forged. Where the hell did you even find someone to do such a thing? Her logical mind tried to formulate an ad for Craigslist while her heart fought with the idea that their one night together might have been a dream too.

She reached for her running gear, pulling on sweatpants and her old RCAF hoodie, combat boots instead of runners. She grabbed her knit gloves and headed downstairs and out the airside door. She'd learned to run in combat boots and never really adjusted to running shoes even when she could afford the best. They never felt right, and she was thankful for the boots when she spotted a light dusting of snow.

Without much of a warmup, it took half the runway length before she hit her stride. Each of the old runways in the Army Air Corps standard triangular layout was five thousand feet long. If she kept to the apron side of the triangle, she'd complete a three-mile run in one lap. Today though, three miles or thirty, she knew she couldn't shake off the feel of Kiva in her arms, in her bed, in her heart, and ran harder.

Yesterday Kiva had left the hangar with her journals and her thoughts, all of them. She wanted to earn Kiva's trust and needed her to recognize the truth from the fiction Ian had created and her sister and father had bought into. In a way, letting Kiva read her innermost thoughts was far more intimate than any lovemaking session—except it was one-sided. Without any form of reciprocation, she felt exposed and alone.

Maybe that was for the best. It was time to set this whole Kiva fantasy aside. She was trying to figure out how she could do that when she spotted a car in the distance. It looked to be stopped next to the old shack beside the hangar. She hadn't been in that building yet, couldn't find the key to the lock. The guys offered to break it open, but after peeking through several breaks in the wood siding, they all agreed the place looked empty and they all had more important things to do.

She had just made her last turn on the triangular course, with five thousand feet to go, when she spotted Jesus making his way to the visiting car. With her luck, it would be a county inspector sent to fine her for having a dilapidated building on her property. She shook her head at that thought. *Look around, buddy.*

Considering how bad things were all over the county, including the town of Illusion Lake itself, there was no shortage of structures in need of attention. Of course, the difference was she now had money to do something about it. No wonder Ian and who knows who else were so motivated to make this work. Even if she stopped his little plan to corner the property market and shape the look of a new and prosperous Illusion Lake, there was still a vast amount of county real estate at stake. The money from those sales, if done right, could benefit everyone in the county.

Of course she knew it wouldn't work like that. Only a few people would benefit long-term. For the rest, it would be a temporary feast, then a permanent famine. Still, people would never listen to a warning of something that might not affect them for three or four years. People always thought they were the exception to the rule. Almost always everyone paid in the end.

At a hundred yards she slowed to a brisk walk, wanting to catch her breath before reaching the man Jesus was waiting with by the empty shed. That didn't bode well. She imagined he would have allowed the man into the canteen for a coffee if he wasn't a threat. She pulled one glove off, offering her hand in a no-nonsense greeting. "I'm Elliott Snowmaker. What can I do for you?"

The man smiled warmly, shaking her hand and offering his card. "Jon Martinez, from the Colorado Bottling Company. I'd like to discuss the renewal of your contract."

She read his card carefully before passing it to Jesus. Deciding to play it cool, she asked, "Do you have a copy of the expired contract with you?"

"I do."

Before he could get in another word, she asked Jesus to show him to the canteen. "I'll join you in a few minutes," she promised, heading upstairs. In her room, she called Mac and asked him to do a quick search on the Colorado Bottling Company and meet her upstairs in ten. She stripped from her running gear, pulling on a robe, texting Jesus to keep the guy busy while she and Mac figured out why he was here.

Ten minutes later, she had showered and was almost finished dressing when Mac stopped at her door. "He checks out. He runs the water bottling division. They have at least three of their own brands," he read from his notes, "Ponderosa Pines, Aspen Springs, and White River Spring Water. They also bottle for private labels. And they're the largest water wholesaler to New Mexico and Arizona. I couldn't get any current numbers, but as of five years ago they were the number two wholesaler in California and the number four retailer if you combine their brands."

She brushed her wet hair, then shook her short hair loose. "Okay, let's go find out what this Jon Martinez wants with us."

As they reached the stairs, she placed a cautionary hand on his shoulder, suggesting quietly, "Mac, go grab the bolt cutters, cut the lock on the shed, text me what you find." He nodded and turned away from the canteen as she headed in.

She stopped at the counter, pouring herself a coffee and asking Martinez if he needed a refill. She didn't apologize for the delay. In her mind, he was here uninvited, so that meant she owed him no courtesy other than to listen to the reason for his visit.

CHAPTER FIFTEEN

Curling up on the couch hadn't been the smartest idea, but Kiva felt too emotionally drained to climb the stairs and too jacked up on caffeine to sleep soundly. She had closed her eyes with Elliott's innermost thoughts on her mind. Her handwriting was atrocious, and it had taken a while to find the pattern and contend with her sentence fragments. At first she'd even questioned the woman's command of the language. After reading the second book she began to understand. Elliott rushed her thoughts. Her writing never able to keep pace with her mind, she'd resorted to short forms or indecipherable scribbles to get down the gist. When something was important, legally or for future reference, she printed it out in a careful almost machine-like precision. When she was angry or upset, her words were recorded in a deep scratching scrawl.

After finishing the last journal, Kiva could pick out the moments when Elliott was hopeful by the wistful flourish of her penmanship. It was easy to imagine a shrink would have a heyday with it, but she felt something else; she felt comforted. Everything she shared was revealing, open, and without judgment. She talked about their first meeting without blaming their opening animosity on Kiva. She took responsibility for the friction between them, blaming it on her exhaustion and worry.

The last six months had been hard on her, she admitted in the journal. Kiva thought that was an understatement. She also wished she could have brought her elderly grandmother with her to New Mexico and hated herself for not having the money to fly her down to see her little brother's home and the work which had kept him occupied for the last fifty years. She called Kiva feisty, and she hadn't expected that, nor had she expected her to accept the breakfast invitation. She called herself a nerd for going on and on about all the projects in the hangar and boring a beautiful woman to death. And she said something else that shocked Kiva:

"She's brilliant, beautiful, articulate, and way outta my league. Even if she was staying, why would she consider me? And knowing she's going home in a few months just makes her more dangerous. I couldn't do casual with a woman like that. Oh, I know I'd cave if she showed even the slightest interest but good God, the heartbreak would kill me. Why is it I meet her like this and now? It's hard enough to imagine her taking an interest in me but here? Not a chance. And I don't think I can go back there, back to T.O. Maybe in time, but now? What would I do and what would I be to her? The thought. It hurts. I hurt. And nothing's happened. I know better. Still, it hurts to breathe when she's near me and it's impossible to think clearly. Yes, she's my Kryptonite."

Kiva sat up, only then realizing her arms were wrapped around the journal and she was holding it tight to her chest. Carefully placing it back on the table with the rest, she read over her notes. They stopped at the review of their first meeting. She didn't need to make notes, she was there.

What struck her was the difference in their separate recollections, what with her playing that stupid hypnosis game with Shay. She'd followed along to make Shay happy and because secretly she had been wondering what she was waiting for. She was ready for a relationship, a real honest-to-goodness partnership, but unlike some of her friends who had built successful domestic relationships with friends, she wanted more. She wanted the heat of attraction. She wanted the long-smoldering-fire type of relationship that didn't descend into lesbian bed death within a year or two like it had for so many of her colleagues. They seemed to be happy filling their life with more... more work, more activities, kids, or pets.

Reading Elliott's words had been difficult, not because the woman was clearly burning for her, but her own ache. She had denied it for so many reasons, the case, the circumstances, and more. And yes, embarrassingly enough, she had wondered if Elliott was good enough for her. Oh, she was attractive. As a matter of fact, she was precisely the type of woman she had created during the game she played with

Shay. It was like a scene from some stupid romcom where the woman describes her Prince Charming and then a minute later he walks through the door.

She said aloud, "Oh, Elliott, I am so not too good for you."

Her phone rang, the ringtone she'd set for Sheriff Dias. "Hi, David. I'm home and alone. I can talk."

"That's good. Still, I think we should meet."

"Aren't you going to execute the warrant this morning?"

"Yep, in all of ten minutes. I wanted to let you know one of my deputies will call you if we find the evidence. I'd like for you to tell him you're coming over with Elliott to identify her stuff but put him off. Can you insist you can't make it in till about one?"

"Of course. Can you tell me what's going on?"

"Not yet, but please keep that tracker thing refreshed. I know no one here knows the warrant's coming. It's gonna be faxed over at ten to ten. Once we search the bank, I want to see if any of the evidence accidentally disappears."

She checked the time on her phone: nine forty-eight. "Okay. I'll be ready, and I'll warn Elliott that we can't make it in until the afternoon. And David, tally ho."

"Ten-four."

Taking her phone to the kitchen, she plugged it in to charge then decided she better warn Elliott about the sheriff's request.

Elliott picked up and didn't waste time with niceties or preamble. "Your timing's perfect. I've had a visitor and I think you'll want to hear what he had to say."

"Good morning to you," Kiva teased with fondness she didn't immediately realize telegraphed through her voice and even her posture. She warned herself, *Stop behaving like a lovesick teen.*

The gentle laugh she heard in reply lessened her internal scolding. "Sorry, Elliott. I have news too. Can we meet?"

"My door is always open. Or should I come into town?"

She sounded so agreeable. That was the sweet thing about the woman. Even compromised as she was, and however complicated and painful their situation, she never made it personal. "I'd like to come out there. I'm interested in seeing your progress, and I need... Actually we need a place to lay low until afternoon."

"*Oooh*, that sounds interesting. Can you tell me, or do I have to guess?"

Smiling, she teased, "I'm not saying a word until I can see your face." Blushing, realizing what she'd said, she was glad the conversation was happening on the phone. "Just do me one favor. Please don't take any calls until I'm there, and if anyone shows up you can't go anywhere until you finish something you're in the middle of."

"Okay. A mystery and a visit. I'll make sure the coffee's on."

Kiva raced up the stairs to shower and dress. Stimulated and aroused after only a few hours curled up on the couch, she asked herself none of her usual probing questions to uncover hidden motives. This morning she didn't bother. She felt alive and something more. Something had changed for her. She couldn't say what and wouldn't dare. She was singing as she stripped off her clothes and jumped into the shower.

Pulling into the street-side parking area across from the hangar, she smiled to see the exterior painting finished and how good it looked. *Elliott's*, the retro logo read, *Antique, Vintage, and Warbird Restorations. We Provide Aircraft Repairs and Service.*

Well, she thought, I may not have an aircraft but you, Elliott, have indeed repaired my outlook on life.

Striding from the car, she made her way across the access road and in the walk-through door. It was hard to imagine tiring of doing this, coming here. There was something about the place, something that reminded her of hope—or maybe it was joy. The smells of wood lacquers and the pressed canvas were almost enticing. In the slightly green tinge of the mercury vapor overhead lights, the place took on an ethereal feel. Certainly, the look of the tiny biplane on which they were ironing, yes, ironing, the canvas flat, only added to the feeling. Some romantic part of her almost imagined opening the far side air doors wide to a movie set of World War I or perhaps a scene from *Out of Africa*. There was an air of romance that contradicted the reality of war. Or maybe it was the risk of impending loss that made the period so captivating. In times of peril, people were quick to put aside societal norms and just live in the moment. And in recognizing her emotions she too knew her life could include more. How she would go about incorporating it or if she should try, that was the real question.

* * *

The guys had found an old stereo of Elmo's somewhere and dragged it down to the hangar floor and wired in a connection. Mac's phone was plugged in and they were working hard and rocking to Lenny Kravitz. Elliott was stretched over the bottom wing trying to get the fit just right when Mac called down. She turned her head to watch Kiva approaching them. *Is she checking out my ass?* Standing, placing the iron on the nearby worktable, she called to Mac to take over. Mac, she knew, would find any spots she missed.

Taking Kiva into the canteen, she pulled the old steel door shut and smiled. "Sorry about the concert."

"No worries, I can handle a little rock, although for me, Lenny comes in after Melissa and the Wilson sisters."

"Me too," she declared, pouring out the dregs of burned coffee, rinsing the pot, and starting a fresh batch of Columbian blend she'd bought in Amarillo.

Kiva picked up the foil bag, her voice joyfully teasing, "You have been a busy woman. Did you pick this up on your solo drive back in Elmo's Corvette?"

"I did. I hope you know how much I appreciated you taking me up there. And how I missed your company on the drive back. It was chilly with the 'Vette's top down or should I say absent?"

"I'm surprised you didn't freeze to death."

Elliott was grinning, a warmth radiating from her. "Oh, I did. I ended up stopping at one of those western supply stores and buying a Carhartt insulated coat, knit gloves, and a tuque."

"Please tell me you didn't ask for a tuque?"

"Yes, and I had to endure a lecture on everything wrong with the Free Trade Agreement. When I told the guy that axing it prematurely without the new agreement in place had robbed twenty-thousand auto workers on both sides of the border of their jobs, I thought he was going to throw me out."

"Oh my God!"

Elliott was still beaming that warm and silly grin. "The store owner's wife saved the day. She asked if I was paying in real money. When I said, 'Yes, ma'am, real American greenbacks,' she just smiled and told him to carry my purchases out to the car."

Just then the coffeepot spat the last few ounces of steaming liquid into the carafe. She pulled two new mugs down from the shelf. "I even bought some real mugs. I know you didn't appreciate those old-fashioned glass mugs of Elmo's. I've never been fond of them either."

Kiva squeezed her arm, taking a seat at the table. "We need to talk. First there's Sheriff Dias." She explained about his call and wanting a delay. "I have a feeling he's worried not everyone in his department is playing on his team."

"Ouch."

"Yeah, I feel bad. All of this is such a betrayal for him too."

"No kidding. These guys are his friends, right?"

Kiva nodded. "I don't know how close he is with them, but they've all known one another since they were kids."

"How many deputies does he have?"

"It's a small department," Kiva said. "Five full-timers, and the volunteer posse."

"Posse?"

She smiled. "This *is* the Southwest."

Elliott groaned. "Okay. I guess its time for my news. Grab your coffee and follow me. If we're lucky, Zeus's laptop should be finished spitting out the large-scale printouts, and I have a contract I need you to read. Two actually." She poured two more coffees for the guys then led Kiva across the hangar floor to the print room.

Inside, Jesus held up one of the large-scale printouts. "I don't get this. It doesn't even look like the same town, and it's not just that the airport is gone. I mean the lake is half the size. How can that be?"

Kiva was looking over several other documents. "This is interesting. The survey lines for the lakefront properties only stretch to the current lakefront." She stood to help him pin his map to the board, then compared it to the existing one. "This planned road here looks like it's actually in the lake. That is, on the current water side of the shoreline."

Jesus grabbed a yellow highlighter from the desk and traced the planned road. The existing map of the lake up beside it proved it would put the road underwater. "How the hell can they drain enough of the lake to gain a hundred feet of shoreline? I mean, it's just not feasible. Is it?"

Straight-faced, Elliott said plainly, "I think it is."

"Explain?" Kiva asked.

Picking up a green highlighter, Elliott marked the hangar on the current map and then on the development plan. In the second one the runways were gone, but the hangar remained. "One of the papers Elmo had was a hydrology report. I didn't understand it at first, then I found a repair bill for the well pump. About eight years ago, the old military water pumping station gave up the ghost—"

"Wait," Kiva interrupted, pulling several files from her case. "I remember something from the airport agreement... Yes, your great-uncle was, and now you are, responsible for maintaining the airport water pumping system." She read with concentration. "According to this, you must supply water to the Fire Hall and any and all tenants. You can charge them for the water, but not for the maintenance or operation of the pumping station."

With the highlighter, Elliott continued marking an area around the hangar. "This is the pumping station. It's hard to call it that, it's just that little shack on the north side. When Uncle Elmo bought the hangar and most of the land on this side of the runway, he inherited the senior water rights from the military."

Jesus argued, "But how does that change the shape of the lake?"

"It would take removing millions of gallons," Kiva added to his objection. "And wouldn't the spring just feed it back from the aquifer?"

"Yes, to a point. Did we print out a topographical map for the area?" Elliott asked.

Jesus pulled it out of a stack and pinned it up for them.

Elliott traced her finger along the elevation lines, then found a pencil and added the underwater elevations on the lake area of the new development plan. Illusion Lake was shaped like a fat exclamation mark with the tall slender slash bleeding into the fat round period at the bottom. The tall slash was extremely shallow as were the outside edges of the period, but in the center of it was a deep spring, fed from an even deeper aquifer.

"What is the most expensive thing you can pump out of the ground around here?"

Joining them, Mac answered in unison with Kiva and Jesus. "Oil."

"What's more expensive than oil?"

They looked at each other blankly, but it was Kiva who groaned first, getting where Elliott was going. "Water! Bottled water. Shit! But that doesn't explain the increase in land and the huge water level drop off, unless…"

"Unless they plan a huge opening harvest. By pulling a vast amount of water from the aquifer all at once, the water level of the lake would be drastically reduced. They would need a larger pumping station, but they could wholesale enough with the operation we already have and use the proceeds to build a larger, faster processing plant. With that comes new jobs and lots of housing speculation. They already gobbled up all these houses on the lake. If the town then puts in a new road, it allows them to add all new waterfront properties. I'll bet the county has signed options, paid options, for any possible new property created by lowering the level of the lake. For a developer, it would be a wish come true. First they get to sell off all these waterfront properties, and then when the water level falls they can do it all over again."

Kiva nodded. "I get it. They win when they sell off the existing waterfront homes at top dollar, then the water recedes and the county puts in a new road right in front of these premium lots, they sell the newly created waterfront properties and profit again." She stood, tracing the edge of the new smaller lake. "What about up here, where I live?"

"You're in a different situation. Your deed specifically stipulates your property stretches to the waterfront. The more the water recedes the more land you own."

"That sounds like a win," Mac said.

"It does," Elliott admitted, before warning, "Until they reach this stage." She pointed to the last plan layout. "By then, the northern part of the lake will be cut off from the spring. It'll be nothing more than a seasonal creek or marsh. You'll have a four thousand-foot-deep backyard and no place to swim and, worse, if your neighbors sell, you could see a subdivision back there."

"So much for privacy," Kiva lamented, finally asking the million dollar question, "How much water are we talking about? How much will they take to make this work for them?"

Elliott took a big breath. She sat at the computer, opening a scientific calculator app, and worked out a rough algorithm. It was a few minutes before she sat back, answering, "Please understand this is just an estimation, but it jives with what Uncle Elmo put together and what I learned this morning from the water company rep."

Kiva took her hand, very much understanding her caveat. "Just tell us. Whatever you've figured, we'll work with it."

Sighing, Elliott said, "Almost eight billion gallons."

Mac choked, "Eight billion! As in a thousand million?"

While they tried to figure out the implications both to the town and the environment, Jesus got out his phone and Googled the price of wholesale bottled water. "Hey, guys. I think you need to hear this. According to the Beverage Marketing Association, the price for wholesale water today is a buck-ten a gallon."

"But," Mac tried to argue, "that's got to be good for the town. Like, wouldn't it bring in a bunch of jobs and stuff?"

"Not long term," Elliott said. "A water processing plant would mostly be automated. At first they would need lots of people to build the plant and then to get the big harvest done. That would also create jobs building houses, stores to support the workers and a whole lot more, but once they had the primary surplus sucked up, they could only take the amount the aquifer could produce every year. As the lake is already showing a natural reduction, I assumed the current local needs are already taxing the environment.

"That was until I read the expired contract Elmo had with the water company. I didn't understand what he was referring to in his notes until now. He was selling water but stopped when he realized the damage it was doing. With global warming and the drying out of the local environment, the rain and snow we get here would never be enough to replenish what's been taken."

"And that's where his money came from, selling water?" Kiva asked.

She nodded. "And it's why the banker and your dad's law partner knew about the money, the water contract, and the value and size of the aquifer."

Jesus pinned up another map, this one showing the region the water aquifer serviced. If you took a broad brush and painted a diagonal line starting in northern New Mexico and continuing southeast to Dallas, Kiva thought, you would have the region marked out.

Jesus asked incredulously, "There is no way the EPA would allow anyone to jeopardize the water supply for the whole of Dallas-Fort Worth, would it?"

"From what I can tell, Elmo's water rights were originally those given to the military base—with no limitations. And they passed those rights to Elmo, allowing him to harvest as he chose. The water bottling companies must monitor applications, because he had several reps on his doorstep the day the sale for the hangar closed."

She handed the old contract to Kiva. "Elmo refused to renew the contract when he realized the effect it was having locally. In his notes, he mentions how much the shoreline has receded. He also mentions that banker guy and Ian Guerrero pressuring him to reconsider."

Kiva stood, wrapping her hands around Elliott's shoulders, needing to hold on. "They need your well to get started because you hold the senior rights. You know that means you can pull as much water as you want before considering the needs of this or any other municipality. How many gallons can that shack of a water pumping station pull?"

"Four hundred and seventy-four thousand imperial gallons a day."

Jesus was back on the development plan, asking Elliott to draw out the area of the aquifer. Then he pointed to the area he'd outlined with the green highlighter. "That's why they've marked the runways as industrial but have only added one building, probably the intended processing plant." He asked, "Why don't they simply drop new wells along one of these smaller runways? I mean, you already said they only have to maintain one."

Elliott sighed. "I think that's one of the problems. Even as much as the EPA has been gutted, I'm not sure they could get another unlimited permit, not with Dallas being dependent on this aquifer too. You can't run the well dry for seven million people without some blowback."

Kiva stepped up to the plan again. "I'm not an expert on water laws, but I have a feeling that even if they could bribe enough officials to get permits, anyone with more senior water rights, meaning you, could shut them down. Water is serious business in New Mexico. I mean the permitting system alone…"

Mac was still having a hard time with it. "I don't see a problem. I mean if it brings in jobs… Yeah, it sucks for you, Kiva. Your house won't be on the lake anymore but you're getting a whole whack of land in exchange, so…"

Elliott stopped him. "It's not that. Yes, this will bring in all kinds of people, and some will make good wages, but in two, max three years, when the water is gone, they'll be out of work and sitting on properties they can't sell. The only people who will make any money is the consortium who've grabbed up the land."

She pointed to the existing lakefront. "They'll sell the existing houses, then build and sell the new properties on the new land and wholesale all the water. When they're done, they'll walk away with billions, the profits from the water sale, the building boom, and the property sales, and then when the people who moved here have lost everything, the bank will foreclose, and the investors will have those properties back in their portfolios too."

Kiva shared her sentiment. "Guys like Ian Guerrero, Gent Koehler, and whoever else they're involved with will walk away owning the town and have hundreds of millions, maybe even billions of dollars in their pockets. The rest of us will be left with nothing of value and not enough water in the system for daily use. There won't be enough for grazing cattle, much less watering the lawn or anything we take for granted."

They stood in silence, until Elliott finally warned them. "Guys, you can't breathe a word of this. That's an order."

They both nodded their understanding. "You got it, Cap," Jesus responded before leading Mac from the room.

Turning to Kiva, pulling her in without thinking, she found no resistance. Kiva allowed herself to be pulled in even tighter and silently held on.

"You calculated it out. Didn't you?" Kiva asked. "The time it would take to drain the lake down to the level that would allow them to create a new shoreline."

"Twice, to make sure. They couldn't do it with the existing pumping capacity. Not with the airport wellhead, that would take forty-five years. They would have to either bore a much larger hole or drop another ten wells out where the runways are. I'm guessing it's one of the reasons they want the hangar. It's big enough to house additional pumps and hide several wellheads from the EPA. And they could just run delivery pipes out to the pumphouse and pretend for the world they were just maxing the wellhead we have."

There was no need to say more. Kiva would understand the implications to the environment, the community, and the danger to them. Even if they wholesaled the water at half the going rate, Ian and Gent's consortium would still be looking at over four, maybe five billion dollars in profit. Most people would do just about anything for that sort of money. Men as desperate as Ian and Gent were capable of the unthinkable.

"I think we need more help," Elliott said.

Standing with her arms still wrapped around Elliott, Kiva asked, "You think I should bring in a bigger firm?"

Tipping her head back just far enough to see Kiva's face, Elliott shook her head. "If you think that could help. But I was in fact thinking of more muscle, both here and at your place. Kiva," she added gently, "I'm worried sick about you being out there alone."

Kiva sank back into her arms, her head pressed against Elliott's cheek. "I know," was all she said.

CHAPTER SIXTEEN

Kiva watched Elliott pull up to the house, pleased to see she was driving the beat-up Jeep. The weather had turned cold again, and she didn't want to see her driving that old 'Vette. Not only did it have terrible brakes, it didn't have a top. The frame for the soft-top was there, but not the rotten canvas Elmo had stripped when he rescued the car. Like all the work in the hangar, he'd kept a journal of his find, where he had acquired the car, the condition, all the work completed and the repairs he wanted to do. For an elderly man, he had one hell of a to-do list. It did make her wonder if there was more to his untimely demise than what met the eye. The death certificate had listed congestive lung failure caused by prolonged and antibiotic-resistant pneumonia. Yet, the more they were learning, the more she was beginning to question everything and everyone.

Opening the door before Elliott had to knock, she helped her slip off the heavy canvas work jacket with its lambs wool collar and lining, hanging it up and appreciating the soft inside layer. "This must keep you warm."

"Warmer than that guy out there." She gestured toward the new security team outside.

"I tried talking them into coming in but they insisted they can do their job better staying out there."

Elliott offered a thin smile and Kiva gave her a hug. There was no denying how lovely it felt to be in her arms. She was just the right height, and she was warm, always so warm. She pulled her in and held her tight.

"David Dias won't be here for an hour or so. I made green chili. Are you hungry?" She felt Elliott tremble in her arms and leaned back to understand. The look she saw explained everything. Elliott was indeed hungry, just not for food. Holding her hand, Kiva led her to the couch. She held on while they settled in. "I don't know what we're doing. I know I said we couldn't, but I don't want to stop. It's just...I don't want to start something we can't finish." She grinned, adding, "In an hour."

Elliott let out a long showy breath, blowing her bangs from her eyes. "*Phew.*"

"Can we talk?"

"We can. We probably should. It's just..."

Sighing, Kiva acknowledged her concern. "I know." Leaning in, she gave Elliott's cheek a soft peck. "First I want to thank you for the added security. I wasn't expecting you to shell out to protect my family's house too."

After the revelations the water bottling rep had delivered, Kiva had driven to Santa Fe, catching a commuter flight to Dallas to apprise the city officials of the situation. She also met with a private security company, the type that specialized in keeping cattle and oil barons safe. She already knew of their reputation but thoroughly vetted their service before contracting them to protect Elliott, the hangar, and by extension the airport. Elliott had insisted on adding Kiva and her family home to the contract, dismissing any argument.

That done, she had spent the night in the Dallas Hilton, using the time to draft a new agreement for the water bottling company. It wasn't like they wanted to sell them any more water, but it occurred to her that a contract would be one more layer for Ian, Gent, and their consortium to fight their way through. She limited the harvesting days, the size and number of trucks, and added so many limitations including specifying which brands their water could be sold under that she marveled when the company returned it signed before noon the next day.

Now that she was back in Illusion Lake, David wanted to sit with them both to discuss his investigation and what they should do next.

He was worried, and so was she. On top of that, Elliott was sick to death of the idea of making more money off the town's single resource.

"I want to share that money, you know, whatever we make from the new water contract. I want to share it with the town. Is there a way to do it, so no one knows it's coming from me?"

Thinking about it, Kiva was sure they could figure it out. "What have you got in mind?"

"I was thinking about a youth center, but I want something that will serve the whole community. Maybe a community center with services for everyone, you know, seniors, battered women, kids…I don't know."

Kiva smiled to think of Elliott's brand of philanthropy. Inclusion seemed to be the word that fit. "I think what you're trying to say is, you want to build something that everyone can benefit from. Have you got a figure in mind?"

Shaking her head, Elliott said, "I have no idea what's involved, how, or where. Maybe that empty store on the main drag? I'm not ready to put a limit on it. At least not until we have an idea what the town, well, the whole county needs. I would like to plan it so whatever the water harvest is making will cover the operating expenses. That way we know there will always be money to run it."

"Sound and generous."

"But?"

Sighing, Kiva explained, "Whatever you do will not be enough for some people. And if you do something, it will lead to speculation, and that can only open this whole can of worms. Once the truth is out, there'll be no holding back those people who think you're profiting from what's theirs."

"So basically, I can't win. If I try to help, I'm the asshole stealing their water, and if I don't, I'm still the asshole keeping them from profiting from what's theirs."

She watched as the realization hit Elliott hard, her disappointment as clear as Illusion Lake itself. Sitting back, Kiva could admit she didn't have a solution. At least not yet. The only play they had required involving the Dallas-Fort Worth Water Authority, and so far they didn't seem that concerned. Her meeting with them had gone well, but she had a feeling, two of them, actually, and both left her uneasy.

One was the idea that they didn't understand the threat. The other and more daunting was the belief that they didn't care, or was it something far more sinister? That would mean they knew the plan and were set to profit from it too. And they would, twice over. She had failed to track down just who else was involved with Ian and Gent's consortium.

As public servants, the Water Authority board members could cry for attention when the water dropped to a dangerous level, and they would need to raise a water tax to cover the new and rising costs. A lot of new expenses could and would pass under the nose of auditors when everyone's eyes were on solving the supply and demand equation. People rarely understood that most public officials made their money not from the pitiful salary they received but the expenses they could charge back. And then there would be the profits and backroom kickbacks from new contracts. Towns and cities along the aquifer route, from their county all the way to Dallas, would have to buy water from the same companies who would be vying for the contracts to suck it up now. It was a cycle of greed that wouldn't end until there was no water left and even then, the backroom deals would never stop. It was already happening in some places in California and Arizona.

"I'm so sorry, Elliott."

She shook her head. "Not your fault. I have to admit, I'm starting to feel like a greed magnet or conduit or some such shit. Like all people see is an opportunity. Maybe I've got some sign on my head that says, 'fastest route to…to…' I don't fucking know."

"Hey, now! That's not true." The look Elliott gave her almost broke her heart. Taking her worried face in her hands, she wanted to reassure her and help her feel something… anything would be better than this. The look she read in those expressive blue eyes said everything. Elliott wanted to kiss her.

Slowly, so slowly, she moved closer. Like a spooked fawn, Kiva held her breath in anticipation. Finally, soft lips found hers, a featherlight brush.

Kiva's phone chimed and she broke away to look at it. "That's a text from my sister. She never texts…"

Elliott at once recognized the change in her posture, in her attention. "Something's wrong." It was not a question.

Kiva was tabbing in a reply as she answered. "She's at the hospital with my father." Without looking up she asked, "What time is it on the East Coast?"

"Half past midnight."

"Damn it, Shay! Pick up."

Elliott asked quietly, "What can I do?"

"My father had a heart attack. That's why I'm here covering for him."

She nodded. "I know." At Kiva's sharp look, she added, "You told me the other day. And you told me your sister is a doctor. That's got to be good, right? I mean, if you're going to have complications who better than a doctor to be there when it happens?" Judging by the expression on Kiva's face, it wasn't the smartest thing to say. Before she could stick her foot in any deeper, Shay's ringtone sounded.

"What happened? What's… Oh Jesus, Shay! You scared the crap out of me… Are you sure? What's causing the stress increase? I mean… Okay! I'm listening…"

Elliott took a seat on the couch and listened too. Even though it sounded like the scare was a false alarm, there seemed to be a long list of directives requiring Kiva to break out one of her ever-present yellow legal pads and make notes.

"When did he call the office… No, I've been careful not to ask Sofia for any of those files. I've been pulling them after she leaves work and when Ian is gone too… No, of course not. I would have said something…"

Kiva sighed aloud, taking a seat at the kitchen island. "And Sofia was sure Ian didn't have the files in his office… He's right. I better go over now… No. He needs to rest. I'll take care of this… Yes, but don't let him near the phone until he's had a good night's rest… Yes, I promise… Right. Love you too." She ended the call, shoving her notes and the pad back in her bag.

Elliott stood, understanding their evening was over. "So, he's going to be okay, right?"

"Well, I might kill him, both of them, for scaring me half to death but yes. It was a false alarm. Something about stress and scar tissue and something-something levels." She set her bag on the entry table, pulling on her jacket and handing Elliott hers. "I have to go into the office. I'm sorry to end our night like this."

"Its okay. You need to follow your dad's lead. Should I call the sheriff? I can have him meet me at the hangar."

"It would be a relief if you could handle that while I work on this." Now smiling, and stepping closer, Kiva wrapped willowy arms around Elliott's neck. "Now kiss me, then head home. If I get into any trouble, I promise you'll be the first to know."

CHAPTER SEVENTEEN

Kiva woke from a dream of being in Elliott's arms. Reaching for her phone, she quickly checked the time, worried she had overslept. Sheriff Dias would be exercising new warrants this morning at six a.m. including arrest warrants for Gent Koehler, Jose Koehler, and good old uncle Ian. She had promised she and Elliott would be in his office by nine. That was when he wanted them to be available if needed.

Last night in her father's law office, it hadn't taken her long to find that the list of files he had dictated was indeed missing. Ian wasn't stupid enough to leave any potential evidence lying around.

She had just decided she would head out to the hangar and surprise Elliott for breakfast when a vehicle pulled up outside. Who... it wasn't even six-thirty. Before she could struggle into jeans and a tee, pounding on her door had escalated to a frantic crescendo. Kiva raced downstairs, two at a time, pulling the big oak door open to a breathless and red-faced Sheriff Dias and the security guy who looked exceedingly uncomfortable. Nodding to the man at his post, she closed the door behind the sheriff who charged in, wheeling on her. "Why the fuck would you tell them we were coming! You stupid... You've blown everything!"

"What are you talking about?" Kiva demanded.

"Like you don' know! They're gone! Fucking Gent Kohler is gone. And your buddy, Uncle Ian. He ransacked the office; his house is emptied out and—"

"Stop!" Kiva ordered, knowing the best way to deal with a cop was to act like one. "Calm the fuck down and get your head in the game! There is no way I would have informed anyone. Come on, Dias. Where's the upside for me, or Elliott?" At the mention of Elliott's name, she watched as he considered the implication. "Don't even think it, David. Just calm down and tell me everything. And then maybe, just maybe, we can figure out where the leak is coming from." She turned her back on him, stomping towards the kitchen, very much a woman on a mission.

"Where are you going?" he demanded in the wake of her retreating backside.

"I'm making coffee!"

He harrumphed. "Yeah. Okay. Maybe I overreacted."

"You think?" she asked accusingly. "Come on, Sheriff. By now you should know better. Any chance this came from one of your deputies? No offense to them, but maybe one has a previous loyalty you know nothing about?"

"Kiva," he said. "Listen. I'm sorry. I was outta line."

She nodded. At least he didn't attach a condition to his apology. She hated that shit.

"I'm sorry too. This is hard on all of us." Pointing to a stool at the kitchen island she ordered, "Sit. The coffee will be ready in a sec, and we need to figure this out. Why don't we start by listing everyone who knew the warrant would come through and what time that was?"

He took out his memo book and read through the details he'd been tracking just in case this happened.

"So, you were already concerned. So much so, you're keeping notes down to the minute."

"Listen Kiva…" He had dropped the angry look, and now the condescending tone disappeared with it. "Here's the thing. When we moved on the bank last week, I didn't like the way some of my men acted. Even though we were executin' a warrant, some a' them was walkin' around like we were the ones breakin' the law. The search was half-hearted at best and none of 'em found anything. I had to go into the back room and toss it myself to find the laptop and phone. If I didn't have that tracker app goin' on my own phone, I woulda assumed they searched the place proper and you and Elliott was wrong about that stuff ever bein' there."

"And you would have been mad as hell," she added.

He nodded.

"How did you organize the search? Did you use some standard procedure or assign sections of the bank to certain officers?"

He waited while Kiva poured the fresh brew and he took a sip. "I assigned them in three parties. Two ta' cover the tellers. I knew they wouldn't be stocked that early but wanted to be prepared, you know, in case Gent Koehler walked in while we was executin' the warrant. I was on the branch manager who opened up for us, and the other two were the ones doin' the actual searchin'. I had them start their sweep like a clock, startin' at the front door, twelve o'clock, and workin' around the dial."

Kiva went to her briefcase and retrieved an ever-present pad of legal paper, then sketched out the basic layout of the small branch. "If memory serves, the building doesn't have much of a footprint. Here are the main doors. Then the public area takes up most of the center. The tellers are over here, the service counter is here, and the loan officer's desk is here." She added a counter to the left of the doors, the loan desk to the right and the teller counter about midway back. She added a square behind them. "Okay, the vault is here, but I don't think it goes all the way back. What else is back there?"

He took her pen and turning the pad around, added the remaining details. "This here is Gent's show office."

"Show office? As in he has another?"

"Yeah. Downstairs is a full office. I'll draw that out in a sec. Let me finish…" He added two more details. "Here's the admin closet, behind the vault. The vault is only for show. They call it the day vault. Over here are the stairs down and a washroom. See, when you look at that app thing, it looks like Elliott's stuff would be in the admin closet, but there's one right below it. I was surprised. I had no idea they had a full office downstairs. Anyway…" He ripped the top sheet off and began drawing a new layout. "You come down the stairs here, and you have a kitchen, another washroom over here, the real vault right under the upstairs vault, and Gent's real office. The second storeroom is in the same place downstairs, just bigger. It was full of old equipment and reams of junk. Honestly, it was a good place to hide that stuff. If I hadn't known what I was lookin' for I never…"

His radio squawked to life. He clicked the mic pinned to his epaulet. "Dias here."

"Sheriff, we got a problem."

"What the hell now!" he growled off mic, then pressed the transmit button again ordering, "Talk to me, Santos."

"We got a fire! We think it started next to the law office, but it's moving fast. Fire department's on another call. They say it'll be twenty minutes before they can get back."

Kiva shared a look with him. Arson looked to be a standard tool in their opposition's playbook. Thinking out loud, she asked, "What about the volunteer fire department. The guys who man the airport?"

Dias shook his head. "It would take them longer than that to reach the airport and drive back."

"What if I call Elliott? She and her guys can drive that old pumper and rescue truck into town."

"Do it," Dias ordered. "Santos, evacuate the block, the entire block. Have Connie call everyone in, we need roadblocks. Shuffle anyone stuck inside the perimeter over to the restaurant."

The radio was uncomfortably silent. When it finally cracked to life, the deputy sounded overwhelmed. "Sheriff, there's already a crowd growing, already too many for the diner."

Kiva offered an alternative: "Hobson's?"

He nodded. "Santos, get them roadblocks ordered up then open the old Hobson's Furniture store. Hold everyone there. That's your command post till I get back. You hear me?" He was already halfway to the door. "And Santos, get dispatch to call in the airport volunteer firefighters. Tell 'em to come straight to the fire. Their equipment is coming to them. Understood?" The deputy squawked his affirmative.

He turned to Kiva who had completed her call and was pulling on her boots and finger-combing her hair. "Elliott and her guys are moving. As long as they can get that old REO Speedwagon started without too much fuss, their ETA is eight minutes."

"Good," he nodded, adding, "Leave your car here. You can roll with me. Make sure everything here is squared away includin' that fancy video system. Whatever's going on in town sounds like a desperate measure to me, but if it's just a ruse, I'd be pissed as all hell if they targeted this place. Kevin's one of the good ones. Maybe one of the last ones." He stopped at the door, adding, "Bring your lawyerly stuff, counselor. I'm going to need you to help with witness statements and such."

Kiva turned on the surveillance system and set the alarm, then followed him out the door with briefcase in hand. She couldn't turn back time, but she could be a good and faithful servant to her community and help in this time of crisis. *Interesting. When did I start thinking of this as my community again?*

Slipping into the sheriff's department's 4x4, she tried to recall just which businesses were in the same block as the law office. Of course, they had to target the one part of the strip without empty stores. Why couldn't it have been one block north, with the empty Hobson's taking up most of the block? She knew the answer. Because whatever Gent and Ian were involved with was so big they would do anything to cover it up. To hell with collateral damage. Those bastards and their associates didn't care if they destroyed the livelihood of innocent people, many of whom, she guessed, wouldn't have the type of insurance needed to cover the loss from a fire. Maybe she didn't have a time machine, but she had information and the letter of the law and God help those assholes intent on taking this town for all it was worth. *Not gonna happen, Uncle Ian. It's just not gonna happen, you greedy son of a bitch!*

CHAPTER EIGHTEEN

When Kiva and Dias pulled into town, two facts were painfully apparent. The town firefighters had yet to return from their callout, and while Elliott and her guys, assisting the volunteers, were doing everything they could, they weren't going to stop the fire filling the air with ash and acrid smoke. At best they would keep it from spreading to another block.

The other fact was harder to stomach. People were scared. While the sheriff headed towards the old pumper truck, she made her way inside Hobson's Furniture store. The place, once the largest retailer in town, was close to three thousand square feet of nothing. A few old tables and some office furniture had been left behind, and the deputies had commandeered them, setting up a primary information center near the pinned open and broken front door.

People, those the deputies had rounded up and evacuated, were standing around with no place to sit and nowhere to go. Santos, the only deputy she could see, was arguing with one of the evacuees and looked to be moments from losing control of the situation.

"Deputy Santos," she interrupted. "You can tell everyone to relax. I'm here to take their statements for the insurance money and department reports."

That wasn't exactly why she was there but gambled on the idea that when money was at stake, people tended to pull in their horns. The angry group, she noticed, was in various states of undress. She'd forgotten the stores had apartments above them. Apartments where people had been rustled from their beds and now stood fearfully facing the prospect of losing everything they owned.

Santos, who gave her an incredulous look, didn't get that she was giving him an out. Stepping closer, she quietly spelled out the situation. "These people are in shock. They need food; they need a place to sit; and they need time to digest what's happening." When he finally caught on, she suggested, "Call the Crow Diner. Tell Gale you need coffee." She looked around, adding, "For at least thirty. And food. Ask for whatever she's got ready, cereals, pastries, pies, the works. Then wake up Ted over at the rental place. Tell him we need tables, chairs, and china, all the cups and plates he has."

"That's stuff's for weddings, not—"

"The wind's blowing south. You saw it yourself. If that fire jumps to the next block, Ted won't have any fine china left to rent out." Finally getting it, Santos nodded, pulling out his phone.

Stepping away, she addressed the group which had moved in closer to hear the exchange. "Okay guys, I know this has got to be scary, but we're going to do this together. Deputy Santos is calling for food and equipment, so we can all get comfortable as we—"

She was interrupted by the sound of sirens. They all turned to watch as the regular fire department trucks raced past the store. There were grumbles and insults tossed around. A few angry faces turned to her wanting to know why it took so long for them to respond. She held up her hands. "Hey! I know we all want answers, but the volunteer guys are here, and they were fast. They have the fire contained. As for the regulars, I understand they were putting out a house fire up county. I know it's harsh, but they can't be in two places at once. That's the peril of a small department, and yes it sucks but we're lucky the airport still maintains a volunteer team and they could get here so fast."

Someone in the back groused about how some folks wanted to get rid of the airport, speculating on how screwed they would be without it.

"You're right. We're lucky we still have them, and that old Elliott Moreno's niece has been training her own guys to be firefighters. They're the reason the volunteer guys got here so fast and the reason this entire town isn't burning."

There were a lot more calls, questions and speculation which she again held up her hands to stop. "I only know what you know, but I promise I'll share everything that comes in and we're going to find out exactly what happened. We'll get everyone some help. I promise."

* * *

It was well past noon when Elliott, still decked out in bunker gear, walked into Hobson's, now the command center. She reeked of smoke and her face was darkened with soot and something else. Maybe disappointment. Her only request was for a few minutes of Internet access on Kiva's laptop. The sheriff had already returned and warned everyone that nothing of the block could be saved. Now he was busy with two deputies taking witness statements and generally keeping people calm. Gale, the woman who owned the Crow Diner, was on hand, serving coffee and sandwiches and cereal while Erica Dunbar had shown up on the heels of the rent-all guy with blankets and more forms for everyone to complete. It turned out she was the county's Red Cross coordinator.

Kiva couldn't believe the amount of paperwork these people were facing, and this didn't include dealing with the insurance companies, for those who had insurance. After taking over a dozen witness statements, she knew none of the apartment renters were insured. It was time to put an end to whatever was going on. Gent and Ian were gone, so why had their goons set the town on fire? She was sure it had been started by them or at least the assholes working for them. She finished the document she was working on and stood to take the young couple who had just lost everything over to were Erica had set up shop.

Her first question to Erica was on behalf of the people gathered, some of them still in their pajamas. "Have you arranged for emergency clothing? I know funds and housing will take a bit but—"

"No worries," Erica said, indicating the chairs in front of her table for the young couple. "The thrift store owner is on her way. She'll see what everyone needs then bring it all back here for folks to pick and choose." Turning to the couple, she suggested, "Why don't you guys sit. Let's get started on these forms. Yes, I know it's a lot of paperwork, but that's just how it works. Once I get everything submitted, we can get you some temporary funds for housing and basics."

They nodded, looking too shell-shocked to know what to say or do. Kiva put a hand on the young woman's shoulder, telling her and her partner, "We'll get you through this. The whole town is behind you."

She stepped away with Erica. "Please tell me you can actually get help for these people. Real help like money and a place to live?"

Erica gave her a neutral shrug. "Money takes time. I'll put the paperwork through immediately, but it's not like the state will declare this an emergency. That means someone will have to evaluate needs and that won't happen overnight. As for housing…" She looked around the long-vacated store. "There are no shelters in Mirabal County. This is it, or maybe the school gym. But that'll be the mayor's call."

Kiva groaned silently. Gent Koehler was the mayor of Illusion Lake. With him in the wind, they would need to assemble the town council and push some political boundaries. The worst part was knowing anyone on the council could be involved in torching the place. "Erica, can you call the council in for an emergency meeting?" Kiva added, "Tell them Gent called the meeting."

"What happens when Gent shows up and tells them I lied?"

She shook her head. "Trust me. Gent will not show and if he does, he has a lot more to worry about than who called in the council."

She headed back to her own table where Elliott was still sitting, head down, in deep concentration. She pulled a chair around the table and sat next to Elliott. "You okay? You don't look so good." Elliott's eyes betrayed her thoughts. She was scared, disappointed, and something more. Kiva knew she needed to move to safer ground. "Can I ask what you're looking for?"

"Property records. Can you…?" she asked, pushing the laptop within Kiva's reach.

She looked at the screen and nodded. "You're on the right track. If I remember correctly, the buildings actually stretch over several lots. Yes. Here we are. There are ten lots with four buildings fronting the street…" She halted her explanation, apprehension worming its way inside her. Every building on the block was owned by the same consortium Gent and Ian were working with to drain the town of its single resource.

"I take it that's news to you?"

She pulled up the online copy of the town survey, hoping she was wrong. The lot layout was hand-drawn and scanned in. Understanding now, she had to face a terrible truth. Her father's law practice, housed in the second building on the block, a building he and his partner owned, or at least she thought they owned, was now listed as belonging to the consortium. Mutely, she pointed this out to Elliott. Why had her father never told her?

"You didn't know?" Elliott said more than asked. "Do you want to call him? I mean, it might be better he heard what's going on from you first."

"You mean better I call and get his reaction before someone can prep him for my questions?"

"Easy." Elliott wiped at the soot caked around her mouth. It looked like she'd been wearing goggles, but the rest of her face was encrusted in the stuff.

"Don't touch your face! The soot is probably full of asbestos and other carcinogens. Those buildings were all put up during the fifties and sixties."

Elliott nodded. "It's bad." She said it quietly, just loud enough for Kiva to hear. "Everything's a loss. Contents, buildings, even the cars parked out back. My guys and the volunteers did everything we could, but you can't fight a four-alarm fire with one pumper with a failing pump and one rescue truck. I think we have to assume the other fire was set to get the regulars as far from here as they could."

Closing her eyes, she knew Elliott was right. "The sheriff told me it was a barn fire on an abandoned property. The dispatcher was told squatters were living there. They wanted to be sure no one was trapped before they abandoned it to come back here."

"Was anyone actually there?"

She shook her head. "Dias has a deputy checking it out and he called Mary Rinaldo, the fire marshal, and asked her to get out there first before she starts anything here. Other than the tracks from the fire crew and the sheriff's department, the deputy he sent didn't see anything to indicate people had been out there in years." She rubbed her forehead again then set her hand on Elliott's thigh, rubbing a spot on the heavy turnout pants. "Is this your great-uncle's gear?"

"Yeah, thank goodness it fits me. The pump on that old truck needs constant attention. I'm not sure I could have stayed as close without this stuff. Of course, the boots are two sizes too big, but it wasn't like I have the training to do much more than I did. I wish to Christ I did. I feel like we let everyone down."

"Elliott, no! Don't think that. You kept a sixty-year-old truck operating while a bunch of weekend warriors did everything they could to keep this fire under control. Whoever is responsible for this couldn't have expected you would be here. I suspect they planned for a lot more damage than this one little block."

"Who? Who could have planned this or even started it? Who does that?"

Sighing Kiva admitted she didn't have any answers.

"Go call your dad before someone else does, Kiva. I know you trust him, and I trust you, but it won't hurt to listen to him, to tell him what you think is happening and ask what he thinks we should do."

Kiva stood, and leaned in to give her a quick, chaste kiss on her sweat-flattened hair. "Thank you. Get yourself a coffee or maybe some water. I'll be right back."

Out back on the old furniture store loading dock, Kiva called her dad at her sister's place in Florida. She was relieved when he picked up. Shay wasn't above screening his calls even on his personal cell phone.

"Hey, baby girl! Your timing is perfect. I just finished the back nine."

"How'd you do?" she asked, not bothering to admonish him for yesterday's health scare. As far as she was concerned Shay was responsible for his health, and she was a doctor. If she thought it was safe for him to be on the golf course, Kiva wasn't going to interfere.

"Not bad, not bad. But I must admit, I'm rusty. Of course, I would be doing better if a baby alligator hadn't stolen my ball from the edge of the water trap on the fourteenth hole."

"Oh, the joys of golf in Florida."

"Don't I know it. So, how is work going? Did you find the files I asked for?"

"Actually Dad, that's why I'm calling."

"That's not like you. What's old Uncle Ian done now?"

She sighed. This was always going to be an awkward conversation, even more so now. "Okay, Dad let's start there. Ian is not my uncle, and I'm hoping he's not your friend. Before you interrupt, I need to ask you some tough questions, and I need you to answer. No waxing poetic. First off, when did you sell the building that houses your office and the rentals above it and why?"

"Kiva. It's not really any of your business, but since you're sitting in my office and covering for me, I'll answer. We sold the building last year. We had a great offer from an investment firm looking to redevelop the town. It's a long-term thing, and since I never imagined you would be interested in the practice, I thought it made sense to have an exit strategy in place. If you're asking because you're interested in staying in town, then don't worry. I'm sure we can work out a longer lease—"

"Dad. I don't think that's going to happen. Please tell me if you're involved in this investment firm or any of their dealings?"

"Kiva. What's this about?"

"Just answer me… *please*," she begged.

She could hear him moving around and realized he was leaving the clubhouse, and probably his golf buddies, to go outside. "Ian did encourage me to invest. Frankly, the returns looked good and I wanted to, but I didn't think you girls needed the income and neither of you would want to be saddled with real estate holdings in New Mexico when you're in Toronto and your sister's here in Fort Lauderdale. Of course, I completely forgot about your mother's house being there, but that's something you girls will have to talk to her about. So, short answer, I bowed out. I guess that was a mistake."

"No Dad, it wasn't."

"What's happened?" he demanded. Her father, the pragmatist, was back.

"Ian is gone, along with Gent Koehler. As in run-for-the-hills gone. And the building, well, the whole block, is nothing but charred ash. I'm really hoping your records are backed up and paper files stored off-site?" She listened to a long silence. "Dad?"

"Ah, yeah, I hear you. Um, let's start with the office. What the hell happened?"

CHAPTER NINETEEN

Elliott couldn't stand the way her face was itching but had taken Kiva's advice not to make it worse. Then Erica spotted her.

"Oh, my goodness, Ellie! What a mess. Let's get you cleaned up," she said, grabbing her arm and steering her towards the washroom.

"There's no soap or towels. I was hoping…"

"Oh gosh, of course. What was I thinking?" Erica changed course for the table where she had piled a truckload of Red Cross supplies, grabbing several items, handing Elliott a small bar of soap. "That stuff is for babies, so it should be okay for your face. Although it may take a bit to scrub off that caked-on mess."

Getting the soap to build a lather was always harder with cold water, but she worked and worked until she could get some decent coverage. She noticed Erica hovering but couldn't talk with her face caked in soot and soap. Instead she nodded, hoping that was all the invitation the woman needed.

"Ellie, I know you probably don't have any answers yet but what the heck is going on? I mean, first there's a fire out at your place now the darned town is half burned to the ground. I know it's not all bad for me. If anything, I'm going to have my hands full getting these folks and businesses resettled but, I mean, should I be scared? Thing is, this place may not be much, but it still feels special to me. We may not all live out there like Kiva's family does, but we all feel a connection." Taking in the filthy T-shirt that Elliott was just turning right side out, she ordered her to wait a sec and disappeared.

Elliott felt a little self-conscious standing in a public washroom with her shirt off, the suspenders to her turnout pants hanging from the loose waist. With the bunker pants, fire boots, and only her sports bra on, she looked more like someone waiting to pose for a calendar than any sort of firefighter. Erica returned with a few tees, all used but clean. While she pulled on a black one that read *Reba McEntire, Cowgirls Don't Cry*, Erica rested her backside against the other sink and continued from before, "I know they call it Illusion Lake. For me, it's always been more like tranquility lake. Maybe some old-timer got here back in the day and saw it when the water was glassy, or all iced up, but it's no illusion. It gives me a real peaceful, tranquil feelin'. I dunno how else to explain it."

Considering the situation, Elliott wanted to share what was going on and get Erica's take, but another part, the part warring in her head, advised her to hold off. After everything that had happened to her over the past few years, she had zero confidence when it came to reading people. Well, maybe she had done well with Kiva. She certainly lucked out there. She said, "Then I guess we need to find a way to help these people out. Afterward, we can put our heads together and see if we can come up with something, some way to create some jobs." She took in Erica's surprised expression before turning for the door. She was halfway back to where her bunker coat hung over Kiva's chair when some guy, across the empty store, started yelling.

"That's her! That's the bitch who started the fire! Deputy! DEPUTY! THAT'S HER!"

Elliott stopped in her tracks, looking around to see who he was fingering. The focus of his vitriol was her. Just behind her, Erica stepped away as if worried she would be encompassed in the accusation. She shouted, "You? You did this?"

"What? No! I just spent the last six hours trying to help put it out!"

Her accuser stormed up to her and started pushing an angry finger to her chest. One of the private security people Kiva had hired rushed in, stepping between her accuser who was aggressively pushing the frozen Elliott. He shoved the man back and took up a defensive posture, but it didn't stop the deputy from moving in and questioning the man who said she'd started the fire. Once he repeated his statement that she was the arsonist, another accuser stepped forward followed by another. Suddenly there was no shortage of people who imagined seeing her carrying gas cans into the law office at five a.m. and driving away as flames began to lick at the windows.

Unable to stop a train wreck in motion, the private guard resigned himself to shielding her from the angry mob as the deputy roughly tossed her across Kiva's work table, cuffed her hands behind her back before dragging her out to the street. Some of the crowd followed and she took a few shoves and hits the private security guy couldn't block. One man got close enough to spit on her while another kicked her low in the ass, delivering a painful blow between the legs. That one almost took her down but the pain from the handcuffs and the deputy hauling her to her feet by raising her hands high behind her back checked her fall and gave her a new shock to manage. At the store's pinned open doors, another deputy blocked the exit so the occupants wouldn't follow. The crowd, half pushing and half dragging him from the door, was enough to motivate the deputy with her to double-time it to the sheriff's office across the street.

They had almost reached the doors when the sheriff himself caught up. "What the hell's goin' on?"

"She's the one who did it, boss. I got all kinds of witnesses says she set the fire!"

Pushing the deputy away, he spun her around, unlocking the cuffs with his own key. "Jeezus, you dumb fuck. She didn't do it. I know exactly where she was when the fire started, and she was nowhere near here. Didn't you hear what she had to say?"

"I got witnesses! They're all sayin' she did it!"

"Better witnesses than me?" Sheriff Dias demanded before asking the stricken-looking deputy. "Who are your so-called witnesses?"

Across the street, angry victims were spilling out of the empty furniture store. Recognizing the threat, Dias nodded to the deputy. "Go find your witnesses and bring them over here right now. I want their sworn statements." To Elliott, he suggested in a kinder tone, "Better we get you inside until we know what's goin' on."

She didn't need to be told twice. Stepping into the county sheriff's office was like stepping back in time. A small waiting room was divided from the rest of the space with a handrail-topped spindled fence, swinging gate included. Not wanting to risk staying too close to the windows she pushed through the gates, only then realizing the private security man was right behind her. He must have been worried too;

he was pushing her into the sheriff's office. She sank into a chair in front of a marred wooden desk while he peered through the only other door, announcing it to be a private bathroom.

"You need to get back out there and find Kiva," she ordered. "Who the hell knows what's going on and I don't know where she is."

He got on his radio to check in with the other members of his team. She couldn't hear the responses with him using an earpiece. Finally he reported. "She's still on a call, out on the loading dock. I have two guys watching her. She's safe for now."

"For now," she reiterated. Not at all confident things would stay that way. "What about my guys?"

"They're on their way in here. We'll bring Ms. Park over too once we have an escape route set up."

Before she could contemplate just what that meant, the sheriff stormed in, and the private security guy stepped out of the office, closing the door behind him. David Dias tossed his badged cowboy hat on his desk, eyeballing her with concern. "Tell me you spent the night with Kiva? I mean, it sounded like you might when we talked last night but if I'm wrong…"

"No," she said. "Her sister called. That's why we canceled. Something about her dad having a panic attack. She went back to the office to pull some files. I headed back to the hangar. My guys and the security detail can confirm that. I was there until you two called this morning."

He slid into his seat. "Your security people said the same thing. And I had a fella on you too. Just checkin'. Good to hear we're on the same page, although…" Huffing, he shook his head. "I've known Kiva since she was a little girl. I feel like I'm supposed to rip a piece offa' you for trying to take advantage. Don't eyeball me, little lady! I can be all protective if I want!" He huffed again, rubbing a hand over his short gray and black bristly hair. "What a goddammed shit storm."

"I hate to ask, but who identified me as the arsonist? I mean, he must be on Gent or Ian's payroll."

He nodded. "My deputy is trying to find him, but I'm guessing he hightailed it out the minute he set the mob on you."

"Erica was just steps behind me. Maybe she knows him or at least the folks who jumped on the bandwagon to get the crowd worked up so quickly." Seeing his face, she softened her stance. "Hey, I get it. These people just lost everything. It's normal to be mad and need someone to blame."

He shook his head. "You just spent all mornin' helping fight that fire. Not to mention committin' your own resources and staff to do it. It earned you at least a few seconds of defense. I can't stomach what's goin' on in this town. And now the way folks are actin', it's no wonder you don't feel you can tell them what's really behind all of this. Yesterday I was thinkin' you were outta line not to trust these folks to manage the lake like a rare and precious resource it is. Now I'm thinkin' I was dead wrong."

Before he could explain further, Kiva pushed through the door, with Jesus and Mac still dressed in their bunker gear, on her tail. "You okay?"

The sound of glass breaking in the front of the sheriff's office had him storming from the room with Jesus and Mac backing him up. The security man placed himself in the doorframe like a last-ditch roadblock. From outside they could hear shouting and more glass falling. This wasn't new breakage but more like the guys were clearing the remains of glass still sticking to the frame of whatever window had been broken.

Dias's voice carried over the cacophony, ordering the crowd to listen to him. He challenged anyone present who saw Elliott Snowmaker in the area before the fire started to step forward and swear out a statement on penalty of law. Suddenly, all those folks who were sure she had been there weren't so sure. Yes, he confirmed, she arrived first with the airport volunteer firefighters, gearing up to fight the fire but before then, could anyone really swear she was there? People grumbled. A few angry folks still tried to make a case for her being there earlier, but he challenged them with ire, explaining he had a deputy assigned to her protection and knew for a fact she hadn't been in town all night. That didn't silence everyone but forced them to back down.

Listening from the open office, Kiva told her, "I was on the loading dock talking with Dad when Erica came at me like a bat outta hell. I guess when she couldn't get her hands on you, she decided I had to answer for her being nice to you."

"I'm sorry."

"Don't be. I had the pleasure of telling her you were with me last night and went home late with your security detail in tow. You did go back to the hangar?"

"Yes. I'm sure security can give you a full report."

"Fine. I'll go get my things, and you can swear out a statement."

Kiva slipped past the young man assigned as Elliott's security detail who was still standing sentry in the doorway. Moments later, he pressed a finger to his earpiece, telling her, "She's getting the detail's records for last night. And just so you know, the sheriff still had a deputy tailing you. Between us, them and your men, it won't take much to straighten this out."

She had spotted the none too subtle deputy on the way home from Kiva's. She nodded her appreciation.

* * *

It took an hour before Kiva was back in the sheriff's office. She had interviewed the deputy assigned to follow Elliott and spoken individually with the leader of the security detail and the men assigned to Elliott herself. She quickly read through their overnight report and interviewed Mac and Jesus, both of whom took offense at her questions until she assured them the effort was to protect Elliott.

Heading back to the office with her notes and her laptop, she reflected that if anyone looked suspicious, it should be her.

Last night, when her sister's call came in, she'd been given a long list of items her dad wanted her to pull from the office. He had received calls that night from both his law partner Ian Guerrero and his old friend Gent Koehler. Both spun desperate stories of Kiva being waylaid by an unscrupulous Elliott Snowmaker and both men had insisted he be involved and get the airport property settled. Kiva's sister had taken him to hospital the moment the stress of not knowing what was happening at home had spiked and his worry for Kiva had sent his vital signs back into heart attack territory. Everyone was pointing at Elliott, yet here she was, the actual person who had been at the office alone late last night, and it was her father who had secretly sold the building to the very people involved in the plan to exploit Elliott's water rights.

Kiva slipped into David's vacated seat to sit across from Elliott. Before she could decide what to say or where to start, Elliott quietly stated, "I'm ready. Should I begin with last night when I left your house?"

Before Kiva could say another word, Erica Dunbar charged in, pushing under the arm of the security guy standing guard in the doorway.

"You little bitch!"

"Erica?" Kiva stood. "Whatever it is that has you so charged, dial it down and think before you say another word."

"Oh, I get it. You and missy here are all lawyered up? Is this what I get for being a friend? You two and whatever it is you got goin' here is gonna damned well ruin me. You know I depend on these folks around here to make my livelihood, and you two have all but destroyed my good reputation!"

Kiva bristled at the accusation. "Erica, what the fuck are you talking about?"

"You saw what's goin' on out there. It don't matter what you two do or did. All anyone's gonna remember is me being all friendly with you two and that's the end of me. I just finished telling your girl here how attached I am to this place. You two must'a been having a hoot at that! I stuck my neck out for you and I even called that emergency council meetin'. There's another thing that'll make me look a fool!"

Not bothering to ask Elliott about the conversation she had apparently missed, Kiva stepped closer to the broiling woman. "We're your friends. Geez, Erica, we've known each other since kindergarten. I promise, we, Elliott and me, we're not up to anything, but we are trying to stop something, something that could destroy this town and bankrupt everyone in it."

Before Erica could round on that or Kiva could explain more, the sheriff cleared his throat. "Erica, settle down! There's a lot of business that needs to be said, and you need to hear it but so does the town council. Most of 'em is here already. I want you to head on over and get things rolling. You too, Kiva. You can report on the statements you've got and how many folks are homeless and with no one and nowheres to go. That'll give them something to chew on till I get there."

Arms crossed in defiance, Erica stuck her chin out, pointing to Elliott, "What about her? She's got a lot to answer for."

"Yes, she does," he confirmed. "I want to personally ask the council to give her and her boys a commendation for all they done today. Then we're going to play back the evidence from the airport fire. Then I got some security footage from here to share. And I'm thinking you should keep your accusations to yourself till you see what I found."

Backing down but still belligerent, she demanded, "How are we supposed to call a meeting without Gent?"

He shook his head. "Gent's long gone, so you better figure it out. You got Kiva here, so maybe she can check the bylaws and figure out how to proceed. Listen to me. I don't care how you get that meeting goin', but get it goin' anyway you can. Ellie and me got a lot of information, some that's gonna be hard to hear, and they need to do more than listen. We're gonna need some decisions made and they need to be made now while the town's still standing. Understood?"

She grimly nodded. Kiva stepped up to her, offering tentatively. "Are you comfortable heading over to the town hall with me?"

Erica nodded again. "This better make a whole lot of sense and soon."

"Sense I can't guarantee, but it looks like the answers are on the way." She led Erica out of the office and hoped Dias would take Elliott out the back way so she didn't have to face the confused and angry crowd. She had plenty of witnesses to Elliott's whereabouts, but no one would take her at her word. She still worried about the depth of the sheriff's allegiances. The security guys were outsiders, and even though they were vetted and well respected, it didn't mean everyone would believe them. It was just a matter of time before someone suggested they were paid to say Elliott was at the hangar. Sometimes, accusations were all anyone ever heard.

CHAPTER TWENTY

By the time Elliott and David Dias entered the town hall, the meeting was edging towards chaos. He grabbed her by the arm, propelling her through the angry crowd, pushing away a few of the aggressive town folk who attempted to get in her face. They passed through the wooden gate into the well, where the judge's desk, witness podium, and jury stand had been replaced with six raised desks for the town councilors. The chairman's desk, with the placard announcing Mayor Gent Koehler, was unoccupied.

Elliott wasn't surprised to see Kiva at the presenter's podium and looking very much like the litigator she was. She still looked confident but stressed. Not having someone to chair the meeting was clearly challenging the council and infuriating the crowd.

Sheriff Dias stepped up and behind the chairman's desk. Grabbing the gavel, he took command of the meeting, slamming it down and warning them all, observers and council alike, that he would not tolerate any more outbreaks or mischief. He asked Kiva to get Elliott set up with her computer while he continued with his own report of the current situation downtown and what his investigation of the hangar fire had revealed. Elliott marveled to see how quickly he took command and how no one, not even the council members, objected to him taking over for the absent and missing mayor.

Kiva, reaching for Elliott's hand, pulled her close by suggesting she could access her Cloud-stored files from Kiva's laptop, explaining quietly to her that the room had a widescreen display as she connected the HDMI cable. Standing there, she logged on to her Cloudserver, seeing her client screen doubled on the wall display left of the mayor's desk. She whispered, "Just how much do you want me to share? I mean, they're already gunning for my head. Do you know there are men outside with guns at the ready?"

Kiva nodded. "Easy, Ellie. Most of them are the sheriff's posse."

"Most?"

"Yes, but I'm counting on Dias to keep control, and you can win these folks over."

"How the hell…" There was a level of desperation in her voice, but her face showed readiness to play her part.

"Easy, Ellie," Kiva repeated. "And no worries, I'll lead; you just give them the basics, and we'll play it by ear."

At the sheriff's signal, Kiva played the edited version of the dash cam footage taken the night of the hangar fire. It was the same version the fire marshal had played for him and the court the day Elliott stood accused of setting that fire too. It was interesting to be standing at the podium, watching the councilors and the town folks crowded in the long rows of benches and lined up all around the edges of the chamber. Kiva's hand was on her back and gently rubbing small soothing circles. She certainly had nothing to do with setting the fires, she told herself, yet in a far more nefarious way, she was the cause. How would things have gone if one of her cousins had inherited old Uncle Elmo's business? All were deeply invested in their lives, families, and activities at home. Any of them would have handled the situation over the phone, accepting Ian Guerrero's offer and liquidating the estate sight unseen. They would have taken his word at face value, pocketing a small reward and considering themselves lucky.

Meanwhile the town would have experienced a short upswing. People would have built homes and taken advantage of the expansion of jobs that would generate more business and more opportunities. Everyone would have believed prospects had turned around for good and just as the residents and newcomers were getting on their feet, the water levels would start to drop, all while the pumping plant went online and the automation process began replacing the people who had helped build the facilities. Soon they and the support workers would find themselves unemployed.

As the shoreline quickly receded, the property values would begin to plummet too, along with the retail and service jobs that had sprung up to serve the expanding workforce. The *coup de grâce* to the town would be the complete automation of the pumping plant, and the new shoreline that could potentially be eaten up by large showpiece estates for the few executives with any interest in spending time enjoying what would become their private lake. Erica Dunbar, like the rest of the town, might not comprehend just how fitting the name Illusion Lake was.

Elliott had to present the situation accurately but with care. Most people could listen to theory but getting them to take the long road, especially if all the rewards looked to lie in a separate closer direction, was next to impossible. She remembered her grandmother complaining that people voted with their pocketbooks, fixated on small dollar items while ignoring the long-term risks that would take the most significant bites from their tax dollars. She understood how hard it was to think of doing right for your grandchildren's futures when you couldn't pay the rent or feed your kids.

Elliott took a deep breath when the sheriff signaled for her to begin. "Thank you, Sheriff, councilors, and ratepayers, for this opportunity to speak on the Illusion Lake situation and its effect on the future of the town and Mirabal County. The information I'm about to share is technical and in places difficult to understand."

She pushed the new county plan layout onto the big screen, then thought better of her choice and began with a series of pictures she'd had the guys take just days ago.

"Hey! That's my house!" one of the councilors interrupted.

"It's a beautiful adobe home on an impressive lot. Did you build it yourself?" she asked.

"What? Yeah, why? What's your point?"

"You like being on the lake?"

"Of course. Get to the point!"

She moved onto the next picture, a two-story farmhouse with a classic fieldstone foundation and red tin roof. "I bet this place has been in the same family for several generations?"

From the second-row bench, a woman stood, all but spitting with rage. "Four generations! Why?"

"You still pump your water straight in from the lake?"

"'Course. There's never been a need to drill a well."

Elliott, nodding, put up another photo. This one was of an apartment above the main street offices. The picture was taken yesterday from the back alley, depicting a new set of stairs and a second story deck, with dormant planter boxes hanging all around the railing.

A man and woman standing along the wall, moved closer to the rail. "Hey! That was our apartment!"

Next, on the big screen, she showed the current plan layout for Mirabal County. On it, she circled the three black squares that represented the house pictures she had just shown them, and the apartment location. While the plan was just black lines on a white page, she had already added blue to color in the lake to make it easier for folks to comprehend what they were seeing.

"This is Mirabal County as we all know it today. Last year, your mayor and bank president Gent Koehler, local lawyer Ian Guerrero, and several powerful figures joined together to form an investment consortium. I know some of you have heard they intend to redevelop the airport property into a gated community. That must sound pretty good and would have brought in some much-needed construction jobs."

Next, she showed them how the final town plan would look if the consortium had managed to accomplish their scheme. In it, the lake was half the size. The existing properties, including the few she had highlighted, were either gone or cut off from the new privatized Illusion Lake. "This is the aim of the consortium. They have purchased all the available waterfront options around the new lake—"

"Wait!" the councilor who owned the adobe house interrupted. "How the hell could they change the lake? You just can't drain it off, it's spring fed!"

Instead of answering, she pushed open a blank Word document and, in a font size big enough for everyone to see, typed: *Harvest 8,809,500,000 Gallons*. She waited for that to sink in, then read the number out loud to be sure they understood.

"The consortium's main goal is not to build houses or create jobs. As a matter of fact, any jobs that might be created will be short-lived. Within a year, they will have built an automated water harvesting plant and within another two, sucked more than eight billion, yes, billion with a B, gallons of water from the lake. Yes, Illusion Lake is spring fed from a deep underground aquifer. This aquifer isn't just the source of water for the lake. It supplies over eight million people with the necessity for life." She pulled up the NOAA hydration chart then overlaid it on a map of New Mexico and West Texas. "What you're looking at is a map of all the places the aquifer supplies water and all the people who depend on that water. Illusion Lake is just one tiny part of what is at risk."

Questions were being shouted, and the sheriff was trying to settle them down. Kiva touched her shoulder, stepping close and whispering in her ear, "Please put the new plan back up. I want to help revisit the location of people's homes."

Elliott nodded and changed the picture on the big screen. There was still a lot of shouting going on.

Sheriff Dias was banging the mayor's gavel. "Ms. Park is representing the town. Frankly, she's the only lawyer we can trust, and she's been sharing everything she's found. She can answer that question better than I can."

Kiva turned to face the townsfolk. "The central question is simple. How much water can the town safely take from the lake? The simple answer is none. The lake is already receding from over-harvesting. We can't take more without causing major changes to the landscape. And even if we didn't care about the outcome, it's not all ours to use as we please. Think of the aquifer as a great big underground lake. And unlike Illusion Lake above ground, this underground water system stretches all the way to Dallas. I'm sure the good people of Dallas-Fort Worth would have something to say about losing their water supply."

While the debate continued, Kiva quietly asked Elliott, "What would you do?"

She had already thought long and hard on the subject. Picking up Kiva's pen she made some notes in the form of points on a new page of the legal pad. When she was done, Kiva raised her eyebrows. "Why don't you suggest this?"

She shook her head. "I'm an outsider. It has to come from you."

"Ms. Park. Kiva!" the sheriff interrupted their *tête-à-tête*. "You've been on this from the start. Why don't you tell these folks what we're suggesting?

Unsurprised by Dias throwing her the ball even though they had yet to find a solution, she turned back to the townsfolk and the councilors. Beside her, Elliott stepped a few feet away to give her the floor and clearly signal Kiva was their leader in this situation.

"The underground water supply may belong to more than eight million residents of two states, but Illusion Lake belongs to all of us, and we belong to it. Mirabal County is our home, and as the ratepayers here, we are the landlords and share responsibility. We could allow the consortium to continue unchallenged and try to live with the fallout and be forever impoverished by our inactions—or we can fight back.

"This consortium, whether operating within or outside the law, is a business and businesses don't like to lose money. They've already outright purchased several properties and the rights to just about everything else. I for one do not want to see our lake forever changed, nor do I want to see just a few folks become ultra rich while the rest of us lose everything we have."

Elliott had to hold back the smile as she watched Kiva in her element. It would be so easy to love this woman. Would she get the chance? Whether she had said it or not, Elliott knew she was not going back to Canada or the airline or any airline for that matter. Restoring aircraft had never been on her radar, and maybe in a few years she would tire of the challenge. But what about Kiva? Watching her lay out her plan for the town, speaking of her desire to right this ship. Was it enough to keep her here? At that moment Elliott understood it would be up to her to present it to her as a possibility. Is that what she wanted? Did she have feelings for Kiva? No doubt, but were they enough? They needed time. Time was everything and maybe the plan she had just suggested was enough to entice the town and maybe Kiva too, in getting to know her, the real her.

The debating, questioning, and planning went on for another two hours. By the time they were done, most of the town had accepted that Elliott was not involved in setting the fire. She was relieved that the question of how and who had been taking water so far hadn't been raised. The other outcome was the appointment of Sheriff Dias as interim mayor. His first official act was to appoint Kiva special counsel to the county in the matter of the consortium and the newly named Illusion Lake adaptation plan.

With everything decided, and despite Elliott's plea not to go for the quick win, the people wanted to be assured of a portion of the spoils. She understood how that could be appealing but worried about how Kiva would pull it off. The plan Elliott had suggested in her points note depended on them being able to wrestle back control and on Elliott herself being recognized as legal guardian of the existing harvesting permit. She was willing to continue with that responsibility, and, of more interest to the people, to equally share the proceeds of all profits any water harvesting created. Now her only question was, could she trust Kiva and Dias to make sure the people got what they wanted now, without her surrendering their future?

CHAPTER TWENTY-ONE

Kiva relaxed into the old clawfoot tub in the master bath. She'd had long days before but nothing like this. Outside the bedroom door, she could hear Mark and Andi getting their kids settled in for the night. They would be living with her while another family, now homeless, stayed in their little cottage. Before the town meeting had wound down, the topic of housing all the displaced residents from the fire had been raised, and Mark and Andi had been among the first to offer to share their little home. But it made more sense for Kiva to open her mother's house. She knew her mom wouldn't mind. She had, after all, invited her ex-husband a decade ago to return to Illusion Lake and take up residence in their one-time family home. Adding a few homeless townies wasn't an issue, but trust in this situation was hard for her.

Her mind automatically turned to Elliott. She assumed they could stay together out at the hangar, but Elliott had already left with the guys to fuel up the fire trucks and return them to the airport. She wasn't surprised to know they were uneasy about leaving the hangar unguarded.

That's when Mark approached her, wanting to help with the housing issue, asking her to consider putting up Andi and the kids.

He'd bunk with his friends so that she would be more comfortable having only another woman in the house. She smiled at his logic. "Andi and the kids, and *you* are welcome in the house. I'm ashamed I didn't think of it myself."

She'd moved to the master bedroom, ensuring privacy with the adjacent bath and full balcony overlooking the lake. She had been going to continue to stay in the guest suite, but Andi insisted she consider her need for quiet and a place to work and take the master. Now, enjoying the old deep tub and listening to the kids rip around the house, she was glad Andi had insisted.

If only Elliott could be here to enjoy it with her. Elliott had handled herself so well during the council meeting. She'd stood tall even when most of the town believed she was involved. Part of her wondered why Elliott hadn't fought the accusations harder, but after talking with Sheriff Dias and the arresting deputy, it became clear that she never had a chance to explain. She was surrounded and then in cuffs so fast even Kiva was surprised by the speed. Of course, the original accuser, the instigator who had whipped the town folks into a feeding frenzy, was nowhere to be found. Dias believed, and she concurred, that he was probably a plant, meant to do just what he had done, take attention away from the consortium's efforts while placing suspicion squarely on Elliott. And it had worked.

* * *

Sitting at the table in the canteen, hair still wet from the shower, Elliott pushed around a bowl of uneaten green chili the guys had made. She could feel Jesus and Mac watching her, but thankfully they knew enough not to ask. She listened absently as they discussed the REO Speedwagon and possible fixes to the failing pump and other snags needing attention. The discussion about keeping the fire trucks working even if the repairs came out of her pocket would ordinarily interest her, but the fire trucks belonged to the county, and today the people of the county had made their feelings clear. They didn't trust her and all the repairs she paid for, and all the time she and her guys had put in meant nothing. All in all, the difficulties she'd faced in the last year had one common denominator: her.

"Is it me?" she asked the guys, startling them.

They shared a look before Jesus cleared his throat. His tone was diplomatic as he answered, "Cap. You're being targeted. Plain and simple. They had a plan, and you screwed it up. Looks like their strategy to turn things around is to make you the bad guy."

Mac continued. "He's right. And as far as folks around here go, well, they don't know you. They know Koehler and Guerrero. Hell, in their eyes those guys are pillars of the community. If they had half an idea how high this thing goes, who knows how they would react?"

"He's right, Cap," Jesus said. "People don't take kindly to having their beliefs turned upside down. And no offense but most of these folks are good old boys if you know what I mean. To them you're an outsider, a woman, and a gay one too. Some folks just can't wrap their heads around all that."

"What about you?" she asked without emotion, and still feeling very much defeated.

She watched as the guys stalled. Finally, Jesus answered. "Captain, ma'am. You saved us, gave us a job, three squares and a bunk. You get us, you're a veteran too, you know what it's like." He ducked his head slightly, explaining, "We heard the nightmares. We got 'em too. Maybe most folks don't get that, but we do."

She merely nodded.

"You okay?" Mac asked.

"I've got what my Nanny would call 'runaway-itis.'"

"You thinkin' about that flying job in Bangladesh?"

Staggered, she asked, "You know about that?"

They shared a look all over again. It looked like the guys could never decide who should speak their joint thoughts. This time it was Mac who confessed. "Sorry Cap, but sound really carries in this place. We heard you on the phone with that recruiter last week. It sounded like you were pretty firm you wanted to stay here."

Jesus nodded, adding, "If that ain't the case, we would understand. We wouldn't want you to turn down an opportunity on our account."

"It's not like that. Besides, I'm not good with turning tail and running. I'm just…"

"…Feeling like you been so far out on point for so long, and with no one covering your six."

She nodded to the analogy. "Yeah." Then she sighed. "And I just can't see the Whiskey X-ray letting up."

They nodded, understanding the WX acronym meant she was in heavy weather. Mac stood, gathering their plates and removing their coffee mugs. He returned with the bottles of premium booze he had found stashed in old Elmo's room. Jesus helped, grabbing glasses and the ice tray from the fridge.

She shook her head. "That won't help."

"We know," Jesus agreed, "but it won't hurt."

That cracked the first hint of a smile. Examining the bottles, Elliott added two ice cubes to a glass and pointed to the twenty-year-old scotch. "I think Elmo would be glad to see us putting his good booze to use. He had such hopes for this place. I keep wondering if he died of pneumonia like the nursing home said, or if it was really a broken heart that killed him."

While Mac poured tequila into his glass, Jesus went for the bourbon. Once their glasses were full, they raised them in unison, and Mac offered, "Here's to our two nations' flags. Colors that never run."

Elliott raised her glass. Scotch wasn't her thing. Still, it was smooth and rich as it burned through her haze. *What the hell.* And hell was where she felt she'd landed.

CHAPTER TWENTY-TWO

Kiva was halfway through her morning routine when she remembered she didn't have an office to go to. That didn't mean she didn't have work to do. Rejecting the dress suit she had planned to wear, she grabbed jeans and a soft cotton button-down from the stack of clothes she had moved from the guest room. Striding downstairs, she was still trying to figure out where she would be meeting her clients going forward much less where she could settle in to conduct the work the sheriff and council expected her to complete. In the kitchen, she was pleased to see Andi had just finished getting the kids fed and was pushing them towards the door and the scheduled school bus pickup.

"Coffee's made."

"Thanks Andi. Where's Mark?"

"He waits with the kids for the bus. He especially likes going out there these days. It gives him a chance to check in with your team, and I think it makes him feel like he's part of something again."

Kiva sipped at her coffee, leaning back against the counter as she considered what Andi had just shared. "I thought things were getting better?"

"They are. They were. I mean, he was doing really well with maintenance contracts, especially on the seasonal properties and landscaping. But now that so many people have sold those places out, the new owners aren't interested in his services."

"I take it those are all places the consortium bought out."

She nodded "Over easy, up, or scrambled?" she asked while pulling out the makings.

"Scrambled, if you don't mind, and let me help with something."

"Okay, grab place settings and tell me if you've figured out where you're moving your practice."

Opening the cupboard, she pulled down three plates. "At the moment, no. I have one appointment today. I figured I could take it at the Crow. There's not much left. Even the sheriff's office is boarded up, not to mention already overcrowded. It's too bad Gent Koehler is a suspect, or I'd ask him about using his basement office at the bank. There's even a separate entrance."

While Andi poured the egg mixture into a large pan, she said, "Mark and I were talking about it last night. He thought you might consider the airport."

Kiva groaned quietly. "As much as I'm sure Elliott would be happy to accommodate me, I just can't ask. Besides, the place may be huge, but every last inch is dedicated to some aspect of old Elliott Moreno's business. I'm not sure his great-niece is ready to shake up the flow he designed."

"Actually, it was the old Fire Hall that Mark was thinking of. Evidently, besides the dorm upstairs, the ground floor includes office space. I guess it was used by the Air Force fire chief and maybe the admins. Mark says there's power and water out there so they can service the equipment. Even the old furniture is still there. It's not fancy. Sort of pre-seventies utilitarian but it's an office, with a waiting room. All you'd need is a phone and maybe Sofia back on reception. I mean if you feel you can trust her?"

"Yes. There's that. I'd forgotten about Sofia. I'm responsible for her job. If I'm not bringing her back, I'll have to let her know."

Andi dished out the eggs, adding bacon to each plate. Kiva took her seat at the island across from Andi who had just put Mark's plate in the oven to keep warm. "I'm not sure who I'd have to approach about using the Fire Hall."

"Well let's see… you're the special counsel to the council. It sounds like that would be your job. I mean, who else is there to ask?"

With her fork halfway to her mouth, she had to grin. "You know your talents are wasted at the Cash and Carry?"

"Yes, but I set my hours, and it's a zero-stress job. Besides, you need me there where I can take the pulse of the town and keep you informed."

She said it with a straight face, and Kiva realized she was serious. Deciding to test her, she asked plainly, "Okay, tell me this. What do folks around her think of Elliott? Elliott Snowmaker, not her great-uncle."

"Now you're talking," Andi said with a grin. "Some think she's stuck-up, but most think she's on the shy side like her uncle. They don't really understand what she's doing out there at the hangar, but they never understood what old Elliott was working on either. They just knew it brought money in and kept the airport open. I don't think the mayor, ex-Mayor Koehler or Ian Guerrero, ever understood how important the airport is to the people around here."

"Explain?"

"It's like having the airport keeps the town open for business, or at least in the business of opportunities. Without it, people worry Illusion Lake will become nothing more than an out of the way backwater no one takes an interest in. You never saw how half the town went out there when old Elliott had the test pilot come down to fly his rebuilds. And when a buyer would fly in. *Wow!* Last year, someone came in on a fancy private jet. That had all the kids out. Another time, some guys flew in in an old World War Two bomber. I can't remember what kind it was, but everyone in town went out for a tour. Some even paid to go for a ride. The talk around town is that young Elliott is almost ready to test fly a real old one. One with double wings. You don't know how many people are asking me to tell them when that'll be."

Kiva sat back, only then realizing she had polished off her breakfast. "I had no idea. After yesterday..."

"Kiva. Can I make a suggestion?"

She was not sure she wanted to hear it, but curiosity and Andi's insights intrigued her. "Sure."

"She seems nice, and kind, and just what you need."

"You know?"

Andi smiled, "It's not like there are a lot of gay girls around here. Well, except for Erica, and that woman is way too high maintenance. I mean she's pretty, but God, she needs to bring it down a couple a dozen notches."

She grinned her response. "So, you don't have a problem with Elliott?"

"Hell no! I think that woman may have saved this town and I'll be sure to straighten out anyone still walking around thinking otherwise. Consider it my job. Okay?"

Kiva nodded. "I may have to put you on the payroll."

"Hardly. You've put a roof over our heads and given us a footing in this town. But if you feel the need to do more, Mark could use a reference. I don't know if Elliott could use another hand out there, but I have to say he never stops talking about everything she's got going on."

Finishing the last of her coffee, Kiva set the mug down, offering, "I'll make sure Elliott knows Mark is interested. If she can't use him, he'll be my number one on the list for new jobs to help get the town turned around."

"And I'll keep my ear out for how folks are leaning."

CHAPTER TWENTY-THREE

As planned, Kiva met her one appointment at the Crow. Once they were finished, the other diners wasted no time cornering her and pushing for answers. As much as she believed they all deserved to be heard, she also knew this was no way to get anything done. Finally making her escape, she headed straight for the boarded-up sheriff's office.

The place was busier than usual and chaotic. Bypassing the desk officer and the admin trying to manage the small crowd, she headed straight for Dias's office, knocking once before letting herself in. She hesitated in the open door when she spotted two deputies in with him.

He waved her inside. "Good, you're here. How was your meeting at the Crow?"

Taken by surprise, Kiva shook her head, "How did you know?"

The smile he offered was classic Dias. "This is my town. I know everything."

"All right then, you must know why I'm here."

He nodded. "You need a place to work, and you want to know when my lone criminalist and the fire marshal will finish their reports."

"Well Sheriff, you're a regular Mister Wizard."

Deputy Lozen laughed openly while DaSilva hid his amusement. Dias gave them the stink-eye before returning his attention to Kiva. "Buzz is, the Fire Hall at the airport might work for you, and as a bonus, that's where we put Sofia and her husband. That's not gonna be a problem, is it?"

"You tell me?" she asked.

Instead of answering directly, he turned his head to Lozen. She, in turn, opened her memo book and read from her notes: "Sofia Gonzales. Sixty-two, married to retired schoolteacher Sabastian Gonzales, who is known to the town as Bash. There is no history of unusual contact between them, the consortium, Koehler, or her employer Ian Guerrero. The only real estate the pair own is a small cottage right on Bull Draw off County Road Four. They've rented an apartment over the law office for the last four years, ever since Mr. Gonzales's eyesight began to fail and he lost his driving privileges. The only banking records I could find was a set of joint accounts here in town. Those records are as regular as clockwork with zero exceptions. Neither of them has been out of the country in more than ten years, and other than taking Bash into Albuquerque twice yearly to visit an eye specialist, they haven't even been out of town. The only extravagant expense they have is the eye doctor, but that's partly covered by the health insurance from Sofia's employer, which she contributes to and has for as long as I could find records."

"In other words, she looks clean," Kiva said.

"Squeaky," Lozen confirmed.

"They're staying at the Fire Hall. Why not go home? I mean, their house is sitting there. It's got to be a lot more comfortable than bunking in temporary quarters."

Dias handed her a printout, explaining, "Here's the list of all the displaced folks and where we've got them and how long they can stay." She took the page as he continued, "Sofia and Bash were one of the first ones to trade down. Much like Mark and Andi Coe did. They figured their cottage was a better fit for one of the homeless families and the Fire Hall sort of suits Bash better. It gives him somethin' to concentrate on, which is what Sofia was hoping for. He's offered to man the emergency phone lines. The phone company's supposed to be out there now, addin' lines for the county dispatcher and nine-one-one."

That information came as a surprise to Kiva who said nothing but couldn't help raise an eyebrow.

He smiled, stating simply, "I have my reasons. Now, if I remember right, there's more than enough room for you and Sofia to run your practice and take care of the county out there and still house the dispatch office. It also puts more eyes out there and should ease up on the stress Snowmaker and her guys have been under. I'm also hopin' it makes things real clear to everyone concerned that the airport is county property and county business will not be affected by the actions of a few greedy and disloyal SOBs."

"Wow, Sheriff. Don't hold back."

He grinned, then pointed. "Chief Deputy Lozen here will follow you out to the airport. I know you have your security people out there, but it's about time we show some force too. She's goin' to be hangin' around helpin' get the new dispatch office set up. Anything you need, let her know. And Kiva," he added, once again serious, "when I say anythin', I mean that. Now we got the books open, we found a heap load of Fed money that should have been goin' for emergency services among other things. I mean to fix that straight up."

"Understood." Kiva folded the multipage printout detailing the housing situation and placed it in the side pocket of her attaché. "Looks like I'm off to the airport then. If I need any basics, I'll get Sofia to call here…"

"Just have her contact my admin. Or ask Lozen here. She's on facilitation duty so let her do the facilitatin' while you get to work."

All the way to the airport Kiva debated whether to drop in on Elliott. She was combing through a long list of excuses to visit. She could bring Elliott lunch from the diner, or she could say she was stopping in to let her know she'd be working from the Fire Hall, or maybe she could…she could just stop in. By the time she reached the airport, she simply resigned herself to getting to work and worrying about Elliott later.

Walking into the Fire Hall, she was greeted by Sofia Gonzales who looked to be scrubbing her way through the waiting room. Judging by the before and after comparison, the last time this place was used as intended, smoking indoors was still allowed. "Sofia, you don't have to do that."

"Oh, I don't mind. Besides, if we're going to make this place work for everything you have on your plate, we may as well make it look respectable."

"Okay. What can I do?"

Sofia stopped her scrubbing, placing her wet hands on her hips and giving Kiva a motherly look. "You can get to work. Your office is clean and ready. I just need you to make a list of things you need before I head over to the Cash and Carry. Oh, the phone people just finished up in there. I asked them to set up a toll-free number and the main line like before, but I didn't bother with the private lines we used to have. You never used your dad's and well, Ian…"

"Yes. Good old Ian. How are you doing with all of that?"

The subject looked to deflate her. Finally, she shook her head. "I knew he was up to no good, but I didn't think it was my place to say anything. Now I…"

Kiva stepped closer, resting a gentle hand on her arm. "Sofia, you didn't do this. And having a feeling is not the same as knowing full well what was going on."

"I didn't! Please Kiva, you've got to believe me. I've seen Ian do a lot of less than reputable things over the years, but I never suspected he would be part of something like this!"

Kiva pulled her father's steadfast assistant into her arms. "Don't you worry. I can't imagine what you and Bash are going through. Even Dad's beside himself over Ian's betrayal of you, him, the practice, the clients and the town." Releasing the older woman, she asked kindly, "Are you and Bash okay staying here? I mean…"

"It's perfect. Oh, it may be old and on the drafty side but other than being in town where Bash can get around on his own, this is perfect for him. I think he was hoping to be some sort of help to Miss Snowmaker and her boys, but when the sheriff asked him to consider taking a spot as a nine-one-one dispatcher, well, he was just tickled. He's in with Connie right now, getting a crash course on the protocols."

Kiva looked where Sofia had indicated. "You know, I've never actually been in this building. Care to give a tour?"

Smiling, Sofia nodded, and led the way. "It's bigger than it looks sitting all by itself so far from old Elliott's hangar. This is the old waiting room. I have no idea what folks would be waiting for in a fire station, but it's open to this office. I figured I'd use it as the admin area and reception. I know that makes for a big waitin' room, but I've got a feeling we're gonna get a lot of drop-ins over the coming days."

"I agree. And it's perfect. Okay, where have you got me set up?"

Sofia led her down the long central hall. "Washrooms are on the right here. There are three offices down on the left side, the sheriff said you get the first, and his department would share the second with us. Don't know what that means but I'll leave it to you. Then 9-1-1 is next after that." She waved a hand toward the office meant for Kiva. It was clean with a sizable desk, set in front of a window that looked north towards the lake.

Stepping behind the desk, Kiva set down her attaché and turned to look out the window. Other than the unkempt fields and the lake, she could glimpse the edge of the runway but not all the way to Elliott's hangar. She smiled to see the new phone. Chairs had been found along with a tall bookshelf that looked to be the match of the battered and blemished desk. At least the office hadn't been painted orange or some match to the decade the building was last used.

Sofia followed her eyes as she took in the two-tone Air Force blue walls. "I was thinking we could order some big prints of the county, both now and what them devils had been planning towards and put them up. A real before and after. You know, sort of to remind folks what we're risking here."

"Good idea. Elliott has a large format printer and all the files."

Sofia nodded, pointing out the window. "As soon as I hear the FAA inspector leave, I'll call over and ask about getting copies."

"The FAA?"

Seeing her concern, Sofia soothed, "Bash was talking with the boys last night. Seems she's getting ready to fly one of those old planes they been working on. I'm sure it's all part of what they do over there. He's all excited. Says if things go good today, tomorrow will be the big day. I expect half the town will be out to watch. If so, we should be prepared. I'm thinking that afterward they'll be by here to see you."

Kiva didn't know which troubled her more, the idea that Elliott might take that old bi-wing trainer for a spin or having a line of drop-ins on her door. Trying to keep her tone neutral while she digested the risks, she suggested, "How about showing me the rest of this place?"

Sofia led her back into the central corridor and down a smaller aisle between the washrooms that opened to the old meeting hall. At present it was being cleaned and already housed a few displaced women and kids. Back in the central hallway, they stopped at the third office, the one-time radio room the sheriff had repurposed as the new county 911 dispatch center. Sofia's husband Bash was there and training with Connie, the county's lead emergency dispatcher. After greeting them, they toured the kitchen and a large separate lounge area, finally ending up in the garage section.

"They call this the apparatus floor," Sofia said as she waved her hand at the trucks and people gathered at various chores.

Kiva wasn't surprised to see Mac or Mark, but the number of other people confused her. Chief Deputy Lozen had pulled her 4x4 into one of the empty truck bays, and there were five more for a department with only the two antique fire trucks to fill the space. Waving the deputy over, she had to ask, "Who are all these people?"

"Volunteers. The sheriff was out here last night and told folks if they didn't have a job to go to, they could consider themselves volunteered. The county fire chief and two of his lieutenants are here too. They plan to get everyone organized and do some training."

"All of these people are living here?"

Deputy Lozen looked around. "About half, I'd say. The rest are genuine volunteers. Nothing gets folks interested in helping than feeling helpless after a catastrophe. Everyone wants to be a hero."

Looking around at the faces, she recognized only a few, and the security implications hit her full force. Remembering the time Elliott spent explaining the security levels for airports, she worried that the county, by not locking and guarding the airfield, was already in violation. "Since everyone staying here and those technically volunteering are, as Elliott would say, 'Airside,' I think we need to have a roster, maybe even ID badges."

Lozen seemed perturbed. Looking around she finally nodded. "I get what you mean."

"Do you know all these people, who they are?"

"Mostly," Lozen answered.

Sucking in a deep breath and preparing for pushback, Kiva ordered, "I want background checks on everyone. Then we'll issue ID and let's make it a rule that they have to wear them whenever they're out here."

"I'm not sure how that'll go over. Besides, where would we get stuff like that?"

Kiva reassured her. "Don't worry, I'll order everything." Turning to bring Sofia into the conversation, she added, "Let's set that second office up as security and badge control. That way people expect going forward that the sheriff's department and by extension, the Fire Hall here, requires everyone to check in and pass background checks. I don't want a repeat of the scene we had at Hobson's with some ringer for Gent and Ian slipping in and causing trouble."

Turning back to Lozen she asked her, "Can I count on you to get me a complete list of everyone staying out here, and all the volunteers, and to get those background checks started?"

Lozen rocked back on the heels of her western boots, thumbs clipped inside her gun belt. "I may need some help. We usually send that sort of thing up state to handle. I mean. I can handle the criminal part, look for warrants and stuff but…"

Kiva patted her arm reassuringly. "How about I lend you my investigator? He can handle the rest."

She nodded. "That'll work. I'll get started as soon as these folks get the trucks unloaded."

"I wanted to ask about that," she said, watching as Mac and two other men helped the driver from the appliance store wrestle the most massive refrigerator she'd ever seen from the back of one of three trucks crowding the empty bays. Beside them, several other volunteers and even the regular firefighters were opening box after box and lining them up. Some were marked with the Amazon logo while others looked to be from the Cash and Carry and a few other local stores.

Sofia, always helpful and in the know, explained, "Oh, that was all Miss Snowmaker. She is such a kind woman." Looking to Kiva, she smiled. "Of course you know that. Anyway, she was out here last night with the sheriff, walking around like she was the inspector general himself, clipboard and all." She colored a little as she explained, "I didn't think much of it—*her* last night. I mean we were all tired, and things out here were, well, less than comfortable but she kept promising to make it better as soon as she could. Then about an hour ago, these deliveries started showing up. Blankets, pillows, linens. She even ordered a top of the line washer and dryer set. Mark and the boys just got them connected. It all seems so generous. Well, I guess the county will pay her back, still…"

"Yeah, still," Kiva said, not at all surprised by Elliott's generosity. She shook her head. While she had been at home enjoying a hot bath, Elliott had been here compiling a list of all these people would need just to feel comfortable while they took time to rebuild their lives.

Seeing the boys had the new fridge on a dolly and were pushing it towards the big kitchen without much effort, she called Mark over and stepped aside to speak confidentially with him. "So, I hear you're volunteering for the fire department?"

He nodded sheepishly, shoving his hands in his pockets.

"If it won't be too much of a disappointment, I have a job for you, a paying job." At his surprise, she cautioned, "I don't know how long it will last and it may get uncomfortable…"

He grinned. "I'm already intrigued. When do I start?"

She smiled too. It was hard not to with him. "I need an investigator and someone to work closely with the sheriff's department. You'll be doing everything from helping with background checks to badge control. We're going to have to badge everyone living or working out here. Will you be comfortable with that?"

He just smiled, offering his hand, and asking again, "When do I start?"

Back in her new office, she pulled out her ever-present legal pad and began making a list of everything they would need. She handed it to Sofia, along with her credit card. "See what you can grab in town."

"And the things I can't get here?" she asked, reading the long list, her eyebrows rising.

"Let's follow Elliott's example and try to fill the list locally first. Everything else we can order to be overnighted from Staples or Amazon." Without any fuss, Sofia left her to work. She pulled out her laptop, notes and the few files she had. There was no Wi-Fi. Remembering the phone company technician was on site, she slipped out of her office and was glad to find he was still in dispatch. She explained that she needed broadband and wireless added to the order and was temporarily confused when he asked to which firm to bill the service and installation. It was a good question. She couldn't bring herself to use Deegan, Guerrero, and Park. As much as it was still a legal entity, she didn't want to be associated in any way with Ian Guerrero. She gave him her own name, knowing she could change the bill-to later. Would she? It was time to answer that question, not just for work but for her and Elliott too.

Returning to her new and very empty office, she grabbed her phone.

CHAPTER TWENTY-FOUR

Elliott had spent most of the morning with the FAA inspector. He carefully covered every detail of the final inspection, taking notes and photographs and explaining as he went. He wasn't enamored with everything she'd done but couldn't find fault from a structure or airworthiness perspective. Once done, they sat in the canteen where he completed the inspection certificate and explained exactly what she would need to do to complete the flight testing. He didn't like that she was signing off on the airframe, electrical, and the flight test too, but there was no rule against it, and she was more than qualified, which he checked thoroughly to be sure.

"When will you perform the flight test?" he asked.

"I wanted to do it today, but the boys tell me it's a big deal around here and the people of this town have been through so much I figured I'd let everyone know. So I'll do it tomorrow. Probably early before the winds pick up."

He nodded to the logic. Sampling the coffee she'd poured for him, he hummed his approval. "I'd like to stick around. Old Elliott used to offer me his guest room. Is that offer still open?"

"Ah…" she stalled, trying to decide where she could sleep if he took the guest room and the boys had Elmo's and the old sitting room.

"We're a little short on space...but, yeah. I'll figure something out. It'll be good to have you here."

He nodded, seeming to relax. "Your uncle used to talk about you," he said without elaborating.

She didn't bother to correct him on the uncle thing. She'd long tired of explaining that Elmo was her great-uncle, and in fact, what difference did it make? She had always relegated Elmo to a relative she didn't often see or know too much about. But now she realized that Elmo knew her, cared deeply about her and, much like her grandmother, he was probably the only person in her family who had. How strange was it to have such a large family and understand that only two of them cared at all? She hadn't spoken with her father since her sister's wedding; and her brother? He was always proud to call when he was clean and scarce as hell when he wasn't. As a teen she always imagined her mom would have her back but coming out had disproved that theory and in a big way. That day, her mother had said things Elliott would never forget, but it was the meanness in her eyes and the chill that rolled from her words that had most shocked Elliott. She'd found herself on the street that night, cold, alone, and scared. The next day, after school, she had gone to her grandmother, hopeful but prepared for more of the same. But Constance Moreno Green knew the sting of family hostility and she knew her granddaughter. The next day the old girl went with her to the office of the local military recruiter and signed her joining papers as her legal guardian. Nanny knew the recruiter wouldn't be interested in challenging her claim of legal supervision. Now she had her Nanny on her side and a part time job in the militia of the Canadian Forces. Thinking about it now, she realized Elmo would have been quickly appraised of her situation. She had never given it much thought, but in a way, her grandmother and old Elmo had been better parents to her and better influences on her than anyone else. She owed then so much.

Nanny, I owe you so much gratitude. I promise, I'll soon be able to show you.

How strange to be so far from home to find the family life she always craved. While the thought startled her, it felt good. The only thing that would make it better would be to have Nanny here. She knew the old girl wasn't ready to say goodbye to her friends much less the excellent healthcare available to her in Toronto, but she could offer to fly her down for visits. Yes. It was time her grandmother got to see just what her baby brother had built.

Excusing herself from the inspector, she climbed the stairs to gather a few books, pack up everything she would need for tomorrow's flight: flight suit, long underwear to protect her against the chill of flight in an open cockpit, and her flight bag. She added a change of clothes and then dragged everything to the library. She could bunk on the couch for the night. Returning to the guest room, she grabbed her pillow and stripped the bed. The least she could do was give the guy clean sheets.

Once the washer was started on the linens, she found an extra blanket and took it and her pillow to the library. Although it had become much more than a library. It was her living room and Kiva's occasional office. *Kiva.* She should call her. Late last night after she had placed her orders for all that she needed at the Fire Hall to give those poor displaced people some comfort, she lay in bed unable to think of anything else. After a very long day and a long hot shower, she still couldn't sleep. So much had happened. The fire, the county meeting, the details needing attention, had blurred her desire for Kiva.

It had always bothered her how her parents and their friends could spend entire evenings discussing other people; speculating on their motives, their behavior, their lives, and drawing conclusions based on their assumptions alone. Her family, like so many others, considered themselves superior. They celebrated their own lack of failures, oblivious to the fact that they had never tried anything different from what they knew, never taken a chance. No wonder they looked at her like some weird and stupid loser. Elmo too had been judged by them, and they took pot shots at her grandmother too. Maybe she was a target simply because she was different. The thought took her back to her basic military training.

She and her fellow recruits had one class every afternoon just after lunch. The morning was filled with drill, PT, and other physical training classes, then a big hot lunch which the military called dinner. By the time they entered the too hot theatre, they were exhausted. The instructor warned that falling asleep would come with serious consequences. Anyone who couldn't stay awake during the lecture was to stand. Of course, no one would. No one wanted to be that person.

Midway through the second lecture, Elliott couldn't take it any longer, and even though she was sitting in the center of the second row, she stood. The instructor, mid-sentence, stopped dead, and she quaked silently as he marched to where she stood. She was expecting to be called out and punished on the spot.

"SNOWMAKER! You havin' a hard time staying awake?"

Here it was. Elliott was about to get her ass handed to her. All around her, it seemed the other ninety-eight course mates were tittering, waiting for the hammer to fall. With no way out she admitted her drowsiness, "Yes, Chief!"

Simply nodding, he chewed out the rest of the platoon, implying she was the only one with the balls to do the hard things. He went on to add, "Just remember: You can't fall if you don't stand up! If you don't stand up, you can't get anywhere, and this life you've chosen means you'll need to go places. Learn to take chances, learn to stand up. Never worry about falling or failing. We all do. In time your mates will learn to trust you and you them. Learn to stand up and have their back, and when you do, they'll always have yours."

It was admirable advice and she learned to trust that her squadron mates would always have her back. Civilian life was different though. Who had her back now? Who trusted her? She knew she could count on her grandmother, but there was little she would ask of an elderly woman other than for her love which she received without question. And Elmo too—she now understood how deeply he cared for her and had been there in his own way. Who else? Did Kiva truly trust her, have her back? She refused to speculate on the motives of others, to judge people like her family did. There was only one way to really know.

Once she informed the FAA inspector that his room was ready and the security detail would let him pass at will, she found her phone and tabbed to Kiva's number.

Kiva picked up with a charming greeting: "Hey you! I was about to call. How did the FAA thing go?"

"I... ah, it went well. He didn't like some of the modifications I made, but they're all within standards so, everything passed. All that's left is the flight test."

There was a long silence. Finally Kiva admitted her worry. "That kind of freaks me out. Are you sure you want to do that? I hear old Elliott used to get someone from Albuquerque to come down."

"Don't trust my flying?"

"Ah, no. That's not it. And before you draw a conclusion, I trust your aircraftership too. I just, well, it's an old plane and so..."

"Made of sticks and glue?"

That made Kiva laugh, the sound through the crisp digital line making its way right through her.

"Good description. Listen, I'm at the Fire Hall, do you mind if I come over to do some work? Maybe we could have some lunch and talk?"

"Both sound good. Although it looks like I'll be entertaining the FAA inspector for lunch if you don't mind sharing whatever I warm up?"

"That's not a problem. Listen, do I drive all the way around the field, or can I use the little road beside the runway?"

She smiled to have Kiva ask. "Normally I'd say use the taxiway, but with the FAA here to witness our indiscretions, I suggest you go around. And you might want to put the word out to the kids who race here that tonight might not be a good idea."

"Not a problem. Besides, you've earned their trust. I think they'll more than heed the warning."

That was interesting. At least she could say she had earned the trust of one group. Would others follow? "What about you? Have I earned your trust?" She hadn't meant to ask, at least not on the phone, but there it was, out in the open.

"Oh, Ellie... You have earned more than that and I'm so sorry I've given you cause to ask. Here's what we'll do. I'll run into town, grab lunch for everyone from the Crow and meet you and the guys, and the FAA person, in the canteen. After lunch, we can head up to the library and talk about everything. There's so much I want to know too, and so much I want to share. Sound good?"

"Sounds perfect. See you then."

* * *

Lunch had been a boisterous affair. Between Elliott's guys, Mark, the security detail, and the FAA man, everyone had dug into the mixed bag of sandwiches, grabbing takeout containers of soup and chiming in on how the morning was shaping up. The security detail was mostly worried about the number of newcomers at the Fire Hall, and the FAA guy too was concerned, but Kiva explained her plan to get them all background-checked. She'd already supplied the security detail with a list of the folks, both volunteers and displaced, so far authorized to be at the airport, or more specifically, the Fire Hall.

Elliott took some ribbing for all the stuff she had ordered, especially the big screen TV and the oversized fridge. They compared the fridge to the sixty-year-old unit in the canteen, which she hadn't bothered to update. With its barrel-shaped door and locking pull handle, it was a relic. She had taken the teasing with grace and a few back pats before the guys, along with the FAA inspector, headed back over to the Fire Hall. Up in the old library, Kiva and Mark sat at the desk and built an itemized list of what he would need to do to complete their part of the background checks, then she sent him on his way.

Joining Elliott on the couch, she watched her set aside a binder of poorly photocopied, old fashioned typewritten pages. "You have been nonstop for days now. What are you working on?"

She smiled, looking pleased to have Kiva there. "The operational numbers for tomorrow's test flight." At Kiva's pained look she warned, "Don't do that. It's perfectly safe and I know you don't know this, but I'm good, really good…"

Kiva's laugh lit up her face, "Oh I know you're good! It's the flying thing I'm worried about." As she said it, her hand migrated to Elliott's thigh, rubbing gently back and forth.

"Does this mean we're okay?"

Moving closer, Kiva asked, "You tell me."

Nodding, Elliott seemed reluctant to trust her voice. Instead, she took Kiva's hand in hers, interlacing her fingers and holding it closer. "I…I want you to know, I've decided to stay here. Long-term I mean. I like the work I'm doing. Love it actually, and…" She took a big breath, sucking in air. "I want to see if… well, I know you might go home but while you're here, I mean, if you want, well…"

"Yes Elliott. Me too." Moving closer, she ran a hand through Elliott's too long bangs and pushed them out of her eyes, tracing her fingers over her cheeks and along her strong jaw. "I want you too. I want a relationship, a chance at something more, and…" Seeing her easy acceptance, she sat back cuddling in close. "I had a long talk with my father this morning. I convinced him, without much effort, to dissolve his partnership with Ian. He's not sure when he's coming home. Probably not until spring and he's thinking he'll keep spending his winters in Fort Lauderdale with my sister and her kids, but when Dad's home he wants to continue practicing. How does Park and Park, Attorneys at Law sound to you?"

"It sounds amazing! Perfect even, but what about your job up north?"

"I think they already assume I'm not coming back. Besides, it's not like it'll be a hardship to replace me. Lawyers, even good associates, are a dime a dozen in Toronto. Dad's doing all the paperwork to dissolve his practice today. He's hoping to get the paperwork witnessed and FedEx'd to me so I can file it tomorrow. He's sending his half of the new partnership agreement too so I can file that as well. With luck, we'll be in business before the week ends."

"That's incredible! Can I be your first client?"

Kiva was all smiles. "Let me guess, you need new sales and service agreements? And if I know old Elliott, he already had someone interested in that little plane?"

"Right on both parts, counselor. If the flight test goes well, the young woman will be here Saturday. She's flying up from Dallas with her dad."

"So soon?"

Elliott nodded. "Maybe we can squeeze a familiarization flight in tomorrow afternoon? I've been dreaming of taking you up."

"You have?"

"Well, yeah…" She grinned, color racing up her neck and burning her cheeks.

Kiva beamed. Only Elliott would be open enough to admit what she'd been thinking and shy enough to be embarrassed. "You! Oh, Ellie. Come here." She pulled her close. Their lips had hardly met when someone close by cleared their throat.

"Sheriff!"

He grumbled a greeting, sliding into a chair across from them. They moved apart but held hands. It wasn't like the sheriff didn't know they were involved. "What can we do for you?" Kiva asked.

"Lozen tells me you want background checks on everyone out at the Fire Hall?"

Prepared for pushback, she explained, "I do, and I know it's a lot of manpower you probably can't afford, but…"

He waved her off. "No, I agree. And I got some legal things I need you to unravel. I think I mentioned the feds have been sending us money and equipment. At least that's what's in the books but we never seen hide nor hair of it." His discomfort was more than evident. With the situation or with them? "Kiva. Some of that stuff we was supposed to get is weapons. Assault rifles and the like. This whole thing is makin' me sick."

That answered her question, and now the implication was clear. Much as she was relieved to know he could accept the two of them, the town's situation was not tolerable. "It sounds like we can add weapons trafficking to the list. Have you informed the FBI?"

He nodded, not at all pleased. "They're sendin' down two agents. I gotta tell you I don't like outsiders snoopin' around, especially now."

Elliott asked simply, "What can we do?"

He looked at her carefully. "You already done so much and after the way this town, me especially, been treatin' you…"

"Sheriff, this is my home now. We may have gotten off to a rocky start," she said, looking to Kiva to be sure she knew she was included, "but we're all past that. So, let's get on with doing what's best for everyone. Agreed?"

He nodded, and Kiva squeezed her hand.

"Well then," the sheriff began, "I need to deputize your boys. I know they're on your payroll and I'm not gonna start orderin' them around, but I want all the loose ends cleaned up before the feds get here—"

Kiva interrupted. "I just hired Mark to be my investigator. Will that be a problem?"

"Lozen told me. I'll deputize him too, just to cover our collective butts. And you were right about insistin' everyone stayin' and volunteerin' out here be ID'ed. I know the airport is on county land, but it never occurred to me that operations, and security, are still a federal concern. At least not until that FAA man walked into the Fire Hall. So, do whatever you have to do but do it fast. Understood?"

"Absolutely. As long as Lozen or whichever deputy you assign out here can get the police portion of the background checks done quickly, we can do our part too. What will you do if anyone out here refuses to submit to the background check?"

He harrumphed, before stating plainly, "If they're homeless, we'll have to find some other place for them. If that's the case, hand 'em over to Erica and tell her I'm requestin' the move and fast. If it's one of them new volunteers, and there are considerably more than I'm feelin' good about… Well, we'll just send 'em away. To me it's simple enough. If they refuse to be checked out, we are gonna refuse to let them help out. I got no problems with it. I talked to the fire chief, and he said the same thing. All his guys had background checks run when they was hired, so we'll do the same."

She nodded, glad that was settled.

* * *

While Kiva now had a perfectly good office to use, she had stayed at the hangar, wanting a day to get some serious work done before she started taking appointments. She wasn't avoiding the walk-ins and the overwhelming number of new clients already camping out in the Fire Hall; she just needed time to come up with some answers.

Sitting at the desk in Elliott's library, she was deep in thought. Mark and Deputy Lozen had done a bang-up job rushing through the first of the background checks. What she appreciated most was their diligence. They hadn't skipped any details, and better yet, Mark had an aptitude for the job. He had spent the afternoon at the bank, pulling records for each applicant, meticulous with all but especially those folks he couldn't personally vouch for. And his efforts had paid off. Two of the volunteers' records looked perfectly legitimate. Each was paid regularly, both working for a small contractor outside Mirabal County. Both looked to spend typical amounts and had nothing of note in their credit checks. Other than the long periods of stable employment in a region with long-term employment problems, nothing in their background checks should have caused any concerns. In other words, they were perfect applicants. Until Mark compared their records and found them to be exact matches.

There was no way that two men, even working for the same company, had made precisely the same amount every week, withdrew equal amounts and even used their debit cards on the same days and from the same machines. Even if the two were tied at the hip, the ATM withdrawal records suspiciously lacked transaction numbers, something generated by the ATM company. It didn't take more than a minute for Deputy Lozen to pull the DMV records for each, easily identifying one as the Escalade driver caught on Elliott's dash cam footage. The other, Deputy Santos was ninety percent sure, was the same man who whipped up the crowd at Hobson's, accusing Elliott of starting the fire.

Tapping her pen on the stack of printouts, Kiva considered her options. If records of this quality had been generated and added to the town's bank register, more bank employees than just Gent were involved. He was smart and resourceful, but this would have required someone with computer skills and that wasn't him. Looking to Elliott who was sitting on the couch and staring at her own laptop, she asked, "Why do you think old Elliott moved his account to a bank in Amarillo and not Albuquerque?"

Considering the question carefully, Elliott finally suggested, "Out of state? I mean, I don't know how things work down here. Could that make a difference?"

"Maybe. I bet Gent could have done a search of all banks in the state. Maybe being in Texas was all the separation Old Elliott needed to ensure some privacy?"

Elliott shrugged. "We could call the branch manager in Amarillo. She seemed sharp and on the ball with the attempts to access the account. That tells me they did eventually learn where he moved his money. Maybe we should find out how he transferred his account. I mean, if he set up a wire transfer, Gent would have access to those numbers."

"Old Elliott was smart. I'm betting smarter than that. But you're right. I'll call her and ask. I'm betting he had a high currency draft made up and hand carried it to Amarillo."

"Ballsy."

"That was certainly how old Elliott rolled. I think you get some of that from him."

Elliott grinned, setting her laptop aside and moving to sit in the chair across the desk. "Nanny too. They were fearless in their own way."

Now it was Kiva's turn to smile. "You miss them. Elmo and of course, your Nanny's not gone but she's so far away."

"Yeah, I do. I'm ashamed to admit I didn't know how much Elmo cared or that he followed my career so closely. He always played things down when he was in town like it was just a coincidence that he was visiting when I had something going on. I wish I'd put it together before now. I'm embarrassed at how self-focused I've been, and I wish I'd have known just a bit more about his work down here. I would have loved to be involved before now."

"Maybe that's why. I mean, you now know how proud he was, and all his letters say the same thing. They all reiterate his desire for you to follow your own path. Maybe, and I know this is a simplistic interpretation, but maybe that was so important to him he wouldn't risk sidetracking you?"

Nodding, Elliott said, "Nanny used to tell me stories about their childhood. I think my great-grandfather was a living tyrant. He had the lives of each of his children planned for them from birth. Nanny once told me he used to keep this bamboo rod down the center of the dining room table and if any of the kids made even the simplest mistake during dinner, he would pick up that stick and whack them in the head or face. I know my parents' lack of interest in me can be a sore point, but I think being an outcast was a whole lot easier than being beaten on a regular basis."

Kiva moved around the desk, resting her backside on the front side of it, leaning close to give Elliott a soothing kiss. "This may be the most selfish thing I've ever said, but I'm glad. You're here now and if crappy parentage is a contributing factor, then so be it."

Elliott pulled her along the desk so that Kiva's legs spread around her knees. With both hands in hers, she kissed each one before smiling up at her. "I think that's the nicest thing anyone has ever said about my family." With her strong hands, she eased Kiva's hips down, planting her on her lap. Her arms around Kiva's waist and Kiva's around her neck, Elliott turned their conversation to the subject at hand. "Back to the town's bank," she sighed, looking like she was working the problem. "I'm assuming it may be more compromised than we thought?" When Kiva nodded, she asked, "Who's running the show over there?"

That seemed a strange question. Had Elliott not been paying attention? Gent Koehler was owner and the bank president, but he also had a manager in charge of the day-to-day operations. Of course, Elliott knew that too.

When she didn't answer, Elliott pulled her closer, asking thoughtfully, "I'm asking who runs the place. Not the guy in charge thing. Who is the actual person who gets the daily business done?" Seeming to recognize her confusion Elliott asked a different question. "Who runs your law office at home, and I don't mean the partners. I mean who gets everything done? Who makes sure you have paper and pens, and appointment books, and computers? Who makes the bank deposits and schedules the staff and makes sure the new associates are in the right place at the right time? In the military, in an Air Force squadron, the command structure places the commanding officer at the top of the heap, but the guy or gal that really gets the day to day work done is the squadron chief warrant officer. A good chief will keep the whole squadron humming like a well-oiled machine. That's what I'm asking. Who is really running the bank?"

Elliott took Kiva's silence as an invitation to continue. "We used to have this saying… 'Want it considered, ask the CO. Need it done, see the chief.'"

"I understand. I just never considered it before, and I'm shocked by my elitist thinking. I never…"

"Why would you?" Elliott asked, gently easing her concern with a kiss to her chin, followed by a soft exploration of her neck.

"You…" Kiva was struggling to think. Stepping up and out of the warm embrace, she kissed Elliott's cheek before returning to her place behind the desk. Opening a Google window, she entered the bank name, pulling up their website and scrolling through their menu for a directory. "I'm thinking we're looking for someone who is not a permanent part of the senior management team?"

"That would be my guess too."

"*Hmm.*" She just wasn't seeing the big picture. Picking up her phone and scrolling through her contact list, she said, "Let's see who

Erica's go-to person is." The conversation was thankfully short. When she hung up, she looked perturbed.

"I'm guessing Erica's still not forgiven us?"

"For which part?" Kiva asked, ticking off her fingers, "For being together? For not including her in our investigation? For being at the center of the controversy? For being together?" she added again, smiling at her awareness.

Getting up from the desk, Kiva rounded it for a second time, straddling Elliott's lap. "For being together... I like the sound of that." Leaning in, delivering the sweetest of kisses before resting her forehead against Elliott's and sharing what she had learned from the short call with Erica Dunbar. Delivering a teasing bite to Elliott's lower lip, she soothed it with kisses that deepened. "*Mmm*." It was always a pleasure to kiss Elliott. The woman had a talented mouth. She was especially appreciative remembering the number of women she dated that couldn't kiss worth a damn; something that always stunned her. Enjoying the sensation caused by Elliott's teasing tongue, she hesitantly pulled away. Sighing, she asked, "Do you remember the divorce case I was working on?"

She nodded, instantly serious. "Domestic abuse situation?"

"Yeah. The Murdocks. Erica says Maria Murdock is the person to see if she needs to rush a mortgage application or pretty much anything that needs to get done over there. Even though she's not technically a manager, she's the town's go-to person at the bank."

Elliott, with her arms firmly around Kiva, sighed. "It's never simple, is it? Are you disappointed?"

"I don't know what to think. I mean, I really liked Maria. I thought she stuck it out with Bryan Murdock way too long, but I put it down to her ancestry. She did mention she would be the only person in her family to be divorced."

Elliott's hands untucked her button-down shirt, sliding under it to stroke the smooth skin of Kiva's back. "Do you think she understands what she's doing or was she simply following Gent's orders?"

She shook her head. "I really don't know. I guess Sheriff Dias and I are going to have to have a long talk with her."

"Can I suggest something?" Elliott asked, her fingernails gently teasing lines up and down her lower spine.

Involuntarily, Kiva's eyes closed with pleasure. "*Mmm*, oh, uhm, suggestion?" It was getting harder and harder to pay attention. Elliott's mouth had gravitated to her cheek, and she was making her way along her jaw towards her extremely sensitive neck.

Just when she lost all track of the conversation, Elliott pulled away slowly. She suggested, "Why not invite her out here? Isn't her son one of the kids who helped out during the night of the fire? If tomorrow is really such a big thing, why don't we invite certain kids, you know, ones like hers and the others who race cars out here, and offer them a familiarization flight?" With a caveat, Elliott added, "That assumes the test flight goes well."

Leaning back to look in her eyes, she needed to be sure. "You would do that?"

"Sure. Like I said. If the test flight goes well, I could offer to take a handful of people up. Well," she grinned, "one at a time, and while I'm doing that you and the sheriff could have a private chat with this Maria person and no one at the bank would be any wiser."

Kiva smiled, delivering a deep kiss before asking, "Where is your inspector guy?"

"The boys took him out to that rib place on the highway for supper."

Tipping her head to the stack of linens on the end of the couch, she pointed. "You really don't need to sleep on the couch you know. You could come home with me."

Elliott, mirroring her posture and leaning back to study her eyes, asked carefully, "You're sure about that?"

Combing Elliott's bangs from her deep blue eyes, she nodded, a smile spreading across her face. "I wouldn't ask if I wasn't serious. Ellie, I don't want you to ever worry if I'm interested. I am."

A warm smile spread across her face. "Just like that?"

She pulled her in for a hard, tight hug, whispering in her ear, "Just like that."

CHAPTER TWENTY-FIVE

At Kiva's house, while the kids occupied themselves with a Disney movie in the living room, some of the adults took refuge in the dining room, the only place in the open concept space with some semblance of privacy. In the kitchen, Sheriff Dias and Deputy Lozen doctored their coffees, while Mark and Elliott cleared away dinner. Andi had brewed a big pot of decaf, and, pulling all her notes and findings together, Kiva joined them, escorting the adults into the dining room and pulling the decorative French doors closed. They were soon heavy into a debate, trying like hell to figure out the consortium's next move now that its play had been discovered, even if the town didn't exactly know who all the players were.

Kiva tapped her pen on the ever-present legal pad. "We have the obvious suspects, Gent and his son Jose, Ian Guerrero and his son Maxwell too, and we've identified the guy with the Escalade registered in Texas to the consortium…"

"Don't forget my idiot brother," Mark added.

She nodded. "We also have serious suspicions but can't yet prove Judge McCallum and Judge Tomlinson are involved."

David Dias growled a warning, then acquiesced to the need to name their suspects, even heavy hitters like the two judges.

Kiva moved them to the theory of other key players among the not so big leaguers, including bank record fixer Maria Murdock. While they speculated on her involvement, Elliott, who had begged the kids for a few pages of construction paper, was busy making some sort of chart. As a visual learner, she needed to work out the connections.

Kiva's phone chimed a notice she had received an email from her dad. Tempted to ignore it, she remembered that her father knew exactly who she was meeting tonight and why. "Sorry," she offered, ignoring the others as they chatted about their theories.

Opening the email, she was glad she had. Her dad had been digging from his end, mostly connecting with other lawyers he had known for ages. While those professionals were loath to give up clients or risk even looking like they may have breached confidentiality, their underpaid admins had sworn no oaths. The list of suspects he sent was long and telling. It included members of the Dallas-Fort Worth Water Authority, the judges they suspected, and a few state assembly members in New Mexico and Texas. She had to retrieve her laptop to research a few names she didn't recognize on the list. The last name was the most ominous. "Ah, guys? This last name... It's the SAC for the Albuquerque field office of the Federal Bureau of Investigation."

That revelation brought all conversation to a halt. "You're sure?" Dias asked.

She nodded, handing over her phone with the open email from her father. "According to Dad, this FBI boss guy is not one of the main conspirators. From what he could gather, neither are Gent and Ian. They may not know this, but they're small fry. They may have started this thing as insiders and the only local players, but things have grown so much more complicated."

After both Dias and Lozen read through the email list, they passed it to Elliott, who printed names on the chart she was drawing in bright crayon on the construction paper. Playing show and tell for the group, she held up the first of the oversized pages.

"I've been thinking about this, and I kind of knew they had to have some heavy hitters to pull this off. First, they would need some thousand-dollar-an-hour tax lawyers. And they look to have it with these two." She pointed to two of the attorneys Kiva's father had named. "They would have the wherewithall to create the consortium and the offshore business experience and connections. The consortium would also need the inside on county regulations, real estate and holdings. I think that's where Gent and Ian came in handy. I can't make a connection though."

David Dias groaned. "Judge Tomlinson is from Texas originally. And Judge McCallum is old money. He may be from these parts, but he hobnobs with those rich Texas boys. He hosts a big shindig every year, usually a fundraiser for whichever senator is in his favor. He's got a huge spread down in Curry County. That place is so big, it's got its own runway, big enough to land his G-four."

"A state judge who can afford his own Gulfstream? Holy cow! I definitely didn't expect something like that," Elliott marveled.

"No. But I shoulda."

She nodded. "Well, that gives us the connection, and I see where they would have needed Ian and Gent's insider knowledge." Elliott huffed, speculating, "I wonder if these two even understand how small potatoes they are in the scheme of things."

They all looked to be considering her words when Mark asked, "Maybe we can use that? I mean, they're both in hiding, but neither man has great wealth to fall back on, not like McCallum and Tomlinson."

Kiva agreed, and following his thread, added, "They both must be hurting from all their plans going south so fast. I wonder what it would take to shake them out of whatever holes they're hiding in."

While they debated the wisdom of offering either Ian or Gent a get-out-of-jail-free card, Elliott continued adding names to the charts she had drawn. She tapped her pen next to the crayon-drawn box filled with the name of the FBI Albuquerque special agent in charge. "Sheriff. Is there a way for you to check if warrants have been issued from a different place in New Mexico?"

"Issued for who?"

"Me," she answered quietly.

While he blustered, assuring her that wouldn't happen again, Deputy Lozen was more proactive. Signing into PACER, she found what he was sure didn't exist. "Yep. It was filed today in US District Court, New Mexico." She skimmed quickly through the court document before handing her phone over to the sheriff. "It looks like they're going to try something new. I guess when they couldn't get the arson thing to stick, they decided to go federal. That would take things out of the sheriff's hands."

While Elliott just nodded, Kiva demanded to know more. "To go federal, they would need to prove she crossed state lines in the commission of a crime. What the hell could they be accusing her of now?" She knew she was sounding hostile, but even Elliott laying a reassuring hand on her forearm couldn't dispel her dread.

"Evidently the county was supposed to receive several items gifted through the military programs that give surplus goods away," Lozen explained. "Most are items that can be repurposed by first responders. I guess the consortium is ready to throw Ian and Gent under the bus to keep plans moving forward. The feds are alleging we received weapons and gear that Gent applied for and that old Elliott and now our Elliott here has been selling off illegally. As some of those items are assault rifles and such, the charges include weapons trafficking."

Kiva fumed but could find nothing to say.

Dias, sitting opposite Kiva at the other end of the table, set down the deputy's phone and sighed. "I guess the two feds I'm expecting in the morning aren't coming here to help us but to arrest you." He tapped his fingers on the old dining table. "How much do you think Ian and Gent were expecting to haul in? I mean, if you're right and they're only the local talent, I don't expect a big chunk of that eight billion was ever headed their way."

Elliott agreed. "Actually, I have a feeling they have no idea how much money is involved. Why else would they make such a complicated plan to profit from the new lands the water pullback would create?"

"And," Kiva added, "it's why Ian tried to buy out the hangar before Elliott could see what she'd inherited. I've suspected from the start he had a buyer for those projects. When I was first looking into his aggressive behavior involving the probate, I decided to get a quick evaluation of old Elliott's estate. I was shocked to receive instant offers of a million or more for everything in there. Even as is."

Andi, who had been mostly quiet, addressed the sheriff. "You said Judge McCallum has a huge spread down in Curry County. I'm curious. What would a place like that cost? Not just to buy but run. You know, with a herd and hands, and all the trimmings of wealth fellas like Gent and Ian dream of."

"You mean the whole nine yards?"

"You bet. Country club lifestyle. Membership in the Cattlemen's Association, and all the bells and whistles that come from being among the one percent in New Mexico."

He took a moment to consider her question. "Erica would be a better source on the real estate side but given the lower property values and labor cost here, not to mention we don't have great big wads of millionaires like they do in Texas, I would guess around twenty-thirty mil. More than that would definitely push you up in the Judge McCallum class, and less would still be real comfortable but in the realm of rich hobby rancher, much like old Tomlinson is."

Andi mused, "I wonder how they would react if they knew their new friends were taking the lion's share and were now trying to throw them under the bus. I mean, especially now that their part in this is public. Even if they get away with what they've done, their payout is out the window, and they can't just return to town, pick up their old lives and pretend they're still pillars of the community."

"*Hmmm*," Kiva added in agreement, picking up the construction paper charts. "I bet their allegiances could be swayed if they knew their buddies had set them up to take the fall for everything and for chump change compared to what the rest of the group might gain." She asked plainly, "Only thing is, how do we even get word to them?"

Looking very much like a man with a plan, David Dias stood. Leaning heavily on the dining table with both hands, he explained, "We'll divide and conquer. Deputy Lozen here is gonna head over to Erica's house, ostensibly to ask about large spreads up for sale in the region. While she's visiting, she can drop some hints that Ian and Gent were getting shortchanged in a big way and we're onto the big boys upstream looking to take billions for themselves."

He placed a fatherly hand on the deputy's shoulder, adding, "Make sure you let her know we're all feeling bad for how those old boys been swindled and they could do better if they went state's witness on this." She nodded, and he continued handing out orders. "While yer talking to Erica, I'm gonna be in the office callin' in every favor I have in Washington with the FBI and ATF. I can't sit still and have them send some crooked bastard to scoop up our Ellie again. By the way," he asked, checking his watch, "what time is it in Washington?"

Elliott answered automatically, "Twelve-forty."

He nodded, straightening up. "Guess I better get on the phone and wake some folks up. For now, I need you, Ellie, to stay here out of sight and away from the airfield."

"Uh…" She looked conflicted.

Kiva offered, "Elliott can stay here for however long she needs."

Still looking caught out, Elliott answered, "No. Ah, I mean yes, I can. But I have a test flight tomorrow. I just can't hide indefinitely."

He shook his head, his thumbs clipped in his gun belt and looking very much like he wanted her to recognize his authority. But before he could say more, she explained, "Half the town will be at the airport tomorrow. I can't let people down like that. Especially with how confused people are about me. If I don't show, it will just be one more thing that proves I can't be trusted."

She was getting riled up, and now it was Kiva's turn to calm her down. Taking her hand, she asked the sheriff, "David, what time are you expecting the agents from the Albuquerque office?"

"Not before eleven. They're drivin' down in the morning. Unless they get roused from their beds extra early, I suspect we won't see them much before that."

Squeezing Elliott's hand, she asked her, "Can you be in the air by then?"

"If the run-up and taxi tests go well."

Kiva smiled, her confidence evident. "I doubt you've left anything to chance. I'm betting you'll get that little bird in the air. Once you do, how long can you fly?"

"Four hours, if I really lean her out. Heading east, that would easily put me into Texas or going north maybe as far as Pueblo, Colorado, but the minute I land, the FAA would have me."

Realizing that wasn't the best idea, Kiva filled in the blanks for the others. "And you would have crossed a state line to knowingly flee a warrant. No, that's not what I was thinking. I just wondered how long we could keep you in the air, as in, how much time we have to fix this mess."

The sheriff interrupted. "Last weekend the wife put on an old movie. She's got her favorites and loves to watch 'em." Seeing no one was quite following, he explained, "It was *Out of Africa*, you know, with Redford and Meryl. Anyway, isn't that little plane of yours the same as the one they had Redford flyin' all over the place? I mean, they had him flyin' from ranch to ranch and landin' on folk's lawns and such. Can your little bird do that?"

Elliott nodded. "As long as the field isn't too rocky or freshly plowed, she can land anywhere. I was planning a few off-airport touch-and-goes anyway. Have you got a place in mind?"

"Not yet, but I will by morning or at least Deputy Lozen will." When they all looked at Lozen, she shrugged, just as mystified as the others.

Dias ordered, "Get out to Erica's now. Tell her some of what we talked about, how Gent and Ian were bein' used and only gonna get chump change. Then tell her you come into some serious money. Or maybe say the Tribe's lookin' to acquire some land, and you want to start looking at ranches right away, as in tomorrow. Tell her you're especially interested in unoccupied spreads, something ready to go, that'll close quick."

Lozen stood, looking a little dubious. "She's gonna be suspicious."

"Good!" Dias said with a grin. "That'll get her talking even faster."

After they saw Dias and the deputy out, Andi helped Kiva clear away the coffee mugs while Mark rounded up the kids and dragged them off to bed. Elliott grabbed her bag and sat down at the dining room table. She wanted to go through the flight test procedures one more time and review her test plan. Before she could get settled, Kiva squeezed her shoulders, bending close, and whispering in her ear, "I've got to make some phone calls but if you don't mind my company, why don't you finish your work upstairs? There's a big desk and much better lighting."

She followed Kiva out of the dining room and up the stairs to the master suite. "You moved bedrooms?"

"It made more sense to put my few things in here than move all my dad's stuff out." At the uncomfortable look on her face, she asked plainly, "Elliott, what's wrong?"

"Nothing," she said, all her attention on the documents she was pulling out of her knapsack.

Slipping up behind her, Kiva wrapped her arms around her waist, pulling herself flat against a rigid back. Elliott covered her hands and began gently rubbing her thumb back and forth. It was nice but in contrast to her still rigid body. "Okay, it's something. Don't freeze me out." When the pause stretched on and on, she asked simply, "Elliott?"

"*Eh…*" Finally, she turned in Kiva's arms, wrapping hers around Kiva's slim waist. "It's nothing like that. It's… Okay, this is going to sound silly, juvenile even, but… this is your dad's bedroom, bed…"

Unable to help herself, Kiva laughed good-naturedly. "If that were true, I'd be a little freaked out too. But no worries. When we were kids, this was my grandmother's room. When my dad moved back here, he still slept in the other suite. I moved his stuff in here so I wouldn't have to sleep in my childhood bed. Not that I would have minded, but it would be on the tight side for the two of us. Of course, the kids are in there now, and it was easier to let Andi and Mark have the other suite. Besides this one has the extra room and the balcony. And I promise you, my parents have never done it in here. Frankly, it's been so long for those two, I don't think it would have mattered anyway." She pointed across the room. "And that's a new bed."

The tension in Elliott's body eased, and she produced a smile, "Childish, I know…"

Grinning, Kiva kissed away the rest of her explanation. When her soft wet lips parted, and a probing tongue met hers, Elliott felt her knees weaken. Finally breaking, she leaned back just enough to see Kiva's deep brown eyes, "*Um*...Did you say you had calls to make? Because..."

Kiva laughed, pulling her phone from her back pocket, and slipping from her arms. "Get your review done while I wake up my dad."

Elliott nodded. She absolutely did want to do one more review before the test flight in the morning. She had previously only done seasonal test flights or tests after a major component had been changed, like when an airplane's skis were replaced with floats. In many ways, the procedures were the same and Kiva was right when she asserted that she wouldn't leave anything to chance. Still, pushing an eighty-year-old aircraft to its limits did feel different.

Across the room, she could hear Kiva on her call, negotiating with her sister to wake their father. She respected Shay's protection but Kiva's need was her need too. The last place she wanted to find herself was back in jail and this time a federal prison, an *American* federal prison where they could move her anywhere in the nation with impunity. Who knows where and for how long they could lose her in the system if key players wanted her missing?

Pushing the concerns for her own welfare aside, she spent the next hour reviewing every out-of-date and old-fashioned piloting brochure old Elliott had collected, then all the modern maneuvers required by the FAA. Once she completed the test flight and signed off on its airworthiness, she had offered to take the FAA inspector for a check ride. It wasn't required, but she considered it a token gesture before an airworthiness certificate was issued, and they could permanently add the tail numbers to the Gipsy Moth. With her flight plan finished, she folded it, clipping it to the top of her old kneeboard, a clipboard with a fabric case with pockets for a flight computer and area charts that would Velcro around her thigh for easy reference. Plugging in her phone to charge, she did the same with the integrated flight tablet she purchased explicitly to augment the instrumentation and streamline navigation and communications in the little Moth. She might not know what to expect from the FAA tomorrow or the FBI for that matter, but she sure as hell planned to be ready for her test flight.

"Good. I take it you're all set for tomorrow?" Kiva asked as she stepped up to the opposite side of the desk, looking at how Elliott had lined up the carefully folded papers on the kneeboard, the special use tablet, and Elliott's phone. "I like the way you always organize things before you can settle for the night."

"I know it's a little OCD, but I can't relax until I know I have a plan for the next day."

"Does it keep you awake?"

"Sometimes. Mostly. Without a plan, I have a hard time figuring out why I should bother getting out of bed."

Kiva nodded her understanding, making her way around the desk, and pushed the desk chair back far enough so she could straddle her lap. She enjoyed being able to sit like this, fun and intimate at the same time. Grinding back and forth as if adjusting for the most comfortable spot, she watched Elliott's face, the pleasure she invoked. Arms around Elliott's neck, she took her time, running her fingers through her soft shaggy hair. Pondering everything she knew about this complicated woman, she said quietly, "I keep forgetting the hell your last year has been."

"*Umm.*" Elliott didn't seem to register the statement for a long pleasurable moment. Finally, she nodded, her hands wrapping possessively around Kiva's waist. "I keep wondering how I let things unravel so far out of control. Honestly, it makes me feel stupid."

"Does it make you worry about me?" she asked.

"Not in the least."

There was such sincerity in her words that Kiva couldn't help pulling her close, as close as she could. She whispered, "I think you set your sights far too low with that last one. I don't know why, but I know it wasn't you."

Elliott groaned, her head resting on Kiva's shoulder for a long time. Finally, she confessed, "I thought I saw a bit of myself in her. You know, the kid from the wrong side of the tracks makes good? And to cut me some slack…"

"Which you should definitely do…"

"Definitely; except it's my Achilles heel." She sighed. "I don't understand deception. I mean, I get it, but why? That's the part that confuses me. Then there's you. Why would you be willing to take on a project like me? I mean, I'm still the kid from the wrong side of the tracks, or Don River in this case. I bet all the years you lived in Koreatown you never set foot in Regent Park."

Kiva, her hands, still brushing gently through Elliott's blond hair, took in her blue eyes so dark with need. "You're right. Of course, most of the kids I went to Jarvis Collegiate with were from Cabbagetown and they intimidated me. And law school was worse. By my final year, I think I was the only person in my class that wasn't from Forrest Hill."

Elliott gave her a quiet "Ouch," but smiled too. "You must think I'm…" She was unable to complete the thought.

Kiva leaned back to be sure Elliott was listening to her every word. "I think you are joyful and insightful, reserved and kind, all in an accepting and generous way. I also think you took too much responsibility for the failures of your relationship. That you can't see, much less understand you were being played." She brushed her cheek. "Elliott. It happens. There are people out there who are just wired so differently. I saw it so many times with my young offenders. Sometimes it was the kid, and I would cringe to think of the kind of adult they were becoming. Sometimes it was a parent or adult who influenced them, and I would report the situation to the Children's Aid. That's about all I could do."

"That must have sucked."

She nodded, finally disclosing both to herself and Elliott, "It's why I can't do it anymore. At least not full-time. There's a part of me that's just like you. A part that doesn't understand the machinations of hate and greed and wanting to wound others. It's taken me a long time to understand people of that ilk are not wounded souls needing a healing hand. Their behavior is in their nature; their victim act is a method to lure you in."

"Well, I feel like an ass for being attracted to someone like that, and it's shaken my belief in my ability to judge the character and intentions of others."

"Good. Ellie, that's a good thing. We both need it right now to get through this situation. And believe it or not, the town is coming around to you. Knowing how they've been misled by those they trusted, this gives us the added empathy to help heal them and fix this entire situation."

"I wish I could figure that out... the fixing part."

"Yeah." She planted a slow, soft kiss on Elliott. Teasing her bottom lip then sliding her tongue along before pulling away again. "My dad and Shay are very impressed with you."

"What?" Elliott said, confused by the change in topic. "After reading the fake journal and all? Do they even know where I'm from?"

"You should have heard Dad once he had the real facts. He believes that if you have what it takes to survive growing up in Regent, serve honorably, and achieve enough that people are trying to take you down, you must be something special."

"And what about his daughter? What does she think?"

"Shay?" Why did Elliott care what her sister thought?

Pulling her in even tighter, Elliott spread Kiva's legs to pin around her hips. She almost bucked when her crotch moved against Elliott's middle, making it difficult to concentrate. "Oh *you!*"

Elliott smirked, her lips migrating to Kiva's collarbone, nipping and soothing her way towards her neck. "*Hmm?*"

"I..." She rolled her hips feeling an uncontrollable twitching deep down. "*Mmm*, Ellie... Would you think I'm a bad person if I say I want you to fuck me?"

Elliott broke away, staring intensely into her eyes. With a grin, she warned, "Not until you tell me what you think of me."

Kiva groaned, her arousal making her rock on Elliott's lap. Inhaling hard, she uttered, "I think you're too good for me, too good for this town..."

Looking amused, Elliott asked, "But?"

"But...but you're here, and I want you. I want you to touch me, and I want you inside me."

Elliott lifted her from the chair, carrying Kiva effortlessly across the room and setting her on the edge of the bed. She stood between her open legs, pulling her own T-shirt over her head and dropping it on the floor. Unzipping her jeans, she revealed a sexy pair of boy shorts, a match to the bra she wore. Elliott kicked them free, telling her, "Kiva, I want you naked. Every inch of me wants to see you and touch you."

Between Elliott's words and the musky smell of her arousal, she thought she would come on the spot, it was hard not to react to every twitch between her legs.

Elliott sank to her knees, pulling her into her arms. Her lips found her collarbone again, and moved down, kissing the back of the hands Kiva held in place over her bare breasts. It wasn't as if this was the first time, or that Elliott didn't know just how flat-chested she was. Looking into her eyes, Elliott admitted with a grin, "I'm a leg woman myself, but just between you and me, there is nothing sexier than small tits."

Kiva couldn't help but laugh. "Oh my God, I can't believe you just said that!"

Elliott answered with her lips and then her tongue, finding a pebbled nipple between Kiva's fingers and teasing it hard.

Kiva's head fell back, her hands finally releasing to allow Elliott full access. She combed her fingers through Elliott's hair, pulling her head closer, adoring the sensations being drawn from her sensitive breasts, arching her back as that marvelous tongue laved, sucked, circled, and teased each nipple. Elliott's hands migrated to her waist, tracing up and down her jean-clad thighs. The down strokes scraped along her outer thigh while the return movement was gentler, gliding tantalizingly closer and closer to her center.

When Kiva began inching towards the thumbs stroking her inner thighs, Elliott stood, looking just as aroused as Kiva. "Not so fast."

"Ellie, please..."

Tracing a single finger, Elliott began at her lips and moved straight down her neck, her chest, only stopping at the waistband of her jeans. Kiva lifted her hips and Elliott ripped her jeans down and free, tossing them aside. Hooking her finger under the elastic of her remaining French cut bottoms, Elliott's grin gave the game away. "Back. If you want me. Lie back on the bed."

Kiva shuddered. She shifted herself back across the bed while Elliott's finger held in place, peeling away her last defense. With Kiva naked and stretched out on the bed, Elliott peeled off her own bra and her shorts. She moved like a predator, kneeling between Kiva's open legs and moving up above her on all fours.

"Tell me what you like."

Feeling shy, Kiva didn't answer.

In response, Elliott lowered herself.

The sensation set her aflame, she bucked, arching her back and letting out a deep guttural response. "Oh fuck!"

Elliott trapped her mouth in a deep kiss, ravishing Kiva, her tongue exploring every inch. When her mouth followed her hands back to those sensitive breasts, Kiva sucked in air, her aching need surged higher. Releasing Elliott's hair, she bunched the bedding in her hands, fisting the sheets. A hand had migrated down and fingers now stroked gently between her legs.

"Please Ellie, please...don't make me beg!" With the sheets fisted, she was desperate for Elliott to be inside. Two fingers did just that, slipping in and curling. It was all she could do not to scream, semi-conscious of the kids in bed just down the hall. Feeling Elliott's mouth abandoning her breasts, she raised her head, taking in the deep pool of blue staring back as she made her way down her body. "Oh God!"

"Not God, baby," she said nipping at the taut skin above her mound. "Just me. Just you. Okay?"

"Okay? Oh, *oooh* yes, Ellie. Yes, it's okay!"

Elliott's mouth dipped, tasting, exploring, finally settling on her clit. With her fingers still in Kiva, she continued her slow thrusts in and out, her fingers always curling back when inside and hitting that one irresistible spot while her mouth sucked, her tongue licked, and her one free hand continued to tease a breast.

Kiva's orgasm exploded like electric shocks, shock after shock, each ripping through her core, her body, her mind, her very existence. Then Elliott was beside her, scooping her into her arms, holding her, soothing her as tears ran down Kiva's cheeks.

"I'm right here... You're so beautiful, so amazing. I'm here."

"Good God...Ellie," she finally squeezed out.

"I'm here. I've got you."

An aftershock ripped through her, and she was astonished to feel Elliott's body respond in kind.

"Are you... Did you?"

Brushing her lips against her forehead and along her temple, Elliott admitted, "Not completely. Nothing your personal attention wouldn't fix."

The grin that spread across her face felt entirely out of character, almost foreign. "I don't know what you did, but it was...oh my God! I have no idea how to follow up on something like that." She could smell her own arousal on Elliott's face, as she tipped her head to look at her.

"Making love isn't a competition. And yes, I want you to touch me, but I won't die if you can't. Just touching you, having, sharing what we do is beyond anything I could have imagined."

Comforted, fearless, and beyond aroused again, Kiva rolled onto Elliott, kissing her possessively. It had never been like this with anyone else. She couldn't get enough of her. "Think I might just keep you up all night."

Below her, Elliott's hands, glided down her back. The sounds she made were appreciation, desire, and pure want. "I want what you want, everything you want."

Kiva fought to control an orgasm on the brink of taking her again. No way would she come without taking Ellie with her too. Her need for the woman below her was primal and all-encompassing. "I want you like I've never wanted anyone."

She slid her hand between Elliott's thighs finding her wet, open and inviting. She was slow and methodical in her exploration as Elliott squirmed and moaned and begged. Before she knew what was happening, the orgasm she had been holding back exploded, and Elliott's too, riding out wave after wave along with her. *Lovers? Is that what we are, all we are?* It didn't seem like enough, and in that moment, she knew it never would be. With Elliott they had more, were more, and she wanted that, needed what they could be.

The sheen of sweat that covered them both was a shared outer skin. Her body dissolving into a need for sleep, Kiva uttered the words that had been rattling her mind. "I think I need you."

She felt Elliott's arms tighten around her, her sleepy voice echoing her emotions, saying what she needed to hear. "I'm here. I'm right where I want to be...and I'm not going anywhere...for as long as you want me."

"*Mmmm*, I know it's too soon. Ellie, I know. Just know that yes, it's what I want too."

Elliott's lips found her temple, delivering featherlight kisses. "Perfect...*mmmm*, just perfect."

CHAPTER TWENTY-SIX

The convoy of cars heading from her house to the airport made Kiva smile. That, and Elliott's acute embarrassment when they had gone down to breakfast to find the house crowded with people. Besides Andi and Mark, two of the security team were just sitting down to breakfast. The two women had both taken some kindhearted ribbing. Once they headed outside, it became clear they all needed their vehicles even if they were all heading to the same place. Elliott's Jeep led the way with Mark riding with Kiva, and Andi and the kids following in their minivan. Two of the security teams, in their big SUVs, brought up the rear like parental geese, overseeing them all.

Mark was riding in with Kiva to take the opportunity to get a jump on the day's duties. When her investigator in Toronto called, she was glad he had. "Hang on Yves. I've got Mark in the car with me. Give him a sec to get a notebook out."

"*Bonjour* Mark. Good to meet you." Yves's voice, and his deep French accent, came through crisp and clear on the car's integrated hands-free system.

"Hey, Yves. Thanks for the tips you sent down yesterday. Big help, man."

"*Merci*. Ah, Kiva! I am having some difficult news for you."

Yesterday when he called, she had all but forgotten she'd requested he investigate Ian Guerrero and the situation here in town. That seemed so long ago now, and she had already uncovered more than she ever wanted to know. "No worries. I already know there are some heavy hitters involved, but anything you can add would be appreciated."

"I 'ave a list. I traced this 'ere consortium off the shore. They made many stops, but they are not so smart as Yves. They make a mistake when they bank at St. Maarten *et* Saint Martin."

"Where the hell is that?" Mark asked.

Kiva explained, "It's an island in the Caribbean. One side belongs to France and the other to the Netherlands." Slowing her speed as they passed through the gutted town, she shook her head at the devastation the fire had delivered. Then said, "Saint Martin isn't exactly known as a money shelter island."

"*Oui*. This is correct. But Caymans has been very diligent since the American subprime mortgage crisis did much damage to them. All the islands too. Many banks 'ave failed. Most have been bought out by national banks with no such damages."

Kiva huffed. "Let me guess. Canadian banks? And that's how you lucked into your information?"

"Oh, my Kiva. Luck is not part of my good works," he teased.

"Wait!" Mark interrupted. "How come Canadian banks didn't take a hit? I read the entire world's financial systems were hurt."

Kiva slowed her Mustang to follow Elliott as she turned onto Airport Road. "Not Canada. Their banking laws are so much different. Simple explanation, Canadian banks can't trade in commodities that can't be sold or used by the public."

"You don't have mortgages?"

Over the car speaker, Yves's laugh was easy to hear. "Almost, my friend. It is something that is very old-fashioned here. One must have a great amount of cash for down payments and taxes. Lots and lots of taxes."

Kiva shook her head at the description, but it was basically accurate. "Okay, Yves. Go on."

"I find the shells, the many companies, start at St. Maarten on the Dutch side but they pick a bank on the French side. *Oui*, one of ours. Your *maire*?"

She helped him, calling on her high school French to suggest, "Mayor?"

"*Oui*, yes. Your may-*or*, 'e is only on this board and so was this partner of your papa but not after. They are, as you say, small fries."

"Listen to you, using English slang." She had forgotten how much she enjoyed working with Yves, both his accent and his humor. "Can you send us a list of who is named in the corporations? I'm curious, do any names add or fall from the list along the path of shell corporations?"

"Yes. This is 'ow the may-*or* and partner are. They are listed on the first as company officers, but they vanish from the next. I am thinking they do not know this."

Mark was nodding vigorously. "I bet we can use that. Are you sending all the corporate papers?"

"Everything, my friend. I have sent to Kiva, links to the cloud."

"Yves, can you send links to Mark too? He can have access to everything."

"Yes, this I do now." They could hear a keyboard clacking in the background. While he typed, he explained, "Now, I also find property both real and other. Some 'ave been gained from the county. Some *extraordinaire* weapons, vehicles, and *avions err* aeroplanes. I have designations, but this is not my business. I think you 'ave an *aviateur* who can help wid this. Yes?"

She exchanged a look of concern with Mark and asked Yves, "What are the designations for the weapons and the aircraft?"

"Two C-*Vingt-et-un* 'uron, six grenade-launcher, and *vintgt-huit* ah M-16."

"Twenty-eight! Are you telling me they have twenty-eight fucking M16 assault rifles?"

"*Oui*, and *deux*, ah two 'urons. This plane I do not know."

As they approached the airport gates, a long line of traffic stretched out before them. "Yves. I'm going to have to call you back. Me or Mark. Something is going on up ahead."

He signed off without fanfare.

Mark, still struggling with Yves's accent asked with irritation, "What the hell is a Uron?"

Slowing the car, she was trying to get a look at what was holding up the traffic. There was never traffic here. There was never traffic at all. "I think he meant Huron." She tossed him her phone. "Search Google for the civilian designation for a military C-21 aircraft."

Following Elliott's example, Kiva pulled around the long line of cars and was pleased to see Andi follow and of course the security detail right behind. At the gate, now manned by the sheriff's posse and one deputy, they were waved through without delay. The deputy on duty explained that the sheriff wanted all visitors to sign in. That was new, and she wasn't sure if that was for the FAA's benefit, the FBI's, or for the situation. Either way, it couldn't hurt.

The street side parking, always vacant, looked to be full. Elliott pulled her Jeep over and parked in front of the hangar doors. Kiva waved as she passed. Elliott was in work mode, and she and Mark had a trail of corporate documents to dig through and a warren of weapons to report to the sheriff. If Ian and Gent and whoever they were involved with had those weapons here and were desperate, who knew how things could escalate.

As they made their way around the bottom of the triangular runways, Mark related what his Internet search had found. "A C-21 *H*uron," he said, putting extra emphasis on the H. "Is the designation for a Beechcraft Super King Air. Geez! They're a bit on the big size for traffic spotting. I think the commuter plane Andi took last year from Amarillo to her parents' place in Austin was smaller than this thing."

With the parking lot across from the Fire Hall just as crowded as the one at the hangar, she drove up the side-access laneway and was pleased to see the security detail pull in behind and take a blocking position.

Airside at the Fire Hall, the scene was just as chaotic. Most of the folks milling around had handwritten nametags stuck to their jackets. It wasn't perfect, but until they received their badge maker, it would do. It was the number of people that concerned her. She knew folks liked to attend a test flight, but this was unexpected especially since it was still a quarter to eight in the morning.

Mark stopped her. "Look," he said, pointing across the field. The hangar doors were open, and it looked like the guys were pushing out the little blue Gipsy Moth, with its classic silver wings, but that wasn't what caught her eye or Mark's.

"What the hell?" Parked on the apron next to the FAA inspector's Beech Bonanza was a long sleek turboprop. "Is that the same…"

"No way," Mark said. "I don't know what that is but it's twice the size of the airplanes we're worried about. Think it's the FBI?"

"More like ATF." They both jumped, turning to Deputy Lozen, who had snuck up behind them. "Counselor. The sheriff's in our office." She tipped her head to Mark in recognition that they were sharing the space. Looking at Kiva, she said simply, "He needs you right away. And I need you, buddy, to help make sure everyone out here is ID'ed. We haven't got the badge stuff yet, so Sofia gave me a box of mailing labels to use."

As they followed her inside, Kiva asked about the ATF. "When did they arrive?"

"Not long ago. Been here 'bout ten minutes. The sheriff called your detail. They said you were on the move, so he's being patient."

"Patient, my ass," she huffed, following the deputy through the open apparatus floor. "How many agents?"

Lozen whistled. "A whole squad, all in tactical gear. Don't know what or who they think they're gonna take on, but the sheriff sent DaSilva and Santos over to the hangar to make sure no one touches our girl."

Kiva nodded, knowing Lozen was referring to Elliott. As much as she wanted to call and check on her, she was confident the security detail, not to mention the deputies, would have already warned her of trouble. This had to be part of the missing funds and weapons the sheriff had already identified. At least she hoped so.

She stopped before the closed office door, turning to Mark, ordering, "You two use my office. Print out everything Yves sent us and get fact sheets on the identified weapons and aircraft." Thinking about it, she added, "Better make extra copies." She removed her pen and yellow pad from her bag and handed everything else over to them. It held her laptop, and he would need it to access the new documents.

She tapped on the door to the office Lozen and Mark were assigned to, and entered. "Good morning, Sheriff. I see the Bureau of Alcohol, Tobacco, Firearms and Explosives has decided to join us."

The office designated for joint use by Mark and Deputy Lozen featured a built-in, U-shaped worktable fitted to the walls, and several chairs. It wasn't the ideal place for so many people to meet but considering the number of civilians wandering around the place, it was probably the only empty room. With the sheriff were four federal agents. Two were in jeans and T-shirts, and without their obligatory blue windbreakers, they might have been mistaken for bikers or drug dealers. The other two were kitted out in tactical gear. "Care to bring me up to speed?"

Sheriff Dias stood, looking relieved by her arrival. "Gentlemen, this is our county special counsel, Kiva Park." Waving a hand, he said to her, "This is the ATF. They were just trying to explain why they were here and not looking for the men who ripped off this town, diverted funds from our emergency services for over five years, and procured equipment from the military ten-thirty-three program that we've never seen."

She nodded, not bothering with the offered chair. "I'm curious myself. Unless it's to explain where those military items actually went, including twenty-eight M16 assault rifles, six grenade launchers, and two Beechcraft King Air turboprop airplanes?"

There was silence in the room. She kept quiet and still while they exchanged looks and were not altogether successful in hiding their discomfort.

Grinning at the long silence, the sheriff continued. "Like I said, you boys aren't working with some country bumpkins here. We got a good idea who and what. We're way ahead of yer accusations. Now you gotta choice. You can drop all the posturin' and listen up or get on that fancy plane the DOJ's lendin' you and get your keesters back to Phoenix where you all belong."

After another round of silence, one of the suits spoke up. "Look, Sheriff. We have good intel and—"

"You got nothin'! Nothin' but more crap from the same folks who cooked up this here whole mess. Now, what's it gonna be? I'm expectin' the FBI to be here soon. Either you back down and listen up, or Ms. Park here will save all she's got for them and you boys can sit on the sidelines while the first draft takes to the field and makes the winnin' play."

One of the agents in tactical gear leaned over, whispering in the ear of the oldest agent, the one in jeans and pristine motorcycle boots, who remained quiet. Kiva thought: *So that's who's in charge.* Then he nodded, offering, "Let's hear your evidence."

Kiva agreed with a nod. "First, let's move to the old day room. There's a large meeting table in there, and we can work like civilized people and help ourselves to coffee. And believe me, I have a lot to cover, but first I want to check on Elliott's progress. I don't want to miss her test-flight takeoff."

"Elliott Snowmaker?" the guy in the tactical battle dress demanded. "You're knowingly going to let her flee?"

The sheriff just laughed at his indignation. "I'm going to join Ms. Park here in watchin' that young woman test fly a little bird she's been rebuildin', and if you want to stop her, you and your boys'll have to go through me, my department, half the town and this feisty little filly here!"

The ATF men exchanged looks but didn't argue.

"Good choice," the Sheriff said, leading them to the day room and the promised incentive of coffee.

* * *

Decked out in a flight suit over her long johns and wool socks, Elliott struggled into her old ski-doo boots, zipping them up. She stuffed pencils, a small pad of paper, spare gloves, a backup paper VFR chart of the area, and her old trusted Jeppesen CR-2 circular flight computer in various pockets. Shaking off her unease at so many people being present, she pulled on her flight jacket, grabbing her kneeboard with its backup flight test plan already attached, along with the integrated flight tablet, and her helmet. She pocketed her phone. Technically, she couldn't use it in the air, but if things went south, she would have it on the ground.

Outside, she was pleased to see people were respecting the apron boundaries. Well, mostly. Many had taken the opportunity to stroll around the V-tail Bonanza, not to mention the DOJ's de Havilland Dash 8 that stood towering over the Gipsy Moth. It was hard to believe they had both rolled off the same factory floor, only eighty years apart. The guys had already rolled out the Gipsy Moth and fueled her up. That was an arduous task using jerry cans, and she was diligent as she strained the fuel to test for sediment. The walk-around was repetitive, but she took her time, paying as much attention to the little bird as she would have when she was still flying 737s.

Finally ready, she climbed in, then asked Mac, who was acting as her ground handler, "How is this website thing you set up going to work?"

He leaned against the fuselage, explaining, "Jesus connected the radio room transceiver to his laptop and added an audio relay to the website. Anytime you broadcast on Unicom, anyone listening to the website feed will get to hear what you're saying."

"But not if I switch frequencies or I'm on intercom?"

"No, ma'am. The radio room transceiver is set for the local traffic freq, and that's all they'll get."

"And people actually want to hear me read through the flight test details?"

His eager grin gave away his interest, and everyone else's it seemed. "You have no idea how many folks want to be part of this and just listening in is about all they can do. I think it's… Well, I think everyone just needs to feel like something good is happening around here."

"Tell me the FAA inspector is on board with this?"

His face lit up. "It was his idea."

"Huh. Who knew?" She gave him a half grin as she strapped in and got settled. "Okay then. It's gonna be boring, but if everyone wants to listen, then I'll broadcast my checklists and the operational numbers as I identify them. Time to get this party started," she added, pulling on her beat-up old military issue flight helmet, and plugging in to the new integrated Nav/Com tablet mounted inconspicuously below the antique instrument panel.

Mac trotted around to the nose of the plane, ready to pull the prop to start. Holding up her handheld VHF radio, he announced on the Unicom frequency, "November One-Niner-Two-Niner-Delta, clear for start up."

Craning her neck, she double-checked the area. Covering her mic, she called out nice and loud, "CLEAR!" Then reached out of the cockpit to the contact relay switch. Flipping it to the On position, she advanced the mixture knob, then opened the throttle a smidge. "Contact!"

CHAPTER TWENTY-SEVEN

Elliott was having fun along with the whole airport listening in to the back and forth discussion with Jesus. He was in the radio room, and as the Gipsy Moth didn't have an actual modern Pilot's Operating Handbook, she was committed to recording all the operational numbers and creating her own. Elmo had collected a wealth of historical documents, which she had studied in depth, but the various booklets were nothing more than copies of pamphlets from multiple flying clubs that had popped up all around the British Empire during the roaring twenties. None were for the exact model she was flying, and of the few operating notes, she was sure the differences had more to do with the liability each club was willing to assume.

The only genuine pilot's manual she had came from the fledgling Royal Australian Air Force and applied to the first edition of the Tiger Moth. It provided airspeeds and maneuvers identified as stalling and spinning, which was helpful even if it was written for a slightly larger airplane with a more powerful engine. The only pamphlet she had for a Gipsy Moth like hers came from the London Flying club and was for the metal tube-framed Gipsy. Under the headings for stalling and spinning, she found, typed in all capital letters, the warning: DO NOT ATTEMPT. That wouldn't apply to the flight test today, as she not only had to attempt these maneuvers, she needed to record the operational characteristics and the flight speeds for reach one.

Having finished the run-up and taxi tests, Elliott broadcast the results as she went. Now, zigzagging her way towards runway 21, she had a moment of quiet to enjoy the fit and feel of the little cockpit. The air was only sixty degrees and even without heat in the open aircraft she was more than comfortable. She grinned to think the dopamine gates in her brain must be open. Then the radio crackled to life with a new voice.

"Illusion Radio, Stingray Police One, five miles west, inbound full stop."

Listening to Jesus reply to the approaching police helicopter, she had to wonder if they were surprised to hear someone was monitoring the Unicom frequency. Their immediate response belayed that hope. "Illusion Radio, Police One. Contact the sheriff and have him meet us on landing."

"Police One. Illusion Radio. On arrival, air taxi to the Fire Hall, at the button of two-one. Meet the local LEOs and ATF on arrival. You have traffic, a de Havilland Gipsy Moth preparing for takeoff. Runway two-one is active; advise you stay west and expedite your landing from the south. And Police One...approach with caution. There are civilians on the field."

Listening to the long delay before the cops answered, Elliott knew the pilot was disseminating all the information Jesus had delivered. Which item they were discussing she couldn't guess. Stopping on the taxiway, just feet from the runway, she checked the cockpit, her instruments, and then the open runway and the airspace both leading to and from it to be sure it was clear. Then wasted no time. "Illusion Radio. November One-Niner-Two-Niner-Delta. The active is clear. Rolling."

"Two-Niner-Delta. Illusion Radio. Tallyho, de Havilland Gipsy Moth, on your maiden flight."

That wasn't exactly standard, but this was uncontrolled airspace, so she grinned as she steered the eighty-year-old trainer with the rudder pedals, and gently pushed the throttle to takeoff power. Elliott held the center line with precision born of skill and practice, a grin lighting up her face. The only thing that could have made this better would be sharing it with Kiva. She noted the tail lifted at thirty knots. With another aircraft in the pattern, she would wait to report that fact until they were on the ground and the frequency was clear. She could see the sleek Agusta 109 Stingray closing in fast and was heartened to realize they were heeding Jesus's directions and staying out of her way. With the tail in flight position, forward visibility was unhindered. It was easy to feel the Gipsy lighten when she reached forty knots. The old girl wanted to fly. Rather than wait for the numbers she found in the Tiger Moth manual, she eased back ever so slightly on the stick and was rewarded with a perfect rotation at forty-five knots. Her original plan was to touch back down immediately and repeat the process several times to nail the speeds. With the New Mexico State Police arriving in their big fancy helicopter, she decided staying in the air was a better bet.

Elliott had no sooner started a left turn to exit the pattern when another aircraft announced its approach. This one used a standard tail number. It wasn't until she was on the downwind leg that she could see the approaching Aero Commander, the "US-EPA" large lettering across the high wings impossible to miss. There were now more aircraft on the field than Illusion Lake had probably seen in the last few years combined. *At least the people who came out to watch are getting their money's worth.*

* * *

Deputy Lozen trotted into the room, slamming some papers on the long Fire Hall dining table, next to where the Sheriff was sitting. "I got it!"

Kiva could only be thankful for the reprieve. At that moment, the lieutenant from the State Police, along with the special agent in charge of the ATF, were in a heated argument with the newly arrived special agent leading the EPA's Criminal Investigations Unit. The only other element crowding the room more than their alphabet of law enforcement was the compounding of tactical gear-fueled testosterone and egos. Local, state, and two federal agencies… She didn't care who, only if they could follow Elliott's mantra: "Make a plan. Make it work."

When the sheriff interrupted the argument to point out that his deputy may have found where the guns and equipment received through the federal 1033 Program were stashed, a whole new argument started. This one was centered around who had the most appropriate aircraft to clandestinely survey the property in question. While they carried on like a bunch of schoolboys, Kiva looked to Lozen who was standing across the room just as miffed about how the morning was shaping up. She had wanted to be outside to witness Elliott's takeoff. Mark, sitting beside her, was streaming it from the website, all because she was forced to play referee to a bunch of men who couldn't or wouldn't see the bigger picture.

Once she caught Lozen's eye, she leaned towards Mark. "Do you think Elliott could handle a quiet flyby?"

He nodded. "I know just how to get the details to her without having to transmit everything over an open frequency."

"Good. Go. Talk to Lozen. She's smart. She'll get this and don't come back till it's done." She watched him get up quietly, taking her coffee mug and his, like he was just heading for the kitchen. And Kiva was right. Lozen must have read her mind as she followed him out without a backward glance.

Looking back at the heated faces gathered around the table, Kiva normally would have broken it up by now and instilled a little reality into their situation. Instead, she sat back, rereading the report her Toronto investigator had put together and researching on her laptop the legal statutes as she went. Water was one of the most complicated issues under the three levels of law, and that was only part of the case. Corruption of local officials, fraud under the provisions of the 1033 military program, were two of the areas she was researching. Now she had to consider if the consortium had broken any laws in their attempt to monopolize the local real estate market and if investment laws had been broken especially with the men involved in squirreling money offshore. These were all complex issues and far more than one criminal attorney could tackle. To do this properly, she'd need a team. A tax lawyer, and someone familiar with investment banking.

While the alphabet of law enforcement refilled on coffee, she slipped out for a quick discussion with Maria Murdock. Now, back in with the boys, she had Maria's input to consider. Maria had admitted, without prompting, to fraudulently creating banking records at Gent's orders. Gent Koehler had used her impending divorce as leverage, convincing her he could and would have the judge in the case grant sole custody of her children to her abusive ex. Now knowing Judge McCallum was involved, Kiva realized it wasn't an idle threat. Banking laws would play into the case as well. She felt sorry for Maria for her part in this but more than that, she was angry. After her years in Juvenile Defense, she had tired of the way men used their power over kids and women. Regardless of the laws broken or jurisdiction of offenses, this whole thing was nothing more than a group of men, power players, taking advantage of people with little or nothing with which to fight back.

By the time Mark walked back in with Lozen at his side, the officers and agents assembled had begrudgingly decided to have the state police do an overflight in their helicopter. Evidently it had the best equipment of the three substantially outfitted aircraft gathered on the field. She smiled to think the town folks had gotten a much better show today than anyone could have expected. Most thought they would get an up close and personal look at the FAA inspector's Beech Bonanza, old Elmo's Corvette which the boys had pulled over to the Fire Hall for everyone to see, and of course the Gipsy Moth.

She watched as Mark paired his phone to the brand new large screen TV, one of the many items Elliott had bought to make the place more comfortable for the town's displaced residents. When he resumed his seat beside her, he nodded, saying quietly, "All queued up, counselor."

Kiva stood, taking the room and brooking no complaints or objections. "While you were all arguing over jurisdiction and who has the bigger equipment…on your airplanes, Elliott Snowmaker made a quiet flyover and captured these images."

The room broke out in pandemonium. Cries of foul, and complaints of how Elliott might have tipped their hand, not to mention lost opportunities, abounded. Before she could rein them in, the sheriff lost his cool. He smacked his coffee mug down hard on the table, breaking it into big pieces. "This is my town," he shouted, "and you sons-a-bitches are my guests! I don't care if you don't like that Ms. Park here went around you's. We got bigger problems and I for one want to see what young Ellie come up with a whole lot more than I want to hear any more bull crap from you lot!"

Kiva stifled a grin and began scrolling through the shots that had been sent to them. Elliott had taken them with her phone and not all were good. Some were nothing more than blurred ground shots that looked like something taken with a shaky hand. Of the few that were clear and captured the ranch Deputy Lozen had identified, the photos more than told the story. It was easy to see the place had once been a thriving horse center with several large round pens that looked recently worked. There were two barns, one of which should have been filled with equines, but seemed to be housing horses of a different kind. Two Humvees were easy to spot, including the men working on them. The second barn, which she suspected would normally hold the winter stores of feed, hay, and straw bedding, had the tail of an aircraft poking out and another parked beside it. Kiva was able to zoom in, and the high-resolution Elliott had used let them read part of the tail number without difficulty. The second aircraft had no numbers on it, so she turned to the pilots from the various agencies to identify it.

"That's a Super King Air," the EPA's pilot/agent announced. Speculating for the group, he added, "With no markings, it could be one of the two the ten thirty-three Program gave to the town." Both he and the pilot officer from the state police stepped closer, conferring about the half-hidden plane. It was good to see at least two members of the diverse group working together. When they both agreed, the EPA agent explained, "It could be a Challenger or a Gulfstream. Without seeing the rest, it's hard to tell, but if that's the trailing edge of the main wing and not the edge of an overhead door… then we'd both put money on the Gulfstream. G-four, G-five-hundred, we can't be sure without seeing the rest but definitely a Gulfstream."

Dias nodded, weighing in. "We know someone who's got himself a real nice G-four. Only one in these parts. Good bet that's Judge McCallum's bird."

By the time Kiva had tabbed through all the pics Elliott had taken, they'd counted over twenty cars and trucks, and more than a dozen armed men looking like they were patrolling the theoretically empty compound. Finally seeing their group begin to work together, Kiva reiterated what they should have all read by now in the reports. "Among the over one hundred items the county was to receive through the military equipment program were twenty-eight M16s, six grenade launchers, eight Humvees, two Beech Huron Aircraft, one ARFF certified Oshkosh Striker, and enough ammunition, grenades, surplus uniforms, and office equipment to run a full company of light mechanized cavalry including air support. And as we can see from the shots, one of the King Airs is absent. It could be stuffed in the pole barn ahead of the G-four, it could be grounded somewhere else, or…" She left the thought hanging for them to speculate.

"Gentlemen," she continued. "We have a unique opportunity here, but the laws are complicated and overlapping. If any one of your agencies thinks you can pull this off on your own I'm here to tell you, you are mistaken. If we want to shut this down and I certainly have had enough of these people threatening this town and working to exploit the county from several angles, then we have to work together. Now, I'm going to go take a statement from Maria Murdock on the banking fraud and, hopefully, get a moment to witness Elliott Snowmaker landing her eighty-year-old Gipsy Moth. When I return, I would like to hear that you have organized a working group because it is the only way any of our separate sides are going to shut this down and see justice done."

She walked out without looking back, giving Mark a subtle signal to stay. She knew he would text her if the situation deteriorated or if luck was with them and the various players set their separate agendas aside, deciding to focus on the greater good.

* * *

When Elliott turned final for runway 21, she was ready for the audience. Still, the size of the crowd was disquieting. Including what looked to be a platoon-sized police contingent. She reminded herself that she'd had an audience for every landing she'd made in her old job— having passengers on board was sort of the same. Today it looked like she had a whole lot more than the one hundred and thirty-six people her Boeing 737 held, to witness her every move. She shook it off. Because she'd taken straight to the air on takeoff, she needed to spend some time in the pattern now, so announcing her intentions was probably the only way to keep everyone from stressing. Pressing the push-to-talk button on the stick, Elliott explained on the air that she needed to complete at least three takeoff and go-arounds but didn't bother to tell them what they would entail.

Keeping the center line like a pro, she settled the little Moth into a perfect three-point landing right on the numbers. She slowed almost to a stop, then gently accelerated to quietly lift off again. That one was textbook, and she rattled off the numbers for Jesus to record. She followed with three more, including a sideslip from downwind to simulate an emergency, then followed with a dead-stick landing.

Now there was just one more to do. As she came around again, she had to trust that Jesus and Mac had done their jobs. She did trust them, but this was something different, even for her.

* * *

Kiva stood between Mac, Deputy Lozen and the guy from the FAA. He had been explaining every detail of the test maneuvers Elliott was flying. It was comforting and nerve-wracking all at once. She had almost screamed watching the little Gipsy tip on its side in the middle of the way through the sequence, turning as it fell to face the other direction. Then, at what looked like just feet from striking the ground, leveling off and landing without effort. Beside her, the FAA inspector grinned like a proud papa bear. He turned to Mac, who was recording the whole thing on his phone, asking for him to share a copy of the video. He wanted to show it as an example of how it was done.

Over the two-way radio she was holding for Mac, Elliott announced her final approach to land full-stop. Kiva had just learned today that meant a plane was announcing its plan to land and park. She sighed in relief. Then she watched in horror as she realized Elliott wasn't aiming at the runway the way she had for all the other tries. Raising a hand to shade her eyes, she finally asked, "She isn't lined up. Shouldn't we warn her?"

Mister FAA just nodded to Mac, who kept the phone aimed at the airplane as he explained, "She's already done off-airport approaches, but now she actually needs to land on something other than nice even asphalt."

Practically choking, understanding what that meant, Kiva listened as Mac assured her that he and Jesus, and a few other volunteers, had walked the length of the grassy field to the left of the runway. They had marked obstacles, clearing the grass around runway lights and old taxiway signage and were sure she could see everything on her approach. Someone had been there just yesterday, chopping back the unkempt inner field. They hadn't mowed the grass down, but they did take a quick pass with a brush cutter. It was far from the manicured lawns she had seen in the YouTube videos she'd watched to get an idea of what to expect.

As the Gipsy neared, the FAA man grunted that she would need to add more power if she planned to hit that heavy grass and not ground loop. Kiva didn't know what a ground loop was, but it sounded bad. A split second later, they could hear the engine of the Gipsy Moth rev up and the attitude of the plane change. Moments later the front wheels cut through the tall grass with ease, then slowed quickly. Elliott turned the Moth, taxiing towards them. Lozen and Mac warned everyone back, until the pristine little blue and silver biplane spun around almost in front of them. Then the engine cut, and the only sounds coming from the little plane were the odd pings of the engine cooling. Until the cheers and applause began from every onlooker.

The triumph on Elliott's face as she jumped down from the rear cockpit was clear. So was her joy. Yes, there was no question, this was what she loved. Kiva knew it. She'd seen that look before... Just this morning and of course last night. Was that what they had, something as powerful as the very thing that kept Elliott going even through the worst of days?

Oh, Elliott! I think I may just love you too.

CHAPTER TWENTY-EIGHT

By late afternoon a lot had happened. The FAA inspector had taken his complementary check flight and signed off on the airworthiness certificate, and Kiva had pulled in the marker Elliott had earned when she saved the life of Congressman Rodriguez during her misguided incarceration in the Lea County Correctional Facility. Now they would get their task force. Kiva left the sheriff to work out the details with all parties involved while Elliott took her flying. She was made to believe by Elliott that it was her most important in a day full of joyrides.

Once Kiva was back on the ground, she was pleased to realize she enjoyed the flight much more than she imagined. She then spent time drafting the terms of the multiagency task force. The EPA would take them to a federal judge both they and the ATF used and trusted. Her motion included everything needed to issue a warrant for those involved in usurping the military 1033 Program and stealing weapons and more.

Kiva hadn't thrown in everything they had, knowing they needed to hold back some cards until they could see who and what the raid delivered. While the joint law enforcement team strategized, she was on the phone with the US Attorney for the State of New Mexico.

The sheriff was pulling together the law enforcement agencies, but the new task force needed a legal team too. And with an AUSA assigned, she opened her email to see responses from both the AUSA and Congressman Rodriguez's chief of staff. Each were salivating at the prospect of recovering some of the money that had been misappropriated from the county's emergency services budget for the last five years. And she was given permission to bring in a tax lawyer, plus they were talking about the banking laws and who they would need to cover that side too.

With Kiva as the only bona fide criminal attorney and the lead for the county, everyone agreed she would command the legal team. Now she weighed in on an argument over who would head up the actual task force. The ATF believed their man should be in charge and the others all balked.

She had raised the question with Elliott while enjoying their short flight together. Kiva had been more than surprised at how comfortable the little plane was. She had expected an open cockpit to be noisy and windy. Of course, the sound was dampened by the flight helmet Elliott insisted that she wear. The tiny cockpit windscreen, which she had assumed as mostly decorative, did its job too, leaving her feeling safely ensconced in the front seat.

"Look, there's your house. Can you see it?" Elliott asked over the intercom.

Kiva had seen aerial photos before, but this wasn't like that at all. Following the shoreline of the lake, they couldn't be more than two or three hundred feet from the house. The dusting of snow that had blanketed the place just days ago had melted in the warmer temps, and they were close enough that she could see the melt draining from the eaves. The man on duty from the protection detail was recognizable as he walked around the house to get a look at them. Kiva waved as Elliott rocked the wings to let him know it was just them. Once they passed south of the house and cleared the lake, Elliott pulled the nose up and climbed, explaining she needed a little altitude before she could hand control over.

Panicked at the prospect, Kiva jabbered while she worried, asking Elliott who she thought should command the task force.

"Simple. Sheriff Dias."

"After all he put you through?"

"Especially. Look, I know Dias put me in a bad position and God knows I could have racked up some serious charges in there, but he was acting on bad intel, bad intel some of these others are still sitting on. He may be a bulldog of a man with an ah-shucks front and an old boys' drawl, but he's dedicated to this town and determined to see the right thing done in a challenging situation."

They leveled off at 3,500 feet, and Kiva took the time to look around at the empty fields as Elliott made what she called clearing turns.

"Okay, Kiva. I want you to put your feet on the rudder pedals. Just rest them down and let yourself feel what I do."

She did as instructed, at once feeling much more comfortable.

"Okay, first thing you need to see is the horizon and how the engine cowl and your windshield intersects it. Once you see it, memorize that picture. That's what straight and level looks like."

"Got it!"

"Good. Okay, now put your right hand on the stick, nice and easy. Nothing happens fast in a Gipsy Moth. All your moves should be slow and gentle. Like you don't want to spook her."

That image made her smile. Did it describe Elliott's early approach to her or her pursuit of Elliott? Either way, the exercise warmed her as much as the woman did. They spent what felt like just minutes, with Kiva learning the very basics. She had been flying in straight lines and easy turns and even climbing and descending when Elliott asked her to look below. She had been so intent on watching the horizon and keeping the wings level that she had completely missed the airport. Elliott talked her through their entry into the pattern, insisting Kiva keep control as they completed the downwind checklist. It wasn't until she turned to make the landing, with the long runway stretched out before her that she started to balk. "Elliott! Shouldn't you take over?"

"Easy now, counselor. You're doing great and I'm on the controls with you. Just keep listening, and you'll have your first landing to add to your logbook."

"What?" Elliott had thrown a lot at her. Nothing she couldn't handle but the thought that she could somehow log the flight as if she were a real pilot seemed impossible at best.

"Oh. Didn't I tell you?" Elliott sounded so innocent. "I ordered you your own flight kit. Easy there. Now tell me. Does it look like we're flying down to the runway or it's rising up to meet us?"

"*Aah*. Oh my God! It does look like it's rising up!"

"Good. Now tell me what you feel. Not your nerves but how your body is reacting to the airplane."

With only what looked like fifty feet to the runway, she had to force herself to relax and interpret her body's feedback. Once she quieted her mind, it took only a second to understand. "Holy shit! It feels like someone has me by the butt of my jeans and is pulling me down!"

She could hear Elliott chuckle over the intercom. "Now you know what they mean when they say, 'Seat of the pants flying.' Okay, I need you to stay loose on the stick and follow me through on the flair."

Kiva had no idea what a "flair" was but followed along. The runway was racing towards them, and it was all she could do not to fixate or scream. At what seemed like just a few feet, Elliott pulled back slightly, bringing the nose up and making it impossible to see forward and she guessed that was the "flair." Kiva could feel the engine power fall off even more than it had been for the approach and was surprised when all three wheels squeaked down a second later. She was shocked to see how fast the Gipsy slowed, almost coming to a stop before she felt and heard the engine power increase.

"Keep your feet on the rudder pedals, that's how you steer on the ground," Elliott explained, suggesting, "You'll need to steer in an S pattern to see what's ahead of you. Can you see the Fire Hall?"

They had just passed it, so that was easy. "Got it."

"Okay. You might as well taxi over there. And listen to the radio for Mac's directions. He can see where the people are, so he'll know what's safe."

Steering was much simpler than she imagined, but Elliott was right, you couldn't see what was in front of you. She listened as Mac guided them safely closer to the Fire Hall, then Elliott led her through the shutdown, which was simple too. The prop stopped immediately, and they sat listening to the engine ping as it cooled. Then Elliott asked her if she enjoyed it.

"Are you kidding me? That was amazing, fantastic!"

"I was hoping you would say that." Elliott was now standing on the tarmac, leaning against the front cockpit and grinning up a storm.

Kiva removed Elliott's personal flight helmet and handed it to her. In exchange, she accepted the headset usually offered passengers, connecting and hanging it as directed. "Now what's this about you ordering me flight stuff?"

Elliott gave her a shoulder raise like a tween would say "whatever," before her smile gave away her joy. "I was so hoping you would like this."

Standing on the leather upholstered seat as she had been shown, she backed out of the cockpit, stepping from the lower wing onto the ground. Kiva could admit her legs were shaky but not in a bad way. She swung her arms around Elliott's neck, not caring about the crowd witnessing their every move. If the town didn't already know they were involved, they might as well learn about it now. She planted a warm kiss on Elliott's lips, pleased beyond words to realize there was no protest. Yes, that was Elliott, her Elliott and unmistakably, they were on the same page. "You!"

Still grinning up a storm, Elliott said, "I have to take her across the field and refuel before my next flight, but I want to be sure you're okay before you head back into the storm."

Still in those protective arms, she knew without a doubt this was where she wanted to be. Maybe it was too soon to say it, but she was feeling it and hoped beyond hope Elliott was too. "Ellie, I'm walking on a cloud. Your cloud. I hope you know that?"

Pulling her in tighter, Elliott said just loud enough for her to hear, "I'm crazy about you too."

* * *

Sometime during the day, the guys had found enough time to dismantle the antique sleigh bed from Elmo's room and move it to the former guest room for Elliott, setting it up with the new mattress and linens she had ordered. How they found time, with so much going on all day and so many people wandering around airside and wanting to have a peek at the other projects old Elliott had begun, was a mystery to her. And, they'd found enough time to set up the two new double beds she'd ordered, one for each of them. One for Elmo's bedroom, which was now assigned to Zeus, and another for Mac, allowing him to convert the old sitting room to his own private quarters. They had both expressed their amazement and gratitude before leaving for the evening, intent on keeping Mark's wife and kids company. Mark had been asked to tag along with Sheriff Dias on the unofficial task force's raid of the not so empty property. Considering the number of armed men she had spotted on her flyover, she was worried too. At least the sheriff hadn't insisted the newly deputized Mac and Jesus join them on the raid. Although, she was sure, they would have preferred that. Instead, they chose to keep Andi and the kids company. Elliott could only hope Mark knew enough to stay back. His official place on the task force was as Kiva's investigator and he was there to act more like a CSI, recording the raid and their findings.

With her new bed squared away, Elliott made her way downstairs, setting the table for the dinner Kiva had gone out to the Crow to pick up for them. As her mind wandered, she did think about Gale, the owner of the diner. When did the woman sleep? The place was open from early till late and catered to whatever the town needed. She had even purchased a pizza oven when the last pizzeria closed. The Crow was the last surviving restaurant in town, and it looked to thrive even when Illusion Lake didn't.

She was trying to decide if she should open one of the bottles of wine she'd picked up the other day or wait for Kiva to return. Was Kiva in a beer kind of mood or would wine be better? Hearing what sounded like the airside walk-through door open, Elliott stepped out into the canteen, eager to welcome her back. Instead, she felt a wire loop around her neck and someone pulling it hard. Her immediate reaction was to try and pull it from her throat. Her brain uselessly registered the weapon as a garrotte. When her muscle memory kicked in, she pushed back hard, knocking her attacker into a wall with enough power to force him to loosen his grip. She turned sharply, driving her elbow into his face. He dropped the garrotte and slid to the floor, wailing as his nose began gushing blood.

The shock of seeing Ian Guerrero again confused her enough that she didn't sense the second attacker approach from behind until a millisecond before the butt of a rifle met the back of her head.

When Elliott came to, she was zip-tied to one of the canteen's old chrome chairs. Ian was standing in front of her, a bloody rag that looked to be packed with ice pressed against his nose.

"She's awake," his accomplice announced unnecessarily.

Looking at him and seeing the familial resemblance, she could only assume this was Maxwell, the eldest of Ian's sons and the sheriff's abusive son-in-law. "Great. The dynamic duo, Ian the bent lawyer and you must be Maxwell, his wife-beating son."

While Ian ignored her, the son took her characterization personally, wasting no time in slapping her face.

Elliott let her head fall, stifling the pain from the contact. Looking up, she sneered at him. "Did I hit a nerve, Maxie?"

He hauled off and slapped her again.

"Enough!" Ian growled. "We need her to be able to talk if she's going to transfer the money."

"Bitch!"

"*Oooh*! So articulate. Plainly, you're not the brains of the operation. Are you, Maxie pad."

He raised his fist, like that would intimidate her. When she just laughed, he punched her in the mouth. She shook her head. Spitting blood and what felt like a broken tooth she aimed it at his fancy cowboy boots. He swore, moving in for another shot, but Ian pulled him away.

"I told you to hold off! We have to get her to call in the wire transfer first. Then you can have all the fun you want."

Elliott spat her blood at them both. She was sure it was just from the split lip and probably what she suspected was a broken molar. She made a mental note to bring that up with her dentist and almost laughed out loud at the thought. "Ian," she said, "what the fuck are you doing here? You do know that half the state is looking for you."

"And whose fault is that? We had a good plan here, and you had to mess it up! With your reputation, I thought you'd be smarter. We could have made a place for you, you and Kiva too, but no...you had to be a little goody-two-shoes, just like your uncle. Have you any idea how much money you've pissed away?"

She smiled at him. "Actually, I do. Do you?"

He sneered. "You really are a piece, aren't you? If you'd just stayed out of this, you coulda kept that nice nest egg old Elliott set aside for you. Now you're going to transfer it to me. It won't make up for the thirty mil I was set to receive, but it's a start."

"Thirty million dollars? Really?" Elliott was shaking her head. "You actually have no idea how much your compatriots were shortchanging you. Do you?" she demanded. Her mouth was bleeding and it was a strain to talk with her split and swelling lip.

Ian ignored her, setting her phone on the table, and placing a piece of paper beside it. "Now you're going to call that fancy bank up in Amarillo and have them transfer everything your uncle left you to this account."

"Trying to sock more money into that Dominion Bank account? I have to say it was not so smart to use a Canadian bank, even if it is on St. Martin."

"What's she talkin' about?" Max asked his father.

"Shut up!"

Elliott could see her words had affected him. "Yeah, it didn't take Kiva long to trace the money, much less the corporate trail offshore. I must say your friends screwed you pretty good on that one. What with erasing your names from the corporate boards and all. Of course, that might help you in court."

"What are you talking about? I set up the corporations. I should know who is and isn't named as officers!"

She shook her head again. "See, this is where you screwed yourself. What gave you the idea you had the experience and wherewithal to create an untraceable offshore setup? I mean, the guys who partnered with you, the moneymen, must have laughed their asses off. Between taking the lion's share of the profit for themselves and leaving you on the hook for all the laws you've broken…" She sighed. "So sad."

Looking even more riled, Max was screaming, "What the fuck is she talkin' about?"

Elliott grinned as best she could, answering for Ian, "Oh, Maxie. It seems dear old dad made a mistake in his calculations and gave up an eight-billion-dollar payday for a measly thirty mil. How sad is that?" Max glared at Ian, who tutted that she was wrong but looked shaken nonetheless. "Let me guess, you let Gent convince you that thirty million was a fair share?" She knew Gent was just as clueless, but he wasn't here.

While Max and Ian argued about whether Gent was trying to rip them off, she carefully pulled the plastic zip-ties around her wrist tighter. They were already too tight to slip out of and too loose to break with friction. She would tighten them as much as she could with her fingers, hoping she would get the chance to break from the chair before Max or Ian decided to use the M16 lying on the counter. As much as Elliott knew stalling was the right thing to do, she was scared for Kiva. She would be back from the Crow any minute now and if she walked in on this, there was little hope anyone would find them until too late. If she was forced to call the bank in Amarillo, she had a plan for that, but she knew that even if the wire-transfer was stopped, there was every likelihood they would kill her, thinking it had gone through, or doing it when they realized it hadn't.

Deciding it was better to face their anger than risk Kiva walking in on this, she pushed them. "The clock's a-ticking, boys. The branch will close in five minutes. What's it gonna be? Take my uncle's hard-earned money or maybe we put an end to this whole mess. I bet Kiva could negotiate a deal for you both, you could even try turning state's witness against Gent and the fellas who planned to walk away from this with eight billion, that's billion with a B, dollars while you stand as the potential fall guys? Tick, tick, tick."

Now it was Ian's turn to slap her, delivering an angry backhand.

She laughed it off. He was a featherweight compared to his kid. And he was too riled to appreciate how much her words were affecting him.

"Just dial the goddamned bank!"

She grinned, even though it caused her to split open her lip further. She licked at the blood, offering, "Ah, I'm kinda tied up right now."

Max looked like he was ready to get back into the slugging game when even he realized she meant she was literally tied up. He grabbed the phone, demanding, "What the fuck's the number, bitch!"

Elliott raised her voice, "Like I fucking know! What? You can't read through a contact list?" She had been keeping a watch out the door with just the corner of her eye and was pretty sure she had spotted what had to be the shadow of someone coming close. Amping up her game, she was determined to be heard, but mostly she wanted Kiva as far from this as she could get. "Let me give you a fucking hint, asshole! It's listed in my contacts under B for bank or in your case B for all the billions your friends were willing to rip off without you!"

Max rounded on her again, but this time Ian stepped in between them, warning her, "Settle down this minute! And don't even think you're going to get on that phone and warn whoever answers up there. Yer just gonna tell them to wire the contents of the account and use that number." He tapped his hand on the paper sitting on the table in front of her.

"Dad. Are you sure?" Max looked panicked.

"She's lying! Our bank account is good."

"Then how the fuck did she know the name of the bank?"

Elliott couldn't help herself. She wanted to hear how Ian would convince himself of any of this. "Yeah, Dad! How did I know the name of the bank or that Gent was ripping you off? Or that the corporate papers dropped you from the list of officers, or that you were getting ripped off on your fair share, especially since you're the one who put this all together?"

Ian looked stuck between wanting to take the credit for putting the plan together and challenging her on whether everything had indeed fallen apart.

"Tick, tick, tick."

On the other side of Ian, Max was screaming again, "Fucking make her shut up!"

"Oh, come on, Maxie-pad. You don't mind if I call you that, do you? I bet you got called that in school too." She grinned even though it hurt like hell. "Now let me explain in simpleton terms even you can understand. You want me to shut up, but I can't make a wire-transfer if I can't talk. Where's the logic in that? Oh, that's right. You're not much for logic. I heard you prefer to do all your talking with your fists. Isn't that how you communicated with that petite little thing you married?"

He raised his fist again.

Undeterred, Elliott kept poking the bear, "Huh, huh? Come on, Maxie-pad. Tell me, are you one of those guys who is so intimidated by women you can't get it up unless you beat the shit out of her first?"

He pushed Ian hard to get to her, but Ian held him back, firing an order, "Just dial the fucking bank and put it on speaker."

Max did as he was told. According to the canteen clock, it was two minutes to six and the phone rang five times before a harried voice picked up. "Amarillo First Texas Bank. How may I help you?"

"Hey, there. It's Ellie Snowmaker. I have to wire some money. Can you help me with that?"

"Technically we're closed. Can you call back tomorrow?"

At the look on Ian's face, not to mention Max, whose head might blow, she tried again. "Actually, is the branch manager in? I'm Elliott Moreno's niece. I'm sure she'll understand this is important."

"Oh! I'm so sorry. I didn't recognize your name. Mr. Moreno was such a wonderful man. I am so sorry for your loss."

"Thank you. I miss him too."

"Let me get the manager. I'm not sure she can do anything, but she can explain better."

"Thanks." She listened as the call was put on hold and instrumental versions of the top forty replaced the teller's voice.

"So," Elliott asked the two men, "whatcha gonna do if they won't put it through tonight?" Hurt as she was, she was amused at the situation they'd put themselves in. It wasn't like they could wait till morning. The guys would be back by then, and the potential buyers for the Gipsy Moth were due to arrive long before the branch would reopen. Judging by their shared looks, they knew it too.

Before either could answer, the branch manager was on the phone, "Ms. Snowmaker? I wasn't expecting your call. I thought you decided to keep your accounts here?"

"It's Ellie, remember? And well, a girl can change her mind, right?"

There was a small pause as the manager considered her words. Elliott had been on the phone with her more than once, always insisting she addressed her as Elliott, and using a much more formal tone. The last call was just days ago when she had transferred some cash into a trading account and run the first payroll for the guys. "Yes, of course. What can I do for you?"

"I need to wire-transfer all the money in my account, and I'm going to give you a transfer number. When you're ready. Just let me know which number you need first."

"Okay...I'll need the transfer and routing numbers first. Have you got those?"

"Yep!" She read the numbers, practically singing them to a happy tune. When asked for the account number, she sang that too. Both men looked at her like she was crazy but didn't dare say a word.

Once the numbers were recorded, the manager explained, "I just need you to answer some security questions. Are you up for that?"

"You got it. Bring it on."

"Mother's maiden name?"

"Moreno," she answered without hesitation.

There was a slight pause, then the manager asked, "Name of the elementary school you attended?"

"Lincoln Primary."

The next pause was even longer, but Elliott kept her face looking ever so relaxed, knowing the branch manager was searching for a way to decide if this was a hostage incident or if she was drunk. Either way, she was betting the transfer wouldn't be made. Now all she could hope was the manager had the cleverness to not tip her hand.

"Okay. Last question. I just need your four-digit pin code?"

"Oh, that's easy. Nine-two-nine-one." Elliott almost sighed in relief to know she had recited it backward accurately. She also hoped banks here used a backward pin the same way banks did at home.

The answer was almost immediate, "Okay, Ellie. I've got everything, and it's all approved. I'll just send it up to the main branch first thing in the morning, and they'll make the transfer for you. And I'll call you then, to let you know when they'll send it. Is there anything else I can do for you?"

"Ah," she hesitated, watching as Ian gestured madly. "So, I'm guessing it can't be done tonight?"

"Sorry, Ellie but no. I'm not authorized to send a wire of this magnitude and even if I could, which I can't, the system locks me out at six p.m. I'll need you to be patient until morning. Can you do that for me?"

Understanding the message being conveyed, Elliott answered, "I get it. I'll just have to hang on as best as I can. I look forward to hearing from you."

* * *

Kiva was making her way in from the street side door when she heard Elliott's raised voice and her dropping the F-bomb in every sentence. She stopped in her tracks, thinking she might be having a heated phone call, until she heard other voices coming from the canteen. She knew Mac and Jesus had already left for her place, and both her and Elliott's security guys were outside. She set the takeout bag down and inched her way towards the canteen. Careful to not get too close, she identified the two other voices: Ian and probably his disgusting wife-beating son, Maxwell. Stepping back cautiously, moving as far from the canteen as she dared, she began by silencing her phone before texting the security detail. She'd have their asses for this. Yes, several hundred people had been on the field today but that didn't change things. They should have inspected the hangar after all the visitors had left. She'd replace them before she wasted time trying to figure out if they were involved or just incompetent. She would have sent a text to the sheriff too, but he was on the raid, and Elliott's guys were about as far as you could get from the airport, having dinner with Andi and the kids at her place.

She kept texting the security detail, knowing they wouldn't risk texting her back. She let them know she was safe and where she was hiding, then explained that Ian and Max were in the canteen with Elliott. She couldn't tell if they were armed, but they had to have some leverage on Elliott. There was no way she would be intimidated by those two.

CHAPTER TWENTY-NINE

Connie, the head dispatcher, was on duty in the new 911 office at the Fire Hall. Usually she would have the place to herself, but the raid had everyone on edge. Bash had already completed the day shift but sat with her, listening to the radio chatter along with Deputy Lozen, who was none too happy to be sidelined. The sheriff had argued that she was the most experienced deputy and the only one he trusted to protect the town and the rest of the county while he was otherwise occupied. She didn't buy it but believed that Dias had all the backup he could ever want. And as a bonus, she had convinced the other agencies involved to leave behind a spare radio for each of their guarded frequencies. They didn't have the range of the base set that monitored the county frequency, but Jesus and Mac had rigged connections to some of the old antennas still mounted on the roof. It wasn't perfect, but they could hear everything going on. And it sounded like the bad guys had a mole or at least a lookout. Someone had warned them the ad hoc task force was inbound. When the state police helicopter arrived, only minutes before the ground force, Judge McCallum's G4 was just turning onto the dirt runway.

State Police Stingray One hovered over them, keeping them in place, while the ATF's Dash 8 landed in the adjoining field and backtracking and disembarking with their aircraft now blocking the G4 from takeoff.

Even just listening to the radio reports was exciting. Hearing everything streaming in from the various agencies all at once took a little getting used to, but Connie and Bash had the ear for it. Lozen could tolerate it because the idea of the raid was exciting, and she wanted to know those SOBs were caught dead to rights.

Kiva's legal assistant Sofia, however, found the whole experience was giving her a headache. She kept herself busy, delivering coffees for them and to the regular fire department personnel who were on the apparatus floor training the volunteers. Thankfully, the two single moms in residence with their kids were all set up in the day room, enjoying a Disney movie with their little ones. She had just returned to the dispatch office with refills when the phone rang.

Connie huffed under her breath. "Guess it's back to work for us." She put her headset back on and punched the button for the call. "9-1-1, What's your emergency?" She listened patiently, her eyebrows climbing up her forehead. She waved frantically to Lozen, pulling her headset off as she set the call to speaker. "You're on speaker with the chief deputy, ma'am. Please tell her what you just told me."

"I'm the branch manager at Amarillo First Texas Bank. I just received a call from Elliott Snowmaker. She's the woman who…"

"Yes, ma'am! Deputy Lozen here." She checked her watch. It was almost ten after six. A little late for a banker. "We all know who Elliott is. What can we do for you?"

"I think she's in trouble. She just called and requested a rather large amount be transferred to an offshore bank."

"How large are we talkin' here?"

There was a pause, before the woman answered cryptically, "Let's just say, low to mid eight figures." By now Bash had lowered the volume on the radios and everyone, including Sofia, was glued to the sound of the banker's voice.

"We have procedures for this," the bank manager continued. "When I went through the security questions, she got them all wrong, but they kind of sounded like they could be correct. At least if you didn't know the woman. And when I asked for her security pin number, she recited it backward. I didn't know what that meant. I had to look it up. Evidently, it's a security thing for Canadian banks. Citing your pin backward to a call center tells them you're in a hostage situation and being forced to divulge your banking details!"

By the sound of her voice, the woman was truly concerned. "Okay," Lozen began carefully, first pointing to the dispatchers. "Bash. Get her security detail on the phone now. Connie, ping her cell phone. Let's see if she's still at the hangar." To the banker, she asked, "What did you say to the request?"

"I gave her tentative approval but warned I couldn't actually get it done until morning. I gave her a song and dance about it being after six, and I was locked out of the system and that I would call in the morning before I put it through."

Finally letting a lungful of air escape, Lozen praised the woman. "You did everything right. Did you hear anything else that can help us?"

"I'm so sorry. I know she was on speaker phone. I could hear an old fridge kick in and out. I didn't click into that until she answered the security question about her elementary school being Lincoln Primary. I know she's American, but I remembered her telling me she grew up in Canada. I'm having a tough time believing they name their schools after American presidents, even a great one like Lincoln."

"Good observation and the fridge thing tells us she's probably at the hangar. The canteen has a unit that's got to be older than me." Seeing both Connie and Bash waving frantically, she put the banker on hold, passing the handset to Sofia, and suggesting gently, "Sit with her, keep her calm, and take a statement. You know the drill. You've helped Kiva do it enough…"

"Oh my God! Kiva?" Sofia had taken the handset and pressed it to her ample bosom.

Before Lozen could address that concern, Connie cut in, explaining, "The security detail is aware, knows where she is. She's in the hangar, but she overheard Elliott before she entered the canteen. They have her hiding and sending texts every minute or two." She added with concern, "The detail's just planning their entry."

"You order those weekend warriors to hold their position until I get there! If they fight you on this, remind them, they're the assholes who let…Who the hell has her?"

"Kiva thinks it's Ian Guerrero and maybe Maxwell too," Connie answered. "She didn't get close enough to see but judging by what she heard, she's sure they're armed. And she's sure Elliott must be in restraints."

Lozen nodded. "I agree. I don't see that woman not puttin' up a fight. Especially with our Kiva somewhere nearby."

Bash rang in, "You got that right!" Sitting at the new computer, a match to Connie's, he had been allowed to install an adaptive app for seeing impaired users, allowing him to listen to the results of his searches and keystrokes. "I pinged Ian's phone. It's off or dead but Maxwell… Well, we all know that boy was never the smartest. He's in the hangar or at least his phone is."

"Good work, everyone." Lozen might have felt like she was leading the junior varsity into a pro game but so far, they were delivering exactly what she needed. "Okay, let the detail know I'm on the way over. I'll meet them street-side. Connie, you call the sheriff. Call him. Don't use the radio. Tell him I've got this covered. Bash, call Mac and Jesus and get them back here. Everyone stays off the radio and no one sends a text, not to Elliott or to Kiva. We can't risk spooking Ian or that idiot Max. Got it?"

She gave Sofia a hug, promising, "I'll get our girl safe and back to you. I promise. Now, would you mind keeping the bank lady company on the phone?"

Not waiting for Connie's update to the sheriff and his possible reaction, Lozen double-timed it to her unit, and with the lights off raced along the runway towards the hangar. She silently diverted to the street side access, easing up beside one of the big black SUVs used by the security detail. It looked like they had pulled in all their men except the one who was probably sitting on his hands, guarding Kiva's house and swearing about not getting in on the action. With her unit shielded behind the SUV, she slid from behind the wheel, motioning them to join her.

The man she knew, the one she had been introduced to as the detail commander, unfolded a hand-drawn layout of the hangar. "From what Ms. Park has texted, Ms. Snowmaker is in the canteen with a minimum of two assailants. We believe they have some leverage over her and that she is either incapacitated in some way or they are holding weapons on her, probably both."

"Agreed. I believe the assailants are Ian and Max Guerrero. First things first. Where have you stashed Kiva?"

"She's hunkered down in that little plane they flew today." At Lozen's raised eyebrows, he protested, "We tried to talk her into leaving, but she wouldn't risk opening a door or heading up the stairs. She said it's too easy to hear when someone is moving up or down either staircase."

"Agreed." She looked over the layout. "The canteen is a choke point. Even with superior numbers, it would be a mistake to engage them there. Especially if Elliott's tied up or unconscious. She could easily end up a human shield or a bargaining chip. Neither is acceptable. Agreed?"

He nodded. "It's exactly what we've been thinking, but we're not sure how to lure them out without them taking Ms. Snowmaker out first."

"*Hmm*. I think I do." She looked them over carefully. "Which of you men have seen action? And in action I don't mean *Call of Duty*."

Only two nodded, each delivering a quick and dirty of their military experience.

"Can we send Kiva a text message without risk?"

"We have. I mean after she assured us that she had silenced her alarms and all volume. And deputy, just in case you don't know this… she's on the ornery side."

Grinning, Lozen nodded. "Oh, I know. Her big sis and I were besties the first year of high school. Whenever Kiva decided she wanted to hang with us, there was no shaking her, no matter how hard we tried. Okay." She tapped on the layout plan. "We need to get at least one of those assholes out of the canteen. So, here's what we'll do…"

* * *

Hunkering down in the Gipsy Moth, Kiva listened while Maxwell argued with his father. He was agitated about the hold on the wire transfer, while Ian was trying as hard as he could to figure out if they could leave and trust the transfer would go through, take Elliott with them for insurance, or just shoot her now and hope the bank manager didn't call in the morning before the money was sent.

From what she could gather, all that kept them from shooting Elliott right now was the prospect of losing her money. According to her father, Ian was seriously in the red. He had shelled out for a house for Max as a wedding gift, paid for his two younger sons to attend some Ivy League university, and then lost dearly in his divorce settlement. That did make her grin, knowing Ian would have been too proud and stupid to know representing himself in his divorce was a big mistake. If Ian was as deep in debt as her dad thought, she was pretty sure he wouldn't risk killing Elliott, his golden goose. *Would he?* Nothing about his behavior smacked of smart.

The phone clutched in her hands vibrated silently. Checking the message, she was both freaked and relieved to know the detail was about to breach. At least Lozen would be leading them in. She had been Shay's best friend all the years they lived in Illusion Lake and had always maintained contact. Lozen was a combat veteran of the US Air Force, having served three tours in Pararescue before returning home.

She trusted her the most even if Lozen was ordering her to stay where she was. She had a role to play now, even if it was from her hiding place. Kiva's job was to pretend she had just arrived from the Crow with their now cold dinner. Lozen had even written a sort of script for her. All she had to do was stay cool and wait for each prompt then read her script convincingly. Acting wasn't her thing, but with Elliott's life on the line, she would do it, delivering an Academy Award-worthy performance.

Relax. This is just like court and delivering the coup de grâce when no one sees it coming.

While she waited for the go-ahead, she ran a hand around the leather cowl roll of the cockpit, admiring the hand stitching and the amount of attention and detail Elliott had committed to the work. That was just like her, all in and never looking back. It wasn't as if Kiva hadn't spent time thinking about them, but for the first time it was more a serious consideration. Elliott had committed to her, and while she knew she could and would enjoy stepping up their relationship, in the back of her mind she knew she could back out if things didn't work out or if Elliott asked too much. She could always get in her car and head back to Toronto. It wasn't like she'd ever seen herself settling down here. She wouldn't call her childhood home a backwash but compared to Toronto, what did it have?

Elliott. It has Elliott.

Her phone vibrated in her hand. Lozen and the detail were in the hangar. She shook her head, then let them know they had achieved stealth. At least she herself hadn't heard a thing. Taking several deep breaths, she texted back that she was ready. *Ready for Step 1*

She listened as someone opened the airside door and banged it closed.

Line 1 GO!

"Ellie baby! I've got dinner!"

She could clearly hear muffled sounds coming from the canteen. Then the tone of Elliott's almost strangled voice shocked her. "Kitchen!"

That wasn't what Lozen had planned for, and she was sure it was the last thing Elliott wanted too considering she never called it that. Knowing she needed to keep to the scripted plan, she called out, "I'm going to take dinner up to the library. Grab some beers and meet me upstairs!"

Footfalls on the steel staircase immediately followed her words. She tried but couldn't tell if they were made by one person or two in accurate synchronization.

Her phone vibrated again, and the message was clear. *Stay where u are. Keep ur head down!!!*

The Park family did not produce foolish children. As much as she wanted to rush in and save Elliott, she had hired these people for this reason. And with Chief Deputy Lozen leading them, their experience would surpass anything she could do. She had done her part. Now she had to keep her head down and hope beyond hope that Lozen's plan worked.

* * *

Elliott watched the two Guerreros argue; father and son, aggressive and pushing in each other's face. Deciding to pour a little water on the fire, or was it gas, she hissed at the pair, "You harm one hair on her, and I will find you, and when I do, I will rip your dick off and shove it so far down your throat, it'll be sticking out your ass!"

"Fuck you, bitch!" Max said a little too loudly, garnering more heat from his dad. Ignoring his old man, he warned. "Just you wait. After I fuck her skinny ass straight, I'm gonna fuck you up good too."

The threat did nothing to Elliott, and she wouldn't let him see her concern for Kiva's safety. "Guys like you are all the same. You're so threatened by powerful women, rape is all you can come up with to deal with it. Well, I'm so glad you're into it because once they get your little white ass in prison, some big motherfucker is gonna make you his bitch. Nothin' like a taste of your own medicine, eh, Maxie-pad?"

He hauled off and hit her viciously for the umpteenth time.

It took her a minute to recover and raise her head. She spat out some of the blood in her mouth and once again aimed for his fancy boots. She couldn't help but wonder how many times his kids went to school hungry so he could have those boots. Continuing to taunt him, she suggested, "Come a little closer, Maxie-pad. I want to spit on your ridiculous shit-kickin' boots again."

He backhanded her hard, hissing, "Stop calling me that!"

Ian stepped in between them, "Knock it off! You need to get upstairs and take care of that girl. And no!" he warned. "No having fun." At his son's crestfallen face, he amended his order. "Once we have the money, you can do what you want. In the meanwhile, we have to figure out how to get these two out of here without alerting that joke of a security team outside. Once we get them to the compound, we'll secure this one, and you and the boys can teach little Miss High and Mighty exactly what girls are for."

"Ah, what's the matter, Ian? Upset that Kevin's little girls turned out smarter and more successful than all of your idiot sons?"

He shook his head, distaste more than evident. "I don't know what the fuck Kevin was thinking when he wasted all his money sending his spoiled little bitches to university much less graduate school."

"I don't know," she teased. "A doctor at the top of her research field and a very successful criminal litigator... Hmmm. If I were you, I'd be sucking up to Kiva in hope she might represent you when this all goes south. And I assure you, it absolutely will."

Now Ian looked like he would hit her. Instead, or maybe because of it, he ordered his son, "Put a gag on that one, then get upstairs and tie the other one up." Once the gag was on Elliott, he stepped closer, his grin purely evil. "And son, you go ahead and teach that little half-blood bitch any lesson you want."

Elliott vibrated with anger. She had one move but couldn't risk it with both men in the canteen. It was all she could do to hold back her anger. She watched Max open the fridge and grab one of Elmo's beers. From the counter he grabbed a handful of plastic cable ties, the same type that bound her wrists and ankles to the kitchen chair. There wasn't much time. She needed to wait until Max was at least on the stairs before she used the friction maneuver she learned in the military and broke the cable ties. Her next choice was to either take on Ian or go for the M16. An assault rifle was a clumsy weapon in close quarters. Better to take Ian down and keep him away from the rifle. If she could subdue him, even for just a minute, she could grab her phone and call for help. Just then, Max returned, grinning and picking up the M16. *Fuck!* That helped her situation here but it sure as hell complicated her planned rescue of Kiva. *Shoot me then, you useless little motherfucker. I will not let you put a hand on her.*

As she listened to Max make his way up the stairs, a sort of calm resolve washed over her. No matter what happened, she was stopping this now. Ian, taking his son's example, opened the fridge and was hunting around when Elliott used all her force, standing from the chair and pulling her wrists up and in front of her all at once. The cable ties binding her wrists broke, the looser ties around her ankles did not. Undeterred, she lunged for Ian, chair and all, not caring if it made things more difficult for her. Knocking him down, they both hit the floor. Elliott was introducing Ian to her fist when they heard shouts all around them and from upstairs. As Ian cried out from having his already broken nose hit the fridge, a single gunshot rang out from above them.

It scarcely registered, as Elliott hammered her fist into Ian's face again and again. Still swinging, she was pulled to her feet, with one of the security guys cutting the plastic ties around her ankles to set her free. Without waiting, she raced for the stairs, taking two at a time and calling out for Kiva. Deputy Lozen and one of the security men were standing in the long corridor next to the library door.

Lozen had her head turned, speaking quietly into her shoulder mic, so intent on her duty she might have missed Elliott's frantic approach if she hadn't been shouting out for Kiva. Instinctively, Lozen covered the library door, leaning in to block the coming charge. The detail commander was with her and moved into a blocking stance too.

Elliott broke through the two like she was making a desperate two-minute warning Super Bowl play, then stopped dead. She took in Maxwell Guerrero's bleeding body, then looked around the room, frantic to find Kiva. How long had the bastard been alone with her? Was she safe? Was she dead? How many shots had been fired? The M16 lay on the ground. Had it been fired? She was sure she'd only heard one shot. Could she testify to that?

"Where the fuck is Kiva?" she demanded.

"I'm here, Ellie. I'm right here."

Elliott turned to see Kiva standing behind Lozen and the detail commander who were still blocking the door. Slipping back out between them, she stood inches away from Kiva. "Are you okay? Did that little bastard touch you? I mean, I'll kill Ian if…"

"It's okay. I'm okay." She wrapped her arms around Elliott's neck.

Elliott couldn't help but pull her in, enveloping Kiva in her arms. Finally able to breathe, she lamented, "I'm so sorry you had to see that." She had turned Kiva in her arms so she couldn't look at the dead body of her potential attacker. Looking over Kiva's shoulder, she felt only relief to see someone had dispatched the abusive little prick. The thought that he might have put a hand on Kiva made her feel sick.

"It's okay. I didn't see anything. I was downstairs the whole time, hiding in the Gipsy Moth. It was Deputy Lozen who walked up the stairs pretending to be me. She was waiting when he came up."

Nodding to Lozen, she mouthed, "Thank you," refusing to release Kiva from her hold. When Kiva leaned back to look in her eyes, it was all she could do to hold it together.

"Oh, Ellie. Your face—"

"It's okay, I'm okay."

"I'm okay too, and now we're going downstairs and I'm going to take Ian's confession. Care to be a witness, or would you like…"

"I am not letting you out of my sight." Finally feeling like she could start to breathe again, Elliott realized the absurdity of clutching Kiva so overprotectively. She was a capable woman who had handled the situation perfectly. "How did you know?"

"You." She smiled, almost purring in her relief. "When I came in, your voice was raised and I knew something was the matter. I also had a good idea you were acting out for me?" she asked, running a soothing thumb over her swollen, bleeding lips, the rising bruises on her face and swollen eye. "God, you must have an iron jaw."

Beside them, Lozen teased, "It goes with her cool head. Your banker called," she explained. "Kiva here figured things out first and called the detail. Then the bank lady called 9-1-1. She was impressed with how cool you played it."

Before she could say any more, her radio squawked something in her earpiece. She pressed her shoulder mic, answering, "Send them in," then turned her attention back to Elliott and Kiva. "Mac and Jesus are here. As deputies, they can take over guarding the scene and wait for the coroner while I take Ian's statement. Kiva," she added, "you've been through enough for tonight. We can wait until tomorrow for you to interview him…"

"No. No worries, deputy. I'm ready. Just give Elliott and me a few minutes please?"

Lozen nodded, and Kiva took Elliott next door to their newly refurnished bedroom, closing the door behind them. "You! I was worried sick. Before I take you downstairs and put some ice on your face, oh, and your hands and wrists, please tell me you're okay… Oh, Ellie, please… Are you… Did they?"

"Hey." Elliott held her at arm's length. "I am now. Max got aggressive with me. Slapped and punched me a few times, but that was it. I guess I'm not his type. All he talked about was what he was going to do to you. It…"

Kiva huffed, enfolding herself in Elliott's strong arms. "You would have killed him first."

"Yes! I know that's a bad thing to say, but it's all I could think to do."

"I was just climbing out of the airplane when I saw you charge up those stairs. I admit to praying Max was already dead but decided on the spot that if you killed him, I would mount the defense of a lifetime."

"You would take my case?" she asked, careful not to press her aching jaw against the head resting on her shoulder.

"*Mmmm,*" was all Kiva said. Finally looking up, her eyes wet, she declared, "Elliott Snowmaker, I don't think I understood until I realized you were in imminent danger just how much you mean to me. I've been playing with my feelings, trying to understand them but the idea of a commitment... I knew I wanted you now, in the moment, but the idea of, well, forever..."

Kiva trailed off, and Elliott listened to her silence. Finally she asked the one thing that scared her more than the two desperate men combined: "And now?"

"And now..." Kiva leaned back to look in her eyes, "I want forever."

Seeing Kiva's face, her beautiful face, her lips, and her soft brown eyes, she couldn't help but beam. "What a coincidence. While Max was tormenting me with threats against you, all I could think about was what I was going to do, not just to stop him, but afterward. I wanted to protect you, that's undeniable even if you didn't need it, but there was so much more." She huffed at her inarticulate shyness. "I suck at expressing my feelings, my hopes. I just..."

"You have hopes for us?"

That drew a chuckle. "You, Kiva Park, from the right side of the Don River. I have incontrovertible and unquenchable hopes for us, for now, and for as long as you'll have me."

"*Mmmm...*" Kiva nestled back in her arms. "It seems you don't suck at this at all. And just so you know, Elliott Snowmaker from the wrong side of the river. I am hopelessly in love with you too."

EPILOGUE

Kiva stood on the parade reviewing stand just behind David Dias, the new mayor of Illusion Lake. Five months was not a long time to right the crimes that had been perpetrated against the town, she reflected. Charges had been filed, arrests made, and all the major players named. No one would escape justice. Still, it was going to take years for the cases to work their way through the system. Kiva wasn't surprised when Ian Guerrero turned state's witness but when Gent Koehler was arrested during the compound raid, the first words out of his mouth were "plea deal," while Judge McCallum, now disrobed, screamed obscenities at him. How ironic that McCallum felt betrayed by Gent when he was the one making sure he and Ian only walked away with pocket change. Still, Ian and Gent were cooperating and providing the FBI, EPA, ATF, the New Mexico Police, and the new county sheriff with documents and emails. The most encouraging of the updates was learning that McCallum had been named a flight risk and denied bail. He now found himself in the same Level Three detention center to which he had relegated Elliott back when he, Ian, and even Gent thought she could be manipulated into giving up all that Elmo had left her. Instead of him ripping her off and sending her away, she had risen to the challenge and with Kiva's help and Mayor Dias backing her up, she had become the unofficial savior of the town.

The best news was that Illusion Lake was getting some major upgrades. The first would be a new community center being built right on the spot where the old Hobson's furniture store once stood. It had already been demolished, with the Hobson family donating the lot to the town. Today, David Dias and several others would formally break ground on the new center which of course was being built with funds Elliott would secretly supply. The rest of the town, or more specifically the burned down block, was bogged down in red tape but that wouldn't last much longer. Even New Mexico state representative Rodriguez was on hand and working hard to approve the town's exercising of the federal eminent domain regulations to allow Illusion Lake to reclaim all the properties scooped up in the consortium's efforts to profit from the town and Elliott's inherited senior water rights. Legally, the town, and specifically special counsel Kiva Park, were inundated with claims for support and umpteen offers to buy land in the recovering county. Realistically, it would take years to unravel the mess Ian, Gent, and their heavy hitters had created.

Today was the Fourth of July but judging by the turnout for the parade and planned activities, it would be remembered as the day Illusion Lake reopened for business, and everyone wanted to celebrate. Kiva was watching Dias, who stood front and center on the podium beaming with pride as the new sheriff wheeled by, driven through town in Elmo's Corvette. The kid behind the wheel was the young man who had handled Elliott's Jeep the night of the hangar fire and was one of five boys and two girls who were completing summer internships with her. Sheriff Lozen, resplendent in her new uniform, including a David Dias-styled police issue Stetson, was sitting on the shoulder of the passenger seat, looking both honored and shell-shocked.

Behind her, the airport Fire Hall's old REO Speedwagon pumper truck, decked out in tri-color raffia, was being driven expertly by Mac. Jesus, driving the airport's rescue truck which was also appropriately decorated for the occasion, had opened the parade to cheers from the crowd.

These days there was no need to worry for the fate of the airport, as the specially designed aircraft firefighting truck, the Oshkosh Striker the county was gifted with under the military 1033 Program, had been located and immediately pressed into service. Mirabal County and the town of Illusion Lake now had a real airport, which was attracting the attention its residents had always hoped for. With the two Super King Airs in county possession, Elliott had argued successfully that they could be converted for civilian operation and either sold or leased, and she had offered to foot the bill. Her only demands: that they add another hangar to the airport and fuel storage. They indeed had and were immediately rewarded when both official visitors and tourists to the region started to trickle in.

That attracted other airport tenants. The most surprising one was the State Police. They had been in the process of choosing a new home for their aviation division. Only Kiva had known that Illusion Lake was on their radar. Elliott, who was just as good a hound at hunting out aircraft deals as old Elmo, had come to her and asked her to write a plan. In it, she'd offered the police two proposals they couldn't resist. She would pay to have a small operations building added to the airport, and gift them a cool little spotter plane she had picked up at auction. They readily agreed to the five-year contract. Two months later the Australian-built Seeker landed at the field, taxiing to what the new airport plan called Hangar Three, shutting down and parking beside the Agusta helicopter, call sign State Police Stingray One.

There were other changes too. Kiva kept her office at the Fire Hall; after all, why not? The majority of her work was for the county and the Fire Hall had the added benefit of being close to Elliott. Dias had promised he would make sure there was office space for her and her father in the new multipurpose facility the town would build on the leveled block of land that had once housed her dad's office along with small shops and above-store apartments.

Later today, Elliott, along with Kiva's father, and even her sister Shay and her kids, would be on hand for the official groundbreaking ceremony. The rebuilt block would host a youth drop-in center, the upgraded sheriff's department, and new apartments and small storefronts. Her dad was still intent on setting up an office in town but liked the idea of having her at the airport while he would cover the more mundane needs of the county's residents. It would take the better part of the year to get the community center built and more than that to have the other block released to the county. No matter how long it actually took to get started, everyone believed in the project, and in the mayor now leading the town. In the meanwhile the new construction jobs just for the community center had the whole county buzzing. Once the outstanding properties were sorted out, Kiva expected the excitement to hit a crescendo. Yes, everyone in Illusion Lake had something to believe in. In a way Ian and Gent had given the town what they needed, just not the way they'd intended.

Kiva was holding Elliott's small handheld transceiver when it squawked to life. She looked down the parade route, noting the ladder truck from the regular fire department wasn't that far off and bringing up the rear of the parade. After it passed, Mayor Dias would say a few words to the crowd then invite them to enjoy a barbeque, before witnessing the groundbreaking for the new building. Kiva stepped back a few feet, pressing the transmit button. With the little radio pressed to her mouth, she said clearly, "You're good to go." All she could hope now was the FAA didn't bust Elliott for this stunt.

As the ladder truck was nearing the parade stage, the sound of the big radial engine of the newly rebuilt N2S Boeing Stearman could be heard. Like most of the crowd gathered on the street, Dias stepped forward, looking up and asking, "Is that Ellie heading this way?"

He never would call her Elliott, and she had given up asking. She'd now relegated him to the same select group as her Nanny. Turning to the elderly woman next to her, Kiva offered her hand. She was sitting in one of the soft VIP chairs set on the shaded side of the stage and Kiva helped her move forward to the edge so she too could witness what her granddaughter was about to do. While she held the radio in one hand and Nanny with the other, she wished she had a third and could cross her fingers. *Maybe I can cross my heart?*

As the ladder truck passed the stage, the street began filling with people. The restored Stearman, painted in the historic US Navy yellow with its big blue tail and the fat red stripe around the middle, flew past them low and slow. That wasn't too much of a surprise for these people; Elliott was always showing off her rebuilds for the town. What caught everyone's eye was the huge American flag she towed behind the airplane. Elliott had explained that it was just like dragging a banner into the sky and would require a lot of power to hook it and pull it into the air. Once there it was just finesse that would keep her vertical and waving patriotically in the wind. And she was right about the reaction. First, the sight of the enormous flag brought a hush over the crowd. Veterans of all ages and first responders in uniform stood tall and saluted. Then the cheers started.

Kiva grinned up a storm, and Nanny too. When she chanced a look to see if David Dias was upset that Elliott had blatantly broken several air regulations to make the very, very low and slow pass over the town, she caught him wiping away an errant tear.

Nanny—Constance Green, the last survivor of the ten Moreno siblings—smiled at them both. "That girl loves to do right." Turning to Dias, she warned, "Now, if you try to write her a ticket for speeding down Main Street, I'll be the first to put you over my knee."

David Dias just nodded, before offering, "Yes, ma'am. I mean no, ma'am, I mean…"

Laughing joyfully, Kiva patted him on the back. "No worries, Mr. Mayor. Believe me when I say there isn't a day that goes by when she doesn't have the same effect on me." She tipped her head to the gathering crowd. "Time for your speech and for Nanny and me to sneak back to the airport and pick up a certain pilot."

He nodded, looking out on the folks gathering to hear him speak. Quickly looking back at Kiva and Elliott's grandmother, he called to her, "Kiva. Tell her…tell her she done good… Again. And tell her, tell her I'm proud, proud to call her, well you's both know what I mean."

She beamed, nodding.

Turning, she offered her arm to Nanny who accepted her support without protest "What do you say we go get our girl?"

Nanny squeezed her arm as they carefully stepped down the back stairs of the stage. "I'd say it's about time."

Bella Books, Inc.

Women. Books. Even Better Together.

P.O. Box 10543
Tallahassee, FL 32302

Phone: 800-729-4992
www.bellabooks.com

CPSIA information can be obtained
at www.ICGtesting.com
Printed in the USA
JSHW021417190621
15977JS00003B/9